Parthian Books
The Old Surgery
Napier Street
Cardigan SA43 1ED

www.parthianbooks.co.uk

Originally published in Wales as *Paris* (2013)
© Wiliam Owen Roberts
Translation © Elisabeth Roberts 2017
All Rights Reserved

ISBN 978-1-910901-81-6

Cover design by Syncopated Pandemonium
Typeset by Syncopated Pandemonium
Printed in the EU by Pulsioprint SARL

Published with the financial support of the Welsh Books Council

British Library Cataloguing in Publication Data
A cataloguing record for this book is available from the British Library.

This book has been selected to receive financial assistance from English PEN's PEN Translates programme, supported by Arts Council England. English PEN exists to promote literature and our understanding of it, to uphold writers' freedoms around the world, to campaign against the persecution and imprisonment of writers for stating their views, and to promote the friendly co-operation of writers and the free exchange of ideas.

www.englishpen.org

for Manon

'But we are émigrés, and for émigrés all countries are dangerous.'

IRMGARD KEUN

I

1925–1927

1925-1927

I.

Larissa Kozmyevna Alexandrova and Bruno Volkman were married at the Church of Saint Nicholas in Rostock in September 1925. It was a traditional wedding, if a very one-sided affair, and as she watched her sister and Bruno kneeling before the priest, Margarita had had to swallow the lump in her throat as she thought of their mother and father. Margarita was the only bridesmaid, and Larissa had no choice but to ask their old neighbour from Berlin, Gospodin Gregoryevich Smurov, to give her away. They hadn't been able to find Alyosha's whereabouts in Paris. Margarita had written to his Uncle Artyom, but he didn't have any idea where he might be living, any more than he knew what he was up to. He promised to make enquiries amongst the émigré community, but wrote back to say that, apart from a vague rumour that Alyosha might have left Paris for Prague, which he had been quite unable to verify, nobody seemed to know a thing about him. Of course, Aunt Inessa – Alyosha's mother – and her husband, Alexei Alexeivich Dashkov, had been invited, but they'd sent their excuses. So as all the guests were from Bruno's side, apart from Margarita and Gospodin Gregoryevich, it made sense to hold the wedding in Rostock.

It was a hazy day, oppressively hot even though the sun was obscured. The reception for family, friends and neighbours was

3

held at the family home, and after the service, more than fifty guests spilled through the house and out onto the veranda and garden. A large marquee had been erected, festooned with ivy and flowers, with long tables laid ready for the wedding break-fast. Afterwards, a few of the guests followed the old tradition of smashing crockery before the bride and groom, and then to much laughter and applause the couple set to sweeping the broken pieces up, vowing that nothing would ever come to break up the home they would make together. Later on, the band struck up and couples flocked to dance the polonaise.

Bruno and Larissa were to honeymoon for three weeks in the small town of Graal-Müritz, half way between Rostock and Stralsund, on the Baltic Sea. The destination was the bridegroom's choice, though his mother had made all the arrangements. Margarita often wondered why the woman was quite so involved in the young couple's affairs, but buttoned her lip in the company of Larissa. Bruno's mother clearly adored her only son and had spoiled him. His father seemed pleasant enough. A little old-fashioned in his dark suit and stiff collar, a monocle in his right eye, and streaks of silver in his hair, his great delight in life was sailing his yacht on the Baltic.

When the time came for the young couple to leave, they were given a rowdy send-off. Bruno's best man, Norbert Schmidt, and the rest of his fellow medics from the hospital whistled and hooted when he turned to kiss his new bride before they waved their final farewells. As Margarita smiled and clapped along with everybody else, she mused how she could so easily have chosen to be the one wearing the veil and the orange blossom.

2.

It had been in an open air café-bar in Berlin, some five months earlier, that Arnulf Stradler had asked for her hand in marriage.

'I'd consider it a great honour,' he'd told her before going on to list what he could offer her: love, a home, and the security of belonging. 'I know,' she'd answered simply, and had felt sorely tempted to accept; a decision that would have made so much sense had some deeper currents of emotion not swept her in a different direction.

'Will you?' her boss had asked after an agonising moment.

She'd requested some time to consider. How much time, he'd wanted to know? For how long could she avoid giving him a decision, and put such a vexing question out of her mind? She'd asked for a month and he'd seemed about to demur, but must have decided against it. Arnulf Stradler was on the whole an equable man, and was ready to be patient, as he believed that all things came to those who wait if only they were deserving. As Margarita had grown to know him better, she had seen that underneath the rather stern and haughty exterior there lurked a soft heart. The other girls in the factory would certainly have thought him perfect husband material, and an even better potential father for her children.

'Fair enough,' he'd said as he placed some small change on the table, a disappointing tip from a disappointed man. For Margarita's part, as she'd turned for home that night, all she'd been able to see before her was a long and pot-holed road, full of pitfalls and puddles – one which would be difficult to navigate.

3.

On the Sunday afternoon before the wedding, the two sisters had visited their mother's grave at the cemetery of Saint Konstantin in Berlin. There were only a few other lonely individuals about, and the crunch of their shoes on the gravel carried clearly on the late August air as they walked along the paths between the graves. On one new tombstone, a young woman lay prostrate, her long dark hair tumbling all about her, her arms spread out, fingers gripping the marble edges, while two small children in summer clothes ran around her in circles.

After praying for their mother, who had died the previous January, Margarita and Larissa made their way to where their uncle, Fyodor Mikhailovich Alexandrov, was buried. A chaffinch was perched on the headstone, and even when they approached, he stood his ground. Margarita could see the black spot above his bill, the blue-grey feathers on the top of his head and back of his neck, and his conker-coloured breast. His rump was green and his wings were black with two white ribbons across them. He flicked his head as he hopped sideways along the top of the tombstone, as if he was guarding it.

Larissa whispered that she thought it was Uncle Fyodor. 'I think he's trying to tell us something.'

Her sister replied, 'He wants you to be a happy bride on your wedding day, Lala.'

'Do you think so?'

'I do, for sure. Doesn't matter if Alyosha is there or not. It's your day.'

'I hope it all goes well.'

'I'm sure it will be just perfect. You love Bruno, don't you?'

'I love Bruno more than anything in the world.'

They placed their little bunch of flowers on the grave and stepped back.

'Perhaps the chaffinch is trying to tell us how to find Alyosha in Paris,' suggested Larissa.

'Or Prague.'

'Or wherever he is – we've no idea, have we?'

They both fell silent.

'Do you think Artyom really did try and find him for us?' asked Larissa after a moment.

'What makes you think he might not have done?' Margarita looked at her sister in surprise.

'They weren't on the best of terms, were they? When Alyosha left Berlin last March he swore he wouldn't go near Artyom when he got to Paris, and that he'd never ask him for anything ever again.'

'Yes, I know,' said Margarita, 'but that was only because he'd got it into his head that Artyom had helped Aunt Inessa to get rid of Grete. I think he was in love with her, but of course you can see why his mother didn't want him involved with a chambermaid.'

'What did they do to her then?'

'Paid her off to leave Berlin. That's what Alyosha thinks happened, anyway. Though he didn't know for sure.'

The chaffinch seemed to be listening to their every word. Then, in an instant, he was gone, and although Margarita scoured the sky for him, he'd been too quick for her. She craned her neck to see if he was perching in the chestnut tree, but there was no peek of him among the leaves.

4.

Back in Berlin after the wedding, Margarita soon received a long letter from Larissa saying how happy she was with her new husband; their world was perfection, their love unassailable. She described how Bruno always started the day with calisthenics, performing the exercises naked on the rug in the middle of their room. He spent most of his day fishing, while Larissa went riding over the sand dunes down to the sea, following the water's edge across the beach. She described their hotel and some of the other guests – the wealthy wool importer and his wife from Hamburg who had bought them champagne when they found out they were newlyweds, and some Russians who knew Aunt Inessa and often lunched with her at the Russian Exiles' Club in Berlin.

In the final paragraph, Larissa came up with a proposal which Margarita knew she was in no position to refuse. On their return to Berlin, the young couple were due to move in to the new house that Bruno's parents had helped him to buy. There was plenty of room for Margarita too, and Bruno had told Larissa he would give her sister a home with them. On reading this, Margarita felt a sense of relief that she no longer had to stay in her miserable apartment, and even better, that she could escape Gospodin Gregoryevich, who had developed feelings towards her since the wedding, although she had made it as clear as she possibly could that she had no interest in him at all.

Apart from anything else, ever since she had turned down Arnulf Stradler's marriage proposal, she had been living hand to mouth. Following the rejection, Margarita had found a letter waiting for her on her desk at the carpet factory. The contents had made no sense to her so she'd taken it to her superior, who explained that Stradler, Gebhart & Roessel were going through a difficult period and economies had to be made.

She had immediately gone to see Arnulf in his office. He'd been icily polite, speaking to her stiffly, never moving from his chair, but he'd made it quite clear to her that she no longer had a job. She'd returned to her desk to collect her few things, then left the building. As she'd walked down Mohorenstrasse, she'd felt a burning sense of injustice which left her limp with exhaustion, and so had decided to ask for advice – although she was not a member – at the offices of Germany's biggest union, the *Allgemeiner Deutscher Gewerkschaftsbund,* finding the nearest office to her apartment in the Berlin phone book.

The next day she'd met with an official, a middle-aged, pleasant man, who, after giving her a cup of tea, had asked her whether she had any insurance payments against periods of unemployment. When she'd shaken her head, he'd informed her that she'd better try the *Volksfürsorge,* a welfare agency that sometimes gave financial assistance to people who were out of work. Margarita had pressed him to act on her behalf in the face of such an injustice, but he'd explained that the union had battled long and hard with all sorts of employers who had acted in a similar fashion. The trouble was, the union was so short of funds, it was trying to adopt a more conciliatory approach, especially given how much unemployment there was. Slightly aggrieved, Margarita had said that the least he could do was send her ex-employer a letter of complaint, but he'd reminded her kindly enough that, actually, there was no such obligation given that she was not one of their members. With a sinking heart, she'd realised that she would have to embark once more on the soul-destroying task of finding a job.

At the library on Leipzigerstrasse each day, Margarita was soon expert at turning straight to the situations vacant column in every newspaper. She attended a few interviews but with no luck, and admitted to Larissa that she was starting to feel depressed. Her sister was very sympathetic and persuaded Bruno to buy tickets for some of the performances at the Kroll Opera House, to try and raise her sister's spirits with music. Margarita and Larissa managed to see Otto Klemperer conducting *Tristan und Isolde* and the singing and beautiful staging enabled Margarita to lose herself in the wonderful spectacle for a few hours. On another occasion she managed to get herself a cheap ticket to the Philharmonie concert hall on Benenburgerstrasse, where Wilhelm Furtwängler from Leipzig was conducting.

But more often than not, she spent her evenings alone, feeling that her life was going nowhere.

5.

One morning, she spotted a small advertisement which puzzled her. If Berlin's Academy of Fine Arts was looking for life models, why advertise in *Die Rote Fahne* of all places? It seemed a little incongruous. Her heart sank a little at the thought of standing naked in front of a roomful of students, but it was paying work.

She was interviewed by a young lecturer who introduced himself to her as 'Bi'. Otto Bihalj-Merin – Bi – was a strange-looking individual, his thin lips contrasting with a wide, high forehead, and eyes that shone like stars. His accent was unfamiliar to her.

'From Zemun in Hungary originally,' he explained. To her surprise, she was offered the afternoon session immediately – from two to five. When she took off her clothes and stepped out from behind the screen, seven students faced her – two women and five men. She was told to lie on her side on the *chaise longue* and look up towards the high window on the opposite wall. Every half an hour she was allowed to take a break and move around a little to ease her aching muscles. It was very dull, but when Bi paid her at the end of the session she felt it was worth the effort. He told her he that he'd been lecturing at the academy for two years and that he'd placed the advertisement in *Die Rote Fahne* in the hope of doing a favour to a comrade. From the first, Bi took it for granted that Margarita was a communist and this tickled her, but she decided not to disabuse him, especially as he offered her more modelling sessions.

After that, the lecturer took a lively interest in her and would give her copies of *Die Linkskurve*, as well as *Die Kommunistische International* and *Inprekor*. She came to look forward to their discussions, and she often found herself pondering over some of the questions he posed in his thick accent, such as why the working class was having to pay the price for the failure of the Kaiser and the governing class in the 1914–1918 war.

'Is that right? Is that fair? They started the war after all – so they should be the ones to pay the reparations from their own pockets.'

One evening, as she was returning to her apartment after

attending a lecture with Bi at the Marxist Workers' College on the communist interpretation of visual art, she thought she heard her name being called.

'Margarita Kozmyevna!'

From the hurly-burly of the Kurfürstendamm, a man was striding towards her.

'Margarita Kozmyevna! I thought it was you…'

She recognised the thin little moustache ('a pimp's moustache' according to Larissa), the black button eyes and the full, boyish lips. Sasha Belelyubskii was an old school friend of her father's. He wore a light-blue jacket with a striped silk handkerchief of claret and blue in the breast pocket, and a matching bow tie. He hugged her and insisted on taking her for coffee.

'No, after you indeed,' he said as he opened the café door for her – he was as painfully courteous as ever. Lighting his cheroot as they waited for their coffee to arrive, he said, 'I want to hear everything that's happened to you.'

'There's not really very much to say, apart from that my sister is engaged to be married.'

He blew his nose neatly. 'Little Lala? Really? How wonderful.' He blew his nose a little harder. 'I remember her like this.' He held out his hand level with the table. 'As if it were yesterday. And your mother and father too… your dear father. So sad to think of him. He made such a huge sacrifice for his brother, giving himself up to the Cheka like that. To risk his life so that Fyodor could go free. Kozma Mikhailovich, what a man he was – they don't make them like that anymore, I'm afraid. So honourable, so dignified. Did you ever find out what became of him in the end?'

Margarita shook her head, swept by a sudden sadness as she remembered what had been.

'Not a word?'

'Not one.'

Sasha looked mournful. Margarita's father had disappeared

into the hands of the Cheka in 1918, and had never been heard of again. Since her mother had died, it was only Larissa who occasionally reminisced about him, but even she mentioned him less and less. Meeting Bruno had given her life a new direction and had let her put the past and its sorrows behind her.

'How Kozma Mikhailovich doted on the two of you,' said Sasha Belelyubskii through a plume of cigar smoke. 'He told me that often enough...'

Margarita rather doubted it, as her father had never been one to discuss his feelings. She felt that Sasha was just saying it to comfort her. His eau de cologne was overpowering and, combined with the cigar smoke, made her feel a little nauseous. She remembered her mother complaining that he was never without a cigar in his hand. Ella had disapproved of his habit of dying his hair as well – sometimes a light blonde, other times a dark henna, almost black. There was something very feminine about him, and the general verdict back in Petrograd was that he was rather odd, the type of man who laughs at a funeral and cries at a wedding.

'Thank you for your letter of condolence,' she said, searching for something to say.

'Ah, you received it? I'm glad. My apologies for not coming to your mother's funeral. But I had other things to attend to at the time. At least she is at peace now, removed from this miserable existence.' He suddenly looked stricken. Sasha Belelyubskii was a bachelor, and thought the world of his own mother. He adored her in fact, would have gladly died for her, and talked about her constantly. Unfortunately, (the reason never became clear to Margarita) he had left her behind in Russia when he fled for Berlin in 1920. This was still an enormous source of anguish.

Once he had calmed himself, they shook hands and made their farewells outside the café. Margarita watched him disappear from sight, striding down the street quickly and purposefully, like some fervent Christian eager to exit this world for the one beyond.

6.

Bruno and Larissa returned from their honeymoon brown as nuts and full of love. It took very little time for the sisters to fetch Margarita's few belongings from her apartment and install them in her new bedroom on the top floor of the newlyweds' handsome house on Ackerstrasse. It was very conveniently situated, and Bruno and Larissa could walk to the Charité hospital across the park. Larissa had kept her nursing job for now, though Bruno was pressing her to take on fewer shifts so that she would have plenty of time to look after their new home.

After the cramped and dismal apartment, living in such a comfortable and spacious house was a delight. Margarita would have been perfectly happy to stay in every night, but she was aware that the newlyweds might value some time alone, so she made an effort to go out whenever she was asked. Which is why she found herself getting ready rather reluctantly for an evening of poetry readings at Café Leon on Nollendorfplatz. In the old days, Larissa would have been the first to put on her coat and go with her sister, but her husband didn't think much of such evenings. Bruno had no time for poetry, although there wasn't a sport he didn't love watching or participating in – cycling, boxing, wrestling, sailing, fishing, and even women's wrestling on occasion. But Margarita had observed that Bruno was generally reluctant to let his wife go out in the evening without him, even with her sister. He also didn't like the fact that they spoke to each other in their mother-tongue.

'Are you talking about me behind my back again?' he would, ask, half teasing but half serious.

'We'd never do such a thing, darling,' Larissa would answer, kissing him fondly.

'German is the language of this household.'

'But we've always spoken Russian to each other, from the cradle,' objected Margarita, 'I don't see a reason for changing.'

'Not even out of respect for someone who doesn't understand a word of the language?'

'It would show a little respect to the two of us if *you* bothered to learn a little of our language. I'd be more than happy to teach you Russian.'

'Thank you Margarita, but that seems rather pointless when you and your sister speak German so fluently.'

The elder sister said no more, for the sake of the younger. Later, Larissa came to her room and said, 'I know it's a lot to ask, but would you mind not...? When Bruno is about? Could we try not to speak Russian together?'

Margarita put the brush down and, sighing softly, turned to face her sister, 'If that's what you want...'

'I just hate to make Bruno feel uncomfortable... especially under his own roof...'

The poetry evening was held in the upstairs room at Café Leon. As Margarita reached the top of the stairs the first person to greet her was the old poet Podtyagin. He was a little confused and thought her mother was still alive until she gently corrected him. But a puzzled look entered his dull eyes, and he complained that there was always something new in the world, and it would be such a comfort if things could only stay as they were.

These poetry evenings were nothing more than an attempt to recreate a little corner of Moscow before the revolution. In the room, the same old voices surrounded her, as the same old homesick, peevish crowd had come together to reminisce and squabble as always. For some reason, every émigré seemed to despise most of his fellow émigrés. Why did people in exile become so thin-skinned and petulant?

In an interval, Gospodin Gregoryevich beckoned to her, indicating a spare place next to him on the banquette. Reluctantly, she went to join him.

'How are the young couple?' he inquired.

'Very well, thank you for asking.'

'And how are you, Margarita Kozmyevna?' he scrutinised her, 'Still looking for work?'

She had no intention of telling Gospodin Gregoryevich about her life modelling.

'Why don't we arrange a little evening together?' he asked. 'Wouldn't that be lovely? The four of us? Bruno, Larissa, you and me. How about it? We could play cards like we used to do when you girls were my neighbours. What do you think?'

The next poet was about to begin, so Margarita was spared from giving an answer. In the next lull, Gospodin Gregoryevich started talking about her mother. 'At Weinstock's. That was when I first saw her.' He sipped his beer. 'I hadn't been working there long. It was only a temporary post, though I was hoping it might lead to something more permanent. I was in my element working in a bookshop. Just the smell of all those volumes… there's not a more delicious smell in all the world. Your mother would come in to browse and I'd make an occasional suggestion. Things I thought would interest her.' He sipped his beer and pondered. 'A very private woman. That's the impression I had of her.'

'Shy, certainly,' Margarita murmured.

'Yes, a little, now that you've said.'

'Yes.'

'A shame she passed away here in Berlin.'

'To be buried so far from her own country was her greatest fear.'

'A great shame.'

'Mmmm.'

He was sitting far too close to her, and every time Margarita shifted away he simply sidled back up to her, filling her nostrils with that familiar smell of old cigarette cards that he always seemed to carry with him. Clearing his throat as he always did when he was nervous, Gospodin Gregoryevich leaned towards her, gazed into her eyes and said intensely, 'Who among us can achieve the best life without suffering some pain?'

There was a pleading look on his long face as he waited for her answer, but as the silence grew he became overcome with embarrassment. Blushing deeply, his whole body seemed to convey his awkwardness, and although he started to apologise for speaking out of turn, and for daring to… he trailed off, looking like a man who had fallen in his own estimation.

For a while after his confidence, the two of them sat looking at the rest of the room in complete silence. Margarita turned to wondering idly why it was that death so often stalked her dreams, so that she would wake half suffocating, as though it had grabbed her by the throat. From when she was a little girl, she had lived with the fear that accompanied the first realisation that she would one day die, that everything that she was would come to an end. But what was she going to do until then? How was she going to fill the days and the weeks, the months and the years?

Gospodin Gregoryevich eventually managed to start another conversation, telling her that occasions such as this brought to mind evenings in the Pokrovskoye-Streshnevo, on Stoleshnikov Street in Moscow, the café where all the journalists used to gather. How they'd drink and debate there all night long, in a thick miasma of tobacco smoke, until the place reeked like burnt wool. He proceeded to list all those who had frequented the place with him: Andrei Bely, Ivan Shmelev, Konstantin Balmont, and of course Ignatiy Potapenko, the best short-story writer in the world. All of them now exiled the length and breadth of Europe.

'We'd drink coffee from those great big enamel mugs. It didn't matter how much sugar you spooned in, that coffee always tasted bitter. What was the name of the one who used to dye his beard?'

By now Margarita was thoroughly bored.

'He really was a sharp-tongued, malicious little man. Do you know the one I mean?'

'I'm afraid I never lived in Moscow…'

'He'd practically hiss as he spoke.' Tapping his fist on his knee, with his eyes tightly shut, Gospodin Gregoryevich sighed. 'I can't for the life of me remember his name. My mind is like a sieve! But malice was his middle name, that's for sure. What *was* he called? I wish I could remember… perhaps it will come back to me.'

The greatest attraction at Café Leon that evening, and the last to perform, was Igor Serveryanin. As he began to recite his poems, a few threw the traditional red rose at his feet in tribute. At one time Igor had been achingly fashionable, in the vanguard of Russian modern poetry, and he had clung to the same stylistic tics ever since, which to Margarita's ear were, by now, a little stale. The language existed as sound but without much sense. His philosophy was that so many secrets hid within each and every word – even the simplest – but familiarity made people cloth-eared, and only by reminting a word within an oddly new context was there a hope of rediscovering its true depths once again.

It was a bravura performance, as Igor did his utmost to turn the familiar into the unfamiliar. There were powerful verses of trains rushing to the front, flashing through Russian stations where platform after platform of women wailed, and gangs of soldiers sang, the sound of mourning in every note of their accordions. The younger members of the audience seemed to love his verbal experiments, but for Margarita, there was more substance in the longing of his early, more traditional poems, those he had written to his sweetheart. To the communists of course, he was nothing but a dilettante poet, a self-obsessed bourgeois scribbler, out of tune with the new rhythm of the Soviet Republic, which demanded a very different type of poetry. But Igor was nothing if not stubborn, insisting that only the true visionary could distil life into art.

When he finished there was thunderous applause, foot-stamping, and whistling, culminating in loud bravos. Margarita closed her eyes as empty talk surrounded her once more. Gospodin Gregoryevich was so dull. They were all so very dull. She listened to somebody calling the communists thieves and hooligans, recounting how they used to dress up like soldiers in order to encourage the real soldiers to desert, while their mother country was at war in the summer of 1917.

'That's where the heartbreak started, you're quite right…' someone moaned.

'And those Petrograd thugs,' a hoarse voice weighed in, 'those pigs from Kronstadt lording it over us in the streets, interrogating us all, asking us who we were and what class we came from. The downright cheek of it. What right did those sailors ever have to demand that kind of information?'

A reedy voice piped up. 'I remember my dear brother coming home on leave one Christmas, and hanging his sword on the door hook as he always did. When it got dark, we could only light the one lamp in the kitchen, and the family would all sit around the table in the half-light to talk once we'd cleared the food away. But over in the corner, that golden hilt of my brother's sword shone like the star above the stable in Bethlehem, a symbol of hope to me that Russia was not going to be overrun by Jews and communists.'

I remember, I remember…

The same old story.

The same old song going round and round.

Margarita couldn't stomach any more remembering, and thought if she stayed she really might scream. Murmuring her apologies, she hurried down the stairs, walked quickly through the café, grabbed her coat, and stepped out into the night.

In bed that night, the realisation came to her that she had changed. She had left the people at Café Leon behind her, and she didn't have the slightest wish to ever spend another moment in their company. She no longer felt herself to be a part of their world. Her horizons were wider now. She was determined to create a new life for herself.

7.

The bar had enormous mirrors along the walls which made her feel that she could step through to an eternity of other bars. There were various potted plants about the place and one palm tree. It was already quite full, and the tobacco smoke tickled her throat, as practically everybody was smoking.

'Norbert Schmidt is here already,' Larissa told her, pulling her sister after her into the room. 'Look…'

She looked over to where Larissa was pointing and saw Norbert sitting next to Bruno, dressed in a smart, light-blue suit, white tie and grey leather shoes, his fair hair neatly brushed.

'What have you said to him?' she asked suspiciously.

'Nothing. I just noticed how well the two of you seemed to get on at our wedding, so I thought it would be nice if you met again.'

'We had one dance together. That's all.'

'You can have another dance with him tonight then. I'm sure he'll be delighted.'

'Oh, Lala! No. Seriously, what have you said to him about me?'

'Hush, behave…'

As they joined the group, Bruno was in the middle of a spirited account of a new surgical procedure – an abdominoperineal resection – and was explaining rather graphically how the first surgeon attacked the tumour from the abdomen while the second surgeon cut from below, through the perineum. Margarita grew paler and paler and when Larissa squeezed her fingers, they were like icicles.

'Are you alright?' she asked. 'Gretushka?'

Margarita swallowed the bile that had risen to her throat and slowly the urge to vomit receded. Bruno laughingly apologised when his wife gently berated him, but he found it difficult not to talk shop. He looked handsome in his well-cut suit, though he always dressed a little older than his age and there was something rather stately and ceremonious about the way he conducted himself publicly, as though he was very aware of his own standing and worth. But he had a small mouth, a boyish one with soft lips, which gave Margarita the impression that he was a weak man.

Within no time, the doctors were discussing a gastroen-terostomy and the best ways to avoid bruising of the stomach. Their voices swelled as the evening progressed, and Norbert proclaimed that everything he'd learnt in his lectures was pretty much useless when it came to surgery, with all the complications and variables that could arise. That was when a doctor showed his mettle, and it wasn't always easy to keep a clear head in such stressful situations.

They were there that evening to celebrate Norbert's birthday, and all the doctors were determined to enjoy themselves. Larissa introduced her sister to some of the nurses she worked with – a lively group of young women, happy to have an opportunity to socialise with the doctors.

'Bruno thinks I should give up working completely now I'm married,' Larissa told her when they had a moment alone.

'Really? Why?'

'He's mentioned it a few times. None of the other wives work. I think he'd much prefer it if I didn't either.'

Margarita sucked on her cigarette. 'Well, it's up to you. What do you want to do?'

'There's a lot to be said for it, of course. There's always so much to do. I never thought running a house would be so time-consuming, even with a maid.'

'Lala, that doesn't really answer my question.'

'I know… I suppose whatever makes Bruno happy, that's what makes me happy too.'

'But you enjoy nursing. You don't have to pretend with me. I'm your sister.'

'I adore nursing…'

'Well, there you are then. You've just answered my question.'

Larissa threw a little glance over to where her husband sat with the other doctors.

'But Mama never worked, did she?'

'No. But she was brought up in a different age. She never would have wanted to go out to work. Things have changed since her day. It would be a shame to give up your work when it gives you so much pleasure.'

'It's not that simple.'

'And the company as well. You'd miss that more than anything, I'm sure. Why don't you keep working until you have children?'

'Yes… perhaps you're right… I'm not sure, we'll have to see… I'll have to discuss it again with Bruno.'

'Well, at least let him know how much it means to you.'

Later in the evening, some medical students arrived and Larissa motioned with her eyes for her sister to look over to a round table where a rowdy group of them were drinking, smoking and laughing.

'See the one with the scarf?'

Margarita looked at the thin young man, with dark skin and darker eyes and said, 'What about him?'

'He was on our ward this week. He's called Simon. Don't you

think he's the prettiest thing you ever saw? Look at those curls. And his eyes. Did you ever see anything so delicious in your life?'

'Larissa,' chided Margarita quietly.

'I know, I know. But you know, we all have our little fantasies, even we married women. She lowered her voice, 'But honestly, if I wasn't… I really would be tempted…'

The students soon left for some other bar, and at around ten o'clock a small band started to play and the first few couples took to the floor.

'I wouldn't be surprised if Norbert comes over in a minute,' said Larissa, sucking her cocktail through a straw.

'I'm not much of a dancer, as you well know.'

'It's only an excuse to get close to someone, that's the important thing.'

'What have you and Bruno said to this man about me? Seriously?'

Her sister smiled and raised an eyebrow suggestively.

'Lala, why must you meddle in my life?' Margarita felt suddenly irritated.

'I'm just trying to look after you. You don't want to be on your own forever, do you?'

'I'm happy as I am, thank you very much.'

'You've had nobody since Stanislav Markovich. When did he go back to Russia? It was ages ago.'

'I don't remember,' answered Margarita, though she remembered it all very well.

'It must be two years ago at least.'

She hadn't even told her sister that she'd come across Stanislav Markovich again, when he'd been on a visit to Berlin and had been giving a reading from his newly published novel at the Marxist Workers' College. He had read for almost an hour, the lamp on the podium casting dark shadows under his eyes. As she'd listened, Margarita had quickly realised it was semi-autobiographical. Lenin was the guiding light at the centre of everything, as Stanislav recollected his own encounters with Vladimir Ilyich when he was living in exile in Paris before the 1914–1918 war. He'd brought the man vividly to life: how he loved Pushkin and Beethoven, and walking in the mountains. He'd portrayed a generous personality with a complicated nature, somebody who chose to dedicate his whole life to liberating the working class and creating a new society unlike any other in the history of the world. He'd finished the reading by describing touchingly the feelings of immense public grief in the bitter cold of Lenin's funeral in January 1924.

Over coffee afterwards, many had been eager to talk to Stanislav, and Margarita had observed him from a distance. What had brought their romance to an end was Stanislav's insistence on going back to Moscow, where he thought a better future awaited him. Margarita had understood his ambition, his hankering for a career with prospects after living hand-to-mouth for so long in Berlin. He had begged her to go with him, and she had considered it very seriously, but in the end the thought of leaving her mother and sister had made it impossible.

Eventually, Margarita had approached him. Stanislav had stared at her in stunned disbelief for a moment before recollecting himself. He'd introduced the dark-haired young woman standing next to him. 'Lyuba, this is Margarita Kozmyevna... Margarita, this is my wife.'

'I've heard so much about you,' Lyuba had smiled; she'd had unusually green eyes.

'Good things, I hope...' Margarita had replied, half smiling at Stanislav.

He'd taken out his pipe and told her that he and Lyuba had been living in Paris for some months, where he'd been trying to establish himself as a novelist. It was not the easiest life, and it was only by doing a little lecturing and journalism that he'd kept the wolf from the door. They were living in a shabby little hotel on the Avenue du Maine, with the usual narrow dark stairs, smelly corridors and threadbare rooms. Under the window of their room was a *pissoir*, with a wooden bench nearby where lovers came to hold hands and kiss and cuddle for hours. He'd spend hours at this window every day, trying to write and staring out at the world. On the other hand, he spent his evenings mostly in the Rotonde, discussing literature with Mayakovskii and like-minded writers. Their aim was to produce art as a force for good in people's lives, promoting a new, communist, world-view.

'An artist's lot is not an easy one,' Stanislav had claimed.

'He has to take on all sorts of dreary commissions for newspapers,' Lyuba had added.

Margarita had been curious. 'So you didn't stay long in Russia in the end then?'

I travel to and fro at the moment. I'm not an émigré, I'm a Soviet citizen. That's what's on my passport.'

'It's good to know where you belong in the world,' Lyuba had said.

'And what about you?' he'd asked. 'I never would have expected to see you here of all places.'

Margarita had smiled. 'I'm not as prejudiced about the Soviet Union as I used to be.'

'It's good to see you in any case.'

'Likewise.'

Margarita was pulled out of this reverie when Larissa gave her an admonishing little punch on the arm. She caught a sudden glimpse of herself in the mirror facing her and realised with embarrassment that she was beautiful. Sometimes, she'd look down at her legs and be surprised that she had any at all, as she normally hid them under long skirts. Why was she so ashamed of herself? Larissa was always telling her she had a good figure and should show it off.

'If you could just manage to put a smile on your face you might find yourself in luck tonight,' her sister teased.

'Larissa, I really don't need any of your kind of luck. I'm very capable of looking after myself without any interference from you.'

Larissa was used to her sister's protestations, but as far as she was concerned there was nothing sadder than seeing her sister go off to concerts or the pictures all on her own.

'Look, he's looking over, now smile, can't you? Here he comes…'

Once her sister was on the dance floor with Norbert, Larissa went to sit with Bruno. 'Could you undo the button of my collar?' he asked her, and she complied. 'That's better. Gracious me, it's stifling in here,' he complained, stretching his legs out in front of him, and flicking the ash from his cigarette. They watched Norbert and Margarita dancing.

'Has he said anything?' asked Larissa eventually.

'Not really.'

'But he must have said *something,* surely?'

'Just that she wasn't his type.'

Larissa couldn't hide her disappointment.

'Why not?' she asked.

'He likes girls with a bit more padding up top. He thinks your sister is a bit flat-chested. And he has a point.'

'Big breasts aren't everything.'

'But for Norbert they're important. Along with other qualities of course.'

'Do you think the same of me then?'

Bruno turned his sweaty face to look at her.

'Do you think I need more padding here?'

'What makes you think that?'

'So you do.'

'No, of course I don't.'

'I can tell that you do.'

'I've never said such a thing.'

25

'But you suggested it, Bruno.'

'I did no such thing. We were discussing your sister.' He raised his voice in irritation.

'But it applies to me. I'm even smaller than she is. I'm not good enough for you. I know I'm not.'

When Margarita and Norbert joined them at their table, it was obvious that Larissa had been crying. She tried to laugh it off when her sister asked her quietly what was wrong, but her eyes still glistened with tears.

The next day, after Bruno had left for the hospital, Larissa confided in Margarita that she'd been pregnant but had miscarried a few days earlier.

'Does Bruno know?' asked Margarita.

'No, thank heavens. And he mustn't either. I don't want him to think that I'm useless…'

'Of course he won't think that. You're not useless Lala.'

'I just don't know sometimes why he married me. Someone like me. He deserves better. What did he ever see in me?'

'Don't talk like that darling… look, you're just upset. There's no need to worry. You're both young and healthy. You have plenty of time ahead of you.'

8.

Margarita kept to her new resolution of deepening her understanding of communism. She read and studied, and went to as many of the lectures at the Marxist Workers' College as she could. In the absence of any other choice, she continued to work as a life model, which at least gave her plenty of opportunity to discuss ideas and ideology with Bi, though she now knew plenty of other communists.

But although Margarita had begun to see the world in a fresh light, certain questions still troubled her. Foremost among them was how could anybody be so absolutely certain about things? Life for her was random, a matter of chance. Perhaps it was possible for people to live as though they were free, but there were other forces working against ideals and dreams, smashing them to dust. She so often felt that her own life was as insubstantial as tissue paper. Bi dismissed her concerns and taught her to concentrate on what was fundamental.

'What is democracy?' he asked her.

'You tell me.'

'The right to cast a vote for political parties which are no more than clones of each other, and whose only disagreements revolve around the best way to uphold capitalism. For communists, on the other hand, the history of mankind is a journey towards its emancipation.'

And so he went on. The more he talked, the more she learnt. It was Bi who persuaded Margarita to join the German Communist Party. 'The most important thing is to commit to action,' he told her

'Do you think I'm ready to commit?' she asked him, gratified but doubtful.

'Of course you are.'

'But I'm worried that I just don't know enough yet.'

'About what?'

'Marxism, I suppose.'

'You know enough. You know you do. There's something else stopping you. What troubles you? Tell me.'

She hesitated, oddly ashamed. But Bi persisted and in the end she admitted her fears. 'Everybody who joins a political party has to give up their freedom of opinion to a certain degree. But that's especially the case for communists, who must be under Party discipline at all times.'

Which was entirely a good thing, according to Bi. 'There's

nothing that ruins individuals more than individualism,' he told her firmly. Independence of opinion only led to sectarianism and schism. Strict discipline was vital to keep the Communist Party strong and united.

'Look, I want to ask you one simple question: do you want to see a better world being created?' he asked her.

'Yes, of course I do.'

'I'm glad to hear it. But the truth of it is, nobody can create a better world single-handed. So the trick is for the individual to harness his will to the will of the working class in order to join the struggle for equality and justice. Walking the communist path isn't always easy, but what other choice do we have?'

He scrawled a name on a piece of paper and put it in her hand.

'Go and see her – and tell her I sent you.'

Margarita did so the following day.

9.

A thin girl told her she'd go and fetch Hedwig for her and disappeared through a light blue door. Margarita sat and waited on a wooden bench. *Who would have thought?* she marvelled, yet what she was doing felt like the most natural thing in the world. Eventually, Hedwig emerged and Margarita stood up. Margarita expected her to shake her hand, but she didn't; there was something very direct and informal about her.

'Nobody calls me Hedwig now apart from my mother and Bi. Call me Vicky.'

She led the way to an office where three women were typing. Vicky stamped Margarita's membership card and welcomed her to the ranks of the German Communist Party – the KPD. Holding the card in the palm of her hand, gazing at the little gold hammer and sickle, Margarita was amazed at how simple the whole thing had been. As she left the building for the summer sun on Bülowplatz, Margarita walked with a spring in her step, joyful in the knowledge that she now belonged to a movement that looked to the future, not back to the past.

Over the next few months, Vicky and Margarita became firm friends, spending hours in each other's company. Vicky lent her books and pamphlets and every lunchtime Margarita would diligently pore over *Die Rote Fahne* in some cheap café and then leave it for whoever else might care to read it. In any event, she didn't want to risk taking it home with her, for fear of giving Bruno and Larissa some inkling of her secret life.

Every Thursday evening she'd make her way to the Schünemann bierkeller, where her cell held their weekly meetings in a back room. Aside from Vicky, who was the co-ordinator between the cell and the KPD, there were three or four other earnest young woman in their twenties, like Margarita, but the rest were men. Most of them were unemployed, with families to feed, and had the defeated look of hunger and exhaustion about them. There was also an intense but mild-mannered young man, who taught Latin in a school in Lichtenberg and who always chewed the end of a pencil; a journalist; and a ginger-haired youth whose complete inability to sit still annoyed the older members. They all smoked throughout the meetings almost without exception.

Keen to show her commitment to the cause, Margarita often spent her Sundays with her comrades, going door-to-door in the working class neighbourhoods of Wedding and Neukölln, distributing pamphlets and selling communist publications. Sometimes it was difficult not to be discouraged by the lack of interest, and at other times they had to bolt down the tenement stairs to avoid a good kicking. But often Margarita was welcomed, and she felt she was truly beginning to spread her wings, in the company of others who felt the same as she did.

One Sunday morning, she came face to face with an old friend from her days working in a cake factory when she had not long arrived in Berlin from Russia. Her friend hugged her and invited her in to the apartment, but when her husband saw the pamphlet in Margarita's hand, he snatched it from her, tore it to pieces, and bellowed at her to get out.

'Aldrich, she's my friend!' remonstrated his wife, pink with embarrassment.

'Do I have to tell her again?' he said belligerently, straightening up, his fists welded to his thighs. 'Get out, I said.'

He'd been a solider in the *Freikorps*, and hated the Reds, with their lying Jewish-Russian sloganeering about some mythical international brotherhood. The only socialism he recognised was the socialism of the trenches – that's where true German solidarity had existed among working men. He still felt that sense of brotherhood, every bit as strongly as the implacable hatred he felt towards those bogus socialists and rapacious Jews who had stabbed their treacherous knife into the back of the army in 1918.

'Now get out, and don't you dare show your face here again you stupid bitch.'

The door slammed shut.

10.

Margarita was always careful to keep her KPD membership card hidden, and most of the time managed to guard her tongue against saying anything that might upset Larissa or Bruno, who after all were providing her with a roof over her head. She had realised over the months that her brother-in-law was not as politically neutral as she first thought, and was in fact an old-fashioned nationalist, who voted for the *Deutsche Nationale Partie*, though he wasn't a member. Prior to that, he'd voted for the Catholic Party, as all his family were Catholics. Although he never proclaimed much on the subject of politics, and found the whole idea of going out canvassing for any political party rather vulgar, Bruno was highly suspicious of socialism, and positively antagonistic towards communism, ever since someone at the hospital had told him that they had nationalised the women in Russia so that they belonged to everybody. When Margarita had protested that this was completely absurd and obviously untrue, he'd told her that she could take it from him that it *was* true.

'Where did you hear such a thing?' she'd demanded as he repeated the claim over supper one evening.

'I can't remember.'

'You can't remember because it's nonsense, that's why.'

Affronted, Bruno had insisted that the information had come from a very reliable source. Things had become heated and Larissa had tried to intervene, but to no avail. Bruno loathed losing an argument, and would never admit defeat, even when he was on thin ground, always insisting on having the last word.

'Have you ever stopped for one second, Bruno, to ask yourself why you think like you do?' Margarita had asked him challengingly.

'Because this is how all sensible people think,' he'd answered unhesitatingly. 'Communism is nothing but an abhorrent chaos. Anyway, what makes you so very interested in my beliefs all of a sudden?'

Margarita had refused to let it go. 'What do you think is more important? The past or the future?'

'What?'

'What's more important?'

'What do you mean, woman?'

Margarita had explained that many people felt the need to cling to an apparently perfect past when faced by a world which seemed to be changing too quickly. They preferred to distance themselves from the present for some fantasy of a perfect society which had never actually existed. What led even perfectly intelligent people to think like this was insecurity and fear.

'Me? Frightened?' He'd been clearly affronted. 'Frightened of what?'

'Of change.'

'Rubbish!' Bruno had laughed. 'I've never heard such rubbish in all my life!'

Margarita had asked him quietly, 'Why won't you think about what I've just said?'

'Who's been feeding you all this tosh about change, eh?'

'You're too conservative to realise how conservative you really are.'

Perhaps it was his need for security which lay behind his choosing to marry young, Margarita had mused to herself. But she had learnt one important lesson: the sheer futility of challenging her brother-in-law. It was wiser to stay silent.

II.

It was Vicky who first mentioned Margarita to her boss, Erich Lange. After reading other members' reports about her, he was impressed enough to pass her name along to Ernst Thälmann, the Chairman of the KPD and a Reichstag member.

As everybody was leaving at the end of the cell meeting one Thursday, Vicky told Margarita that she was expected at a meeting at the KPD headquarters on Bülowplatz the following day.

'What time?'

'Half past six.'

'Why?'

'You'll see.'

Margarita arrived far too early, well before six, and was made to wait almost an hour and a half. As the fingers of the clock approached half past seven, the building was still full of busy people, with no sign of anyone going home.

Vicky eventually ushered her to an office on the third floor where a middle-aged man in a grey waistcoat told her, without any introduction, that he'd be interviewing her.

'Interview?' she said, bemused.

Vicky caught her eye before leaving, and grinned.

Later, as they left the building, Margarita turned to Vicky and said, 'I'm not sure if I should take it.'

Vicky paused a moment to light her cigarette, 'You'd turn down an offer like that? How could you?'

Margarita had doubts about her own capabilities.

'You don't have any choice but to accept. Think about it. You and I will be working together from now on. Momentous events are about to happen. There's going to be a revolution. Of that, I'm absolutely convinced.'

Margarita duly began working at the *International Arbeiter-Hilfe*, the IAH, a movement under the wing of the KPD. But although it was a full-time post, the salary was so pitiful it meant she had no choice but to continue to live under the same roof as her sister and brother-in-law, which she thought might become problematic.

She raised the matter with Vicky who just said, 'You're getting the same as everybody else. Money doesn't grow on trees you know.'

Margarita decided her only option was to lie, so she told her sister she had found a position with an insurance company a stone's throw from Bülowplatz.

'Are you enjoying the work?'

Oh yes, she could truthfully say, she was enjoying it immensely.

Although the hours were long the work was pure joy – a combination of planning policy and strategy in the office, and political activism out on the street – and for the first time in her life, Margarita felt that she was doing something truly worthwhile.

She was sent to Potsdam, to cover the court case of some junker by the name of Rittmeister Gunther von Kunz, who had shot a young worker in the face. The provocation for this had been catching the man picking mushrooms at daybreak on his estate. This wasn't the first occasion von Kunz had stood in the dock, for a year or so previously he had beaten two young girls black and blue with a leather strop for gathering kindling on his land for their mothers. What did Rittmeister Gunther von Kunz assert before his equals? That he would never dream of shooting an upright citizen, but he didn't give a damn about shooting the two barrels of his gun at society's scum. Of course he was found not guilty; Margarita wrote that the verdict was a foregone conclusion. After all, Potsdam was a city loyal to its ancient Prussian heritage: everybody knew as much, and knew too that the chief of police, the judge, the jury, and every other member of the legal system shared the same ideal of justice, which was that its ultimate purpose was to protect the sanctity of ownership, and that justice was only a means of maintaining order to the advantage of those who owned the most. The report of the court case was Margarita's first article in *Die Rote Fahne*.

'You can never reconcile property rights with social justice,' Vicky maintained. 'Because the first will always stamp out the second.'

Margarita was still in awe of Vicky's energy and her commitment to the cause. She felt she needed to prove her mettle, especially as her boss, Willi Munzenberg, came down heavily on anybody he thought was slacking. Her daily routine included organising conferences and meetings. Sometimes the meetings would be held in indoor venues such as cellar jazz bars, stinking of sweat and smoke, but others were held out on the streets. This world of discussion and debate, notwithstanding the petty squabbling and malice, which often curdled the atmosphere, was pure delight to Margarita.

12.

The minute she was through the front door, Larissa couldn't wait to give Margarita her news.

'You'll never believe who I saw today.'

Her former governess, Duchess Lydia Herkulanova Vors had been brought to the hospital bleeding badly. Margarita was all agog and Larissa was wide-eyed as she told her sister what had happened. Duchess Lydia's mistake had been to put herself in the hands of some backstreet abortionist in Wedding.

'You should have seen her, the woman had made mincemeat of her…'

'Please Larissa, you can spare me the gory details.'

Her sister complied, knowing that Margarita would have been horrified if she had described how the woman had managed to perforate the womb with her steel knitting needle, and then compounded the damage by using forceps to extract the foetus, bringing a good lump of innards along with it onto her kitchen table. Either she was blind drunk, or she thought she was pulling on the umbilical cord, but when she realised she simply stuffed as much as she could back in, although she at least had the grace to run to her neighbour for help, a woman in the same line of business as herself. The neighbour took one look at the bleeding Duchess and ran into the street to flag down a car, knowing the ambulance would arrive too late to save her. So she was rushed to hospital on the back seat of an old Hispano-Suiza which had seen better days. By the time they manoeuvred her from the motor car onto the stretcher Duchess Lydia was in agony and close to death. She was immediately taken to theatre, and was lucky enough to have an excellent surgeon operate on her. As it happened, Bruno was under his tutelage and so he had been tasked with dispensing enough cold puffs of gas to anaesthetise Duchess Lydia for the duration. Although the surgery was successful, Duchess Lydia was very weak after losing so much blood, but to their surprise, she rallied. When she first regained consciousness and opened her eyes she swore she could see her husband – murdered by the Bolsheviks – standing in front of her. She said he was covered in blood, but that he held her hand and urged her not to give in, to fight for her life...

'Of course, nobody understood a word of what she was saying, but Bruno knew she was speaking Russian, so he asked one of the nurses to go and fetch me,' Larissa explained to her sister. 'When I arrived, she was delirious, raving about how the communists had stolen all her possessions, how she wasn't good enough for her husband, and then crying out for his forgiveness and swearing on her life to stay a widow until the grave in order to preserve the sacred memory of their wedding day. Don't you think that's so sad?'

'Who was the father?' asked her older sister.

'She didn't say a word about that.'

Larissa came home with daily bulletins about Duchess Lydia as she slowly recovered her strength. After a few days, she was well enough to receive visitors, and when Margarita went to see her during her lunch hour she found her sitting up in bed, reading.

'Dear Margarita Kozmyevna, what a nice surprise. Are these for me? How lovely, thank you.'

A nurse took the flowers to put in a vase. Margarita didn't want to stay longer than necessary as the smell of hospitals always made her feel queasy, and she was glad when Larissa joined them. Her sister had already warned her that the official version of events was that a burst appendix had brought Duchess Lydia to the hospital and Margarita was happy to maintain the fiction, although the three of them realised that her secret was no secret at all.

'I have so much work to do,' Duchess Lydia told them. 'I'm trying to arrange a conference in Munich for the Monarchists towards the end of November or the beginning of December. We need plenty of time to make sure we arrange it properly. And I'm meant to travel to the south of France this month, to Antibes, to see none less than the Archduke Nicholas Nikolayevich. I'm to ask him personally if he'll grace us with his presence.'

She told them sadly that she thought this might be the last chance to bring everybody who loved Russia together as one, in order to decide how best to move against the Soviet Union, because the communists were gaining increasing diplomatic recognition from more and more countries as the lawful government of Russia. Personally she would never recognise the Soviet regime and she was convinced that it was still possible to defeat the enemy if only they all pulled together and acted as one. She reasoned that the communists were no longer driving the revolution but that the revolution was driving them. The ideal of social equality was an empty aspiration – merely a bloody fantasy, because the attempt to make equal what God had created as unique was at the heart of modern paganism.

'Which explains why life will always be unfair, girls,' said Duchess Lydia in the confident tones of the governess she had once been. 'There will never be a classless society, for the simple fact that man can't meddle with something he didn't create in the first place. Russia is befuddled with these ridiculous ideas about social justice but the truth is that the individual is nothing and the Soviet state is all-encompassing.' Margarita was practically wincing with the effort of keeping her thoughts to herself. Of course it was possible to create a classless society. Did Duchess Lydia want to be a member of a society that encouraged personal greed, or one that created fraternal feelings, based on every member working towards a common goal? And on the tip of her tongue was another question she longed to ask, 'When was the last time you saw the rich queuing at the baker's door?' And then: 'Was that acceptable? Would the poor be destined to queue from century to century for evermore?' Everybody was only too familiar with seeing Berliners snaking around the doors of various food shops, with every shopkeeper a paper millionaire, while the poor struggled to buy even the heel of a loaf.

'Will you two join us?'

'Of course we will,' Larissa answered quickly, 'Won't we, Margarita?'

'No,' she replied crisply, 'I don't think I'll be able to attend your conference in Munich.'

'Why ever not?' asked Duchess Lydia, rather taken aback.

'I've only just started a job after a long period of being out of work. It won't be possible to have time off.'

'What a shame. Perhaps Larissa can come on behalf of both of you.'

'I'd love to,' Larissa said, then paused slightly before adding, 'but I'll have to ask Bruno first.'

Duchess Lydia took a hand of each of the two and squeezed them. 'You two are such good girls, and you always have been.'

13.

By the autumn, Margarita's new life had not gone unnoticed at home. Larissa was curious about her comings and goings, the long hours at the office, and the weekends when she was out from Friday evening until late Sunday. Margarita's excuses were wearing thin as the months went by. What really made her sister and brother-in-law suspicious was that she never mentioned meeting anybody, and she never once brought anybody back to the house.

One day, Larissa came across her sister's collection of books, which included Marx, Bukharin, Zinoviev, and Rosa Luxembourg. 'According to her, she's reading so that she can understand the way the enemy thinks,' Larissa told Bruno that night as she pulled her nightdress over her head.

'What's there to understand about that lot?' he asked irritably as he brushed his teeth with his back towards her.

'Quite.' Larissa plumped up her pillow vigorously.

Bruno put the brush down and swilled water around in his mouth before spitting it out into the sink. 'A good honest Berliner. A hardworking young German. That's what your sister needs. He'd soon put a stop to her stuffing her head with all this Marxist rubbish.'

Larissa didn't have the slightest inclination to make love with her husband when the light was turned out, but Bruno was feeling amorous. She turned her back on him, but he pushed his hand under her nightdress and reached for her breast, which was always over-sensitive. Although she'd told him often enough not to squeeze so hard, he never listened, and kneaded away as he always did. Then he tugged at her nightdress, pulling it out of the way over her thighs rather unceremoniously, and pressed his erection against the cleft of her buttocks, his body heavy against hers. He began to thrust, licking and biting the nape of her neck.

Larissa murmured 'Don't!' without much conviction, as she did every time. She felt weary and too tense to be able to relax, but she knew Bruno wouldn't leave her alone until she gave in. He grunted laboriously and rubbed his fingers over her forehead and down the length of her face. He squeezed her tightly around her middle and pushed two of his fingers into her mouth. She resisted, trying to free herself from his hold, but Bruno only pulled her harder.

'No…'

'Why not?'

'I think I'm expecting …'

Bruno froze.

'But it's early days. I didn't want to say anything. Not for a while…'

Bruno touched her cheek lightly with his little finger. 'Why ever not? It's wonderful news.'

'I was too afraid.'

'Afraid of what?'

'That I'd lose it…'

Bruno hugged her, pulled her closer and kissed her tenderly on her forehead.

14.

A crowd of twelve thousand filled the Sportplatz in Berlin for the opening rally. The main speaker was Heinz Neumann, who delivered a powerful speech, in contrast to Ernst Thälmann, who was rather hesitant and uninspiring. But the biggest coup had been persuading Kurt Weil to sing – and his performance did not disappoint.

The *International Arbeiter-Hilfe* had organised every aspect of the two-day conference. Nominally independent of the KDP, Willi Munzenberg was in fact their taskmaster, and had overseen everything. They'd worked day and night for many weeks – Margarita harder than anybody. She'd been the first in every morning and the last to switch off her desk lamp every night. Once, she was so exhausted she fell asleep with her head in her arms, waking with a start in the early hours in an eerily empty office. If the purpose of the rally was to raise awareness, promote the cause of the working class, disseminate the ideas of the Communist Party, as well as attract more members and win votes from the Socialist Democratic Party, then their hard work had paid off a hundredfold. For Margarita, perhaps the biggest thrill came when the deputation from the Soviet Union was welcomed onto the stage, led by a blonde young woman called Masha Ivanovna Baburina.

The following evening, after another full day of events, Masha introduced a Soviet film in the Mozart-Saal. It was located in the Crimea, so familiar to Margarita from the summers of her childhood. As she watched, she could almost feel the heat of the sun on her shoulders and the taste of saltwater on her lips. She gazed longingly at the waves of the Black Sea, where sprightly soviet youths dived into the surf after a long day netting fish or harvesting fruit. There were some scenes in Yalta too, and she was instantly steeped in memories, longing to walk through the town's small market once more, past the fat, red-faced women sitting on wooden stools next to their stalls, their cheeks shinier than their apples, their sleeves rolled up to expose their strong arms, their knees spread wide, talking and touting, laughing and cuffing the head of any small child foolish enough to try and swipe something with their small hands, 'get-out-of-here-or-you'll-really-catch-it-and-don't-even-think-of-snivelling-to-your-mother-because-she'll-only-clout-you-harder'. Margarita could practically smell the piles of ripe cherries and apricots, the big bunches of herbs, and the fish lined up in neat rows on the wooden counters, open-mouthed and glassy eyed, their scales gleaming through sprinklings of coarse salt. And that cacophony of voices exhorting you to taste, to try, to buy, and the samovar boiling away, and the sun boiling even hotter, though you knew the sea was just waiting to wash away the accumulated heat of the day and make you deliciously cool again.

Talking to Masha Ivanovna after the screening gave Margarita a deeper understanding of what was really happening in Russia. It quickly became clear that hope now filled the people's hearts as society strode confidently towards establishing full communism.

There were obstacles in their path to be sure, but it could only be a matter of time before the ideal of a classless society would be realised. As Masha said, she and her two brothers were a testament to how far the Soviet state had already succeeded; born into grinding poverty, her brother Mishka now worked for the government's housing department in Moscow, while Boris was an engineer in a factory in Sverdlovsk. Masha spoke of her mother, who'd worked for the local soviet at the height of the civil war, delivering messages on her bike until a neighbour betrayed her to the Whites. They interrogated, tortured and raped her, but she didn't give away the name of a single comrade. In the small village where she grew up, every year the schoolchildren still remembered her sacrifice, and paid tribute to her in a day of song and dance.

Masha told her of the pitiful living conditions the three siblings suffered following the death of their mother and how they had struggled to survive throughout the rest of the civil war, three little *bezprizorni* – homeless waifs – stealing rides on trains, wandering the country, finding shelter wherever they could. It was the Komsomol who rescued them, giving them back their dignity as well as a meaning, value and purpose to their lives. Had the working class under the leadership of the Communist Party not won the war against the White Armies, her life would have turned out very differently. She had no doubt that it would have been a miserable existence.

'In what other country in the world would three orphan children have had such opportunities to make the most of their talents?' she asked.

Here she was – Masha, daughter of a poor peasant family – leading a deputation to an international conference in Berlin. That was a wonder in itself. As for the unemployment in the bourgeois countries that their deputation had been hearing so much about, this was something that had disappeared forever in the Soviet Union. There was more than enough work for everybody.

Margarita admired her dedication and her faith in the Revolution and thought about the sacrifice of her mother who refused to betray the cause.

Every martyr is a witness to the truth.

15.

Willi Munzenberg wasn't a man to rest on his laurels. He had already come up with a clutch of fresh ideas to advance the cause, and Margarita's next task was to arrange a symposium, to be held over a weekend, for the intellectuals to thrash out a definitive analysis of the international situation – and whoever else she invited, it was vital that Kai-Olaf be included.

Acting on a suggestion of Vicky's, Margarita rented a house out in the country, on the outskirts of a small village to the north of Torgau, on the banks of the river Elbe. The two of them travelled there together on the train from Berlin one cloudy February day. They were arriving a day before the others to make the beds up, get in supplies of food and drink and other necessities, and make sure the place was aired. Smoking incessantly, Vicky was uncharacteristically quiet during the journey, staring out through the train window. Margarita tried to start up a conversation with her, but got no further and so let her be.

When they arrived at the house, Margarita was enchanted by the place. The trees were still bare but she thought the winter seemed to have loosened its grip a little and that there might be a sniff of spring in the air. After living so long in Berlin, she'd forgotten how silent and dark the country could be at night, the high sky above her head as clear as an angel's mind.

Vicky was clueless when it came to cooking, so while

Margarita prepared some fried liver and potatoes she sat by the table smoking away, still uncommunicative.

'Are you thinking about tomorrow?' Margarita asked.

'No. I'm thinking more about yesterday.'

She looked a little pained and Margarita felt it indelicate to probe any further. She finished cooking and served the food. Even when she was eating, Vicky had a lit cigarette to hand by her plate.

'This kitchen hasn't changed a bit. The same beams, the same cupboards, even the cups and plates are the same. Just like the last time I was here. I recognise the crack in this cup... look.'

'When were you here before?'

'A few years ago.'

Vicky never went on holiday, and Margarita was curious what had brought her here.

'I came here on my own. Apart from when Emerick visited.'

'Who's Emerick?'

'He was my husband.'

After they'd eaten, Vicky told Margarita about him. Vicky and Emerick had been members of the German Independent Socialist Party. This was the party which came into existence because the Socialist Democratic Party had failed to do enough to oppose the 1914–1918 war, but by 1920, there was a growing tension in the ranks as more and more of the membership – following the Russian Revolution of 1917 – wanted to join the Comintern.

When a formal offer came from Moscow to establish the KPD, there had been strong opinions on both sides, and fierce disagreement. The danger was that the Independent Socialist Party would split in two. Emerick had been firmly against accepting Moscow's conditions, but Vicky, far less sure of the best way forward, and anguished in trying to reach a decision, became desperate for some quiet time to herself, away from the hurly-burly of her working life.

'That's when I decided to come here on my own – to give myself time to think, away from the noise of everybody arguing.'

She'd go to sit by the riverbank and listen to the sound of the frogs in the bulrushes, trying to clear the muddle in her head. After dark, she'd return to the house, but would often still be lying fully awake as dawn broke, listening to a couple of cockerels in the distance challenging each other. In the end, she'd decided the best way to order her thoughts would be to write a pamphlet. In the tranquil kitchen, with the Moscow Comintern's twenty-one conditions in front of her on the table, she'd put her mind to work. The most important thing was to be honest with herself and everybody else and to face up to the mistakes of the past. She'd reviewed everything that had happened since the start of the 1914–1918 war. The truth was that the 1917 revolution had been a success. A communist government was, by now, well established in Russia, while the efforts of German workers had come to nothing. What was the reason for their failure?

The German proletariat were just as determined, that was clear – but they weren't as ruthless. Vicky thought back to January 1919, not long after the Kiel sailors had raised the red flag, in that period of activity when the first soviet committees were being established the length and breadth of Germany. She'd remembered arresting Frankfurt's chief of police, the Kaiser's man through and through, a hater of socialism. What had she done? Locked him in the cellar of a hotel, and tried to reason with him, tried to appeal to him with logic. What would Lenin have done? Shot him in the head without wasting another minute on him. He was an enemy of the cause, nothing more.

After a week on her own, Emerick had visited and told her he'd be very reluctant to accept the Comintern's twenty-one conditions. What about the Independent Socialist Party's right to independence of opinion? How would that be preserved? And without that independence, what dignity remained, forever more at the mercy of the whims of the bigger Russian party? Such a system wouldn't represent the supremacy of the working class at all, but supremacy *over* the working class by a distant bureaucratic clique in Moscow, with no knowledge of the political situation in Germany.

'Moscow is the last city of Asia,' he'd said.

'The first city of Europe,' she'd replied.

They couldn't even agree on that, let alone anything else. He'd left the next morning, leaving her with Rosa Luxembourg's pamphlet on Lenin to read.

But Vicky's own pamphlet soon went on sale. Her main argument was that if the German Independent Socialist Party failed to join with the Comintern, it would gradually decline and become irrelevant. At best, it would become a safe little party of reform instead of a truly revolutionary movement. Emerick had been furious and became even more so when Vicky had started to visit the local branches of the Party to make her case, which was that the only way to bring about a revolution like 1917 was to accept the Comintern's conditions and create a Communist Party in Germany.

In Emerick's opinion, the days of utopian romancing were at an end – if they had ever existed. Hadn't Karl Marx himself argued that the best hope for a socialist revolution lay in the developed capitalist countries, and not in a poor Russia with its primitive way of life? There wouldn't be a need for a dictatorial soviet party if a strong industrial working class existed in Russia. The experiences and traditions of the workers of Western Europe were very different, and it would be a step in the wrong direction to follow Lenin. Far better to follow an independent path towards socialism and social justice, even if that made it necessary in the short term to accept the capitalist system and work for change from within it, step by step. Unlike Vicky, Emerick did not regard reform as a dirty word.

Vicky for her part had seen this as the inadequate response of a party which, while sincere in its aspirations for social justice, was too ready to compromise. Yes, there were people with a clear vision within the Independent Socialist Party, who wanted to use the state to remedy social ills, but it also contained hypocritical and ambitious petit bourgeois who viewed socialism as nothing more than a ladder to high office and privilege.

It all came to a head in the October congress of 1920. With the future of the German Independent Socialist Party at stake, feelings were running high. It was a momentous occasion, a fateful hour – Zinoviev himself had come all the way from Moscow, and his address to congress lasted four hours. The Menshevik, Yury Martov spoke against him but he was a sick man, a shadow of his former self.

Vicky and Emerick, both prominent, respected members of the Independent Socialist Party, had taken their places at the front of the stage, as much in disagreement with each other as two people could be.

Husband and wife.

Emerick had spoken from the heart.

Vicky had spoken from the heart.

They had walked off the stage apart.

When the motion had gone to a vote, the vast majority had been in favour of accepting the Comintern's conditions, and from that moment in Halle, a new party was born – the *Kommunistische Partei Deutsch*. The German Communist Party.

16.

Some of the faces were familiar to Margarita from the IAF conference, but there were other comrades that she didn't know. The first through the door was Fritz Globig. Small, but with a self-important air, he had a reputation for creating bad feeling and dissent, and thoroughly revelled in his ability to stir up a hornet's nest. Vicky had warned Margarita about him, and she decided to give the owner of those knitted brows and pugnacious expression a wide berth.

The next over the threshold was Peter Maslowski, clean-shaven, straight-backed even though he was well into his sixties, followed by his latest girlfriend, Ulrike. She was younger than him by almost forty years, though she had already married and divorced. When Margarita greeted her with a kiss by the door, she smelled of face powder.

There were several delegates from the Baltic countries – Estonia, Latvia and Lithuania – and one from Luxembourg. Yannick was a tall youth, thin but broad-shouldered, with fair hair that looked as though it hadn't seen a brush in quite a while. He had a voice to split rocks, well used to shouting its way through arguments.

The rest came in twos and threes. Kai-Olaf was the last to arrive. He had the bluest eyes Margarita had ever seen in her life, and his head was as bald as an egg. By now, Margarita was experienced enough to know that Kai-Olaf wasn't his real name, but his name in the Comintern. According to Vicky, Kai-Olaf was a highly experienced agent.

'What kind of experience exactly?' asked Margarita.

'You'll hear that from him I expect,' came the reply.

Nobody had much inclination for sleep that first night. They talked long and late, and time slowed and quietened, the moon high in the sky.

Margarita was the first up the next morning, and was just starting to collect the dirty glasses and overflowing ashtrays when Kai-Olaf padded barefoot into the kitchen. She was a little tongue-tied around him, and realised that she felt a little shy. He offered to make her some coffee, and she managed to say that she was surprised to see that he was so full of energy after such a late night, and his long train journey from Italy to Torgau the previous day.

'Travelling is so tiring,' said Margarita as she sat down to roll herself a cigarette with the tobacco from Vicky's little tin.

'I'm never tired.'

'Lucky you.'

'Yes, I *am* lucky.' And he smiled at her.

There was nothing shy about him: he was an extraordinarily confident young man.

'I do some calisthenics, to keep fit.'

'And they tell me you write poetry as well?' Margarita asked tentatively.

'They?' He brought the coffee pot to the table and smiled again.

'Vicky.'

'You mustn't listen to everything Hedwig says about me.' He poured the coffee into two cups. 'I haven't written any poetry in a long time. Wish I could, but I have no time, unfortunately. To write poetry, a man needs to be left in peace.'

Margaret held her cup in both her hands and sipped her coffee, waiting for him to continue.

'Then again, I don't know if poetry is relevant to anything anymore. When I read the stuff that's being published, it seems so old-fashioned and sentimental. I often ask myself, *do these people live in the real world? Don't they have eyes? Ears?* Poets should be stung into writing poetry and excited by the world around them. But the vast majority of them just wallow in the past, because that's safer. Anyway, political action is much more important. Do you agree?'

'Yes, I do...'

'Good.' He smiled again.

Kai-Olaf was convinced that Europe would be facing another

war before long. 'Within five years, perhaps less. Unless we manage to stop the capitalists from starting it.'

Vicky was next to appear, as Margarita and Kai-Olaf were preparing breakfast for everybody. She looked exhausted, and was coughing badly, though the first thing she did was light a cigarette. Peter and Ulrike were the next two to join them. He too was bleary-eyed from lack of sleep, and accepted the coffee Margarita offered him gratefully.

Over the following two days, they discussed the situation in the Soviet Union, as well as the revolutionary possibilities in other countries – Germany, France and China in particular. Kai-Olaf gave a presentation on the fragile underground Communist Party in Italy. The essence of fascism, he told them, was to wage war against freedom. Mussolini had even claimed that people were sick and tired of freedom, and yearned for order and purpose. He said that the best freedom for the Italians was freedom in chains. In a nutshell, he argued that freedom must be sacrificed to protect freedom, as only the fascists were capable of stopping communism. Mussolini's revolution was a nationalist revolution, and the main objective of nationalism was always to oppose the unity of mankind in the name of some narrow concept of liberty.

'We've a long way to go yet before we beat them,' Kai-Olaf told them sombrely.

He explained how capitalism had succeeded in re-establishing and strengthening itself throughout Italy in the wake of the imperialist war, in spite of many difficulties. Then, he turned to Germany. He mentioned the Spartacist Uprising of January 1919, and Rosa and Karl's murder at the hands of the *Freikorps*. How the Treaty of Versailles had placed a huge burden on a people already struggling, with its requirement of the payment of crippling reparations. *C'est l'Allemagne qui paiera,* as the politicians of the Quai d'Orsay had proclaimed – the Germans were to pay for everything.

After every individual presentation, they split up into smaller groups for further discussion. Margarita found herself in the same group as Peter and Ulrike, though she would have preferred to be with Kai-Olaf. She could see him in the adjoining room, sitting on his haunches. Vicky was there too, and Margarita heard her open the discussion by stating that no revolution would succeed without the army on its side, and asking whether there was a realistic chance of that happening in Germany. But it was as much as Margarita could do to concentrate on all the arguments and counter-arguments of her own group.

That evening, it was Margarita's turn to make a presentation. She chose 'Women and Communism' as her title, and it was largely based on the writings of Alexandra Kollontai. For Kollontai, socialism meant far more than the nationalising of heavy industry. The strongest emotion in Europe for a century and more, she argued, was fear: fear of new ideas; fear of change; fear of the enfranchisement of women. This accounted for why some men remained tied as tightly as ever to the apron strings of old certainties, such as Catholicism or Calvinism. Socialism, on the other hand, sought to transform people's relationships with each other. It called for the eradication of the traditional pattern of the family: the paterfamilias, who owned everything, and the wife, who wasn't even allowed to own her own opinions.

Margarita's presentation received a warm reception, and that night after dinner, the men agreed they should be the ones to wash the dishes.

17.

A hungry-looking young man named Paul chaired the plenary session the next day. He had a little white mouse with pink eyes with him, which scampered all over his back and down his shirt.

Paul adored his little mouse, and called her Rosa. Margarita knew him slightly from those Sundays in Berlin spent knocking the doors of Neukölln and Wedding. He was an unemployed printer, originally from Düsseldorf, and spent every second of his time working for the KPD. He was the most committed of all of them and had sacrificed his entire life for many years to the communist cause. He had no other relationship – apart from Rosa – and he could be extremely impatient and sharp-tongued, especially if he thought somebody was slacking, and so had offended many comrades. Although he had never criticised her personally, Margarita had never warmed to him and felt the feeling to be mutual.

If the discussion threatened to drift, Paul was the one who brought it back to the core issue. They were discussing the situation in France that morning, and he was highly critical of the French Communist Party, who, as far he was concerned, was a sieve, losing members as fast as they poured in. Lack of discipline was to blame, with everybody coming and going as they liked.

'In contrast to our French comrades, I expect one hundred percent from everybody,' declared Paul, 'including Rosa.'

'Mr One Hundred Percent,' became his nickname. That afternoon, Ulrike wrote *100%* in chalk on the back of his waistcoat.

'Why are you laughing? What's the joke? What's so funny?' he said irritably, to suppressed snorts of laughter. 'Come along, come along. The revolution will never happen like this.'

Margarita had noticed how, from that first night when Kai-Olaf walked through the door – ducking to avoid hitting his head on the low lintel – Vicky's eyes were constantly fixed upon him, following his every move. As Vicky never had more than a coffee and a cigarette for her own breakfast, Margarita couldn't help asking her if she had her eye on Kai-Olaf. Vicky answered sharply, 'What makes you think that?'

'Just the way you behave around him.'

'You don't understand anything. The cause is more important to Kai-Olaf than any woman's love.'

18.

On the Sunday night, they had a farewell party. Margarita put her hair up and changed into her green dress, after agonising if green suited her. When she came down to the kitchen, Kai-Olaf was bent like a blacksmith over a horse, a wine bottle between his thighs. The cork came out with a satisfying pop, and Kai-Olaf looked up and passed her the bottle without seeming to notice what she was wearing or how she had done her hair. On the table was bread, butter, pork pâté, cheese, cake, a couple of bottles of rum and a regiment of wine and beer bottles.

It was bitterly cold outside, but it was all cosiness and rosy cheeks inside the house. The wine and the beer flowed, and they had a sing-song, with Peter Maslowski accompanying on his banjo. They sang the chorus of their favourite, 'The Trumpet of the Revolution', over and over. Margarita glanced around the room, which was filled with laughter and noise. There was Vicky, with her characteristic habit of throwing her hair back impatiently from her forehead as she spoke, only for it to fall back a few moments later. Everybody was chatting nineteen to the dozen, apart from Paul, who disapproved of parties as a bourgeois distraction, and was in his room with Rosa. But for the rest of them, that night, capitalism was nothing but a passing cloud to be blown out of the sky by a stiff breeze.

As the night went on, many of them exchanged stories of how they had become communists. Margarita sat between Vicky and Ulrike listening, breathing in the smells of tobacco smoke and beer and wine and sweat: the familiar smells of these long nights with the comrades. There were a variety of reasons for joining the party. Yannick shouted at the top of his voice that it was the 1918 uprising which had got him involved. Fighting on the streets of Berlin in 1919 with the Spartacists pulled Ulrike in to the cause, and Karl and Rosa Luxembourg's sacrifice convinced somebody else. The bloody insanity of the Imperialist War. The loathsomeness of the Kapp Putsch in 1920. The human cost of the hyperinflation of 1923. The strikes. The famine. The poverty and the unemployment which stunted so many thousands of lives.

It was Margarita's turn. After Vicky had refilled her glass, she began to tell them her story: how she had met Stanislav Markovich Feldman and been swayed by his arguments for returning to the Soviet Union (she said nothing of their romantic involvement), and then how Bi had encouraged her to learn more. How attending lectures and reading books like *The ABC of Communism*, which explained the nature of historical materialism, had been a revelation to her. How she had gradually come to see the truth of the Marxist analysis of society.

She noticed Kai-Olaf gazing at her with those unnervingly blue eyes.

After speaking, Margarita felt suddenly tired, and she leant her cheek against Vicky's shoulder. The wine was making her head spin and the words of the next speaker floated past her in a blur. She felt overwhelmed by a feeling of sadness. She thought of her sister, and had a pang of envy that she would become a mother in June. Sometimes she wondered whether, in her heart, that was what she most wanted too.

She snapped back to attention when Kai-Olaf started to speak. He mentioned a man called Jan, but said most of them already knew what an important influence he had been, so he wouldn't bore them with it again. But there had been another experience, a personal experience, that had taken place outside Lvov, in Poland. Kai-Olaf had been working for the Communist Party in

Moscow, and was staying in the city on his way back to Berlin. It had been a Sunday afternoon, one of those days that stays in the memory – a blue sky without a single cloud and the sun shining as though for ever. He had joined a group of students and other young communists for a picnic on the riverbank, under the leaves of the hazel trees – a chance to paddle and catch minnows. Most of them were Jews.

Kai-Olaf had been telling them about the situation in Russia, when they had heard a sudden bellowing. The next minute, a gang of youths wearing the badge of some Catholic organisation had been upon them. They had kicked and punched everybody indiscriminately, like madmen, their violence implacable, beating flesh to a pulp and turning the picnic into a bloodbath. Two of the brutes had chased Kai-Olaf into the middle of the river and had held his face under the water, shoving it against the stones of the riverbed and screaming at him to show them his cock. Even after they'd satisfied themselves that he wasn't circumcised, they had beaten him just the same. If he hadn't managed to free himself and run for his life, they might well have killed him that afternoon. For months afterwards, he felt guilty that he'd saved himself but left the rest to their fate.

He'd already made a vow to promote the work of the Communist Party to the best of his ability, but this incident hardened his resolve even more. Here was the only party committed to purge the world of the hatred which was so deeply ingrained in Poland, Hungary and Romania, and even in France and Germany – a hatred that had been nurtured and allowed to flourish for centuries by a corrupt and venal Catholic Church.

'What's between you and Kai-Olaf?' asked Margarita when she and Vicky finally went to bed late that night.

'Nothing.'

'Vicky, I'm not a fool so don't treat me like one. I can tell there's something.' She got into bed. 'When did you first meet him?'

'You really need to know right this minute?'

Of course, she did, she was itching to know.

They lay there in their bunks in the dark, and Vicky began to speak.

The first time Vicky visited Moscow was for the Comintern's Congress of 1921. At the same time, Emerick was in Vienna for the European Socialists' Congress, where he and Otto Brauer, the leader of the Austrian Social Democrats, hoped to establish an International Workers Union as an alternative movement to the Comintern. Although Vicky and Emerick were still married and living under the same roof, since the Halle congress, they were barely speaking to each other.

The visit to Moscow renewed Vicky's hope, and on her return to Berlin, her article condemning the International Workers Union as a movement of liberals, petit-bourgeois, reformists and fools was the lead article in *Die Rote Fahne*, which then offered her a permanent position on the paper. The Social Democratic party wrote a coruscating response to her article in their own newspaper and subsequently both the *Leipziger Volkszeitung* and *Freiheit*, the Independent Socialist Party's paper, wrote critical pieces as well. However, Vicky's pamphlet was responsible for persuading some members of the Independent Socialist Party to defect to the KPD and the Comintern. Her husband Emerick told her she was nothing more than Lenin and Karl Radek's little poodle and, as his wife, she was making his own position untenable.

What was more important to her? The KPD or him?

Vicky told him it was only a matter of time before what now remained of the Independent Socialist Party returned like a little bird to its nest in the Social Democratic Party.

'Must you keep spouting that line at me day in, day out?'

Emerick was furious with his wife, but was also increasingly concerned about her health. From when she was a child, Vicky had always had a weak chest, and now the punishing hours she spent working for the KPD had finally caught up with her. Her doctor told her in no uncertain terms that if she didn't rest, her health would be irretrievably broken. Even then, she was reluctant to give in, but Emerick told her firmly, 'The revolution can wait for you to get better.'

The KPD paid for her to stay at a sanatorium in the Swiss Alps. Her room there had a balcony, and the view was beyond anything she could have imagined. She sat for hours watching the play of shadow and sun on the snow-capped summits by day, and, after nightfall, the silvery moonlight dimly reflected on the smooth, silent slopes, with the vast universe above, dappled with a billion stars.

Vicky carried on working just the same – against the express orders of her doctors – writing articles from her bed advocating a United Socialist State of Europe. She had never been more convinced that Lenin was right. A Europe-wide civil war was the only way forward; pointless to live in hope that somehow a communist order would flower from the soil of capitalist goodwill. The workers thought like trade-unionists, in terms of short-term objectives, rather than adopt a more long-term strategy for real gains. Unfortunately, that was how Emerick thought too. But the revolution had a fresh smell – pure and clean like brand new leather. It was imperative to learn from the mistakes of the past. True communism needed tough men and women with a clear vision and an untiring commitment to destroy capitalism and start anew.

Two months went by. Vicky claimed she was well enough to return to Berlin. Easy enough to peddle lies in a letter – letters never betrayed themselves with a blush. But when Emerick came to visit her and saw for himself that she was by

57

no means fully recovered, he suggested taking her to Italy for some sun instead. He reminded her that the last time they'd had a holiday was on their honeymoon three years previously, in 1919, and that had only been a week in Paris. Vicky knew this was a last-ditch attempt to save their marriage, and felt that she couldn't refuse.

They travelled down to Naples, Capri and Pompeii. It was August and the streets were baking. One morning they climbed to the top of Mount Vesuvius, she on the back of a donkey, he walking at her side.

'I love you,' Emerick told her on the summit, his voice a note higher than usual.

'I love you, Vicky,' he said again, as they made their descent.

'I love you too,' she answered.

But when Emerick arrived back at the foot of the mountain, he confessed that there was an empty feeling in his heart.

He took her with him to Rome at the beginning of September, where he was due to attend the International Federation of Trade Unions Congress. That's what was paying for the holiday. As she walked around the Piazza Venezia on her own one afternoon, Vicky saw Kai-Olaf coming towards her. She wasn't sure to begin with if it was him, and she had to shade her eyes from the sun to see him properly. She hadn't seen him since January 1919, when he came to Frankfurt with a crew of sailors from the Kiel mutiny in order to spread the revolution.

What an exciting period that had been. Vicky remembered the heated discussions in the Schleisinger Eck, an old tavern on the corner of Gallus-strasse. She remembered going over to the city barracks, to release the soldiers who had been imprisoned there for refusing to obey their officers. She remembered her elation when the first soviet was elected. Their confidence and conviction grew, but Berlin was slow to react. The revolution was building up a head of steam, but why was the Social

Democratic Party so reluctant to lead it? Why were they so infuriatingly cautious in all their decisions? They should have published a manifesto. But it was the revolutionaries in the Schlesinger Eck who did that, on behalf of the Soldiers and Workers' Soviet.

They distributed the manifesto and thousands upon thousands of people spilled out onto the streets in a sea of red flags and ribbons – men, women, children, all making their way as one to the Osthafen fields on the city outskirts. People were jubilant, feeling in their hearts that the dawn was about to break, that the revolution was bound to prevail.

But staked against the new German republic was the older power of the great estates of East Prussia, as well as the iron, coal and metal barons of the Ruhr.

'Our mistake in 1919 was that we weren't ruthless enough.' Vicky had said this to Margarita more than once. 'That was the lesson I learnt too late.'

Like arresting that wretched Frankfurt chief of police, instead of shooting him in the head. Vicky had been so naive.

On the Piazza Venezia, she and Kai-Olaf had sheltered from the searing heat under the canopy of a little trattoria. Vicky didn't need to ask him; she'd known full well he was there on Comintern business. He'd told her what Mussolini was up to, and how fascism was on the march throughout Italy. He'd been in Bibbiena, a small town not far from Arezzo. Stopping for a drink at a café, he'd been told about a stonemason called Giulio, who had just returned from America, where he'd been working for three years in order to save enough money to marry. One night, he happened to be drinking in the same bar as a group of fascists from Arezzo. They started baiting him, and the leader of the group ordered him to shout 'Evviva Mussolini!' When the young man refused to do it for the third time, the fascist took a pistol out of his belt and shot Giulio dead right there. Within a fortnight, the fascist had been set free, with no charges brought against him.

Three days later, as their train approached the outskirts of Berlin, Vicky told Emerick that their marriage was at an end.

'I know,' he replied, without taking his eyes off the fields that streaked past the window.

Vicky arrived back in the city on the day that Walther Rathenau, the Weimar Republic's Foreign Minister, was shot dead in broad daylight by three Nazis as he drove through the streets in his open-topped motor-car. Vicky knew that she had made the correct decision. The fascists were flexing their muscles, ready to smash all opposition to smithereens.

'I was right, not Emerick. The communist way is the only way Margarita.'

'I agree,' answered her friend. 'The communist way is the only way.'

It would take strength and determination to fight capitalism and fascism – and those qualities were only to be found in the Comintern and the KPD.

'But you still haven't answered my question,' said Margarita.

'What question?' asked Vicky in a sleepy voice.

'What is there between you and Kai-Olaf?'

'I've already told you.'

19.

As he hauled himself up the dark stairs to his room on the top floor, Alyosha told himself yet again that he really must find somewhere cheaper to live. Of course, there were certainly cheaper places to be had in Paris – far cheaper – but they were damp hovels, infested with vermin and lice; places to destroy a man's health forever.

'*Confort moderne*' proclaimed the bold letters on the front of the hotel. But this was a feeble attempt to throw dust into someone's eyes to hide the layers of dust inside. The Hôtel de Nantes was an old building on the Rue du Montparnasse, divided up into a warren of cramped rooms that smelled of rancid fat and stale cigarette smoke. The owner was a portly asthmatic, always with half an ear to the radio, which, when it wasn't making a noise like an egg frying in a pan, crooned from somewhere under the counter in the reception. He would listen to it constantly, day and night, as though he was expecting to hear tidings of great importance. At his feet lay an ugly old dog, a great ball of fur with a head at one end and a tail at the other – a lazy, good-for-nothing lump.

Alyosha was adept, by now, at nipping up the stairs when the man's back was turned, to avoid the ever-more-insistent requests that he pay his rent. It was hard to live outside the world of daily work. But who would be daft enough to take on a Russian with a visa that was due to run out before the end of the summer?

But the rent was now long overdue, so he had no choice but to go out once more with Leonid Kolosov.

20.

Leonid Kolosov was Alyosha's best friend. In Russia, Leonid had fought in Denikin's army during the Civil War, but before that he'd been a painter and decorator in Moscow. Fleeing Russia, he'd had a tortuous journey across Europe, tramping hundreds of miles on foot. On the way, he'd worked for a while as a miner, living in a filthy hostel on the outskirts of Sofia, where he'd been struck down by dysentery. Leonid had made his way along the backroads of the Balkans in the company of other ex-soldiers, to the city of Trieste. From there, they had aimed for Florence, and found lodgings in a garret in one of the old medieval palazzi on the Borgo Pinti. Leonid had hoped he might once more make a living with a brush and paint, but there was no work to be had, and so he and a friend had taken up their packs again.

They'd arrived in Paris with dusty clothes and aching bones. It had been a wonder that Leonid's friend had even survived the long journey. Leonid had spent the next few months shuffling along the streets, looking for work, wondering whether he'd have to spend the rest of his life with nothing better to do than talk to his own shadow.

Eventually, he'd found a job as a *plongeur* in a hotel restaurant on Rue de Vincennes, but soon became fed up of washing the filthy dishes of the three sittings, especially as he was paid the smallest wage for the dirtiest work. To add insult to injury, a pimply French youth had been employed over his head to wear the *frac* and work in the restaurant as a waiter, after he'd been promised the job more than once. Leonid had been gripped by an almost uncontrollable rage, more violent than he had ever felt before, at the sheer injustice of it. He'd collected his wages and left that day, but for his swan song, he'd emptied the till on his way out. It was while he'd been getting blind drunk with the proceeds that he'd met Alyosha, and shortly after becoming friends, they'd become partners in crime. Breaking into houses was much more lucrative than working.

This time, they burgled a substantial house on the Faubourg Saint-Germain, full of paintings of aristocratic ladies and gentlemen with pink cheeks and huge wigs, the family coat of arms proudly on display. Other rooms were decorated with Gobelin tapestries, and stuffed with furniture: gilded chairs and sofas, ornate and heavy, and thickly brocaded curtains framing the large windows. It reminded Alyosha of his former home, the house where he'd been brought up in Petrograd. If things had turned out differently, perhaps he could have whiled away his life in a house like this one.

They had always had a golden rule: that they would only steal money, because money couldn't be traced. But Leonid was beginning to be tempted by small items of large value, which could be fenced quickly and profitably.

'Look at this,' he said, dangling a finely wrought gold bracelet on his finger. Alyosha told him to put it back, but his friend was having none of it.

'Don't you worry; I can get rid of it easily.'

'How?'

'Doesn't matter how.'

'But it *does* matter how. Wait...'

Leonid was already pocketing the bracelet. Alyosha grabbed his arm.

'Oy! Let go! ...'

'You're going to sell that to somebody...'

'Let go of me I said!'

'...who probably knows you. So if the *flics* shake them down they can pin it on you. It's too risky.'

They both froze as they heard a noise from downstairs; the unmistakeable sound of the front door opening.

'Out. Now.'

21.

'I'm bad at remembering names...' his new neighbour, Yury, had mumbled the first time they met, as he stood at the head of the stairs, dressed only in his vest and underpants. He had been to piss in the zinc bucket in the dark little cupboard that passed for a W.C. 'Were you in the civil war in Russia?'

Alyosha said he'd been too young to fight.

'Nobody was too young to wage war on the Antichrist.' The man scratched his underarm with his dirty fingernails and Alyosha backed away slightly from the stink of him, but there was no escape to be had. 'Come into my room, why don't you…'

Reluctantly, Alyosha followed him in and sat on the unmade bed. He would discover that his neighbour spoke about Russia obsessively, and was always going back to the turmoil of the Civil War. He loathed his life as an exile in Paris.

Yury pulled a lice comb through his greasy hair and then examined it.

'When I first arrived, the only place I could find to sleep was in a stable with some poor nag of a horse, clapped out after a lifetime of pulling people in a cart around Paris.'

He shook his head sorrowfully. 'Russia,' he sighed.

It was the Russian landscape he missed more than anything. That and the weather. And the people. He described seeing the sun set above Sukhinichi, a blood-red streak across the vast sky, as the clouds froze above the tiny village of Pruzhana on the fringes of the vast Belovezhsk forest, where open fields stretched across the country, fields of oats, fields of barley, and wide meadows of wild mustard. They'd sat there as the rain soaked the soldiers to their skin.

'There's nothing worse than rain to make a soldier's uniform stink…'

And then it would rot on your back and fall to pieces leaving you half naked. The worst time was when you saw miles of marshland lying ahead of you, and you had to slog through it in the rain, your feet so heavy you could barely lift them, through thickets of grey poplars, dense vegetation, clumps of weeds, under a cold green sky, and no shelter to be found for the horses or the soldiers; the merciless wind pursued them with as much savagery as the Red Army.

Onwards, onwards.

And the communists never far from their tail.

Onwards, onwards.

Until, late one afternoon, a girl in a glade, her big white eyes, her lips open like a scream; nearby, a dog and a small boy, her brother. 'Go and fetch water from the stream,' he orders the boy. He tears his shirt, tears it in two, in three. A young girl in her terror – *What's happening to me? You're having a baby.* He rolls up his sleeves. *What's happening to me?* A scream swallows her words, deafens them as the pains rips through her. The night in flames; sparks in the forest, and her low whimpering mingling with the rustle of the leaves; dry, white lips, the smell of her sweat among the birds, the moles and the sharp scent of a zig-zaggy fox, until something pink spills onto the straw like a piglet.

Yury's stories were nearly all of the same ilk.

'How were we so stupid as to lose Russia?' he'd ask, again and again. On one evening, the man demanded, 'When do you think we'll all be able to go home?' while on another, as Alyosha was combing the lice out of his hair above a basin of boiling water, Yuri begged, 'Alexei Fyodorovich? When do you think the hour will come?'

'Some day.'

'How can you be so sure?'

He wasn't sure at all.

'This is the age of Caesar,' his neighbour raged, 'an age of blood and iron, and we just kick at the wind.'

Yury often felt he was going crazy, as well as bewilderingly powerless and listless; that he was nothing more than his current situation, and that his future was a bleak affair.

Russia, Russia…

His friends in Paris were ex-soldiers from the White Army almost to a man. One of his closest friends was a one-armed twenty-eight-year-old called Fedot. Every time they met, they got roaring drunk together, and reminisced as the big red trumpet of the gramophone sang arias from *Rigoletto*.

22.

Alyosha lifted his head. For a split second in the dense blackness, he had absolutely no idea where he was. But a stranger's fist was knocking furiously on his door. He pulled back a curtain to let the moonlight flood the floor of his room, and stumbled to the door.

Two devils stood there.

He groped for his visa, his *permis de sejour* and his Nansen passport, and stood there, bleary-eyed, as they rifled through them. Neither of them looked as though they were in any hurry to leave, or gave any apology for turfing him out of his bed at six in the morning. Outside his window, a glimmer of light was just inching its way into the sky.

Before he'd left Berlin, Alyosha had spent days running from one counter to another, from office to office on Alexanderplatz, begging for the passport created especially for stateless Russians. Then more endless queues and interviews, before he'd obtained his visa in the office of the French Counsel. A *permis de sejour* could only be obtained on the Paris black market, and had cost him dearly. But his papers were all in order.

The visit had the stamp of a warning about it. They'd been investigating a spate of burglaries, and his name had been passed on to them. They didn't want to accuse him or arrest him ('Not at present anyway'), but they wanted him to know that they would be keeping an eye on him from now on.

'So if you have any common sense…'

'Can I have my visa back?'

'If you want it back, you'll need to go and see this man.'

The name on the card he'd been given was Superintendent Chenot.

66

Alyosha didn't have much choice. Without a visa he could easily be arrested on the street in broad delight, and transported over the border in chains between two policemen. When he showed up at the *Préfecture de Police* on Boulevard de Paris the next morning and announced himself, he was ushered up to an office on the second floor, where a man in his fifties, dressed in a dark suit and a shirt with an ill-fitting collar, sat behind the desk.

Alyosha took a cigarette from the proffered silver case. Superintendent Chenot was clean-shaven, and his fleshy cheeks testified to a life of good eating and drinking. There was some slight defect in his left eye which meant it was always half shut, and he wore a pair of spectacles, with black bone frames. He was friendly enough, made small talk about this and that, although Alyosha hardly said a word.

'Do you know what the secret of policing Paris is?' the Superintendent asked eventually. 'I'd be happy to let you in on it.'

Through a gap in the clouds, a shaft of light fell on the old grey mansard roofs of the tall buildings of the Quai Saint-Michel. Alyosha watched the tourists strolling past the stalls lining the walls of the riverbank. He could also hear the faint hum from the steady trickle of traffic: trucks, motor cars and omnibuses.

'...are you listening to me?' Superintendent Chenot clicked his fingers. 'Small accidents and small men can cook up big events.'

He insisted that Alyosha shut his eyes and try to imagine a gang of men sitting in a room in a building somewhere in Paris at that very minute, plotting some villainy. A burglary. Something even worse, an atrocity. A bomb in a café, perhaps. What did anybody know about these men? How would it be possible to prevent them? Through what method?

'The most important commodity for a policeman,' Superintendent Chenot told him, 'is knowledge. When a man knows all there is to know about his fellow man, he's in a very privileged position. It makes it possible to re-arrange the pattern of events, so the consequences are diverted – but without anybody being any the wiser about the unseen hand quietly steering it all.' Suddenly he laughed – a big heartfelt sound. 'The expression on your face, Alexei Fyodorovich!'

As he lit another cigarette, Alyosha noticed that the policeman's nails were bitten down to the quick.

'What would you like to be?' Chenot asked him calmly from behind his black spectacles.

He shrugged his shoulders.

'Apart from a thief.'

Alyosha denied that he was one.

'Seen your friend Leonid Kolosov recently? You needn't answer, because you haven't. Do you know why? Because he's with us – well he's not with us exactly, but in a cell over in Santé. Mind you, I'm not sure how much of a friend he is to you, really. We brought him in for a little chat after he'd been trying to flog a bracelet over in the Bois de Verrière market, only the stall holder happens to be one of our songbirds. Now… we don't have the evidence against you that we have against your friend. But then again… how will you survive in Paris without your visa? Or your *permis de séjour*?'

Knuckles rapped against the frosted glass of the door and a curly-headed man with a ginger beard came in, shirt-sleeves rolled up and his trousers hoicked up over his stomach with braces. He placed a file on Superintendent Chenot's desk and said he couldn't go any further with it until his boss looked at it.

'I'll telephone you once I've finished, Eric,' Superintendent Chenot looked directly at Alyosha and added, 'I shouldn't be too much longer.'

The curly haired man nodded and left the office.

'Do you know this man?' asked the policeman holding up a photograph in front of him.

Alyosha nodded, 'Baron Wrangel. He led the White Army.'

'And what about this one?'

Yury Safronovich.

'You needn't say a word. I know that you do. You both live at the Hôtel de Nantes.'

He picked up two or three other photographs. 'We have all sorts of people singing to us in all sorts of places – you'd be surprised.'

Yury Safronovich was a member of the *Soiuz Russkikh Ofitservo Uchastnikov Voiny* – the Union of White Army Officers in Paris, which held regular meetings. It was the duty of the Paris police to keep an eye on all foreign groups, never mind who they were. The Reds. The Whites. Mussolini-hating Italians. Arabs. Armenians. Yellow students from Cochinchina, hell-bent on toppling the regime in Saigon. In short, the riff-raff from all continents, who had found refuge here in France, the shit from the gutters of every country in the world. Nobody was going to turn the Republic into an arena for political intrigue, with so much potential for violence. Not on his watch. And now that the Soviet Union and France had restored diplomatic relations, any plotting from the White émigrés was at best a nuisance, and at worse, harmful to French interests.

'So… you do us the odd favour, and you can be sure we'll look after you.'

Alyosha asked what kind of favours he had in mind.

'You just tell us what your friends are talking about. What's on their mind.'

'You want me to be a Judas?'

'You could argue that Judas helped Jesus Christ to bring about God's eternal purpose in the world. So, you wouldn't be a traitor, you'd be a facilitator.'

23.

Zepherine was at home with the baby, but his uncle's wife gave Alyosha a distinctly lukewarm welcome, especially once she understood that he'd come to ask Artyom a favour. He needed to be put in touch with Milko Steiner as quickly as possible, so that he could buy a new visa on the black market.

He offered her a cigarette, but Zepherine made a point of taking one from the wooden box at her elbow, and said curtly, 'I though you weren't on speaking terms with your uncle? But then, you only call by when you want something.'

It was the truth and he didn't have a ready answer. He snuffed his match out between his thumb and forefinger and slipped it into his pocket.

'Is he here?' he asked her.

'No, he's not. He's away on business, and before you ask, I've no idea where.'

'When are you expecting him back?'

'I'm not sure.'

'He didn't say?'

'I didn't ask.'

Alyosha suspected that she knew, but chose not to share the information with him.

'Would it be possible for a message to reach him?'

'Would it be possible for you to stop interrogating me?'

'I want to put our quarrel behind us.'

'Do you now? Well, well.' She swept a wisp of hair back from her face.

'I was at fault to doubt him. It was my mother who got rid of Grete, I realise that now.'

'You took your time to come to that conclusion.'

'Yes, I know. I'm sorry.'

'I hope you're not just saying this to me because you need his help again.'

'Like I said, I was at fault.'

'So what are you living on? Your mother's money? Have you patched things up with her too?'

He had no intention of telling Zepherine how precariously he was living, and the conversation limped on until Alyosha could bear it no more and made an excuse to leave. At the door Zepherine asked him to wait a moment and came back with a letter in her hand.

'This belongs to you.'

Alyosha recognised the writing at once and noticed the Biarritz postmark.

'It arrived… let's see… a while back now. I don't remember exactly when. Better late than never I suppose.'

'Thank you.'

They said their farewells and he left his uncle's house.

He read through his mother's scrawl on a bench in the Luxembourg gardens. The Hôtel Biarritz in Biarritz. What was she doing there? Was she on holiday, or had she taken up residence?

The contents were direct and to the point. Alexei Alexeivich Dashkov had left her for another woman. He had taken advantage of her and stolen her money. He had been opportunistic and selfish from start to finish. She begged Alyosha to forgive her for not listening to him when he warned her; she longed to see him once more, she thought about him constantly, was worried about him and realised how badly she had treated him.

Alyosha was about to throw the letter away, but changed his mind. He decided he was going to reply to his mother.

24.

At the best of times, Yury was a sad and self-pitying creature, which explained why there was always a sour, bitter air about him. He hardly ever laughed. Perhaps he had lost the capacity, as his only reaction to a witty comment was to say 'ha ha', which made him sound even sourer. One of his favourite phrases was, 'Every exile is a chronicler of suffering'.

There was something sickly about him, his shoulders always hunched and his hands usually stuffed up the sleeves of his shirt as if he was trying to keep warm, even on a sunny day. Not only had he been uprooted and thrown to the four winds, many years previously, Yury had been disappointed in love. He had never come to terms with his loss and still lived with his pain, in summer as in winter, day and night, frozen in his misery as the city streamed past him.

'You have no idea how much I loved her.' Like picking at a scab, he insisted on revisiting his memories over and over. 'We were engaged. I remember putting the ring on her finger as though it were yesterday.'

This was in Kiev during the Civil War.

'Look…'

He took a photograph out of his pocket.

'What do you think of her?' he asked, smiling gently. 'Tell me honestly.'

'Very beautiful.'

'Wasn't she?' Yury kissed her image. 'Nobody could hold a candle to her. Then that fucking stinking fucker of a Jew stole her from under my nose.'

His grief for her loss was stronger than anything else. At the time, he'd been running a puppet theatre in Kiev with Tamara Bobrikova, this girl who left him for another man – some journalist by the name of Stanislav Markovich Feldman. Destroyed, Yury decided to join the White Army and go off to fight the Reds, just as the first chill winds of winter were blowing in. It was his attempt at burying his pain, though he nursed a hope that Tamara Bobrikova would see through the Jew, and come back to him one day.

'That hope was the only thing that kept me alive through that winter of mud and blood.'

He wasn't only fighting for Russia, he was fighting to win Tamara back, and he clung to his dream of returning victorious to Kiev to fill his lungs with a pure spring breeze. But Tamara Bobrikova was lost to him forever, and all down the years he still loved her, still desired her, though he hadn't heard a word of what had become of her. The worst of it, what gave him more pain than anything, was that he had lost her to one of Jesus Christ the Saviour's murderers, one of the race who had nailed the Son of God to the cross.

'I used to know him,' Alyosha finally had to admit.

'The Jew Feldman? You?'

He nodded.

'How? When?'

Alyosha told him of his own troubles in Kiev. Then he said, 'He used to see my cousin, Margarita Kozmyevna, in Berlin for a while.'

'Did you ever hear him mention Tamara?'

'No, never.'

Ever since he'd lost her, Yury's heart had darkened, his reason was disturbed and his judgment impaired. No wonder he used to shout at himself so much. Behind the door of his room, he kept a puppet of the devil – one he'd bought in an open-air market in Moscow – and often the two of them would scream at each other for hours, which always terrified any new tenant.

In the meantime, Alyosha continued to report every word back to Superintendent Chenot.

25.

The heat of an Indian Summer had curdled inside the walls of the Hôtel de Nantes, and in his airless room, Yury sat in a stupor on the wooden chair by the open window. An aria from *Rigoletto* played on the gramophone, and every now and again garbled voices, children's laughter, and the occasional whistle floated up from the street.

'You've not much to say for yourself this evening, Alexei Fyodorovich,' Yury said.

Alyosha was standing in front of a little mirror shaving his face by the weak light of the small carbon lamp. He told Yury that the letter he'd posted to his mother in Biarritz had been returned to him that morning unopened, and on the back, in red ink, the hotel manager informed the sender that Madame Dashkov had vacated the hotel without leaving a forwarding address – or settling her bill.

Yury's sympathy and concern were sincere, Alyosha felt more uncomfortable then ever: being a Judas was dirty work. He hated quizzing Yury about his fellow White Army officers, and hated betraying his own people – men who had suffered the blood and agony of the Civil War, men who had lost everything and were living a miserable existence as exiles.

'Are your documents all in order?' asked Alyosha.

'I don't have a *permis de séjour* at the moment, but I hope to have a new one stamped by the end of the month. These things always take time. Why?

'You'd better try and have it stamped before then.'

'I can't pay for it until I'm given my wages.'

'Then don't be in your room on Thursday night. Stay away – all night.'

Yury looked doubtful. 'Why? What have you heard?'

Alyosha felt dirty.

'Are you in any trouble? No, there's no need to tell me, I know you are. You've got yourself into some scrape, that much is obvious. A debt? A woman? Blackmail? What?'

How to answer? Alyosha felt marooned on an island of loneliness where he couldn't share his worries with anyone.

'Come on – out with it. What's troubling you?'

'I can't tell you…'

'Yes, you can.'

Alyosha dithered for a while, and then, under further pressure from Yury, came clean and told him all about Superintendent Chenot.

'Grass on who exactly?' Yury asked. 'Me?'

Alyosha told him the whole story from beginning to end.

'You're playing a very dangerous game.'

Alyosha knew that better than anybody.

'Yes, a very dangerous game. What exactly have you told them?'

'Nothing really…'

'Are you sure?'

'Yes.'

Yury reflected on his predicament and then said, 'You need to clear out of here. Find somewhere else to live. And keep clear of this Chenot for good. Seriously. We already know about him and he's a sly bastard. He tried his best to recruit me last year but I told him where to go.'

That Thursday night, there was much pounding on the doors of hotel rooms in the area as the police worked diligently to round up anybody who didn't possess official papers. On the night of the raid, Alyosha wandered the streets, slipping in to a bar or café when he needed to warm up. He eventually fell into an uneasy sleep propped up against an oak tree in the Jardin de Luxembourg.

This was no kind of life.

Things had to change, but a visa on the black market would cost him an arm and a leg. To pay for it, Alyosha needed to find work immediately, and that wasn't the easiest thing in the world. There was only one thing for it. He would break in to his Uncle Artyom's house.

He kept an eye on the comings and goings there for a few days, and noticed that Zepherine usually went out shopping in the afternoons. He waited until he saw the maid take Bibi out for a walk in his pram at three, and then climbed up to a back window, watched from a branch of the birch tree by a jet-black crow, with yellow eyes and glossy feathers. He smashed the window and climbed into a bedroom. This was where he had slept when he first arrived from Berlin in the spring of 1924. Almost three years had gone by since that day when he first walked into his uncle's house, clutching his cardboard suitcase. He'd vowed to himself he wouldn't go near his uncle, but, as the French bureaucratic nightmare of trying to settle in Paris had engulfed him, he'd had no choice but to go to the house to ask for help, although he'd loathed himself for doing so. He remembered being ushered by his Uncle Artyom down the wide, black-and-white marble-tiled passage, into the square living room, with its magnificent chandelier hanging from the high ceiling. Underfoot had been a carpet and modern, brightly-coloured paintings had hung on the walls. He remembered the suspicious look the fair-haired, buxom young girl had given him.

'My nephew, Alexei Fyodorovich – Alyosha, this is Zepherine. He'll be staying with us for a while,' Artyom had stated, before offering: 'Campari?'

'Perfect,' Alyosha had managed to answer.

'Zephie?'

She'd still been considering him, and eventually she'd asked him exactly how long he was thinking of staying.

'Until he finds his feet darling,' Artyom had answered.

She'd still looked a little sulky as they'd sipped their drinks. Then she'd asked, as if Alyosha hadn't been there, 'Is he anything to do with *her*?'

Her to Zepherine was always Jeanette, Artyom's first wife.

'No.'

Artyom had a son by Jeanette, Dimitri, but the ties between father and son didn't seem very strong. Zepherine was a jealous woman at the best of times so their names were never to be mentioned in front of her.

In his uncle's study, he broke the flimsy lock on the bureau easily enough and started rifling through its contents, making as much mess as he could. Then, he emptied cupboards, drawers, shelves, tossing everything he had no use for on the floor. He stuffed as much loot as he thought he could sell – not as much as he'd hoped for – into his pockets.

He was stopped short for a moment by an old photograph of his mother and his uncle when they were children. Then he came across the deeds to Manoli Les Pins, a villa Artyom had bought in 1921, a few miles inland from Nice. He pocketed the deeds, safe in the knowledge this would cause a great deal of inconvenience to his uncle at some point. He wanted to injure his uncle, injure him as much as he could for stealing Grete away from him. He would never forgive him for that.

He walked out of the front of the house confidently, and strode up the street, past a little old gypsy woman carrying her load of pegs on her back, her colourful rags blowing around her tiny frame in the wind. His head was spinning with elation at his success, and he felt as though for once he had done an honest day's work.

26.

A friend of Yury – an ex-soldier who'd fought with the White Army under Baron Wrangel, but who now worked on the production line in the Renault factory at Boulougne-Billancourt – found some proper work for Alyosha. He also told him that he knew of a room going in an apartment block in Passy, in the 16th *arrondissement*, not too far from Place de Costa Rica, behind the Trocadéro.

'I don't think my feet stink too badly,' said his new co-tenant, 'but if they do, open the window.'

Smelly feet or not, what choice did Alyosha have? He had to find a place to lay low in order to stop being Inspector Chenot's stooge, and so he moved his meagre possessions over to Passy. The new room had an alcove in the wall, which passed for a wardrobe, and a small shelf by the window, where he placed the copy of *The Protocols of the Elders of Zion* that Yury had stolen from the Sorbonne Library, and his father's volume of Catullus, along with the deeds to his uncle's villa.

His co-tenant was out every night driving his taxi, so Alyosha didn't see much of him, which suited him very well. Sometimes Yury would meet him after his shift in the Renault factory, and would attempt to pull his leg in his deeply unhumorous way. 'Don't you think it's ironic that one of the children of the bourgeoisie has joined the proletariat? Eh? Think about it. Before long you and your lot will be the working class. People like you will inherit paradise here on earth, at the end of history with a capital H.'

Alyosha snorted at his friend's idiocy.

'You can snort, but isn't it true?'

One evening, the two of them went to a charitable evening to raise money for a Russian library for émigrés. The author, Ivan Bunin, was giving a reading, along with some other émigré writers and poets, and there was a short musical interlude; some Mozart and Schumann. The evening was well attended, and, after the official programme came to an end, people lingered to drink and smoke and return to their fantasy of going head-to-head with the communists and destroying the Soviet Union. These were the people whose secrets Alyosha had been expected to betray to the police, and he felt very pleased that Chenot no longer featured in his life.

'Alexei Fyodorovich,' somebody greeted him wheezily. 'Dear friend, son of your dear father, how are things with you? What a very nice surprise to come across you here.'

Alyosha racked his brains but the elderly man with a grey moustache and silver spectacles looked unfamiliar. He wore a sheepskin hat, a shabby but well-cut grey fur jacket, and he carried a battered black leather briefcase under his arm.

Suddenly, Alyosha remembered who he was. Yevgeny Karpovich Kedrin had been his father's lawyer for over twenty years back in Petrograd. He'd been a prominent Freemason, as well as a member of the Kadet Party in the last Duma before the 1914–1918 war.

'Alexei Fyodorovich, I couldn't be happier to see you.'

Yevgeny Karpovich took his hand, squeezed it tightly and lowered his voice until it was almost inaudible. He wondered if he could have a private word? They moved to a corner, but it was only so that he could ask to borrow some money. Alyosha had none to give. Yevgeny Karpovich continued to press Alyosha's hand, and changed the subject to talk about Russia. It became clear that he was seething with bitterness, and struggling to find some meaning to his life. Since the revolution, he seemed to have misplaced the person he used to be. Yevgeny dreamt of returning to his grandfather's estate in Turkestan, where he had spent all his summers as a boy, but he could never truly escape the pain of his present, for he was starving in the middle of plenty, failing where he should be succeeding. How was it possible for a man such as himself to retain his dignity in this foreign city?

After Yevgeny Karpovich finally drifted away, no doubt to try to borrow money from somebody else, Yury told Alyosha how the man had enraged half the émigré community of Paris the previous year, when he claimed in the letters page of *Posledniia Novosti* that Tolstoy had stolen the plot of his great novel *War and Peace* from something by Lermontov. The more people took issue with his claim, the more stubbornly he clung to it. The letters flying back and forth became more and more insulting, until the paper had to bring the correspondence to a close, for fear of a libel suit. Alyosha, faced with the long walk back to Passy for the want of an omnibus fare, could not have been less interested.

27.

Nobody could call brushing a mile and a half of factory floor inspiring work. The best of it was spending his days among Russians, former soldiers from Baron Wrangel's army. For Alyosha, hearing his mother tongue all day was a huge pleasure. Still, it didn't make the work any less boring, and he spoke to the foreman in the hope of something better.

After a couple of weeks, he was promoted to screwing the doors of the Renault cars into place, working on the production line for the 8CV, the 10CV and the 18CV models. He was soon thoroughly bored of endlessly tightening screws all day, and went back to the foreman, but this time he was told curtly to get on with it or get out.

On his way home to Passy at the end of his shift that night, he called in at a shop on the Rue de Montparnasse. His fingers slid along the shelf of spirits, and when nobody was looking, he slipped a narrow bottle of Salignac Cognac up his sleeve.

After the foreman had sampled his present, Alyosha was moved up the line to where the motor cars were painted. On either side of him were two men from Khuzestan, their faces empty of emotion under their round caps of white fur. But who should be sitting on the stool opposite, with a small brush in his hand, but Prince Yakov Sergeyevich Peshkov. They had last seen each other on the day the Prince and his fellow White officers left the dacha in the Crimea on horseback, during the Civil War. Accompanying them was his French governess from Petrograd.

Alyosha remembered the sick feeling in the pit of his stomach when Mademoiselle Clementine Babin left him on his own. She had insisted that he stay behind, because the journey back to Petrograd was too dangerous for him to undertake. He remembered how he stood at the door, gazing at their retreating backs as they trotted down the lane. That was the last time he saw Mademoiselle Babin.

Prince Yakov hadn't changed at all. He still had that smooth-skinned face, with those rosy cheeks like a young priest's. As the two worked, Prince Yakov told him what had happened to Mademoiselle Babin.

'She talked about you quite a bit…'

A long time ago, thinking about her used to make Alyosha hot all over, but, by now, she was a faded memory.

'…she was a tender-hearted young woman and her decision to leave you in the dacha weighed heavily on her conscience. She told me several times how ashamed she was of what she did to you. She even wanted to turn back on a few occasions. I had to persuade her how foolish that would be, after we were already so far from the Crimea.'

He told Alyosha how he'd returned to his regiment, which had been heading north, as the battle plan was for the White Army to attack Moscow. But, even with Baron Wrangel at the head of the army, the Whites had been repelled and the soldiers had fled in disarray, despite their officers' best efforts to stop the rout. In the end, Prince Yakov and Mademoiselle Babin had fled too, and had found shelter in a mansion house in the country, in an area that was yet to taste the poison of Bolshevism. It stood on the outskirts of Horlikva, and belonged to a rich merchant called Ryabinkin. When the Prince and Mademoiselle Babin had arrived, they'd been given food and drink, but, with the front so close, the Prince had agreed it was safer for the family to burn his uniform and bury his sword, as those found giving succour to White soldiers were harshly punished. They had come up with a story about the Prince being a blood relative of Ryabinkin, who had been prevented by the war from returning to Paris, where he and his French wife lived.

It proved a short-lived refuge, and, in no time at all, a detachment of Red Army soldiers had arrived on horseback.

'That's when I began to fear the worst.'

When the hammering had begun at the door, Mademoiselle Babin had started to shake. The Prince had taken her hand, and whispered something comforting in her ear, but Ryabinkin had already made up his mind that only one course of action was possible, and had opened the door.

A dozen or so dust-encrusted soldiers had entered the mansion, been greeted by the family, and ushered to the table, where they had been provided with a handsome meal. Ryabinkin had given a short speech, telling them, 'Let us all enjoy the blessings of the table together. I know you will commandeer the house, gentlemen, and everything in it, for the soviet which you will establish in this corner of the world...'

Grunts of assent from the soldiers.

'...and that everything I own, after tonight, is the people's property. So if it belongs to everybody, let everybody enjoy it.'

The soldiers had looked at each other uneasily, suspecting some bourgeois trap, but after the first few glasses of vodka had been knocked back, they'd relaxed, and were soon eating, talking and laughing with the family as though they were all old friends. Ryabinkin was a very funny man, with a vast store of anecdotes to keep them all entertained. The soldiers had been doubled up with laughter, and when the vodka had run out, the champagne bottles had been uncorked, followed by wine, and they'd all drank like there was no tomorrow. It had been an unforgettable night.

The whole thing had been a ruse of course. While the soldiers had been drinking themselves into a stupor, two of Ryabinkin's men had loaded all the gold and jewellery into a specially constructed box hidden in one of the hay carts used on the farm, pulled by two docile carthorses.

Before dawn, when Lenin's men had still been snoring stentoriously, the family, dressed in servants' clothes, had crept out of the house by the back entrance.

'Did you and Mademoiselle Babin go with them?'

'I did.'

'What about her? What happened?'

'That's the thing…' The Prince touched up the motor car with light, delicate strokes, concentrating intensely. 'Ryabinkin had a house in Moscow as well, and before fleeing for the country, he'd buried yet more gold and gems in the garden there. So now he didn't want to leave Russia without them. He really wasn't being sensible, and his wife begged him to join the rest of us in the cart, but he refused. He thought he could get the better of the Bolsheviks, but another word for a man's fate is egotism. He couldn't be talked out of it, and Clementine wasn't willing to leave Russia either, so she left with Ryabinkin for Moscow, though it was Petersburg she hoped to reach in the end. That's when I came to realise that she had just used me for her own purposes. She said – she swore – that she was still in love with your uncle, Kozma Mikhailovich.'

That was the last time the Prince saw Mademoiselle Babin. He never heard from her again and had no idea what happened to her. Later, though, he learnt that his father had been murdered and his brother killed in battle at Ufa, in Siberia, though his mother and sister had managed to flee to Riga. From there, they'd found a passage on a ship transporting bulls to Malmo, and from

Malmo they'd crossed to Bremen by ferry, and from Bremen to Berlin until, eventually, they'd reached Paris.

He'd eventually managed to escape over the border to Lemberg, and went on from there to Gorlice, and, after wearing through the soles of his boots on the long walk across the remains of the Austro-Hungarian empire, had succeeded in reaching Vienna more or less in one piece. Thankfully, a train had taken him the rest of the way to Paris.

For all his enquiries, he never heard one word about the trader Ryabinkin or the beautiful young Frenchwoman, Clementine Babin.

'We've never heard what happened to my uncle either,' Alyosha told him. 'I'm pretty sure he's dead.'

Unfortunately, Prince Yakov and his womenfolk hadn't managed to bring any of the family's wealth out of Russia, and no doubt by now all their possessions had been nationalised for the benefit of the Soviet state.

28.

It was a dry, cloudless night, and clear blue moonlight streamed into Aloysha's shabby room. From the street below, he could hear the spluttering of a motor-car engine unwilling to fire. It went on so long that he started grinding his teeth with frustration. Then, there seemed to be some attempt to rock it to and fro, but the drunken voices swearing and laughing suggested that this wasn't working either. He lay on his bed, too lethargic to undress, trying to still his mind, but the men around the motor car were making too much of a racket.

A second passed. Then another, and another and another, tick-tocking in his ear. He started to count them. He shifted onto his side and stared at the wall.

Later, much, much later, the motor car engine snorted into life, to the accompaniment of shouts and whoops. Alyosha rolled onto his back again, shut his eyes and tried to sleep, but Mademoiselle Babin filled his thoughts, coupled with a longing for those carefree days of his childhood. He remembered an afternoon in Yalta, long ago, when he lay in an old hammock under the palm trees, drowsy with heat, the world heavy and still under a blazing sun. Then Ivan, his father's chauffeur, coming over with a bottle of cold beer in his hand, taking a long swig, and offering to show him how a motor-car engine worked. He could see the golden fuzz of hair on his arm glistening in the sunlight. Then, in another life, Ivan the Commissar at an open grave in a dark orchard.

He preferred to remember Mademoiselle Babin, her breasts jiggling under her blouse. He imagined her naked, beckoning him... Ivan used to try and flirt with her in his clumsy way, and she'd humour him a little, in order to have him at her beck and call. She'd enjoy being able to send him here, there and everywhere on various little errands, but she secretly loathed the man, Alyosha was sure of it. Ivan, with that unique way of talking, as if he was hiding the poison he felt towards mankind just under the surface of the words – he must have made her skin crawl. Alyosha had despised him too, but he did regret not taking up the chauffeur's offer of learning how a motor-car engine worked.

29.

Alyosha walked out of the Renault factory gates at the end of his shift, surrounded by the clattering of the wooden clogs of his co-workers. It was a bitterly cold January evening, and he pulled his beaver-skin cap – a welcome Christmas present from Prince Yakov – down over his ears, and quickened his step through the throng, eager to be home. As he turned the corner at the bottom of the street, he nearly collided with a man in an overcoat, woollen scarf and soft hat. Before he could apologise, he was being bundled into the back of a motor car, which drove off smartly once the door had banged shut.

'And there I was, thinking I'd lost you forever.' Superintendent Chenot turned around from the front seat, and proffered his silver cigarette case. 'How are you, stranger?'

He lit both their cigarettes. 'Perhaps Paris feels like a big city to someone like you, but it's a very small village to someone like me.' It began to sleet and the driver put the wipers to work. 'I thought you and I had come to an understanding.' Superintendent Chenot rapped Alyosha's arm with his finger as he stared at him through his black-rimmed spectacles. 'What's the problem? Why have you been avoiding me?'

'Because I don't want to grass on my own people.'

'But one of your own people has been more than happy to grass on you. How else do you think I found out where to find you?'

'Who was it?'

'Somebody close to you.' Superintendent Chenot replied as he loosened his collar and rubbed the nape of his neck. 'Now then, if you don't keep to your side of the bargain, I'll have very little choice but to throw you out of France.'

Alyosha was caught in a snare, and the wire was tightening around his neck. That night, he went to see Prince Yakov and poured out his troubles.

'Don't go near that factory ever again. It's far too risky.'

'But what will I live on?'

'Don't look so worried, we'll find you something.'

The Prince promised to do his best for him, and he kept to his word.

Alyosha found himself working at the Louvre.

30.

It was early April, and the group he was leading through the galleries was comprised mainly of Germans, though there were a few Swedes, a Danish couple, and a Frenchman. He'd turned exclusively to German until the Frenchman took offence and complained.

His first sight of the girl sent an electric shock through him. It was her hair he noticed first: remarkable hair, bright and yellow, like gorse flowers. Then, her blue eyes and slender body, with its narrow waist and long limbs. She had drifted into their orbit, but wasn't a part of the group, so he didn't have a chance to say anything to her. He hurriedly finished his patter with the usual guff about how art deepened people's understanding of their existence, and transcended the impermanence of life, and then wished them a good day and an enjoyable stay in Paris, hoping to run after her. But some idiot lingered, determined to have his money's worth, asking him lots of tedious questions about this painting and that, then for some restaurant recommendations for that evening, even though he was clutching a Baedeker. By the time Alyosha went to look for her, a new group of tourists had already been disgorged by the omnibus and was waiting for him.

He let them wait. He was terrified that he would lose her; that she would disappear across the squares of Paris, and that he would never see her again. But there she stood, and when he approached her, she calmly asked him when the museum closed. He told her, and she informed him that she'd be waiting for him outside.

'I'll be here,' he said.

'I'll be here, too,' she replied.

Before she left, he asked her name.

'Ludwika.'

Ludwika.

He glanced at the clock.

Ludwika.

He had no idea how he managed to get through the next two hours.

Ludwika.

He could hear his own voice making sentences, one after the other, but it might well have been nonsense for all he knew, and every second mocked him for his impatience.

Ludwika.

His mind was like treacle, but his spirits soared.

Ludwika.

In every painting, he saw her face, and when his hand happened to brush against a sculpted marble thigh, his whole body burned with a sudden rush of heat. He had too much energy, and felt an almost overwhelming urge to skip. He remembered the shape of her head, the exposed nape of her neck, that yellow–gold hair. He thought even the hardest face must melt into a smile if it clapped eyes on that lovely girl.

When Alyosha finally came face to face with her again, he found himself utterly unable to put two words together: his mouth was dry, his mind had unravelled. He wanted to drink her in, scoop her up, touch her, kiss her… he wanted everything at once…

'You're not French?' she asked him.

'No. You?'

'No.'

'I didn't think so, no.'

'No,' Ludwika said, with a sudden little thrill of pride.

Alyosha could see the fine little golden wisps of hair at the nape of her neck. He still couldn't conjure up enough words to form a sentence – so he smiled.

Smiling back, she asked, 'Are you a Berliner?'

'No…'

'But you speak German with a Berlin accent.'

'Living in Berlin for a while gave me that.'

'Hmm… then you're… Russian?'

'For my sins.'

'You Russians aren't all bad.'

'Any more than you… Poles?'

She beamed her assent.

They wandered over to the Tuileries Gardens, and sat on a bench to talk, lingering there as the dusk fell around them, though they hardly noticed. Then they strolled down to the river, and leant against the wall, which still held some of the warmth of the day, to watch two fishermen sitting below them on little stools, still as the statues of the Louvre.

Alyosha was paid on the last Friday of the month so he thought he could just about manage to take Ludwika for supper. He took her to the small restaurant on Rue de la Cité, where Prince Yakov reinvented himself as a waiter every evening after his shift painting cars at the Renault factory came to an end. Alyosha's wages from the Louvre were pitiful and he depended heavily on any tips the tourists gave him, so he was very grateful that his friend managed to leave a few items off the bill at the end of the meal that evening. Thanking his good fortune it was his day off, he arranged to meet Ludwika the very next day.

31.

The church bells woke him early. After the long winter, the city seemed to have been shaken gently awake by fresh spring breezes. The trees were in bud, and the parks and gardens were already colourful with spring blooms. Arriving far too early for their rendezvous, Alyosha went to sit on one of the stone benches to wait for her, among the green leaves and snowdrops in front of Notre Dame, feeling reborn.

He was watching the black-headed gulls bullying the smaller birds, as the crowds started to gather in front of the Cathedral, when suddenly, with a shock of recognition, he saw her coming towards him. He'd half expected her to look different, as though he'd only imagined her, but she was just the same, only her hair was loose, falling around her shoulders. She wore a light-blue blouse with red polka-dots, a skirt and cardigan, and high-heeled brown shoes. There was nothing ostentatious about her, nothing affected. He stood up to meet her, and there were a few seconds of shyness, but then it melted away in their smiles.

'What shall we do?'

'What would you like to do?'

'Don't mind – you say.'

They had to stop to catch their breath at the top of the Cathedral tower after climbing up the dark stairs, and Alyosha, greatly daring, took the opportunity to put his arm around her waist and pull her to him. They gazed out over the city, showing each other where they lived. Then they pretended to be tourists, like the excitable Americans around them, and he solemnly pointed out the Eiffel tower to him, and she, giggling, the Sacré Coeur to him.

He kissed her and it was as if he had woken from a long winter's hibernation, when the feet of the dead had trampled all over his restless sleep, into the most beautiful spring day of his life.

They left the church and followed their noses. Ludwika obviously knew the city well. She took him to the Café de la Paix, her favourite, and they sat outside, sharing secrets and laughing at the people around them – laughing at each other, laughing over nothing, laughing because they were happy. And they held hands, and kissed, their tongues curious, their spirits free. They kissed and they kissed again, and by that evening, Alyosha was head over heels in love.

32.

One evening, Alyosha met Yury in their usual haunt. This was the Café du Musée-de-Cluny on the corner of Boulevard St. Germain, where they would elbow themselves a space between the regulars at the zinc counter and order a drink from Bobo, surely the surliest bartender in Paris. Alyosha hadn't seen his old friend for a while, because he found it so hard to drag himself away from Ludwika. The sky had just emptied a shower of soft rain onto the street, and when a wet Yury stepped into the bar, Alyosha could see at once there was something wrong. His friend looked broken. He was even thinner than usual, his clothes hanging off his bony frame, and he walked very slowly as though just moving one foot in front of the other required enormous effort.

With no greeting or preamble, Yury took an engagement ring out of his waistcoat pocket and then rummaged in his trouser pocket and produced a wedding ring, before putting them both down on the zinc. 'I want you to be my best man,' he said.

Alyosha wondered if he had misheard him. Who was he thinking of marrying? He had never had the slightest hint that there might be a woman in his life.

'You're my only friend in the world,' Yury said sadly, 'You're the only one I can trust,' he whispered, his voice fading to nothing.

A mongrel had appeared at his knee, come in from the street to look for scraps; he shook his wet fur as he licked Yury's hand. Alyosha noticed two ticks, swollen with blood on the dog's ear, about to fall off.

'So who's the lucky woman?' asked Alyosha.

'Don't say a word to anyone.' A smile wreathed his face, 'Do you promise me?'

'I promise.'

Yury's eyes darted here and there as he whispered conspiratorially, 'She doesn't know yet.'

Alyosha, feeling increasingly uneasy, suggested that it might be a good idea to see if she wanted to accept his proposal before planning the wedding, in order to prevent any disappointment and bitterness. But Yury told him she wasn't going to refuse; he was pretty confident on that count. One of her many virtues was that she knew who she was, unlike the majority of women who spent their lives deceiving themselves. For all the chaos that filled the rest of his life, he was convinced that she was going to make a loyal and faithful wife to the end.

'The most faithful any man could ask for...' he reiterated. He spoke of her with a touching tenderness; she was no Tamara Bobrik-ova, ready to deceive him at any moment with a filthy Jew. This one would never treat him shabbily; she wasn't about to run away with some pig and break his heart in two. Then Yury said he wanted Aly-osha to come with him to hear him ask her for her hand.

'Don't you think it would be better for you to do it on your own?'

'She'll be thrilled to see you.'

Alyosha felt this to be unlikely.

'Come along. There's no need for you to worry, she knows all about you already. I've told her everything that's happened to you, the good and the bad.'

'I'm really not sure if this is a good idea, Yury Safronovich.'

'This is the best idea of my life, Alexei Fyodorovich.'

They splashed their way through the puddles of rain until they reached the church in Saint-Germain-des-Prés, and Alyosha would have passed on by, but his friend marched in through the doors. Once inside, Yury insisted that Alyosha kneel at the altar next to him, under the stained-glass windows. Then, he took the engagement ring out of his pocket and placed it on the flagstone in front of him. He put his hands together under his chin in prayer, and asked the Virgin Mary humbly if she would give him her hand in marriage.

33.

The lovers wandered the sunny parks which rang with birdsong. May smelled of clumps of dry horse manure and roses, and the light freshness of spring showers. By the time it had given way to June, Ludwika had transformed Paris for Alyosha into a second Eden. But he resented all the hours he had to spend away from her at his work, and for so little money. He often talked of finding something better.

'What would you do instead?' Ludwika – or Wisia as he now called her – asked him. 'Go back to working in a factory?'

'I can't do that. There's nothing worse.'

He didn't say a word to her about Superintendent Chenot.

Ludwika came of aristocratic stock, and her family owned a large estate not far from Lvov. She described where she had been brought up to him lovingly, painting a picture of the children from the village playing under the branches of the ancient walnut tree in the middle of the square, where the man from Zagreb used to bring his dancing bear every year to entertain them all. At the end of the show, the villagers would show their appreciation by throwing their coins into a hat, and the bear and his master would bow their thanks before ambling away together down the road to the next village. She taught him some of the songs of her childhood. There was one about the Wilia river giving birth to the other rivers – a symbol of Poland's rebirth after living under the Russian yoke, she told him with mock severity, though another time she had tears in her eyes as she described how her grandfather had been sent to Siberia in chains, after the unsuccessful uprising of 1863. Alyosha liked the pretty folksong 'Little Star' – *O gwiazdeczko* – the best, but *Kujawiak* – Wisia's favourite, a song of longing for home – was too sad for him.

She was very proud of Poland's new-found liberation since the war, and she was highly critical of Russia and Austria-Hungary for keeping the country in thrall for so many years. She told him that Franz Joseph's Austria-Hungary was a gypsy camp of an empire – one which had forced all manner of nations into its imperial pen, all huddled together with no space to turn, desperate to escape.

With her, Alyosha learned that at the heart of every real conversation lay empathy. Late one afternoon, he took her to the small church by the Santé Velpeau hospital. It was empty apart from an old woman in black who was kneeling at the rail, and the smell of incense lingered in the air, mingled with the centuries-old damp which penetrated the walls. By the altar, next to Jesus and the Virgin Mary, stood a statue of Joan of Arc, clad in pale bronze, and it was there that he told her about his friend Yury, who was being held in a locked ward at the Maison Blanche hospital.

'Will he ever come out?'

'I don't think so.'

'What sent him over the edge?'

'Russia.'

Ludwika was in her second year at the Sorbonne studying philosophy and music. She knew about things that were quite new to him, and was always happy to share and discuss what she had learnt. Her lodgings were in the Latin Quarter, but her landlord had a gimlet eye, and knew exactly who came in and out of the building. He was a voyeur and a busybody, and would creep around the building, listening at doors and peering through keyholes, and she even suspected him of opening their letters when he could get away with it. She was convinced he would report back to her parents if he suspected Alyosha of sharing her bed, so it was safer for them to sleep at Passy.

Alyosha was ashamed of his shabby room, and felt his Wisia deserved better. He resisted bringing her to his hovel to begin with, but she had insisted, teasing him that he must have another woman hidden away there. She seemed entirely unconcerned by the rough walls and the bare floorboards; to the contrary, they charmed her. Similarly, she found sharing his thin mattress while his roommate was out driving his taxi romantic rather than sordid. Wisia always wanted to hear every tiny detail of any story Alyosha told her about himself. Nothing was too trivial to be of interest and so he did his best to summon up his memories for her, some of pleasure and some of pain. He told her of one of his earliest, a train journey from Simferopol to Sebastopol when he was about six or seven. How he woke and gazed out of the window just before dawn, too excited to go back to sleep and not wanting to miss anything, as the sun started to warm his face and the unfamiliar smell of the singed and parched landscape filled his nose. Then, the train coming to a halt, the leaves on the trees shivering a little as if in greeting. The family had spent the day in the town, where the dry, hot winds had been mercilessly punishing the narrow streets for centuries. He remembered eating his lunch with his parents on the enclosed, glass terrace of their hotel, stuffy even with every window wide open and a canopy under the roof to provide shade. It overlooked a deep, sandstone valley, covered with thick blackthorn bushes. Further down that valley was a famous city of caves, where, long ago, when a different civilisation of people had lived on the edges of the Black Sea, they had carved hundreds of small, dark windows into the rock. Alyosha used to wonder about the mysterious lives of the children of the caves for many years. He often imagined himself playing amongst them, drew pictures, and begged his parents to take him there, but they never did. It would remain a city of the imagination for him forever.

'Will you take me to Russia one day?'

'I would if I could.'

'Do you think you'll ever go back?'

'I don't have much hope.'

'I'm sure the opportunity will come for us to go back there someday,' she said.

'I don't see how, unless the regime changes.'

'That's so sad.'

For Wisia, the idea of never going back to the country of your birth was incomprehensible. He noticed an innocence in her eyes; that innocence, he thought, anchored her whole character. He put his hands on her shoulders and was surprised how warm they were.

'Give me a kiss.'

They kissed for a long time.

She questioned him at length about the maid, Aisha. What had he seen in her? What was it about her that made him love her? *Had* he loved her?

'She was the first…'

Alyosha was forced to resurrect more and more of his boyhood in the face of her tireless questions. He surprised himself with how much he could remember – especially the summers; those holidays in southern Russia, where a narrow spit of land jutted out to sea, providing a shelter in its lee for the sailing boats to anchor. He remembered a three-masted yacht sailing in to harbour one evening, her sails filled with the colours of the setting sun. He remembered the Black Sea lapping against the boardwalk at Yalta, and the trams, with the open-roofed upper decks, and those warships at anchor out in the bay, like a school of fat whales.

'I'd like to go with you to Yalta,' she said.

'I'd like that too, more than anything in the world.'

He told her about the evenings; how all the doors and windows of the houses would be open to the street, so that you could hear snatches of conversation from inside as you walked by. Children's laughter, women talking, the chink of crockery, a few notes from a piano, a dog barking. He remembered the smell of the almond trees – the purest smell in the entire world – mixed with the briny smell from the summer sea. At one time, his favourite spot had been down by the harbour. He used to sit on one of the wooden benches watching the golden haze of a sunset on the horizon sinking slowly into the sea, painting the water in a criss-cross of silver. Then, the last ray of sun would disappear, taking the transparent silver lattice with it, and an inky blue-black would saturate the sky, before thickening into the blackest black, so that on cloudy nights, only the quiet sound of the waves testified to the presence of the sea. That and the occasional silent light from a passing ship.

Somehow these vivid pictures of himself had been preserved, but, in spite of that, he couldn't really summon up that *feeling* of being a boy once more.

'What are you thinking about?' she'd ask. 'You're hiding something; I can tell...'

He wasn't.

'I know you're keeping something back. What? What aren't you telling me?'

'I've told you everything.'

'Every last thing?'

'Bit by bit, yes.'

'Are you sure? What really happened between you and Aisha then?'

She went back over that episode compulsively. Was she really jealous of something that happened so long ago? He was getting tired of her questions.

'So her lover punched you? That sailor, Oleg?'

'Not exactly ...'

'What happened then?'

'I've already told you...'

'Tell me again.'

'It was more of a scuffle, but I somehow punched him and broke his nose. I was in such a jealous rage…'

'Even though he was stronger than you?'

'He was huge. A bull of a man. And a Bolshevik too. But I was too furious to be frightened.'

A silence grew between them

'Do you have a jealous nature Wisia?' Alyosha asked her, running his hand lightly over her naked back.

'Who doesn't? Don't you?'

It was difficult trying to explain to her why he didn't do anything with his mother. He told her about the day the previous summer when he'd been walking down Boulevard St. Michel and had stopped in his tracks, causing a woman to trip as she tried to sidestep him, barrelling into some man whose dog started to bark furiously (this made Wisia laugh). What had made him stop so suddenly was seeing his mother on a poster advertising the picture 'Russia's Altar', dressed in a loose silk robe, bound by her wrists to an altar, her head hanging over the side, her breasts prominent. Standing above her was a brutish-looking individual – a combination of an Aztec priest and Trotsky – holding aloft a shining knife in both his fists, ready to plunge it into her white breast.

Of course, he'd gone to see the picture, but didn't last more than half an hour before he'd staggered out of the darkness into the stifling street, which smelled of the melting tar from the pavement, and the petrol fumes from the double-decker omnibus idling at the kerb while a crowd of tourists boarded. He'd been mortified at his mother's performance. She had made a fool of herself yet again. How would she lift her head up after that? There was more acting ability in the flock of geese she and his stepfather had galloped through in the scene where they fled the Cheka.

He'd headed for the Café du Musée-de-Cluny and nursed a

drink, quietly brooding. It hadn't been a cheap picture, but his mother's performance had been appalling, full of clichéd gestures, the whole thing a ridiculous melodrama about two lovers crossing the border into Russia in order to fight the Soviet regime all on their own.

'If only life were that simple,' he told Wisia sadly.

But, in spite of this new openness, there were things he chose not to tell Wisia. He didn't tell her that he had never been able to forgive his mother and Uncle Artyom for getting rid of his lover, Grete, back in Berlin. Nor did he tell her how he had continued drinking in several other bars after seeing his mother's picture, then spent some of the evening talking to a gang of well-to-do young Frenchmen, their light-hearted, easy banter such a contrast to his own mood. He had soon grown bored with their conversation, but all their boasting about women made him want sex, and he found himself making his way back to the brothel where his uncle had taken him when he first arrived in Paris from Berlin in the spring of 1924, a discreet little place in the Latin Quarter. The madam had welcomed him and rung a little hand bell to summon the girls. They were in just their underwear or a few scant garments, so there was a cornucopia of flesh on display. They formed a *tableau vivant* in front of him, clustered together, the three shorter girls kneeling and the taller girls standing behind them, a smile on all their faces. Alyosha, royally drunk by now, had found it difficult to focus on the girls, but he knew which one he wanted.

'Is Grete here?'

'We have several Gretes here,' the madam said.

'Where? Where is she?'

'Here she is. This is Grete.'

'It's Grete I want.'

'And it's Grete you shall have. Look. Here she is.'

Drunk as he was, he had burst out laughing.

34.

Alyosha may have been able to summon up scenes from his boyhood, but his grip on the recent past was far more faltering. Separating out the events of the past few years, trying to locate them in time and place, was difficult. All those evenings spent in various bars and cafés since he'd arrived in Paris from Berlin were just a fog of different impressions and colours. He struggled to isolate specific evenings, a night when he enjoyed himself – but all that remained was a song or two. Sometimes, he'd try to fish deeper in his memory. What year was it when he used to sit there and watch the sun set over the Black Sea? Could he really remember what anybody said that night with his family in the Hotel Billo in Yalta? The only thing he could remember clearly was a gypsy girl dancing. He remembered the heaviness of her breasts, how they felt when she pressed them against his shoulder, and the fine spray of her spittle on his cheek as she sang, and her voice, something alive and hot. He also remembered the figure of his mother dancing through the shadows…

'You can't fool me, Alexei.'

Why was Wisia so reluctant to call him Alyosha?

'Because you were christened Alexei.'

'I don't like "Alexei".'

They were walking through the pink-tinged dusk, the lights in the bars already burning brightly. In the distance, the words 'Citroën, Citroën' flashed red on the Eiffel Tower. They had been discussing his journey across Russia during the Civil War.

'You'll be Alexei to me forever.'

'So I should call you Ludwika?'

'I like you calling me Wisia.'

A moment's silence.

'Something happened to you in Kiev.'

She wasn't asking – it was a statement.

'Or to that other man then? Stanislav Markovich?'

'No.'

'Why do you go so quiet every time I ask you about it?'

'Apart from being arrested, nothing happened to him. He escaped from Kiev, like thousands of us. Caught a ship from the Crimea. I saw him in Berlin.'

'It's hard to believe everything you went through.'

Yes, it was hard to believe that the old walls of his life had been reduced to rubble by now.

'So much has happened to me. I still think about the people I was with in Russia then.'

He had already told her about Mademoiselle Babin, his French governess who escaped on horseback with Prince Yakov. Wisia had met him when he'd waited on their table at the little restaurant in the Ile de la Cité on that first evening. Alyosha had also told her about Masha, Mishka and Boris, the children he'd crossed Russia with. Where were they by now, he wondered? Were they even alive?

'I look back, sometimes, and feel I've been living some dream. That I'll wake up one morning, and I won't be in Paris, I'll be back home in Petrograd, in my own bedroom, living again with Mother and Father and my little brother and my grandparents, and Uncle Kozma and Aunt Ella and Margarita and Larissa – the whole family all together like before.'

Alyosha didn't have a single photo to show her, and his father's volume of Catullus was the only thing he possessed from that life. But the sun didn't set on a single day when he hadn't looked back at the landscape of his old life. He did his best to preserve what little remained to him, to keep it clear and clean. He tried to file it away in a tidy album in his memory. But what the essence of his memories was by now, he wasn't altogether sure; he felt more and more that all his yesterdays had been warped out of shape by the exigencies of his present.

How could he ever confess to Wisia that he had shot his father's chauffeur, Ivan Kirilich, dead, at an open grave in Kiev? Yet, for all the things he couldn't tell her, he had never been happier.

35.

It was the night of the Montparnasse fair, and people thronged the streets: beggars and pickpockets alongside prosperous families and courting couples, examining the wares at the various stalls, stopping to watch the clowns, acrobats, jugglers and fire-eaters, eating and drinking. It was so full that it was hard work to push a path through the crowds, and Alyosha thought that might be why Wisia was unusually quiet. Even when he won a coconut and a little orange bear with a button nose for her, it didn't succeed in charming her or cheering her up.

'Why are you acting like this?'

'Like what?' she asked curtly.

He decided not to pursue it, and they pushed on through the crowds. A cluster of giggling girls under the blue and red light-bulbs, all dressed up in their finest, were making eyes at a gang of flat-capped lads who were trying their luck at the shooting range. One cock of the walk made a great show of taking his turn with the gun, and was greeted with howls of laughter from the girls when he missed the target every time. Those working-class girls of Montparnasse were a tough bunch, thought Alyosha, who had often seen a slanging match turn to hair-pulling, scratching, and worse.

Eventually, Wisia pulled on his arm and said, 'Let's get out of here.'

She took his hand and led him through the crowd. She was expecting! The thought flashed through his head suddenly. *Wisia is going to tell me that she's having a baby*, he thought, and he felt a strange melting joy at the idea.

There were no free tables at the Café de la Rotonde, so they had to wait at the door for a while until, eventually, the waiter showed them to a table at the back, under a yellow-and-black poster of the Moulin Rouge. They ordered two beers.

'So, are you going to tell me now? Or do I have to guess?'

'On my next birthday I'll be twenty-one.'

He already knew that. 'What else?'

Wisia went quiet once again.

'What else do you want to tell me?'

Normally so talkative, she seemed to be finding it strangely difficult to speak.

'Wisia, what's making you so sad?'

She frowned and stared down at her fingers.

'If you tell me what's the matter I might be able to help.'

She sighed.

'Are you expecting?'

At last, she looked him in the eye – and laughed. 'What on earth made you think that?'

He shrugged, embarrassed, 'I don't know…'

She laughed lightly and then her expression grew sombre, 'You're such a fool sometimes.'

He took her hand. 'But something's upsetting you…'

'I'm not pregnant.' Her tone was flat. 'I made a promise to somebody last year.'

She spoke so quietly, he didn't catch what she said.

'Say that again.'

Wisia repeated her words.

'What kind of promise?'

She looked away.

'Wisia, what promise?'

'I'm engaged to be married.'

Alyosha stared at her, feeling something pressing on his heart, as though a bucket of concrete had been poured onto his breastbone.

103

'He asked on my twentieth birthday.'

'Who is he?'

'His family are neighbours of my grandmother, their estate is nearby… Alexei, don't, let go… your nails… you're hurting my wrist…'

He didn't understand, but what was worse, he was scared of understanding. Wisia was telling him now that the engagement was something their two families had wanted for a long time. She told him that her fiancé, Mateusz Kolodziejski, was the commercial *attaché* at the Polish embassy in Bucharest, an ambitious young man from a good family who wanted to make his mark in the diplomatic service.

'You don't wear a ring.'

'Why do you think?'

He didn't know what to think.

'I thought it was only fair that you should know.'

'When did you see him last?'

'At Christmas… when I went home.'

'But you correspond?'

Her silence confirmed that they did. He felt nausea rise from his stomach and he had to swallow hard or he would have been sick. Since he met her, Wisia had danced through his soul and had possessed it utterly, and now she had released this thunderbolt.

When he lived in Berlin, he heard about a poet who'd been in love with a girl who had finished with him. He did everything he could to win back her love, but nothing worked; in fact the more he tried to tempt her back with his poems and letters, his flowers and gifts, the more she seemed to despise him. The young man was in hell, and even considered suicide. One evening, he went to the café where she worked, ordered a glass of wine from her, tipped his head back to drink it in one, then crushed the glass in his fist until it shattered. What everybody saw next was a man rubbing the fine splinters of glass into the flesh of his cheeks in order to wash away his pain...

He gazed at her, dazed with anguish.

She sighed very softly.

With a huge effort, he dragged himself to his feet to leave, but she grabbed his arm.

'Don't go... no, listen...Wait, listen... don't be angry... I'll be twenty-one in a month's time... Alexei? Look at me... Old enough to know what I want... Not what my father wants, or my mother, or anybody else in my family... But what *I* want...'

He still felt bitterly disappointed as he asked her what that was.

'Do you need to ask? You know what...'

'I'm not sure that I do ...'

'Kiss me, will you? Alexei?'

He felt a flicker of emotion as he leaned towards her to comply.

'That wasn't much of a thing... I want a proper one...'

Wisia swore to him that she had made up her mind to live her own life. Living away from her family in Paris had made her realise that there were other ways of living other than theirs. She didn't have to follow the family traditions, or slavishly accept their old-fashioned morals, or place any importance on her ancestry – any more than she had to listen to her mother's and grand-mother's priests, old men whose minds were still in thrall to the Middle Ages.

Her mother had often told her that a woman's duty was to stay at home, though in the same breath, she would say she believed in the equality of the sexes. But not a superficial equality like the right to vote, or go out to work – true equality meant man and woman had their own place in the pattern of creation: each as important as the other. But in the Sorbonne, Ludwika had absorbed other ideas, and she was determined to claim her happiness, and his too.

These were the sweetest words Alyosha had ever heard.

Wisia intended turning her back on her privileged back-ground to live a different life. She wouldn't deny her true feelings in order to comply with her family's expectations. There was no virtue in a woman denying her own emotions by sacrificing herself to some perceived social and familial obligation. How would she hope to know her true self if she did that?

Out on the streets, the festivities had come to an end, and the coloured bulbs had been extinguished. They walked arm-in-arm through the debris from the fair, pausing every now and then for a long kiss. Their dreams for the future had already bound them even closer together.

36.

When Wisia went off to her lectures, Alyosha always felt a sense of loss. The best years of his life, when he should be laying down a strong foundation for the future, were rotting between his fingers. He yearned to be studying for a degree at the Sorbonne himself. But what hope did he have of that, with barely a franc to his name? Over his dead body would he go and beg a single sou from his Uncle Artyom. Since he'd broken into his apartment and stolen from him, he had done his best not to think of him at all. His only choice was to keep on working at the Louvre, though, by now, he was thoroughly bored of repeating the same old guff day after day. He was stuck, going nowhere, while Wisia was honing her mind, discovering the power of ideas. At least she discussed her subject with him. He felt then that his own horizons were being widened.

She was musical too, and was teaching herself to play the Hawaiian guitar in order to accompany herself as she sang. She was already a gifted pianist, and her deep contralto voice reminded Alyosha of his mother.

'Chopin was a distant relative of mine' she told him.

'On your father's side or your mother's?'

'Mother's.'

She told him that he had written his first piano concerto when he was just twenty, not long before political turmoil in Poland saw him leave his mother country for Paris. She described the three movements to him, the brisk first movement, followed by the romantic second and then the syncopated dance rhythms of the third. One day, they happened to stop at a bar which had an old piano, and she played him some of her favourite passages. Listening to the music, Alyosha reflected that his own life could be divided into three movements: Russia, Berlin, and Paris. But Paris was by far the most important movement, the one which should take him back to the beginning, back to his mother country a stronger man. Would Wisia be the one to somehow make that possible?

She wrote to her mother asking for permission to stay on in Paris in July. She made up something about her tutor advising her to continue her education informally over the summer, in order to see and experience everything that Paris had to offer. For a week or two, her anxiety that her mother would insist on her returning to Poland made her uncharacteristically nervous and low-spirited, and it was as much as Alyosha could do to tease an occasional smile from her. But when the reply finally came, to her great surprise, her mother not only said she could stay, she even arranged for a generous increase in her allowance to be sent. Alyosha had never doubted it, for love was making an optimist of him. He felt fit and healthy, too, and full of hope for the future.

Now that Wisia was in funds, they spent nearly all their evenings in bars. They liked the terrace of the Closerie des Lilas on the Place de l'Odéon, where they'd eke out their brandy and sodas for as long as possible to make them last, kissing and talking, watching the world go by, the café a hubbub of laughing couples, chinking crockery and clinking glasses.

'What do you think truth is?' Wisia asked him on one of these occasions, as she waved away the little cloud of insects that were flying around her. 'I mean, is there even such a thing as one absolute truth? Or just different truths?'

'I'm not sure. Can you give me an example?'

She pointed at two young men in their shirtsleeves. 'Say those two start punching the living daylights out of each other. As you pull them apart they give you two completely different accounts of the events leading up to the first punch. Each of them will have a valid reason for fighting, and they'll both be right. They've both been in exactly the same tussle, but they've experienced it quite differently. You can't call one or the other a liar because they're both saying the truth.' Wisia gazed at him earnestly. 'So what, then, *is* the truth?'

He didn't have a clue.

'In your experience? Is there such a thing as objective truth?'

He thought about it at length. 'To be honest, Wisia, I think everybody tends to see most things in life from their own standpoint.'

Wisia considered this for a moment before asking: 'So, is that a good thing? Or a bad thing?'

'It's not something we have any choice over.'

'But then, how to know anything as it truly is? When I met Marshal Piłsudski for the first time, I found him charming, courteous and affable. He was reason itself in the discussion we had across my father's dinner table, and more than happy to let everybody else have their say. But I've heard people speak about him very differently. They say he's a terrible man.'

'I'm sure you could have said exactly the same about Lenin when he was alive,' said Alyosha thoughtfully. 'If I'd met him personally, I expect I'd have found him pleasant enough. You have to be very astute to know the truth about someone.'

37.

Wisia suggested that they leave the city the minute her lectures were over, for a vacation. Alyosha was allowed a week's leave, so they packed their bags, bought their tickets, boarded the Paris-Lyon-Méditerranée Express at the Gare du Lyon, and headed south. As the train plunged deeper into the dusk, it passed between clay ravines, then on through shallow valleys, which turned from green to purple as they travelled further south. Every now and again, a ribbon of river would appear, and sometimes they'd catch the pale grey waters of a lake glinting in the evening sun.

Their first stay was at Arles, where Alyosha bought himself a cheap straw hat, as the heat was so intense between the white walls it felt as though the sun was stabbing the streets. Then they spent a couple of days in Montpellier, and the following three nights in the small port of Sète, where tanned, athletic-looking young women biked along the quays, the loose cotton skirts of their dresses billowing out behind them, laughing as they went. On their first evening there, Alyosha and Wisia strolled down to the beach after dinner, and sat entwined, listening to the quiet sigh of the waves stroking the sand under the moonlight.

The next afternoon, on the way to the beach for a swim, Alyosha thought he heard somebody call his name, and turning, saw a young man waving at him. He was accompanied by a woman whose face was obscured by a wide-brimmed straw hat with yellow flowers around the brim, and a younger woman in a short summer dress and sunglasses. As they waited for them to reach them, Wisia asked Alyosha who they were.

'That's Vladimir Glebovich Malikov. He was a pupil at the *lycée* next to the Hôtel de Nantes, where I used to live. We used to chat in Russian sometimes when he was on his way home.'

Vladimir introduced them to his mother. Olga Sherbatovna

Malikova was a woman in the prime of life, her whole being speaking of health and vitality. Her skin was tanned a dark brown, so that when she smiled, her even teeth seemed particularly white.

'And you remember Erwana?' Vladimir asked. Alyosha didn't really know the Breton girl who now stood at his friend's side, as Vladimir had only just started seeing her when Alyosha left the Hôtel de Nantes. But he remembered that she wanted to study to become a doctor, just like her father.

'And this is Ludwika.'

His old friend told him there were plenty of other Russian families on vacation in the town, and he invited them for dinner that evening to meet some of them. Alyosha accepted, and that evening he and Ludwika found themselves in a cheap bistro, surrounded by Russians. A man called Rostislav, who hacked and coughed incessantly, much to Ludwika's disgust, introduced himself to Alyosha, and told him that he'd known his father, though, after further probing, it seemed he's shaken hands with him once in Berlin. Later in the evening, Rostislav told him that he had lost a fortune of millions. His companion, Havronya, was a large, fleshy woman in her fifties, but her speaking voice was that of a little girl of six, which Alyosha found disconcerting. Havronya confided to Wisia that she hated her name, hated her life, hated being a widow, and most of all, hated playing the piano in a dirty old *brasserie-concert* in Lille. But she didn't have a choice, as she and Rostislav both lived on the money she made there. They claimed to be brother and sister, but Alyosha knew well enough not to ask too many questions about the lives of other exiles.

Alyosha noticed how quiet Wisia became when she was with people she didn't know. She barely spoke for the entire meal. Sometimes she even looked a little vacant, which he thought might make people think she was rather rude. On such occasions,

Alyosha was always plagued by doubts whether she truly loved him, or whether she wished she was with somebody else.

After the meal they started to sing to each other, folk songs from Russia, Poland and Brittany. When it was Erwana's turn she had a voice to tempt money from a miser's wallet, and they insisted on an encore.

She told them she'd sing a particular favourite of hers: a sad old folk song about sturdy farmers ploughing along with their horses until the sun had set, then scraping the earth from under their clogs on the thresholds of their cottages, exactly as their forefathers had done from beyond memory. But first, she would tell them a story.

In the middle of Brittany one time, in the insignificant town of Loudéac, a dreamy-looking girl stood behind the counter of the *buffet* at the station, her fist against her cheek, staring at a skinny youth with a long neck in a blue collarless shirt, eating bread and drinking cider at one of the tables. He'd placed his scythe against the window frame, and the smell of a harvest sun was strong on his skin. When he had filled his stomach, he rose and admitted that he didn't have a single franc to his name, as the farmer hadn't paid him for his reaping, but after a hard day's work in the meadows he'd been ravenous. He feared the worst, and thought the girl would call the boss for sure, and that he in turn would fetch the police. But instead she said, 'Sing to me. I don't care what, as long as you sing. If you do, I'll let you off.'

He didn't have the best voice in the world, but by the time the song came to an end the girl's face was wreathed in smiles. Nobody had ever sung to her before, to her and only to her, though the entire buffet was listening to the song of the big strong men ploughing with their horses.

To this day, on her birthday, he still sings her the song, as he has done every year since their wedding day.

The couple were Erwana's grandparents.

At the end of the evening, Olga Sherbatovna insisted on settling the bill, though she didn't seem much more affluent than the rest of them. Alyosha and Wisia were returning to Paris the next day, but Vladimir made them promise to look them up in the autumn.

38.

Autumn duly arrived and Wisia returned to her studies, but within a fortnight, a letter arrived from home which brought nothing but unhappiness.

'What's the matter?'

It was from her mother, instructing her to come home at once, as her father was very ill. Alyosha hated to think of her leaving but he realised she had no choice but to pack her bags and leave immediately; it sounded as if there wasn't a second to lose.

They didn't sleep at all that night, just talked through the hours until dawn. The thought of leaving her to go to work that day was so unbearable that Alyosha decided that, even if they gave him the sack, he couldn't care less, he would accompany Wisia to Montparnasse Station, so that he could say his last goodbyes to her there.

'The second I'm home, I'll write to you,' she said.

He asked her to promise.

Of course she would.

But their mutual assurances of daily letters did nothing to stop the cold feeling which seeped through his bones.

'Do you have to go?' he implored.

She hugged him tightly but said, 'Don't make things harder than they are.'

But he found he couldn't leave her at the Gare de Montparnasse, and decided to travel with her as far as Le Havre.

39.

Black clouds hung low in the sky above Haute-Normandie, and by the time they reached the port, it was raining. The town was depressing: grey people in greyer streets and a dull fog hanging over everything. By the end of the afternoon, it had started to pour down, sending them scurrying for shelter into a bar called Lamartine. Wisia was sniffing with cold, the tip of her nose damp and her cheeks drained of colour. Her hair hung in damp hanks over her shoulders and back, making her look prettier than ever, Alyosha thought. He squeezed her hand and pulled her to him, kissing her on her cold lips.

At eight o'clock that night, the *Adam Mickiewicz* had been due to raise anchor, but, for some reason – a fault in the engine or something – this was put back to ten o'clock the following morning. They had no choice but to find a bed for the night, and found a room in a small pension owned by a Madame Bilbaut, a young widow with five children, who had lost her husband in the 1914–1918 war. Her mother lived with her, too – a toothless, tiny old lady who sat in a rocking chair, swathed in her black shawl, muttering continually to herself.

The bed was hard and lumpy, but after not sleeping at all the previous night, they fell asleep almost instantly, Alyosha's nose nestled against the nape of Wisia's neck.

The next day, they made their farewells at the quayside. When Wisia, wearing a hat which made her look older than her age, finally made her way up the gangway, Alyosha felt as though his world was over. He lifted his fingertips to his lips in a ghost of a kiss. At the top of the gangway she turned to stop and throw another kiss towards him, at the same second that he threw her a kiss. They both burst out laughing as they hurled more kisses at each other.

'What?' shouted Alyosha cupping his ear. 'Shout louder,' he

yelled as her words vanished under the screeching of the seagulls. She mimed at him to be sure not to miss his train, though he had a good hour before the next departure. Finally, she raised her hand and threw him one last kiss before stepping away from the rail and disappearing from sight.

Alyosha had nearly reached the station when in one mad impulsive moment he turned on his heel and ran like the wind, ran as fast as his legs would carry him back to the port. Panting for breath, he hurtled into the ticket office – now completely deserted – and bought a third class ticket. A short, wattled clerk with an officious air served him ponderously, his manner as measured as a clock, as Alyosha fidgeted in an agony of anticipation. Hearing the ship's foghorn announce it was about to set sail, he begged the clerk to hurry, but the man proceeded with the paperwork with an almost-unbearable, steady deliberateness.

Finally, clutching the piece of paper in his fist, Alyosha hurled himself along the quayside until he reached the gangway, gasping for breath and in a lather of sweat.

He stayed on deck until he saw the grey harbour walls of Le Havre disappearing in the distance, and he experienced a moment of delightful calm when he realised that the mainland had completely disappeared, and that only sea could be seen all around.

He was going to ask Wisia to marry him.

40.

He decided to bide his time before venturing up to the first class section, and spent the rest of the day dozing in his cabin, down in the bowels of the ship, which he shared with seven smelly fellow passengers. He thought it would be a much easier task, and more romantic, to climb up to Wisia under cover of darkness, and by the time he left the cabin, it was almost midnight. Out on the third-class deck, he gulped the damp air deep into his lungs. The ship's lamps gave out a strangely unreliable light, as though they were shivering in fear of the dark, fading and wilting as they genuflected cravenly before the night.

Moving along the deck was child's play compared to climbing up the narrow and treacherously slippery steps in the face of the gusts of wind which pressed against him. He was suddenly petrified, aware that if he slipped and lost his grip he could fall and drown, without anybody being any the wiser that the sea was his grave. He felt so close to her and yet so distant, but he was a young man at the height of his strength, and he was determined to reach her. He was in the grip of some powerful emotional tide which propelled him upwards and onwards, and as he climbed higher, his confidence returned. The most important thing was that he knew the number of her cabin. Now he couldn't wait to reach her, was already imagining her face when she opened the door and saw him there. The two of them laughing as they lunged for each other, kissed each other, made love. He was on fire to see her, on fire to hug her and kiss her, on fire to feel her flesh once more under his fingers.

After climbing over the rail, he jumped down onto the upper deck. Checking there was nobody about, he crossed over, opened the heavy door, and went down a flight of cast-iron steps. Nobody saw him, and the only sound was the quiet thrumming of the ship's engine. The soft carpet muffled his steps as he walked down the long corridor, which smelled of a mixture of oil and strong polish.

As he was ticking off the numbers on the doors, a tall officer in a dazzlingly white uniform appeared round a corner at the far end of the corridor, walking in a leisurely way towards him, his right hand in his trouser pocket as he whistled Schubert's *Lindebaum* under his breath. Alyosha had nowhere to hide, so half turned away from him by a cabin door, fishing in his pockets as though he were searching for his key. Expecting any moment to be challenged as to why he was skulking around the first-class corridor, Alyosha was mightily relieved when he saw out of the corner of his eye the officer come to halt, knock lightly on a door, and disappear inside. Thanking his luck, he strode eagerly towards his goal. He was outside her door. He stopped and then he realised that it was through this very door that the tall officer had stepped. He double checked the number.

Twenty-six.

That was the number on her ticket.

Twenty-six.

Then he heard a laugh. *Her* laugh, no two ways about it.

His insides turned to liquid and he tried the door. It was locked. He released his grasp on the door handle and tried to calm his spinning thoughts. What did it mean?

Without a doubt, it was her voice he could hear, followed by an appreciative eruption of laughter. Wisia. His Wisia. A dull throb crept over the back of his skull, as though someone had just bludgeoned him. He made to knock on the door, but he was paralysed, unable to speak or act, unable to exert his will. Staring down at himself, he was suddenly overwhelmed with how poor he looked, his jacket with its patched sleeves, his trousers and shoes, so dirty and unkempt, as though he'd been out digging potatoes. He looked like somebody who had been through hard times. His spirit plummeted. What was he doing in first class? He was a man from the third class. That's where he belonged, that was obvious to all.

But he loved her, and so, now knowing what else to do, he stayed, as the night dragged its feet through the darkness. Seconds, minutes, slowly turned to hours, but each hour left him with nothing but the increasingly sour taste of disappointment in his mouth. At some point in the long, oppressive night, the door quietly opened and the officer stumbled out, adjusting his cap on his head. Alyosha, without stopping to think, leapt to his feet and punched him with all his might. He had never in his life imagined that a man's skull was so hard. Pins and needles danced through his knuckles all the way up to his elbow. The officer ducked his head into his hands, the red from his nose staining the white of his jacket, and after seeing the look of mad fury on Alyosha's face, staggered blindly down the corridor until he was out of sight.

Wisia was still standing at the open door, wearing nothing but a towel. She had a curious, nervous look in her eyes, but there was something a little indignant there as well. He was overwhelmed with the urge to choke her, to kill her; he wanted the ship to sink, wanted the world to drown, and the universe to crumble to dust. He didn't want tomorrow, or any other tomorrow to ever dawn again. He waited for her to say something, to try and justify herself – to make some excuse for the long hours she had spent with the man, or give him some explanation, or something, *anything,* but she said nothing.

'Do you hate me that much, Ludwika?' he heard himself ask, the question echoing in the back of his head. 'Do you?'

A fleeting expression of confusion flickered in her eyes but then, in a staggeringly casual way she shook her head. He looked at her intensely, conflicting emotions bubbling up in him. Anger won, and he grabbed her cheeks, squeezing the soft flash hard – and tasted the fear that came from her.

'Don't hurt me...' Her whole body was straining away from him.

'Why?' he asked shaking her violently. 'Why shouldn't I hurt you?'

But he loosened his grip, waiting for a response, for something, anything, that might slake the acid bewilderment bubbling in the pit of his stomach, but again, that maddening silence. He felt her fear evaporate, though he was still full of hate, and still felt a ferocious desire to punish and violate her. The only other emotion she betrayed – by sighing very softly – was that she was a little annoyed with him for being so stupid as to turn up with no warning. Then, he spat in her face, but he missed and the spittle landed in the hollow of her neck – a foul ball of phlegm, fuelled with agony and disappointment. He called her something unforgiveable. He called her something unforgiveable a second time. And then he turned on his heel and walked away.

41.

For the rest of the three-day voyage, Alyosha, like a badly wounded animal, went to ground, cowering listlessly in his stuffy cabin, except when hunger drove him to the third-class dining room to shovel something down before returning to his lair. Only after nightfall did he venture out for some fresh air, pacing the deck as he argued with himself whether he should attempt to see her again or not. He decided against it, because, he reasoned, it was only a matter of time before she would come to find him, to explain and apologise. Invisible bruises were the worst bruises; nothing made them better. Wisia. His own Wisia. How could she? A rock of love turned into a heap of dust. Such a casual, easy betrayal, as effortless as obscuring a mirror with a single breath. *How could she?* That's what floored him, the sheer inexplicability of her behaviour. It filled him with wild feelings of pure hatred, the like of which he'd never experienced in his life.

He would return to the smelly cabin eventually, to the Poles and the two Latvians, who spent their time playing cards, smoking, and drinking for hours at a time. They'd invite him to play a hand with them every now and again, but he always refused, remaining silent and morose, oblivious to everything but his own misery. Anyway, he had no money.

He resisted the urge to see Ludwika again. He had been so sure she would come looking for him, but she didn't, nor even send a message. Nothing. Every time he thought of her, which was constantly, he felt his chest constrict, and sharp blades of disappointment slice his heart to ribbons. Every night, he'd hear the weak strains of the orchestra floating down from first class, playing to the different beats of tangos, waltzes and foxtrots, and would torture himself with visions of her dancing from the arms of one officer to the next, all while he sat on his bunk in a cabin filled with the smell of dirty vests and underpants and stinking socks, listening to a crew of poor workers as they gambled their pitiful wages away.

42.

The screeching of the seagulls at Gdynia was no different from those at Le Havre. From his narrow deck in third class, Alyosha watched her sullenly as she made her way carefully down the gangway, step by step, attended by the officer he had clouted, red glove resting on white glove. She wore a hat and a well-cut coat he hadn't seen before. An equally well-dressed group of people thronged around her the minute she stepped onto the quayside, enveloping her with their greetings and kisses, then whisked her off, a bouquet of flowers in the crook of her arm.

Observing this welcome and the love that came to her part, Alyosha realised that the plain truth of it was that she was home, back with her own people now. What had he ever been to her? Nothing more than a little puppy dog to play with in the park, to throw little sticks of love for him to carry back to her – so that she could mock him.

Was that all he had been? Somebody to while away her evenings with, somebody who made Paris a little more bohemian, perhaps, or even a case of *la nostalgie de la bou*? How had he not seen it? In his blind love for her, he had created some false picture of her. Now he could see her for what she was; she was the daughter of those Polish aristocrats at the quayside. She belonged to them and not to him.

And to her fiancé.

He needed to speak to her, one last time. Hurling himself down the gangway, to the indignation of the sedately disembarking passengers, he looked for her, but she had already disappeared. He ran along the quayside towards the exit gate, but when he saw the wooden hut and the two officials checking everybody's papers, he realised he would have to go through the rigmarole of explaining his lack of passport and visa. When it came to his turn he hurriedly tried to explain himself and gave Ludwika's name as somebody who would vouch for him. An official, who had been listening to his garbled explanation from where he sat at his desk inside the hut, rose and came to join the other two, and looked over the only proof of identity Alyosha had with him – a scribbled note from Ludwika signed 'Wisia.'

'She'll vouch for me.'

He was ushered into the hut where there was a rough table and some chairs.

He had just sat down opposite the two officials when he jerked to his feet again as he saw Ludwika bend her head to step into the back of a Rolls-Royce.

He rushed over to the window and pressed his face against the bars.

'Wisia!'

She turned her head a fraction, half looked around, but then the door closed on her.

'Wisia!' he yelled this time – a long, desperate plea which shattered the silence as the car began to move. He leapt up and barrelled his way past the officials and out of the wooden hut. The Rolls-Royce was coming towards him and he stepped into its path. He was felled savagely from behind, and though he made a feeble attempt to get up, somebody had straddled him and was holding him down. Then, he blacked out completely.

When he came round, they arrested and imprisoned him, but it was a matter of complete indifference to him. He had lost the will to live and as far as he was concerned, they could do what they wanted with him.

II

1927-1928

I.

Dom Narkomfin was a brand new apartment block of reinforced concrete, built in parkland, yet not far from the centre of Moscow. In Berlin, Masha had told Margarita how privileged she felt to be living in such a place, which had its own shops, hairdressing salon, gymnasium and even a crèche. Everything she could ever want was on her doorstep.

When the young official at the entrance realised that Margarita was a foreigner, he phoned through to someone else. By and by, his superior appeared and asked her about the nature of her visit.

'Masha Ivanovna Baburina?'

Was she sure she had the correct name, asked the superior officer. The young soldier looked bored.

'Yes. She told me this was her address. Masha Ivanovna Baburina. Apartment 107.'

A middle-aged woman in a fur hat and coat tightly buttoned to her neck came past the gate and walked by swiftly without catching anybody's eye.

'Where did you say she worked again?' asked the superior officer.

'At the Ministry of Culture.'

'Then I suggest you inquire there.'

Walking back to the Hotel Moskva, Margarita reasoned that the mistake must be hers. What other explanation could there be? She went to her room, pulled off her coat, beret and scarf, and looked through her diary. But the address Masha had written down was the one she had given the young soldier: Masha Ivanovna Baburina, Apartment 107, Dom Narkomfin.

As she stared at Masha's handwriting, Margarita could see her friend clearly in her mind's eye, introducing the film about Yalta. Margarita had been completely mesmerised that night and had felt herself transported home to Russia, so much so, that when the lights came on for the intermission, she had not the slightest inclination to speak German. She wanted nothing more than to nestle into her memories while speaking Russian with Masha.

Margarita remembered her friend's enthusiasm, as well as her wish to learn about their efforts in Berlin. Masha had questioned her closely about the work of the *betriebsräte,* where the communists could offer practical guidance to the factory committees. Margarita had told her about their own struggles: how *Die Rote Fahne* had been shut down by the government and banned for a specified period, and how they had ignored the prohibition and continued to publish it underground. How a court order had put a stop to the KPD conference in Württemburg, at a time when more and more workers were thrown out of work, and how the bosses used the tactics of sacking and shut-outs to demoralise the workers, hoping to intimidate those that remained into not striking, without realising that this might work against them one day, for the foot soldiers of every revolution always come from the army of the unemployed.

Masha Ivanovna Baburina, Apartment 107, Dom Narkomfin. That was her address. Why were they claiming she wasn't there? Perhaps she had moved. She would have to make further enquiries at the Ministry of Culture, as they suggested.

2.

That evening, at the official reception, Nikolai Bukharin, a thin, shortish man with a goatee, a receding forehead and sparse, reddish, curly hair, extended a fraternal and warm welcome to the assembled delegates from foreign communist parties, on behalf of the Central Committee of the Communist party of the Union of Soviet Socialist Republic, on the occasion of the tenth anniversary of the Revolution. The author of *The ABC of Communism* and Politburo member reminded them with a smile that, here in Moscow – the capital city of the communist world – they were among comrades.

The dinner comprised traditional food: bortsch with smetana, shashlik and rice. There was champagne as well as the best vodka, and wine from Abshasin and sparkling water from Kislovodsk, served in elegant crystal glasses. The hundreds of delegates sitting at round tables were served by young men and women in black-and-white uniforms. The six courses were ferried from the kitchens and placed on the white tablecloths in their turn, and then whisked away with great efficiency. When the meal was finally cleared, there was a request for silence, and each head of the delegations was invited to address the company in turn, under the red flags that decorated the walls of the room. Two or three cameras flashed. The French, Italian, Hungarian and Romanian delegates spoke, and then it was Margarita's turn. She had been feeling nervous for a while, and when she stepped up to the round microphone the piece of paper in her hand was shaking. She thanked them for the welcome, and went on to pay tribute to the Soviet Union, the first state in the history of mankind to establish a society which would be emulated world-wide once capitalism was destroyed, and the whole planet – yes, every last bit of it – would live and breathe under a truly humanist social order.

As she went on, Margarita found her voice. She felt proud to be able to report on the progress being made by the KPD, but admitted that they had not yet exposed the Social Democratic Party to all as the fake socialists that they were, betraying the German proletariat time and time again.

They were making good progress in Saxony, Thuringia and Mecklenburg-Strelitz, and there was every reason to hope that the revolution would prevail. As she came to the end of her speech, Margarita raised her voice. 'We have to beat the fascists. We have to beat the capitalists. We have to smash their corrupt order and replace it with a fairer, decent system. Together, we can, and together, comrades, we will be victorious. We will see the dawning of the day when the red flag flies high above the Reichstag.'

Enthusiastic applause broke out. Six hundred glasses were raised in a toast: 'To the tenth anniversary of the Revolution!'

Bukharin held his glass up even higher, 'To other revolutions.'

'Other revolutions.' the room replied as one.

Margarita received a lavish bouquet of pink roses and a little bottle of perfume, which had been produced at the new factory in Yaroslavl.

3.

Margarita was filled with joy to be in the company that night of so many like-minded people, and everybody was so encouraging as they congratulated her, appreciative of her reports of the struggles for the cause. She felt light-hearted with hope; it was so pleasant to be praised for once, instead of hearing nothing but contempt and hatred. Berlin seemed a world away; a city of capitalist greed and rampant inflation, where workers picketed and bosses pocketed. In Germany, there was nothing but unemployment and lives whittled down to stumps, every last twig of hope plucked bare. She had been longing to see for herself how the system in the Soviet Union worked towards a better future, where there was a meaning and purpose and a true worth to everybody's life.

She caught Kai-Olaf's eye as he was talking to Hella Wuolijoka. Moscow had exposed a new aspect of his personality: he was far more gregarious here, and even seemed rather flirtatious. Margarita felt a small stab of jealousy as she gazed at the petite girl's luxuriant black hair and her little snub nose. She'd listened to her story sitting next to her on the train to Moscow. Hella had spent two years at Heidelberg University, where she'd witnessed the rich students at play, those aristocratic sons of the great Prussian estates, whose older brothers had served as officers in Kaiser Wilhelm's *Reichswehr* in the 1914–1918 war. One of their favourite games was to throw small coins, which they had heated until they were white-hot, from the roof of the university to the street below, howling with laughter as they watched beggars and street children pouncing on the coins and then screaming and dancing in pain as they burnt their fingers picking them up. Hella had loathed the place so much that she'd abandoned her studies and moved to Paris. She'd taken an evening class at the Lycée Condorcet to improve her French, where she'd met Xavier, a middle-aged communist who used to know Jean Jaurès, who'd introduced her to *L'Humanité*, a newspaper edited by his cousin. Every day, she'd read it faithfully, and gradually came to see the world, which she had found so difficult to understand, in a new light. She'd begun to take a keen interest in economics, which she'd studied independently at the Bibliothèque Sainte-Geneviève, the famous old library a stone's throw from the Panthéon. There, by the light of a green lamp, she'd read *Das Kapital* for the first time. By this time, she was living in an apartment by the Jardin du Luxembourg, working as a secretary for the head of Kleyer, a German-French metal company. She'd had to learn shorthand, which was useful later on when she returned to Germany, as she was the main contact between the KPD in Frankfurt and the main office in Berlin. It was due to her good work in this capacity that she had been invited to join the delegation to Moscow.

Margarita watched Kai-Olaf as he slowly made his way from table to table, shaking a hand here, squeezing a shoulder there, slapping a back, kissing a cheek. His face was wreathed in smiles, his eyes bluer than ever; he seemed the most relaxed she had ever seen him. Here among friends, he was obviously a contented man. Margarita suddenly felt a little left out; she didn't really know anybody apart from her own delegation. But she resolved to take full advantage of this opportunity to meet as many other communists as she could during her visit.

Kai-Olaf had joined the Italians. That came as no surprise to Margarita as she knew he had worked there. Mussolini had forced the Communist Party to go underground, like moles, to avoid being beaten to a pulp. She saw Kai-Olaf laugh at one of the Italian's jokes, and saw Hella half turn to smile at him. Were they lovers? Hella's attention was taken by somebody else a moment later, and Margarita realised it was pointless to speculate as she had no idea what, if anything, tied them to each other. She had decided to turn in for the night.

As Margarita crossed the hotel lobby to reach the elevator, she noticed Nikolai Bukharin, flanked by two or three young men in leather jackets – obviously his bodyguards. He was talking to Stanislav Markovich. Stanislav caught sight of her and lifted his hand in greeting, motioning for her to wait for him.

4.

Once Bukharin had finished talking with him, Stanislav joined her on a sofa. The conversation flowed easily enough between them. Margarita asked him if still wrote.

'The odd script for a film, when I have the chance.'

'Even after your terrible experience in Berlin?' she teased him. 'Do you remember it?'

'I've tried my best to forget it.'

He had been highly relieved that such rubbish had barely garnered any reviews, he told her, and he claimed that he couldn't even remember the name of the film.

'*Russia's Altar*,' she reminded him.

'Bourgeois nonsense,' he said dismissively as he relit his pipe. Margarita noticed the change in his speech patterns since the last time she'd met him, when he and his wife Lyuba were passing through Berlin. He spoke now with the authority of a man who was used to giving orders and being obeyed.

'So how many of your scripts have they made into films here?'

'One or two,' he said vaguely.

'Anything I might have seen?'

'Perhaps. I'm none the wiser what gets shown in Berlin these days.'

'There's a little picture-house I go to where they show pictures from the Soviet Union.'

Stanislav asked after her cousin Alyosha.

'He's in Paris, too, I think. He must have been there three or four years now.'

'Where does he live? Which part?'

'I'm not sure, we haven't been in contact for a while.'

'Why not?'

'I really don't know, he just seems to have disappeared. Are you and Lyuba still in Paris? Or here in Moscow?'

'Paris. We live mostly in Paris. But I'm often in Moscow.'

'Is Lyuba here tonight?'

'No.'

Stanislav seemed to tense for a moment, then he tapped his pipe and said levelly, 'We've separated actually. Last year. Things became rather… to cut a long story short, I had an affair. Then she had an affair. We tried to patch things up, moved to another hotel in Paris. But something had broken. I've remarried since then. To Tatyana.'

'Happy?'

'Very happy.'

There was a small silence then Margarita heard herself saying, 'My sister has got married too. You remember Larissa? She has a little girl who's a year and a half by now. Ella. For our mother.'

Stanislav said that of course he remembered her, but then stood up rather abruptly.

'You'll have to excuse me.'

Margarita stood up as well.

'Before you go…' she began tentatively.

She explained it had been many years since she had heard anything at all about her father. While her mother was still alive, she would make an effort to ask in various places, but without success. For all she knew, he might be in prison, or dead; she had no idea what his fate had been. For her sister Larissa especially, who had always been their father's favourite and had adored him back, this not knowing was more of a torture than knowing for certain that he was dead. Margarita told Stanislav that she had promised her sister that she would try to find out whatever she could while she was in the Soviet Union. Could Stanislav help her in any way? He promised he'd do his best, and said goodnight.

Margarita unlocked the door to her room and kicked off her shoes gratefully. Sitting on the edge of her bed, she rubbed her toes. She must have walked the streets of Moscow for miles that day. She poured herself some tea from the thermos, and noticed that the fruit bowl and cigarette box had been replenished. By the window, a vase of fresh jasmine filled the room with its scent. Wearily, she splashed water over her face, pulled her clothes over her head and threw them over the chair. But, before she snuggled down into the blankets, she dabbed *Stalin's Breath* liberally between her breasts, wincing slightly at its icy sting.

5.

Alyosha stood in the gloom at the head of the stairs, clutching his father's volume of Catullus in his hand. By now, new tenants had occupied his old room in Passy, a family of Algerians. He'd been handed back the book and his second pair of shoes by a sloe-eyed young man, who'd not been able to tell him anything of his fellow tenant, the ex-soldier taxi driver. Nor was there any trace of the deeds to his Uncle Artyom's villa. Alyosha tied his shoes together by the laces, slung them over his shoulder and left the building. He stood blinking on the pavement of his old neighbourhood for a moment as he became used to the light, and felt the heat of Paris on his face. He walked on and wondered at the abundance of spiders' webs in the leaves of the trees. It was a good hour's walk to the Maison Blanche asylum, and he had a slight feeling of dread as he entered. But his old friend recognised him at least.

'It's good to see you, Alexei Fyodorovich,' Yury Safronovich told him. 'Where have you been keeping yourself all this time? Can you see the change in me?'

Alyosha hesitated for a second before saying that he hadn't changed a bit. In fact, he had visibly deteriorated. His speech was slow and laborious, each word an effort.

'I wish I was a free man, old friend...' he told Alyosha sadly. 'But what of you? What have you been up to?'.

Alyosha decided to keep his experiences in Poland to himself.

'When we see each other next time, I'll be free,' Yury whispered, his soft fingers gripping Alyosha's hand. 'Ask them on your way out if you don't believe me.' As the two of them walked along the gravelled paths in the gardens, he refused to let go his grasp. 'You'll hear from them how much I'm getting better every day. But, if they don't let me go, I'm going to escape from here.'

Alyosha couldn't wait to escape either.

6.

Paris became autumnal. Alyosha's spirits plummeted at the thought of yet another winter of scurrying home through cold dark streets. Another winter of trying to dry damp clothes in front of an inadequate fire. Another winter of catching colds, sweating through feverish nights and waking in the morning in a damp cold bed, teeth chattering and body shivering.

And of course, he was in the same old bind: to obtain his *permis de séjour*, he needed money, as well as having to go through the same old bureaucratic rigmarole all over again. A black-market version would need even more money. But, without a stamp on that precious document, he had no right to live in Paris, and no chance of legal employment. His greatest worry since his return was whether he would be allowed to stay in France.

As he wandered the streets, the soles of his shoes became ever thinner, and he felt as though he was fading away himself, little by little, compared to the vigorous and well-fed people striding past him. Sometimes, he would find himself pierced with jealousy as he saw lovers nuzzling up to each other, whispering the secrets of their hearts.

With nothing better to do, he'd often take to simply following someone until they reached their journey's end. One morning, he followed a girl with a mane of earth-coloured hair, which fell in waves to the small of her back. She looked a most attractive and pleasant young woman, as his grandmother in Russia used to say a long time ago. She was delivering a yellow parcel to somebody.

Alyosha felt a sudden urge to cut off her long hair, hank by hank, and leave it in clumps on the pavement.

He started to follow other heads of hair. This one had light and loose hair, that one had strawberry blonde hair, and for a few streets he followed blue steel hair, thickly dyed. Silver-coloured hair demanded his attention, then salt-and-pepper hair, and white hair, and black hair, and tidy hair, and tangled hair, hair which refused to lie flat however much combing and smoothing it received. He was amazed at the sheer variety of hair there was in the world.

After wandering the streets of the Latin Quarter, he found himself in the Luxembourg Gardens one afternoon, and he lay smoking on the bench in the last of the autumn sun. Around him, the little birds of Paris bathed in the water fountains, hopping and shaking out their feathers. Now and again, the magpies' fighting intruded on his reverie with their hoarse cawing. He watched women in high heels taking their little dogs for a walk, poodles or Chihuahuas dressed like their mistresses, pattering along lightly at their sides. Caressing breezes shivered though the trees, softly rustling the late autumn leaves, until the last bit of warmth from the sun faded away like a sad refrain. For the want of anything better to do, he made his way through the soft twilight to the Seine, to watch the long barges laden with barley and wheat, coal and other cargoes from northern France, from Belgium, from Rouen or Le Havre, chugging along on the yellow-brown waters, past the Ile de la Cité. He crossed a bridge and kept on and on and on, walking until he had climbed up the narrow streets of Montmartre to the bottom of the Sacré Coeur. He walked past open doors and heard women and children talking inside. He could smell mackerel frying, and sometimes something more luxurious – perfume or good tobacco – then the stink of dog shit, but he continued climbing, past secluded gardens guarded by iron railings, until he reached the summit, his armpits dripping, a warm wetness at the small of his back.

Alyosha borrowed a light from a man in a dark red suit, a gold waistcoat and yellow shoes, and fell into a conversation with him. He had a reddish beard, the eyes of a baby and a voice which cracked as he spoke. He'd been a pianist at a picture house for a while, until he'd started drinking too heavily to hold a job, let alone a tune. Alyosha's gaze roved over the expanse of blue-grey roofs extending towards the far horizon, and came to rest on the lights of the world's most famous radio tower winking away in the distance. He smoked a third and then a fourth cigarette, until the sky was dark. The floodlights at the top of the Eiffel Tower started to rake across the night. Before him, the endless city unfurled, street by street, out to the suburbs. Such people beetled along those streets – people from every part of the world. Paris was a complicated ocean where everybody had to learn to swim in its waters – some succeeding better than others.

Had it not been for the kindness of one French consul in Danzig, a man whose dazzling goodness was obvious in his smile, he doubted he would ever have seen Paris again. The Poles had taken him for a spy, and the *Defensira* were convinced of it.

'Don't give us that hard luck story of being on your uppers in Paris. What the fuck do you take us for? Fools? Where are you papers, you little bastard?'

He had spent days doing his best to persuade them he hadn't been trying to slip into Poland unnoticed and that he wasn't a spy for the Soviet Union, he was just a young man in love. Wisia. Her name like a distant echo from somebody else's life.

He shut his eyes: he could still hear that poor girl, the young communist from Lvov, as her whimpers turned to howls in Pawiak prison. They made sure that he could hear her, as they continued to work on him in the next room.

Although he did his best to forget his experience of being

locked up in a cell in Warsaw, he couldn't help but re-run the hours in his head, those hours when he'd been trying to convince them of his true identity. They had threatened to break the bones of each of his fingers in turn.

'But that's who I am...'

Nobody had believed him.

Equally futile were his attempts at forgetting Ludwika, because wherever he turned in Paris there were reminders. The city was full of her. As he walked past solid, respectable-looking houses, he felt like knocking on a door or two to ask about her. Down in the dry warmth of the metro, which sucked people in and blew them back out, he half expected to bump into her. In Montmartre. Around the Louvre. In Montparnasse. As he walked through the Père-Lachaise cemetery one cold after-noon at the beginning of November, he thought he saw her, but when he got closer, the girl putting some white roses on a grave was nothing like her. Wandering the city parks he felt she was there. Turning the corner of the street under a yellow lamp, he still half expected to come face to face with her... One day, he passed that little place on the Rue de la Cité, where they'd spent their first evening together, gradually falling silent as they gazed longingly into each other's eyes. How was he ever going to be able to live without her?

7.

Christmas displays were already filling the windows of the big shops. Alyosha always thought there was something otherworldly about the light in Paris shops. As he wandered around Galeries Lafayette, purely in order to stay warm, the scent of perfume and candlewax reminded him of better days. Around him, he watched parents holding their children by the hand, women with their

Pekinese or Chihuahuas in their little coats tucked under their arms, men on the way home from work carrying flowers tied in pink ribbon, all walking so purposefully and confidently. A person with money in his pocket walks differently from a person with none.

One evening, as people streamed past him, criss-crossing the city streets in their buttoned-up raincoats, the puddles under their feet shining blood-black after a sudden downpour, Alyosha though he caught a sudden glimpse of his mother making her way in the crowd towards the Vavin metro. Could it be her? Had he really just seen his mother in the flesh? He ran after her retreating back, down the stairs of the metro, putting on a spurt to catch up with her as she got to the gates. He grabbed her arm. She turned to look at him and her frightened eyes met his, a fragile woman, half anticipating that he was going to snatch her bag, until fear turned to recognition. But, before she could say a word, Alyosha turned on his heel and hurled himself back up to the clamour of Montparnasse, the cold night stinging his cheeks.

8.

'I couldn't help but hear the conversation at breakfast this morning, Gretushka.'

Margarita was halfway across Red Square with Kai-Olaf. As ever, his knapsack was slung over one shoulder, his hands were thrust deep in his coat pockets, and his blue cap covered his bald head. In front of them were Elfrida and Lornena, and, just behind, Paul, with his mouse, Rosa, perched on his shoulders, was walking with Max and Moritz. Margarita was concentrating on not turning her ankle as she walked across the cobbles.

'Is this the same Masha as the one who came to Berlin, to the conference at the Sportsplatz?' asked Kai-Olaf.

'Yes it is, Masha Ivanovna.'

'So what's the problem?' he asked, and she wondered why he always sounded slightly impatient with her.

'I'm finding it difficult to get hold of her.'

'There's such a thing as the telephone in Moscow,' he turned to look at her with his blue eyes.

'She never picks up...'

'Why?'

'How should I know?'

'Are you sure you have the right number?'

Two sturdy young soldiers holding gleaming bayoneted rifles in front of their noses, flanked the entrance of the dark square.

'This way, come along.' Irina, their official minder, shepherded them together. Obediently, they all followed in her footsteps but Margarita felt a little awkward, ashamed even, as they hurried past the people patiently waiting in the queue. Nobody grumbled, but she caught a few looks of mute contempt thrown in their direction.

As they entered the mausoleum, everybody straightened up instinctively, and Kai-Olaf stuffed his cap into his coat pocket. In the middle of the gloom, there was a ribbon of light, with just one old woman there, her arms crossed on her breast, sitting on a wooden chair, the noise of the world shut out.

Kai-Olaf and Margarita waited behind Elfrida and Lornena to take their turn to file past the place where the Soviet Union's chief architect lay.

'You won't get an answer about Masha from that one,' whispered Kai-Olaf in her ear, nodding towards Irina who was in front of them. 'Not if your friend lives in Dom Narkomfin.' He told her they would wonder why she asking about somebody who lived in a building which housed so many government personnel, and would be sure to think that Margarita was on some dubious mission after some restricted information, especially as she was a foreigner.

'Why on earth should they doubt my motives?' she was rather affronted. 'I'm a communist,' she added, as though that was the definitive answer to everything.

'How many enemies hide behind the same mask, I wonder?'

In Lenin's shadow, Margarita realised that Kai-Olaf was serious. She whispered to him that she would be the last person on earth to betray the Soviet Union in any way at all – she just wanted to know where her friend Masha had gone – that was all.

'Ssssssh!' hissed the old woman on the wooden chair.

'It would have been much simpler if you'd just asked me,' whispered Kai-Olaf as he caught a whiff of *Stalin's Breath* on her skin.

They stood there staring down at Lenin's body, clothed in a black suit, the freckles still visible on the waxy yellow skin, his arms by his side and his hands clenched in two fists. He had a wide brow, a reddish beard, a neat nose and fine lips, and his slightly slanted eyes were wide-spaced. Looking at the length of him, Margarita saw that he was slight. She leant forwards to gaze at his chest, expecting somehow to see a breath, or a heartbeat, some spark of life. But there was none, and she moved along to make room for those behind her.

This was the power which had once sent her fleeing from Russia into exile.

And this, too, was the same power which had summoned her back home.

9.

Alyosha stopped in at the Zimmer, a small bar on the corner of Place Blanche, and ordered a calvados. Leaning on the zinc counter, he plucked the cigarette he had already rolled from behind his ear and lit it. He heard without listening the conversation of the two couples at his side, who were discussing – bickering rather – where to go dancing that night. Alyosha pushed his empty glass across the bar to order another calvados. The barman, looking in need of a good wash, was barely less unkempt than Alyosha himself, and his skin was badly pitted – the result of an illness he'd picked up in Mesopotamia, or so he claimed.

'How are things?' he asked as he poured the drink.

'Same as ever,' Alyosha replied.

When he left the bar, he still had nine francs left in the bottom of his pocket. A few hours previously, a stone's throw from Pont Mirabeau in Auteuil, Alyosha had slipped in to a *maison de retraite* – a home for old people. It was a private establishment, but it still stank of piss and death. He was just scooping up the change from the dressing table in one of the old codgers' rooms as the old man dozed in his armchair, when Alyosha heard him mumbling something, and the next thing he was wide awake, smiling cheerfully, convinced that his son had come to visit, and confused as to why he had to leave so suddenly.

For eight francs, Alyosha knew where he could fill his stomach –a generous *table d'hôte* of *Salade Normande* and a rib-sticking portion of *Saucisse aux Choux* and potatoes, followed by a *Tarte Tatin*, with a good *pinard* of rough red. He was practically salivating as he imagined the steaming plate being slapped on the table in front of him. He had been starving for hours, a stabbing pain which reminded him of the years of famine when he'd wandered the length and breadth of Russia with Mishka, Boris and Masha.

After shelling out for his meal, he still had a franc left, enough to buy himself a breakfast of coffee and two croissants the next day. But his appetite was far from satisfied. Opposite the Moulin Rouge, under three rows of bare bulbs hanging from the branches of the trees above, were wooden tables protected by canopies.

Stacked on these tables in neat pyramids were rounds of Brie, Camembert and Roquefort, bars of chocolate, tins of pâtés and fish, as well as Marseilles soap, bottles of pastis, wine, and *eau-de-vie*. The night smelled of roasting chestnuts, and, next to the stall, a rough-looking prostitute stood stuffing them into her mouth from the paper bag like a child eating sweets.

A black man wearing a white hat was accompanying himself on an accordion, but Alyosha couldn't understand a word of his songs. Where was he from, he wondered: Senegal? Ivory Coast? The Congo? As he headed towards Rue Blanche he was dazzled by the headlamps of the motor cars and taxis, which were unloading their wealthy passengers at a nightclub. Above the door of the Palais de Paris, a light-green awning sheltered the customers from the rain as they strolled from the cab to the club. A doorman dressed as a Cossack rushed to open the doors of the Bugattis and the Hispanos. Two young women stepped out of a Rolls-Royce, giggling as they trotted in on their spindly heels, and a burly middle-aged man with a greying beard followed more sedately, dressed in a superbly cut dinner jacket, white silk scarf and shoes of gleaming patent leather. He had a cigar jammed in his mouth, and his right hand in his pocket. As he entered, the doorman stood smartly to attention and saluted him, but no tip was forthcoming.

Alyosha waited for the Rolls-Royce to drive away before crossing the road to greet the Cossack – Andrei Petrovich Vengerov from Petrograd, former managing director of the now defunct Azov-Don Merchant Bank. They kissed each other three times on alternate cheeks. The shadows under the former banker's eyes seemed darker, and his face gaunter, since their last meeting.

Andrei Petrovich stepped back to look him over and, smiling, told him he looked more like his father every time he saw him.

'So, where have you been keeping yourself all this time, my boy?'

Alyosha had no enthusiasm for recounting his experiences at the hands of the *Tajna Policya* in Gdynia, or of his mistreatment in Warsaw prison, so he gave a vague reply and asked Andrei Petrovich about himself, who told him sadly that the lamps of suffering illuminated Paris more and more for him. He felt such a fraud in his ridiculous, grand uniform, especially when some ex-officer from the White Army should happen to pass. He knew how true Cossacks hated seeing little men like himself parading themselves in front of Paris night-clubs, to provide a little entertainment for over-privileged riff-raff, bringing shame on their good name. Though the truth of the matter was that even true Cossacks had been forced to take whatever work they were offered, however humiliating, to keep body and soul together. He even knew of some who were working on the dustcarts in Nice and Cannes. Nevertheless, Andrei Petrovich felt deeply ashamed, as he'd barely been near a horse, never mind on the back of one, any more than he'd fought for his country. His only connection with Baron Wrangel was when he'd composed a poem dedicated to him and his army, which had been published in a newspaper called *Turel* in Constantinople in 1920. Not that he'd written a line of poetry since the day he buried his wife in Berlin. That was yet another deep well of suffering.

'She lies in the earth of the same cemetery as your own dear father. What I miss more than anything is the sweet sound of her voice. She had such a pretty voice.'

Did Alyosha remember it, the man asked? Of course he did, he lied. They had been as devoted to each other as any couple ever could be.

Alyosha stamped his feet as his toes were frozen. He hoped Andrei Petrovich wouldn't mention his sister, as he didn't want to be reminded about Lazarevna Petrovna – the woman who'd once falsely accused him of raping her in Berlin. He didn't really want to ask after his daughter, Galina, either, as he still hadn't forgiven her for taking her aunt's part and blackening his name to everybody. But Andrei Petrovich brought her up, because Galina had given birth to a little girl called Roksana, who was almost a year old now. She'd been named after her grandmother – his mother. But he feared things were not well between Galina and her husband, Marcel. He implied the marriage had been expedient to avoid the scandal of the child being born out of wedlock, though he was at pains to say that Marcel was a fine young man; nobody could ask for a better son-in-law, even though it was a shame he wasn't Russian. He hoped they would settle their differences, if only for Roksana's sake, but Galina had never been one to confide in her father – she'd been closer to her mother.

'I expect all daughters are closer to their mothers,' he mused. He thought the world of little Roksana, who was just starting to say her first words.

'Me, a grandfather! Who would have thought?' His expression softened a little; he clearly doted on his little granddaughter. 'But who knows what will become of her? What will become of us all? I do worry about what might lie ahead of her…'

A gang of noisy young Frenchman walked by, singing drunkenly.

'Do you still dream of going home, Alexei Fyodorovich?' asked the ex-banker. Not a day went by when Andrei Petrovich didn't yearn to go back to Russia. These days, he attended the Orthodox church on Rue Daru faithfully every Sunday, partly for the service, but also for the company. From one Sunday to the next, he could feel the religion of his childhood grow more important to him. As the months had gone by, he had become more devotional, and regretted how he had neglected his faith when he'd been working in the banking world back in Petrograd. Now, he yearned to be every inch the Christian, as an inch of a Christian was better than two yards of a hypocrite. Roksana had been baptised and accepted into the Russian Orthodox faith at the same church. Galina had attended with him for a while, but she didn't come anymore.

A motor taxi suddenly stopped in front of them.

Alyosha heard a muffled rapping, and saw the driver banging his windscreen in an attempt to attract his attention.

10.

Prince Yakov beckoned Alyosha over and opened the window. It was two o'clock and his shift was just ending. He was famished – would Alyosha join him for something to eat? Alyosha most certainly would. He quickly said his goodbyes to Andrei Petro-vich, and jumped into his friend's taxi, which reeked of mouldy old leather, dirty carpet, wet dog and stale cigarette smoke. The Prince told him he'd been driving without a break for the last fifteen hours. His legs were stiff, his right arm ached from elbow to shoulder, and he had a dull pain in the small of his back from sitting so long. He stretched his head and shoulders back as far as he could, until Alyosha heard his bones crack, and he sighed heavily and rotated his shoulders vigorously to try and ease the ache. Fifteen hours. No wonder his face was a study of pain. On top of everything, Prince Yakov told Alyosha, he could feel the grime of the streets on him, the dirt under his fingernails, the dust on his clothes, and a greasy film on his hair and skin. In fact, his whole body itched.

'But when all's said and done,' Prince Yakov said, regain-ing his customary cheerfulness, 'I shouldn't complain too much about my own misfortunes, even when I'm done in. There are many worse off, and it's important to count one's blessings, never mind how precarious life can be. And this beats working at the Renault factory.'

He drove them to a cheap bistro which stayed open all night.

Alyosha was starving, and was glad they didn't have to wait long before the food arrived. They ate steaming bowls of onion soup with hunks of bread and melted cheese on the top, along with a bottle of house red, but that barely took the edge off Alyosha's appetite, and he was relieved when the fat *patronne,* cigarette in her mouth, plonked some more bread and a *crottin* of goat's cheese on the table. Full at last, Alyosha was ready to talk. As he rolled them each a cigarette, Prince Yakov listened as his friend recounted his recent misfortunes – his troubles with Ludwika, and his misadventures in Poland – from start to finish.

After he had been arrested at the port of Gdynia, he had been interrogated about his lack of passport and visa, and, after telling them for the hundredth time that his name was Alexei Fyodor-ovich Alexandrov, and that his late father was the industrialist Fyodor Mikhailovich Alexandrov, formerly from Petrograd, one of the policemen had slapped him brutally across his cheek, while the other two members of the *Defensira* looked on unconcerned. They carried on with the interrogation all night until daybreak. He was interrogated again for a third and fourth time without a break until the afternoon, a rota of policemen asking him the same old questions which he answered until his voice was noth-ing more than a croak. His head was like cement and he was practically asleep on his feet, but they kept at him just the same, hour after hour, until past midnight. A Russian without a visa or passport, he was clearly working for the Comintern, and they told him that the punishment for spies from the Soviet Union in Józef Piłsudski's Poland was death by firing-squad.

He was dragged out of the room by his hair, yanked along an endless corridor and thrown into a cell. He fell asleep instantly. Later, when it was still dark, he was shaken awake by somebody and given a mug of water and a crust of bread. After that, he was left on his own again, but he couldn't go back to sleep, convinced that, come the dawn, they would drag him out and shoot him. At some point in the small hours, the cell door opened again and he found himself back in the windowless room, sitting on the hard wooden chair in front of the same table, with two detectives from the *Defensira* sitting behind it. During the comings and goings of the next hours, he lost count of how many of them questioned him, but the questions were always the same: why had he lived at the Hotel Adlon for so long? What exactly had he been doing in Berlin? Who gave him the order to move to France? Who were his contacts in Paris? Why choose to live in the Hôtel de Nantes? Why move to Passy? Who did he know in Passy? How had he managed to get on board the *Adam Mickiewicz* without a passport or a visa? And so on and on and on. They interrogated him, first in Russian, and then in German, and he was even interrogated in French for a stretch. The bastards were just desperate to trip him up, to have him betray himself, but Alyosha stuck to the truth, because it was all he had.

They locked him up in another cell, with a low ceiling, no more than a yard and a half high, and pitch black. He lost track of time, but he could hear a voice coming from somewhere above his head, and the clanking sounds of empty buckets from somewhere else. He started to fade away, and lost all sense of self. The blackness and the stillness seemed eternal, until he started to hear time dripping, drop by drop, from some height which didn't exist.

II.

Alyosha couldn't stand up fully and he could only see blurred shadows. He couldn't even see his hand in front of his nose, and he feared for a while that he might have gone blind. When they finally came to get him, it might have been hours or days later, for he had lost all track of time, he was taken to a different room, up some stairs and down a carpeted corridor. There was a substantial round table in a corner, but also two armchairs, a small sofa and a glass cupboard filled with books and documents, and the walls were decorated with paintings of various grey-haired, bearded men, every one wearing a bow tie and gazing prophetically towards some far horizon.

Two men he hadn't seen before began to interrogate him, but it was not long before the door opened. Alyosha watched as an old man shuffled in slowly, his shoulders hunched and wincing slightly as if in pain.

'Is this the one?' asked one of the interrogators, without bothering to take the cigarette from his lips. The old man didn't answer. 'Is this the one?' he asked louder. The old man wasn't sure. 'Take a better look.' The old man slowly shook his head. 'You, move nearer the light. Over here, come on –' Alyosha was hauled to his feet '– stand here so he can see you properly.' Licking his upper lip slowly, the old man scrutinised him carefully. 'Yes? No?'

Finally, he shook his head. The chain-smoking interrogator rose from the sofa with a grunt of irritation, stepped over to the table, pulling up the braces of his trousers, and bundled the old man out of the room.

After a night back in the cell, Alyosha was brought back for further questioning. Although the clouts and kicks that had been doled out to him in the earlier interrogations had been vicious, this round of calm, courteous, quiet interrogation was somehow far more sinister and disconcerting. This time there were five of them: two young uniformed policemen, a young woman at a typewriter, and two middle-aged detectives. The shorter of the two detectives, barely looking at him, said that he was the one. Alyosha wondered what he meant.

'What are you talking about?' he spoke out.

Nobody answered him. 'Who do you think I am?' he persisted.

The taller detective blew smoke out of the corner of his mouth and said, 'Tell us the truth.'

'About what?'

Every time anybody said anything, the young woman dutifully click-clacked away at her typewriter.

'The truth about what?'

They claimed he had been seen in the Café de l'Europe in Warsaw on at least two occasions, sitting at a table with Kornel Makuszyński and Joseph Birkenmajer. It was believed that Ewa Solska was also present, though she had not been formally identified. 'I've never heard of those men, or that woman,' Alyosha asserted, 'I've not set foot in any Café de l'Europe. I've never been to Poland before.'

'There's no point in you denying it, we know all about you.' The taller one was talking. Alyosha had also been seen in a cabaret in the Saxe nightclub, plotting with two members of the Comintern on such and such a day on such and such a time. He was an agent of the Kremlin, and his cover name was Gelendzhik.

'What were you discussing in the nightclub?' asked the shorter detective.

'My name is Alexei Fyodorovich Alexandrov.'

'So you keep claiming, but you don't have any proof,' said the taller of the two, crushing his cigarette into a saucer. 'Not a shred.' He stood up. 'You peddle some pathetic story about jumping on a ship from France because of some girl you've been fucking…'

'Because that's the truth.'

'Sweet Jesus,' muttered the taller detective under his breath, more in frustration than anything else, then gestured at one of the uniformed policemen who placed a sheet of paper on the table in front of Alyosha and gave him a pen. He refused to sign his name. For a while nobody said another word and there was complete silence in the room. Then one of the *Defensira* gave an almost imperceptible nod to the young woman who immediately picked up the typewriter, clasping it to her breast like a baby, and left the room, closing the door behind her. After a few more minutes of silence, there was a knock on the door and an elderly uniformed policeman came in, carrying a kettle with steam wafting out of its spout, and a funnel. Alyosha was informed briskly that they had another of the Comintern's agents in custody. She had slipped over the border from Russia some weeks previously, in order to plot against Józef Piłsudski's government, and was still stubbornly refusing to confess her part in the mission to infiltrate Polish factories in order to organise strikes and agitate, with the ultimate aim of putting the whole country under Moscow's red thumb. She was in the next room, they told him, tied to a chair. The elderly policeman took the kettle and funnel, opened a connecting door and went into the adjoining room, keeping the door slightly ajar.

Alyosha stared at the black type on the form. He knew signing the confession they had written for him was a mug's game. He was under no illusion that, once he did that, it would be the end of him. He knew, too, that they weren't lying about the girl in the next room, because the second the connecting door opened he could smell her: some rough scent mixed with sweat and shit. He heard her say something. Was she speaking German? Polish? Ukrainian? Her speech was too muffled to tell. He lifted his eyes to look at the two detectives, who were still watching him.

'Are you going to make her drink boiling water?'

'Boiling piss,' one of them corrected.

'Her own piss,' added the other, picking his nose. 'We're not animals.'

He could hear splashing and gurgling as the boiling liquid was poured into the funnel, followed by such screams as he'd never heard in his life.

That night, in his cell, Alyosha lay awake in a tormented dilemma, but, by the early hours, he had come to a decision: he would confess that his real name was Gelendzhik, and that he was an agent for the Comintern.

Through the high bars, dawn broke in bruises; his days were numbered. They would bring him before some court, and his name would be in the newspapers for a day or so, reporting a guilty verdict and a sentence of execution by shooting. Then he'd be buried and that would be that.

He felt a strange sense of relief.

12.

Alyosha expected to see his confession waiting for him on the table. Instead, the room was empty apart from a man in a grey jacket and tie, smoking a pipe, who greeted him and offered him a cigarette.

'Let's sit.'

What was this? A butcher tickling his pig before the slaughter?

They sat smoking in what might have passed to an observer as a companionable silence. After a while, the man told him a mistake had been made in his case, that they now believed him and so he was free to leave the country.

This was the last thing Alyosha had expected, and he took a moment to digest it. 'Why this sudden change of mind?' he asked, horribly afraid it was yet another trap. This was ignored, but there was something close to sympathy in the man's eyes as he began to explain the arrangements which had already been made to transport him safely across the border.

Within a few hours, Alyosha was back in Gdynia once again, and that same evening, he was put on board a fishing boat, which crossed the bay to the free city of Danzig, under the authority of the United Nations since the Treaty of Versailles. He'd been instructed to liaise with the French consul, who would help him with his onward travel to France.

Sure enough, he was given a temporary visa which allowed him to return to France, and was told that a passage had been arranged and paid for, although he would have to wait two days. In the meantime, he was given the address of a modest but spotless pension, and the wherewithal to pay for it, and told that a room had been reserved for him.

Freedom had never tasted so sweet. After sleeping soundly, and with a good breakfast in his stomach, Alyosha set out from the pension the next morning to explore. The morning clouds soon dispersed, and the day opened out. He wandered along the streets and found his way to the library. Leafing through the *Gazeta Polska*, he came across a picture of Ludwika which left him shaking and shocked. When he'd recovered his wits, he took the newspaper to the librarian and asked politely whether somebody might be able to translate the column for him. The librarian spoke German and was happy to oblige. He told him that Ludwika, the daughter of the Duke and Duchess of Zawadzki, had married Count Mateusz Kolodziejski, military attaché, in the Polish embassy in Bucharest, Romania. The ceremony had taken place the previous Saturday.

13.

It was an idyllic spot, only twenty miles outside Moscow, in a clearing among the pine trees. The air was resinous, and the birdsong competed charmingly with the thin tinkle of a piano being played somewhere inside the building. Margarita was shown around the kitchen, where a wholesome lunch was being prepared – meat with potatoes and fresh vegetables from the gardens. She was introduced to one of the young cooks, a girl with the traces of a hard life still in her eyes, but who held up her left hand and told Margarita that she had given her wedding ring to the fundraising campaign for the '23 revolution in Germany.

'Why didn't it happen? Who betrayed the working class?' she asked.

Margarita did her best to answer, but the girl made her feel ashamed. She vowed silently to work even harder back in Berlin, to bring about the revolution their Russian comrades were expecting.

The delegation ate their lunch with the young people in the dining room. There were almost three hundred of them sitting on wooden benches at tables, which had been manufactured there, and their easy conversation and laughter filled the room.

It was the young people, and not the authorities, who explained the philosophy behind the prison to their guests. In the Soviet Union, there were no such things as crimes, just personal failings which could be remedied. There was no such thing as punishment, either, just measures to protect society. There was no wall, no lock and no chains. There weren't even any cells. Nobody had to live on bread and water in Bolshevo. There didn't seem to be anybody much to keep an eye on them either. Margarita asked the girl at her side what was to stop them all running away, and the girl explained that the prison had been such a boon to her, that she had applied to her local soviet for permission to come back for a further term. She had even found a husband there, and once his term came to an end, the two of them were going to work in a factory in Perm, as he came from there originally. It was the director and his staff who had found them the work.

Nobody had a bad word to say about Bolshevo. The delegates were all charmed by the place, especially Paul, the only one who had spent any time under lock and key – in Moabit prison in Berlin, for disturbing the peace at a meeting of the Socialist Democratic Party, when he heckled some of the stewards and started a fight.

As they were leaving, Margarita and Hella were each presented with a bouquet of flowers and a skilfully carved wooden model of the prison.

Back in Moscow, that evening's reception was held at the Tretyakov art gallery. Irina, who translated for the German delegation, confessed to Margarita that she was exhausted, as she had been working very long hours for days now, so Margarita offered to help by translating what the artists and judges were saying. In truth, the Germans were flagging almost as much as Irina from the long days and the longer evenings, a hectic itinerary of visiting museums, schools, crèches and factories of all kinds by day, followed by elaborate receptions, dinners, and opera, theatre and ballet performances in the evenings. On the omnibus on the way back to their hotel that evening, Margarita asked Irina about Masha Ivanovna, but she didn't know anything about her.

14.

Alyosha was reading the newspapers in the Russian library one afternoon, when he was tapped on the shoulder. 'Alexei Fyodorovich.'

Looking around, he saw Vladimir Glebovich grinning down at him.

'How are things?'

Olga Sherbatovna, Vladimir's mother, came hobbling over to greet him too, with a book in her hand. She explained she had turned her ankle badly on the kerb of the pavement the previous afternoon.

'Lovely to see you again.'

'And you too.'

Smiling, she asked him, 'We haven't seen you since that evening in Sète. How is Ludwika?'

'Fine I expect. She got married.'

'Married?' repeated Vladimir sounding surprised.

'Yes.'

'When?'

'A while back. To some Polish diplomat.'

He felt a flash of anger as he remembered how he had been so cruelly treated by her, but, since his return to Paris, he felt his feelings towards her were slowly rotting away.

Aware of the disapproving glances from the other readers, Olga Sherbatovna suggested going to Café de la Rotonde. There, she drank Darjeeling tea and the men, coffee, as the endless flow of life passed by. She told Alyosha that she was reading Proust's *À la recherche du temps perdu*, but wasn't enjoying the first volume very much. She never gave up on a book, but she was beginning to lose patience with the author, as so few of his characters escaped his rancour and malice. She felt that there was a humanity lacking in Proust's writing when compared with Tolstoy; the Russian writer's spirit was so much more expansive and liberal, and he showed so much more sympathy for the human condition.

As they talked, it became clear that the widow's circumstances were very much straitened. Her son's education at the *lycée* on Rue Montparnasse had come to an end, and he was trying to pay his way. For the last few months, she had been working in a cheaply rented cellar of an old house on Rue du Bac. The workshop employed half a dozen women, all émigrées, who spent their days painting traditional Russian nesting dolls, where a slightly bigger doll swallowed a smaller one, until every doll in turn was swallowed by the biggest doll of all; that one was always the Tsar or the Tsarina. Painting the dolls was one thing, but then they had to be sold, which was Vladimir's task. Six days a week, he'd take samples around the tourist shops along the Champs-Élysées, but business was slack and orders were scarce. This meant his wages were tiny, as he was paid on commission, and the working conditions in the cellar were poor, as there were only two weak lightbulbs to paint by.

'We're sure to be ruining our eyesight,' sighed Olga Sherba-tovna over her empty cup. 'We'll be blind as moles by the end.'

Alyosha inquired hopefully. 'Is there an opening for another seller?'

'Why don't you ask Duchess Lydia? She owns the business.'

This turned out to be none other than the Duchess Lydia Herkulanova Vors.

15.

It was almost eight o'clock at night, and the cellar was empty. Duchess Lydia was the last to leave every night, and the first there in the morning to unlock the door and set up for the women. Nobody was any the wiser where she lived.

'Alexei Fyodorovich, are you in a hurry to leave? Won't you sit? I'd like the two of us to have a little chat.'

Alyosha had been working there for almost a month by now, but he had never seen her looking so exhausted. She wiped her hands with a dirty old rag, trying to lift some of the paint which stained her fingers. She was still handsome woman, and held herself well, but there was some grey in her hair now, and she had lost weight, so that the widow's weeds to which she remained as attached as a snail to its shell, now hung about her.

Even those ideas that had always been so sacrosanct to her were beginning to lose their grip, as poverty had begun to bite and her self-respect had begun to unravel around the edges. She had invested every centime she had in renting the damp old cellar and turning it into a workshop, in order to give herself some hope of a livelihood.

She told Alyosha how she had been dreaming for years of being able to return to Russia. There had been a time when they had all thought of Bolshevism as some lunatic, whose strength would diminish over time, at which point wiser people could throw him out of the house. Then, she surprised Alyosha when she said that, as for restoring the monarchy, she really didn't see the need for that any more. By now, she would be happy to settle for a Russia under a democratic government.

She told him that she still dreamt of hearing the tinkle of the sleigh-bells as the sleighs sped down Nevskii Prospekt in the heart of winter, when the snow sparkled like a web of crystal and the sun lay low on the horizon, bathing the golden towers of Saint Petersburg in its evening light. She longed to smell the Crimean air, too, and to lie in fragrant gardens listening to the cawing of the birds from the high rocks in the distance.

'Empty dreams… I realise that's all they are now.'

There was no return to be had, and they must accept life as it was, make the best of it, and try to become used to living among strangers. In order to succeed at this, they had to seek other comforts to bolster their souls to the end of their days.

'May I share a secret with you, Alexei Fyodorovich?' she asked, her fingers still stained with paint. 'May I?' She went on to tell him that Andrei Petrovich had asked for her hand in marriage. Vera Muromtseva-Bunina had introduced them at a reading, where her husband, Ivan Bunin, had been one of the poets taking part. Poetry was the language of the heart and emotion, but prose was the language of the mind and reason. That's what Andrei Petrovich had said to her that night. But she had yet to tell her mother, and was dreading hearing her opinion, which was bound to be that she was marrying beneath herself. A former bank manager, indeed!'

'Do you love him?' was Alyosha's question.

She was still scratching away at a speck of blue paint on her nail.

'Marrying somebody is a huge leap of faith, and there is a moral seriousness to the decision.'

She rinsed her hand in a bucket of water and then scoured it vigorously with a scrubbing brush.

'My first husband will be the only true love of my life. But, nevertheless, sometimes I feel so… I don't know how to say this without sounding self-pitying. But, sometimes, I feel so lonely. Especially in the evenings, when it's just Mama and me. Just the two of us, reading or embroidering, and only the sound of the needle pulling the thread through the fabric or a page turning to break the silence. And I occasionally wonder what will happen to me once Mama has passed on to the next life. Or, what *won't* happen to me. I don't know which is worse…'

She wiped her fingers on a filthy rag.

'Andrei Petrovich has lost his spouse, like me. We both under-stand loneliness, and he has respectfully asked for my hand.' She smiled coyly. 'Mind you, I really didn't know what to say when he asked me. It was the last thing I was expecting.' She examined her hands. 'Because it hasn't been so very long since his poor wife was laid to rest on her bed of earth. It was so unexpected, so strange, so… How can I refuse him? And if I do decide to refuse him, will I ever receive another offer?'

'If you're not sure how you feel, nobody can *force* you to marry.'

'No, nobody. Nobody is forcing me to marry, Alexei Fyodorovich. Nobody but myself.'

16.

Paul and his little mouse, Rosa, were sitting next to Margarita. His eyes were two red slits and his breath stank like the gutter of an abattoir. He was always the last to bed and was drinking far more than was good for him. As leader of their group, she had felt it necessary to have a quiet word with him about it, but Paul saw it as an opportunity to challenge Margarita's authority, and drank even more.

'There's been a change of plan,' he told her as he chewed unenthusiastically on his breakfast.

She wondered if he was still slightly drunk. 'Didn't anybody tell you?' He was obviously enjoying himself. 'They've decided to split the group up. I'm meant to lead half of us to Leningrad, and you'll be taking the other half to the south.'

'Where in the south?'

Paul swallowed a mouthful of coffee before answering her. 'Baku. In Azerbaijan. Hot and dry, even at this time of year. From what I've heard, the air stinks of petrol. You can't get away from it, night or day.'

Was he to be believed, she wondered, knowing how he delighted in provoking her. She would be bitterly disappointed if he was telling the truth; she'd been particularly looking forward to this part of the trip, as she would be revisiting the city where she grew up. She was also hoping she might have an opportunity in Leningrad to make further enquiries about her father.

'When was this decided, Paul?'

The waitress poured more coffee into his cup as he replied smugly, 'It's not our place to question these things.'

The girl scuttled away when she saw the nose of the little mouse peep out from under his shirt.

Margarita went at once to see Kai-Olaf.

'What's this I've just heard?' she asked. He thought she already knew about the new arrangement. 'No indeed, I hadn't heard anything about Baku.'

When he saw how crestfallen she was, he suggested she take it up with Irina.

Later that morning, Irina came back to her and told her that the decision had come from a 'high place'.

'I would much rather go to Leningrad than Baku. Why can't Paul lead the delegation to the south?'

Margarita pressed the point home. She had made it perfectly clear from the start how much she had been looking forward to the visit to Leningrad, and she didn't have the slightest inclination to go anywhere else. What she couldn't say was that her promise to her sister to try to find out about their father was very much in her thoughts.

Irina stood politely but impassively, listening until Margarita had finished talking, then just said,

'The decision has been made.'

'Since when?'

'A while.'

'Why didn't I hear about it until this morning then?'

Irina had no idea.

Margarita spent the next few hours fruitlessly looking for somebody with the authority to reverse the decision. She tried to at least extract a promise that she would be allowed to visit Leningrad after being in Baku, and emphasised how important this was to her.

'We'll see what we can do,' was the only answer she was given.

17.

Things were very awkward to begin with when Galina Andreyevna, Andrei Petrovich's only daughter, came to work in her prospective step-mother's workshop. Alyosha hadn't set eyes on her since her aunt, Lazarevna Petrovna, had accused Alyosha of raping her, after he'd refused to smuggle morphine in to her at the clinic where she was meant to be recovering from her addiction.

Galina had chosen to believe her aunt rather than Alyosha, and, worse still, had repeated her accusation to everybody.

Although Alyosha kept his distance, it became obvious that Galina wished them to be friends again. It was Vladimir Glebovich who helped things along by inviting them both to join him for a drink at the end of the working day. In no time, this had become a regular event. One evening, the three of them fell into conversation with a swarthy Sardinian called Camlo. Vladimir soon excused himself because he was meeting Erwana, and Alyosha left soon after, as he didn't have the price of a second drink, but Camlo persuaded Galina to stay and have another drink with him.

A week or so later, Alyosha was working late, packing dolls in the Rue du Bac cellar, when Galina's husband called by.

'I'm Marcel,' he said in a slightly sheepish way.

From nearby, the church clock struck seven.

With an air of quiet sadness, Marcel explained that he was worried about his wife.

'There's no need for you to be, I'm sure…'

'I'm not so sure,' was his honest answer. 'Do you know where she is?'

Alyosha did know. Galina had gone off to meet Camlo again. But he wasn't about to become involved in Galina's complicated life, so he said he had no idea.

18.

As the weeks went by, Galina's body took on a new svelte shape, where previously she had found it difficult to lose the weight she had gained when she was pregnant. Her eyes sparkled, her skin glowed – in short, she was radiant with happiness, and told Alyosha she had never enjoyed a man's company as much as she did Camlo's. She found it so hard to drag herself away from him to go home to make supper for Marcel and the baby. Galina's only concern was that her prospective stepmother, Duchess Lydia, would find out about the new man in her life and tell her father. Then, she confided in Alyosha that she'd been seeing another man for a few months, a bank clerk by the name of Yves. But she realised that Camlo was the man for her now. Camlo knew how to listen to a woman, and he appreciated her more than anybody. He was also a man with business interests here, there and everywhere, and he had told her that he could easily find her better work than painting wooden dolls all day in a damp old cellar. He was always telling her that she was mad to spend so many hours working for next to nothing. Camlo believed in living for the day, not worrying about the future, as pleasure was the purpose of life, not slaving away morning, noon and night.

It wasn't long before Galina had left Duchess Lydia's workshop for a job in a night club called Le Flamant Rose. About the same time, Alyosha was also offered other work, for which he was very grateful, because his sales were so low he was barely making any money. Yet again, it was Prince Yakov who helped him. He'd heard one of his passengers complaining to his companion that he couldn't find experienced staff for his new restaurant, which had just opened on Boulevard Madeleine, and the Prince advised Alyosha to get over there straight away. Alyosha went the very next afternoon, when the tables of the Grand Cercle Muscovite were being relaid ready for the evening customers. The language was Russian and the food was Russian – blinis and caviar, shashlik and stroganoff, and a house dessert called Romanov pudding. The waiters were all dressed in Russian shirts, with golden eagles stitched on the back, and black trousers tucked into the traditional black boots.

Aristarkh Aleksandrovich Kulikov, the owner of the Grand Cercle Muscovite, was an ex–actor–manager from Gavrilovo, on the outskirts of Smolensk in Sycherka, and was immensely proud of his Russian heritage. On principle, he spoke as little French as he could, which consequently remained fairly rudimentary, because, in his heart, he hoped to go home one day. Once he knew Alyosha was Russian, he hardly bothered to ask him about his previous experience, and offered him a job on the spot. He handed him over to his manager, Efim Moisevitch Ovchinnikov, who explained Alyosha's duties to him briskly and showed him around the kitchens. He introduced him to the chef, a pale man who looked a bit of a cold fish, though he tapped Alyosha on the shoulder with a wooden spoon and said, 'Welcome,' courteously enough. It was only later that Alyosha discovered the staff called him 'the Serpent' behind his back.

19.

The Hotel Europa was a modern building, eight storeys high. On the promenade opposite was a tall iron structure with a wide aluminium platform at the top. From here, the boys and girls would parachute off, one after the other. When Margarita had a few precious minutes to herself, she loved to sit out on the balcony of her room on the fifth floor, and watch them climb up the tower with agile speed, then fling themselves thrillingly from the top into the air. Seconds later, shiny white mushrooms puffed up out of their backs and billowed gracefully in the air as they floated down to the soft sand beneath.

At the other end of the promenade, a few people were fishing. One of them spun a net high around his head then, with a quick flick of the wrist, flung it out to sea, centrifugal force and the weight of the leads spreading it out wide and flat, so that it fell cleanly over the surface of the water. Margarita looked beyond him, far out to sea, where the heavy ships, the long tankers, were sailing slowly north to Astrakhan, or to the south, towards the ports of Persia. She shaded her eyes, and it struck her with deep delight that beyond the horizon lay the far reaches of Asia.

The delegation took most of their meals at their hotel, and the standard was every bit as high as the Moskva in Moscow. There was also the same busy programme of visits and receptions. They'd already been to see a modern new clinic for mothers and babies, and five new schools – one Jewish, one Azeri, one Armenian, one Turkish and one Russian. The policy towards ethnic minorities had been explained to them, and it had been stressed how much the Soviet government did to protect minority languages.

But Margarita didn't feel completely happy in the new Baku. With so much black gold spurting from the earth, why wasn't there more evidence of prosperity in the city? Why hadn't the petrol workers inherited the capitalist wealth, those huge fortunes made on their backs during the years before the revolution? In spite of some new housing, most of the population still lived in low mud hovels, while camels and donkeys filled the streets, not motor cars, and goats bleated in the squares. Most of the build-ings were still those of the ancient and primitive East, and the whole city seemed to her to have an air of dusty desolation. As they were being driven to a hospital which specialised in tropical diseases, she asked why living conditions were still so poor for so many, a whole decade after the revolution. She was told (with Irina nodding in agreement) that, while huge improvements had already been made, it was not to be expected that three centuries of Romanov misrule could be put right overnight.

That evening, Margarita strolled through the old city to the Turki Theatre. She did this against the wishes of the local organ-iser, who had provided motor cars to transport the delegation, and Irina had insisted on walking with her.

'There's really no need,' Margarita had told her.

'I could do with a bit of fresh air myself.'

At the corners of the narrow streets, beggars sat in ragged but colourful clothes, pleading in the name of Allah for alms.

'Are you and Kai-Olaf lovers?' asked Irina out of the blue.

Taken aback, Margarita stopped in her tracks and took the cigarette out of her mouth.

'What on earth makes you think that?' she asked

'The way you are with each other…'

'We're comrades. Nothing more than that.'

Irina smiled, but she was blushing. 'I'm sorry, but I thought…'

Margarita laughed to show she was not offended and asked her, 'So, do you have somebody?'

'Not now… I had a boyfriend last year… A student.' Her blush deepened.

'A pretty girl like you – I'm sure it won't be long before there's another.'

There was a champagne reception for the delegation before the evening performance, where they were all introduced to the theatre director, Pamphylia Tanailidi, a tall, slightly hunched woman who chain-smoked small Persian cigarettes, so that she was constantly wreathed in tobacco smoke. She told them a little about the play, and said she hoped the foreign comrades would enjoy the performance.

Next they were introduced to the Azeri, a fleshy man with a young flunky at his side to attend to his needs. This was arguably the most important man in Soviet Baku. Yet again, they were told how things had improved in Azerbaijan since the revolution. The Azeri informed them proudly that it was the first secular Muslim republic in the world. He emphasised the importance of the city, lying as it did on the crossroads between East and West. It stood exactly halfway between Moscow and Pahlavi, and the easiest way to reach northern Persia was through Baku.

Shahnameh, based on Middle Eastern legends, proved a colourful production, full of song and dance. Margarita enjoyed looking at the audience sitting in the stalls beneath her almost as much as the performance. Mostly grubby and dishevelled young people, they showed their enthusiasm and approval noisily and energetically, cheering and clapping at the end of every song and dance.

During the interval, the delegation were shepherded into the bar, and Margarita was introduced to some local dignitaries. But there was little chance to do more than shake hands, as the fleshy Azeri dominated the conversation with an easy authority. A thin-faced man with a black moustache and clean nails didn't take his eyes off her, and as they were all returning to their seats, he quietly suggested that she should come to see him the next day. Margarita felt a small card being slipped into her hand. The name on it was Aznefttrust, and a time had been noted in pencil.

Afterwards, another feast and entertainment had been prepared for them in a restaurant called the National, next to their hotel. The salt fish made Margarita thirsty, and she ended up drinking too much champagne and vodka, so she was feeling tired and light-headed by the time the music started. The musicians were a group of Tartars, and a dozen girls in gold and saffron outfits danced for them. Then, the Azeri insisted on leading Margarita onto the floor, but she found it difficult to move to music which was so unfamiliar to her ear. She tried to imitate her partner's moves who was, surprisingly, as light-footed as a young boy. He clapped his hands above his head as he sang along to the words, and spun her round like a top. Bouncing around drunkenly near them, kicking their heels high, were Max and Moritz, with Irina between them, laughing heartily at their antics. Their shirts were open, their faces were scarlet and their bodies glistened with sweat. Margarita caught a glimpse of Kai-Olaf sitting on his own at a table over in a shadowy corner, gazing at her over a half-empty glass of milk. When the dance finally came to an end, she made her way to his table, and extended her hand to him in invitation, but he shook his head. She leant over and whispered in his ear that the least he could do was rescue her from another dance with the fat Azeri. With a smile, he stood and took her hand.

The next song was slower, and he held her in his arms, but in spite of their physical closeness, Margarita sensed that Kai Olaf's mind was far away. The second the dance came to an end, the Azeri was back at her shoulder, his arms out wide, his head at an angle of false pleading. She had no choice but to step into his arms. The singing and celebrating carried on in an increasingly drunken haze into the small hours.

20.

Sharp sunlight intruded into the room through the mosquito blinds. Margarita felt as though her head was about to split, and her mouth was bone dry. She heard a sigh, which was more of a half-snore, and hoisted herself up onto her elbow to peep over a strip of shoulder, ear, cheek and nose. Breathing heavily into the pillow was Kai-Olaf, and she gazed in wonder for a moment at his bald head. When she slipped out of bed and stood up, she felt dizzy, and a dull pain throbbed behind her eyes. She had to steady herself by leaning her fists against the mattress, and give herself a moment for the light-headedness to pass, before straightening up cautiously. She crept around collecting her clothes as quietly as possible, resisting a strong urge to heave. She tried to piece together the events of the previous night as she dressed, but it was all a complete blur.

She had woken so late that she was only just in time for her appointment. Luckily for her, the Aznefttrust offices weren't very far from Hotel Europa, just a little further down the boulevard.

She hurried past riotously colourful flower beds, tended by men in overalls and white caps, and, short though the walk was, by the time she climbed the stairs of the building, her throbbing headache was worse than ever.

She was asked to wait outside Donbas Hajiev's office, and for the next quarter of an hour or so, assailed by a variety of emotions, she tried and failed to piece together the events of the previous night, which culminated with her and Kai-Olaf in bed together.

Donbas Hajiev was fresh as a daisy, smelling of eau-de-cologne, his black moustache neat as a pin. He greeted her and invited her to sit. She gave silent thanks for the white fan overhead, which dispersed welcome cool air over her back and bare shoulders. A man brought them tiny cups of strong coffee, for which she was even more grateful. The conversation was a little stilted to begin with. Donbas Hajiev had the habit of tapping his knee as he finished a sentence or asked a question, and Margarita found it difficult to concentrate on what he was saying. What became obvious was that he already had a considerable amount of information about her, because every now and again he would glance down at a file which was open in front of him.

After two more cups of the sweet, strong coffee, Margarita was starting to feel a little more like herself. Gradually, the fog cleared in her head, and a clearer landscape came into view. She hadn't been brought to Baku to give speeches, nor to visit schools, apartment blocks, and clinics, nor to stare into a microscope at malaria protozoa – she had been brought there for this. If she wanted more time to think it over, he was saying, he quite understood, but there was so much work to be done and they had so little time to do it. He had heard great things about her, with many testimonials about her dedication to the cause. This was a further opportunity to make an important contribution in undercover work.

Donbas Hajiev had stopped speaking, and without even a moment's hesitation she asked, 'When do you want me to start?'

'As soon as you return to Berlin.'

21.

In the lull between lunch and evening service, the eight members of the Grand Cercle Muscovite staff had to justify their wages by going out on the streets to hand out flyers advertising the restaurant. Alyosha's favourite location was one of the wooden jetties, where the pleasure boats moored to pick up passengers, before continuing to plough their way up and down the Seine. Watching the light softly reflected on the surface of the river calmed his mind like nothing else, and he would usually lose himself in a highly pleasurable reverie, full of sweet memories of his cossetted childhood years.

Often he imagined he was gazing at the Neva, and although hundreds of days of his life had vanished from his memory – days which had left no more trace than the paddlewheels of yesterday's boats on the water – there were some moments which endured forever, moments to treasure, as they reminded him that he had been somebody else back then, with an imagined future quite different from his present. He took a certain comfort from this, because it meant he could perhaps be somebody else again, reinvent himself once more. He just had to keep the hope alive that his circumstances could change, because he himself was capable of change.

Otherwise, to get rid of his flyers, he'd go anywhere the tourist omnibuses stopped, especially outside the Louvre and other museums. This ensured they always had plenty of Americans turning up at the doors of the Grand Cercle Muscovite every night, especially when the tourist season was at its height.

One rather foggy morning, before service had begun, Aristarkh Aleksandrovich assembled the waiting staff and instructed them to invent three stories about their time fighting the Reds during the Civil War. Even the youngest lad, who was only sixteen years old, was expected to come up with something. They were told to emphasise the cruelty of the communists and the bravery of the Whites. In truth, not a single one of them had been anywhere near the front, least of all Aristarkh Aleksandrovich himself, and nobody was very happy at having to pretend, but they didn't dare to object.

In the meantime, Efim Moisevitch had hired a small band of gypsies to sing traditional Russian songs every night. There was a Russian wine list, too, though, in fact, the wine came from obscure vineyards in Languedoc, with Russian labels pasted onto the bottles.

The Americans lapped it up, especially when the main lights were dimmed, leaving just the candles guttering on the tables, and the gypsies started to hum softly, the melody of the violin in the background plummeting suddenly from major to minor in an effort to conjure up the promised 'authentic Russian atmosphere.'

Money poured into the till like water from a pump, and nothing filled Aristarkh Aleksandrovich with more pleasure than the moment when he pulled down the shutters, locked the door, and sat down with Efim Moisevitch and half a bottle of vodka to count the takings. The staff were warned, on pain of losing their jobs, not to breathe a word outside the restaurant about the telling of the war stories, so that their competitors, of which there were several, didn't get wind of it and copy them. The hair-raising stories the staff told their customers become more and more embellished and extreme the more they were retold. They told of men being buried alive, of women raped, tortured and burnt to death before their eyes, of despairing mothers cutting their own children's throats rather than let the Bolsheviks get their filthy hands on them.

But the other Russian restaurants had plenty of tricks of their own, such as bringing in troupes of supposed Cossacks, to plait their arms across their chests, kick their legs, and yell 'Whoa!' Aristarkh Aleksandrovich decided they needed a new gimmick to stay ahead, so he found a retired circus performer to throw twelve inch knives around the head of the sixteen-year-old, who stood shaking, chalk-white with fear, against the wall. But one evening, a clumsy throw took a sizeable slice off the poor boy's ear. Bleeding like a pig, and howling with fear and pain, he was bundled quickly into the kitchen, where the Serpent calmly stitched him up and told him not to be such a girl.

22.

Dirty, melting snow slushed underfoot as the procession of hats, scarves and black coats made its way to the top of the mausoleum where Bukharin, Vorosilov, Kalinin, Molotov, Stalin, Rykov, Tomskii and the rest stood in a row. On the far left of the mausoleum, but slightly lower down, Stanislav Markovich sat with the journalists, bundled up against the cold like the rest of them.

The *Internationale* boomed over the loudspeakers to signal the beginning of the procession. First, seemingly endless columns of infantry marched by, turning their heads smartly towards the Central Committee of the Communist Party as they passed them. Then came the cavalry, the sound of hundreds of hooves clattering against the cobbles filling the air. Then, the roar of tanks and the throbbing of the heavy lorries pulling the artillery, gun barrels glinting with a dull shine. In their wake came the factory workers, each group proud to have been picked to represent their region of the Soviet Union, followed by hundreds upon hundreds of socialist columns – young men and women of the Komsomol, in their white shirts and red kerchiefs, their banners held high, shouting slogans at the top of their voices.

Every inch of the square was one enormous stage, and hanging down over the façade of the G.U.M shops were huge red banners of Engels, Marx, Lenin and Stalin.

Margarita had never seen Paul with such a smile on his face. He was in his seventh heaven, though every now and again he took his vodka bottle from the breast pocket of his coat and took a quick swig, to ward off the cold, he told her. Alongside them in the audience were workers from the factories and mills, as well as officials from various government departments and other institutions who, for whatever reason, had been granted the privilege of being invited to attend. The delegation from Berlin had been seated with the other foreign delegations in a privileged position, but it was freezing cold, and after two hours, Margarita's toes were numb, no matter how much she stamped her feet.

It started to snow. Gymnasts tumbled through the flakes, ghostly figures smiling gamely, though their lips were turning blue, and the spectators all yelled their appreciation of the artistry of their intricate human pyramids before they passed by. Paul pointed at something excitedly and Margarita turned her head in time to see Stalin throwing a snowball at somebody beneath him, and that person throwing a snowball back, and some of the Politburo laughing.

Music blared through the loudspeakers constantly, and every now and then the spectators would spontaneously sing along, Margarita among them. She felt part of a fraternity, one which encompassed not only the communists within the square, but all those millions beyond who were also singing from the same song sheet.

Kai-Olaf didn't take his seat until mid-afternoon, and when he did, he looked sombre.

'Is everything alright?' Margarita asked.

'I've found out why your friend Masha was imprisoned,' he said in her ear.

There was so much noise around them, she didn't catch his words properly.

He sat at her side, his cap pulled low over his ears, his hands deep in his coat pockets, watching the procession. He'd never said a single word about Baku. What did he feel towards her? Did he feel anything? Margarita didn't know what to think or what to do, and kept hoping he would say something, but so far he was acting as though nothing had passed between them at all.

The celebrations carried on for another hour. A dozen aeroplanes flew past the Kremlin in strict formation, followed by four slower aeroplanes flying in circles. Everybody looked up at the grey sky and watched as four dozen men fell from the undercarriage of each machine, like graceful red confetti. But one of the parachutes failed to open, and the entire square watched in horror as the man hurtled downwards, head-over-heels, his arms flailing wildly. Even the Central Committee were like a clutch of open-mouthed chicks as they craned upwards. Then the man plummeted from sight, and the celebrations continued as though nothing had happened.

'Did you see that…?' asked Margarita, shaken.

Kai-Olaf nodded, tight-lipped, without looking at her.

As the procession came to an end, and the square gradually emptied, it was already getting dark, but the lights were on and the militia had lit huge bonfires to keep the pilgrims warm.

Outside, silence reigned, but there was the usual feasting and dancing and singing at the Hotel Moskva that night, the magnificent chandeliers burning as brightly as ever. Paul, Max and Moritz danced in a tight circle, their heads bent as though in prayer, their arms yoked across each other's shoulders. Margarita swept her eyes across the alcoves, where the tables were placed around the room. She had just spoken to Kai-Olaf and was in no mood to socialise. Kai-Olaf had told her that her friend Masha had been sent by ship from Vladivostok to Magadan, after being sentenced to ten years in a Siberian jail. Her crime was spying for the Germans, and her visit to Berlin had been the perfect opportunity to pass on secret information about the industrial potential of the Donbas to the enemies of the Soviet Union. Her two brothers were also part of the plot, and they too were under lock and key.

Although Kai Olaf told her his source was impeccable, Margarita found it almost impossible to believe that this could be true of Masha. Masha Ivanovna? The same Masha who had spoken to her so passionately about the future of her motherland, about the communist ideals she upheld so staunchly? But she had been accused, and a court of law had found her guilty of betraying the cause that was so sacred to millions. Every word that came from her lips must have been a lie.

If Margarita harboured doubts, Kai-Olaf had none.

'But if you'd only met her…' she began.

'What difference would that have made?' he asked.

'Heard her speak as she spoke that night in the Mozart-Saal. I can't believe she'd have done something like this.'

'Double agents like Masha can be very clever.'

'What if they have made a mistake?'

'In a case as serious as this? I doubt it.'

'It's possible surely?'

'They know what they're doing.'

Masha Ivanovna's treachery left Margarita doubting herself, and she felt that she must have been completely politically naïve. Had Masha seen her coming from a mile away? Had she used her as some sort of cover for what she was really doing in Berlin? How had she been so stupid as to be taken in? Kai-Olaf comforted her. 'We all have to learn from our mistakes.'

But she was overwhelmed with shame. 'I've been such a fool,' she told him sadly.

'You mustn't take it to heart,' urged Kai-Olaf. 'Masha can't do any more damage where she is now. Who knows, this might even be her salvation. But think of it this way. Even, if by some strange fluke, she has been wronged, it's a wrong within a proletarian system which is just. The aim of the Soviet Republic is to stop man's exploitation of his fellow man through the creation of a classless society. That's why we can excuse any individual injustice without having to condemn the system. Always remember that communism is underpinned by a completely different attitude from the so-called justice of the capitalist countries, where there's one law for the poor and another for the rich. The bourgeoisie believes that whatever promotes capitalism is good, and whatever puts a stop to it is bad. That's why their praise of freedom and justice is just an empty hosanna.'

Having it all framed like this made Margarita feel slightly happier, and she resolved to follow Kai-Olaf's advice to be less ready to take people at face value without first learning more about them, and even then, he told her, she should remain alert. The enemies of socialism were extremely cunning. There were many who were more determined than ever to see the first workers' republic fail, and would use whatever methods they could to bring about its overthrow.

It had been a long and exhausting day. Margarita had been raised to the rafters by the celebrations in Red Square, and dashed to the ground with the savage disillusionment of realising that she had possibly been used by a spy. Later, she experienced an even greater disillusionment. On the dance floor were Kai-Olaf and Hella Wuolijoka. She was wearing a pretty blue dress with a pleated skirt, and her dark hair was loose and flying around her face as he twirled her round. Margarita felt the sharp sting of disappointment, but when Kai-Olaf caught her eye, she held his gaze levelly for a moment before turning her head away.

More furtively she continued to watch him. He had such a well-chiselled, strong chin, and his blue eyes were as bright as ever. Hella was very beautiful, but as she felt another stab of jealousy, Margarita berated herself. Jealously was a bourgeois emotion. What right did she have to claim another individual as hers alone? He was challenging her to challenge herself. Yes, that's what Kai-Olaf was doing, it was quite clear to her now, and Margarita realised that she still had a long way to go before she could truly call herself a communist.

But she still felt bereft, and without an understanding of anything – least of all herself – she was lost. She wanted to make him happy, but he clearly didn't feel the same. He seemed to have rejected her, so now what? She had her friends in the KPD, her sister, her health, all important things. And yet, they weren't enough – she needed more. At least she was honest enough to admit that to herself. She needed somebody in her life, someone to fall asleep next to every night and wake up with every morning. Was that likely to ever happen? Was somebody going to love her? It was important not to start feeling hopeless, there was enough sadness in the world already without sinking into that trough. She *must* stay hopeful. If there was a clear meaning to history, there had to be a meaning to her life, too. Though, from her own point of view, the future seemed very unclear.

She turned and saw Stanislav Markovich talking to one of the hotel staff. She waited until the young man scuttled off, no doubt to do his bidding, then went over to greet him.

'You're looking tired,' he told her directly.

'I feel tired. It's been a long day.'

'So it has. I'm not staying long. I've promised to meet Panait Istrati. Have you heard of him?'

'No…'

'A writer from Romania, who's very keen for me to introduce him to Mayakovskii. Which I've promised to do, so I'd better not break my word.'

They chatted for a while, and then Stanislav said, 'I've found out what happened to your father.' Margarita waited impatiently while he lit his pipe. 'I don't have good news, I'm afraid.'

She had been fearing the worst in any event. 'He's dead?' she asked.

'About eight years ago. He was leading a special force – a small army within the Red Army – outside Lvov, against the Poles. The exact circumstances aren't clear, but he was shot and buried there.' He coughed a dry cough. 'All praise to him. He was a committed officer, held in high regard. He did his best for the cause.'

Margarita tried to take in the significance of what she'd just been told. She asked when her father had joined the Red Army. Had he become a member of the Communist Party? Had he joined the Red Army voluntarily? Or had he been forced against his will? He had always been so hostile towards the Bolsheviks. Stanislav replied that Kozma had realised that the Bolsheviks were Russia's only possible saviours, and that without them, the empire would be destroyed under the feet of the capitalists. He hadn't wanted to see foreign companies and banks – American, French, British, German or, worse yet, Japanese – fleece the land of all its natural resources, its coal, oil, gold and silver. There were enough forests in the *taiga* to feed the insatiable appetites of the capitalist world for generations.

'It seems Kozma Mikhailovich realised that it was more important to keep these raw materials in the service of the people, rather than fill the pockets of a small band of greedy men.'

Was that really how her father thought by the end of his life? As she did now? What a shame she couldn't have talked to him about it. She'd never find out now what his reasons had been for changing his mind. But it seemed they had both seen the worth of the cause, and had stepped over to the communists in order to contribute to creating a better society than the old one.

Margarita wondered why she felt so calm. She felt no sorrow or sense of loss, but rather an inner release. Stanislav pulled on his gloves, pushing his fingers right to the end, as though he was reproaching the leather for not yielding more space.

'I understand you'll be working for Aznefttrust once you're back in Berlin.'

There was something presumptuous about him. What had she ever seen in him?

'How did you hear that?'

'Somebody in the Kremlin told me.'

'Have you been asking about me?'

Instead of replying, he squeezed her elbow – the first time he'd touched her in Moscow – and declared that they needed first-class people in key places, to prepare for the fight ahead of them in Europe.

'You have an important contribution to make. He squeezed her arm once again. 'And we have every faith in you.' His skin was ashy.

Next day's greatest thrill was seeing the pictures of the Red Square procession in *Pravda*, with Stalin centre stage. Paul insisted that a tiny figure in the crowd was himself. Then Max and Moritz decided they could see themselves too, in among the grey faces and black fur hats. Margarita translated the newspaper reports for them, but, although she scoured all the columns, there wasn't a single word in *Pravda*, nor *Izvestia*, or any of the other newspapers, about the parachutist who had been killed.

23.

They kept trying to persuade Alyosha to pretend to be a prince who was related to the late Tsar, perhaps even going so far as to claim he had been one of those who had disposed of Rasputin's body by pushing his corpse through a hole in the ice into the black river Neva. But he flatly refused, unwilling to have anything to do with such a stupid charade.

His refusal did him no favours with Aristarkh Aleksandrovich, who was still preoccupied with preserving the restaurant's popularity. Alyosha didn't mind coming out with a load of old rubbish about fighting the communists on the battlefield, but claiming to be one of Rasputin's murderers was a different matter. That was not a claim to be made lightly.

But neither was Aristarkh Aleksandrovich a man to cross. He didn't sack Alyosha for his refusal, but he did demote him from waiting on the customers to being a *plongeur,* the lowest of the low. Less money in his pay-packet, and no tips: he was significantly out of pocket.

But Alyosha now spent his days in the company of Marya, Aristarkh Aleksandrovich's wife. She was an unassuming woman, a gentle, plump little thing, with round cheeks, small and pink and appetising as ripe apples. She wore the same black frock with a green trim whatever the time of year. In spite of being the proprietor's wife, he rarely saw her go in to the restaurant. She seemed to prefer to spend her time in the kitchen with the Serpent, working her fingers to the bone morning, noon and night, cleaning and scouring as though she were trying to wash away some terrible, unbearable sadness. Amidst the dishonest *kitsch* of the restaurant, there was an authentic simplicity belonging to her, like something sieved pure and clean. One dark night, in the quiet hour at the end of his shift, she confided in Alyosha about the daughter she had lost as she fled Russia, though in her heart she was still convinced that the child was alive.

But Paris water was hard water. For fifteen hours a day, every day, he would be up to his elbows in it, in a never-ending battle to wash away the grease from the mounds of pans, crockery, cutlery, and glasses, a battle he could never win. After standing on his feet for so long, Alyosha's legs would be like jelly, and his back would be on fire. In spite of all Marya's furious scouring, by the end of service, the kitchen would be pretty squalid: the floor was always covered with grease and spillages, the dirty pans and dishes were stacked everywhere, and there was always a pervasive smell of fat and rotting vegetables. It was a narrow space, with not enough room for them to work comfortably, which added to everybody's bad humour, apart from Marya, who remained serene through everything.

One evening the restaurant was particularly busy, and the Serpent was constantly ringing the bell for service. During a particularly frantic half-hour, one of the waiters wedged the kitchen door open with a bit of wood so that they could bring out the plates of steaming food that much quicker, although this was strictly against the rules, as it wouldn't do for the guests to see the state of the kitchen. Looking up from his greasy sink, something about a couple drinking *vermouth-cassis* caught Alyosha's attention. The woman was dressed in a plunging blue dress, her hair swept up on her head, her crystal earrings shimmering in the candlelight. As she took a sip of her drink from red-painted lips, lifting her eyes languorously over the rim of her glass to look at the man sitting opposite her, he recognised her. It was Zepherine. Alyosha turned his attention to her companion and, although he now had a thick beard, his face was coarser and his hairline had receded, it was his uncle, there were no two ways about it.

His Uncle Artyom.

Alyosha's heart was beating faster as he wondered what he should do. Should he go out and speak to him? He considered for an instant whether he was ready to forgive him for taking Grete away from him, but then he remembered that this was the man who had broken his heart and smashed his dreams to dust.

This was the man who had turned his life into an empty shell. No. He had never forgiven him for taking Grete away.

He never *would* forgive him.

24.

Too agitated to go home, Alyosha went over to the Flamant Rose as soon as he had finished his shift. He would often visit Galina there, because she could slip him past the door without paying, and would usually manage to slip him a gin fizz as she was serving the other tables, warning him to 'drink it slowly' so that he wouldn't look out of place without a drink in front of him.

Le Flamant Rose belonged to Harot and Léonard, two quiet brothers with a murky past, who shared a delight in boar-hunting in the Corbières with the Viscount – his real name was Henri Dupont – a small-arms manufacturer with a substantial bank account at Crèdit de France. He was also a member of the Chamber of Deputies. There had been a rumour going around that his wife had had an affair with some young man in Monte Carlo the previous year, but he had succeeded in avoiding a scandal by paying the gigolo to keep his mouth shut.

'To be suited to politics, you need to be essentially insincere,' he'd told Alyosha one night at the club. 'It's nothing but an unholy mixture of ritual, hypocrisy and compromise.'

Alyosha saw very little of Galina that night. The club was full and the head barman was a tyrant with a gimlet eye, so she was careful not to spend too much time talking to her friend. But she was always happy to see him, and had come to think of Alyosha as a big brother, especially as she was an only child.

He knew a couple of the other waitresses by now as well. Galina had introduced him to Isabelle, a dreamy girl from a small town near Limoges, and Adelina, a round-faced girl from Alsace.

Adelina was a silly creature, with not much personality, and he much preferred Isabelle. According to Galina, they both had their eye on him.

'Try your luck…'

'What makes you think I fancy either of them?'

'You must be looking for someone surely?'

'I'm not sure that I am…'

'Of course you are. Nobody can wrap themselves up in their disappointment forever. Everybody wants to be loved.'

Galina's biggest headache was her husband, Marcel. She was so bored of him, and wanted to leave him, but however cruelly she treated him, he still followed her around like a puppy. How was she going to get rid of him? Yves was still in the picture – in fact the bank clerk wanted her to divorce Marcel and marry him. But it was the man from Sardinia – Camlo – who was meddling with her heart. He came and went like the wind, which drove her crazy.

Alyosha often felt she talked for the sake of talking, because their discussions never led to any firm conclusions, they just went around in circles. But he had found himself telling her about the pain he'd suffered at the hands of Ludwika. Galina called her a bitch, and was surprised how he flinched at the word.

'But that's what she is, a proper bitch,' she insisted, 'to treat you so shabbily. I wouldn't even bother to spit on her if I saw her.'

Did he still love her? It was hard work to kill that feeling. Every time he discussed Ludwika, Alyosha still felt as though some fist was squeezing his heart dry.

25.

Margarita's working hours at Aznefttrust were so long that Larissa barely saw her. She often had to travel to conferences, too, and would regularly be away for a night or two. But when Larissa complained to Bruno that the company was working her sister too hard, he replied that she was lucky to have work at all. She was perplexed all the same. Margarita had told her that she and another girl, Natalya, were both secretaries to the chairman, a Russian from Simferopol called Osip Nikitich. But, if he had two secretaries, why on earth did her sister have to work so hard?

On Ella's second birthday in June, it had been Natalya who delivered a present and a card to the house on Margarita's behalf.

'But she said she'd be here in time for Ella's tea party,' complained Larissa 'She'll be so disappointed, she thinks the world of her aunt.'

'I'm sure she does. Margarita thinks the world of her, too, she has her picture on her desk at work,' answered Natalya, looking slightly embarrassed.

Bruno asked what exactly was keeping Margarita from being able to come to the party.

'There was an important meeting at work that she simply couldn't get out of.'

'Couldn't you have taken her place?' asked Bruno, a little belligerently. Larissa spared Natalya having to answer by thanking her for delivering the present and card.

In fact, Margarita wasn't even in Berlin. She had been sent by Aznefttrust to Hamburg, to meet a sailor who worked for the Woerman Line in a house in one of the suburbs, where she was to hand over a large sum of money from Moscow, which would be transferred in turn to somebody from the Finnish Sailors' Union.

Generally, Margarita's work consisted of sending money or messages to communist cells. She would always travel on a fake passport, even if she was travelling within Germany. Aznefttrust had also sent her to Italy, to a *questura* on Piazza Annunziata in Genoa, where she handed a small diamond over to a sailor who was to sail to Panama, for the revolution in Brazil. Another time, she was sent to Budapest, where she was meant to collect a package to bring back with her to Berlin. It was a small package, not much bigger than her fist, but as she returned to the hotel, she had the impression that she was being followed, and so paused at the window of a café on Andrassy Street. In the reflection, she saw two men on the opposite side of the street halt, too. Her heart started to race as she strode quickly on her way. Shortly, one of the men seemed to have disappeared but the other had crossed the road and was following about ten yards behind her. She was approaching a tram stop and, letting the first tram pass by, she leapt suddenly onto the next, but the man leapt on, too. She tried to quell her mounting panic and, fingering the little package in her coat pocket, wondered what it contained. She got off the tram at the next stop and went into the nearest shop. The young man in a white coat behind the counter had just finished serving a customer and Margarita asked him hurriedly if he spoke German. He did not. French? A little. She explained quickly that the man loitering outside was harassing her, and she a respectable wife and mother of three. The young man took her to the back of the shop without further ado, and ushered her through the door at the back to a yard which opened onto another street. He also promised to send the man packing if he came in to the shop. He must have been as good as his word because she made it safely back to her hotel unmolested.

26.

Alyosha was sitting on his own at the Flamant Rose, drinking a glass of beer, while a couple at the next table were happily celebrating something with a bottle of champagne. Galina had already told him about them: they were Swedish, and styled themselves Baron and Baroness Eklund, but although they lived as a married couple, no rings had been exchanged. He smoked a cigar, and she smoked a cigarette in a long Meerschaum holder, and they both greeted or acknowledged everybody cheerily. They were never short of a franc or two, but nobody was quite sure who they really were, or where their money came from.

Another club regular was Manon de Sainte-Estèphe (or Marie Nérichon as she had been christened). According to Galina, she had once tried to poison her lover, a promising tenor from Rome, and had very nearly succeeded. These days, Monsieur Bougremel, the owner of a silk factory, kept her in an apartment on Rue Chaptal. Once a month or so, he would visit Paris on business, and would beg her every time to move nearer to him. Manon could turn him round her little finger, and would always have some excuse why she couldn't possibly leave Paris. The true reason for her not moving south to Lyon was that she had another lover, a Spaniard by the name of Don Alonso de Zamora y Tinto, who lived in a large house on Avenue Kléber, tended expertly by his butler, a deaf-mute from Montenegro. In return for her favours, the Spaniard had promised to leave her a château on the outskirts of Nîmes, as well as three million francs in an account at Crédit Lyonnais after he died. Little wonder, then, that Manon longed to see the man breathe his last.

'But,' said Galina, 'the maid told her that some other woman has been making house calls lately.'

Manon was sipping crème de menthe at the bar.

'What will she do?'

'Why do you think she's talking to *him*?'

He was Jean-François Ooterelle, a Belgian who had been forced to quit his native soil. He lived under various names in Paris – Jean-Jean Flageolet was one – and made a living through petty theft and fraud. Every so often, he'd turn up at the Flamant Rose, but whenever things started to heat up, Jean-François would vanish for a few weeks to Libya with his lover, Yvette de

Merlanges, a former primary school teacher who was convinced that he was the most innocent and blameless man alive, inexplicably the victim of police harassment.

Jean-François used a walking stick, as his left leg was quite lame from when he'd tried to kill himself by throwing himself over the balcony of his apartment some ten months previously; he'd landed on a Doberman, killing it instantly, and merely broken his hip. The dog had undoubtedly saved his life, but his landlady had been highly unsympathetic, and had thrown him out. The last thing she'd wanted was to have unstable individuals living under her roof. And if he wanted any tips about killing himself, all he had to do was to catch the train to Dubrovnik, walk into the nearest bar, wear a false black moustache, and claim to be a Serb.

From the tête à tête Marie and Jean-François were having at the bar, it was obvious something important was being discussed.

'I imagine it's the easiest thing in the world to kill a man in a wheelchair,' said Galina sagely, blowing a ring of smoke above her forehead. 'A steep flight of stairs, one shove, and there you are. I wouldn't be surprised if that's what they're planning. When people really want something, they're willing to do anything to get it.'

A night or two later, Galina was due to meet Camlo after work, and she persuaded Alyosha to keep her company until he arrived. Over their coffees in the Rat-Mort Bar on the corner of Rue Pigalle and Rue Victor Masse, which stayed open more or less all night, she told her friend that Marcel had finally agreed to a divorce. Yves was still in love with her and wanted them to marry. What did Alyosha advise? He had little to say about it: increasingly he felt that Galina enjoyed being constantly in a state of emotional flux, because that made her life somehow more meaningful. An hour went by, and Galina started to fret about Camlo's non-appearance. She dried her nose with the back of her hand and looked through rheumy eyes at Alyosha. 'I think something must have happened to him.'

'I'm sure he's on his way.'

'Not tonight. I have a feeling he won't come…'

'If he said…'

'He won't come.'

'How can you be so sure?'

'Believe me.'

The time dragged on, with Galina becoming more restless by the second. She was also exhausted. In the end, with her nose running worse than ever, she asked in her little girl voice, 'Will you go and look for him?'

Alyosha sighed quietly and turned his head away.

'Don't then, I'll go myself,' she snapped petulantly, and leapt to her feet, but then half-staggered back down into the chair. They both knew he wouldn't let her wander the streets and bars of Paris her own.

'Alright, alright, I'm going. But this is the last time Galina.' He put on his coat wearily. 'And I mean it this time.' He stuffed the money she had given him into his back pocket and stepped out into the night.

Alyosha eventually found Camlo in a nightclub called Buffe in Montmartre. He was with a woman of course. Camlo winked at him, and introduced him to his companion, an extraordinarily beautiful, blonde, blue-eyed woman from Oslo called Halldora. Alyosha looked on in wonder as she ran her fingers along the gypsy's back, underneath his greasy hair.

'So,' Camlo smirked, 'she can't wait till tomorrow then?'

Alyosha shrugged and Camlo passed him a little packet under the table. He wore a signet ring on his little finger, with a solitaire of at least five carats. The barflies were both envious and admiring of Camlo's ability to bed so many tourists – especially women who had crossed the ocean on bright, white ships to find the romance of the 'real Paris'.

He went back to the Rat-Mort, but Galina had disappeared,

and nobody knew where she'd gone. He stayed for a while, but she didn't come back, so he returned wearily to the room he shared with Stephanos Sourlis. Luckily, he had the bed to himself for what remained of the night.

27.

One Thursday night, after Galina's shift, the take was thirty-five francs short. She swore tearfully that it had nothing to do with her, but it made no difference and she lost her job at the Flamant Rose on the spot.

Alyosha had witnessed her recent deterioration, and her chaotic life worried him more and more. He was very fond of her, but he could see her plummeting towards the gutter. He could also see that Camlo ran rings around Galina, and it made him angry on his friend's behalf. Sometimes he'd be attentive and passionate, other times he'd become unavailable and distant. It drove her mad, as she veered constantly between hope and despair. At such times, Galina would be willing to pay any price for her supply of drugs.

When Alyosha turned to Prince Yakov for advice, as he so often did, his friend told him that it was always dangerous to become involved in another family's business, as, more often than not, meddling only made a bad situation worse. His advice to Alyosha was to stay at arm's length and not to interfere.

'Why must she drag you into all her troubles?'

'I'm her friend. I've known her for ages, since we were children.'

The Prince shrugged. She had people who loved her, who would want to protect her. There was no need for Alyosha to go out of his way to do anything for her, apart from remain her friend. But Alyosha had met Yves by now. He was younger and even more ineffectual than Marcel, so Alyosha didn't think he'd be any match for Galina. As for her father and Duchess Lydia, they had no idea of the real situation. On top of which, there was Roksana to think about. What would happen to her if her parents divorced?

One night, towards the end of August, Alyosha was lying in bed, totally awake. By now, Stephanos was sleeping regularly in the bed of a woman who was married to a captain in the French Army, currently stationed with his battalion in Morocco. Outside, a storm was brewing, the first low rumblings becoming more powerful as it approached, until it ripped through the silence of the stars: thunder and lightning, crack upon crack piercing the sky with a fury so awful, he imagined seeing huge mountains reduced to dust.

How could he stand by and not do anything, as Galina's life went from bad to worse? Every time they met, she was slipping further into addiction. He had no choice but to interfere. He must tell Andrei Petrovich the truth, so that he could make efforts to support his daughter. He didn't want to go behind Galina's back, so, the next day, he went to the Rat-Mort, where she was drinking with Camlo, and told her what he intended to do. She seemed unconcerned, and told him if that's what he wanted to do then what did she care?

'You're such a two-faced, sly little snitch… I always preferred Margarita and Larissa to you…'

He was hurt but understood why she was being so cruel. He searched for the words to placate her. 'Galina, look… Do you remember the two of us going on the train to Potsdam? To that clinic to see your aunt?'

'No…'

'Yes, you do. Don't deny it…'

'I don't…'

'Do you remember what you said to me on the way back to Berlin?'

Far from appealing to her, he had made her livid. 'Who the

hell do you think you are to start preaching at me?' She spat the words out at him.

Camlo squared up, quite the pimp, but Alyosha snarled at him and he backed off.

'I'm worried about you.'

'Find something better to worry about.'

28.

Under the canopy of the Palais de Paris, the liveried Cossack was very happy to see him. Andrei Petrovich told him he'd been hoping that Alyosha would call by, because he had some very hopeful news for him.

'Are you listening, Alexei Fyodorovich?' he asked, pulling a tin of tobacco out of his pocket and taking a pinch to roll himself a cigarette.

Alyosha answered that he was all ears.

'How would you like to make a bucketful of money?'

'A bucketful or a pocketful?'

'A bucketful.'

'I'd be delighted. Who wouldn't?'

'Exactly. Five hundred francs a month? How would that suit you?'

Alyosha blew out a long whistle: that would make him very happy indeed.

Andrei Petrovich smiled, exposing his blackened teeth, which were rotting in his mouth.

'I thought that would make you prick up your ears.'

'How?'

By answering the telephone, dealing with correspondence, keeping the diary up to date, the apartment neat and the wardrobe in order – but more importantly, be available twenty-four hours a day.

'For five hundred francs a month, that's not too much of a sacrifice, is it?'

'It's a handsome salary.' It was also an escape from endless dishwashing at the restaurant.

'I'd have gone for it myself if it wasn't for one thing...' said Andrei Petrovich.

'What was that?'

Only a young man was wanted for the job.

'Well, Alexei Fyodorovich? How about it?'

In his excitement at the possibility of earning so much money, he forgot altogether to mention Galina.

29.

At three o'clock in the afternoon, Artyom was standing outside the prison in Marseille, waiting for the small door within the larger one to open. When it did, he followed in the officer's footsteps, surrounded by the pungent prison smells of vegetables and excrement. Various iron gates were unlocked and locked again until, finally, a heavy door was opened and he entered the damp, dark room within.

There, under a high window, was a plain oblong table and two wooden benches. Sitting on one of the benches on the far side of the table, in grey clothes and wooden clogs, his head shaved bald, his face gaunt, was L'Oreille, an old acquaintance from his arms-importing days. After telling them they had fifteen minutes, the officer sat on a chair by the door, plaiting his arms and turning his head to the side, the better to eavesdrop.

The small man asked at once: 'How did you hear I was here?'

'Doña Rosa told me.'

The *patronne* of the Stockholm bar had told Artyom all about L'Oreille's involvement in the scam to smuggle coffee from

Colombia. It had all gone swimmingly to begin with, as the customs officials were easy enough to buy off, the enterprise had been well timed, and the gang all worked well together. Once they thought the deal was in the bag, the gang had had an unforgettable night of drinking. The coffee had all been bagged up, and it would be child's play to sell it on at a good price with no repercussions.

After that, they'd lain low for a while, and all had been quiet, but it was an unnatural quiet – the kind of quiet which is so close and heavy it even silences birdsong, before August turns into a raging storm. Before dawn one morning, when it had still been dark, the *flics* had battered down two dozen doors all over Marseille with their axes. L'Oreille had been in bed sleeping with one of his girls when he'd heard the wood splinter.

'I should have been with the other one. If I'd been with her, she'd never have squealed. She wanted to teach me a lesson. That's why I'm here, the bitch.'

'Women,' muttered Artyom sympathetically.

'If I so much as looked at another girls' tits, she'd go fucking demented, and start throwing things around. She's a mad cunt, that one. Know what she did once? Put a spoonful of rat poison in my food from some tin someone brought back with him from the trenches in 1918. Must have lost some of its kick, because it didn't do much to me, just made me crap like a racehorse all night...'

Artyom smiled as he blew smoke over his upper lip.

'I don't give a fuck anyway. What are the *flics* going to prove? Fucking nothing that's what. I haven't confessed to anything, and I've got the best lawyer in the business, only he's an expensive cunt.'

'I know. I spoke to him. That's how I got permission to see you today. You doing alright?'

'No worse here than it was in Viterbo.'

L'Oreille was referring to the six months he'd spent in a Jesuit college when he was fifteen years old. 'What brings you back down here anyway?' he asked Artyom. 'Arms?'

'No, I've long since given that up. After the Bolsheviks stole my brother-in-law's factory in Petrograd, I tried to become a free agent with old German stock from the war, but the Versailles Treaty scuppered that.'

'So what have you been living on then?'

'I've been dabbling on the Paris Stock Exchange. Some investments have paid off, others haven't. It's just another form of gambling. But that's not where the big money's to be made.' Artyom glanced over his shoulder and whispered, 'That's why I'm looking for fresh opportunities in North Africa.'

The guard moved restlessly in his seat, unhappy that he couldn't hear.

'Going it alone over there is no picnic,' answered the small man just as quietly. 'Doing business with them is tricky.' He asked for a cigarette, and Artyom lit it for him. 'Don't do it. Too many risks, and you can't trust them.'

Artyom inhaled smoke deep into his lungs consideringly. 'You've made me even more eager to go there now,' he said grinning.

'Fucking hell, you're a stubborn bastard, Artyom. Don't say I didn't warn you.' L'Oreille tapped the table. 'If you're really set on getting yourself killed, go to Place de l'Opéra first, to the Café de la Terrasse. Ask the *patronne*, Madame Trigano, where to find Pierre. Tell him you've been talking to me. He'll give you a few tips.'

'When's your trial?'

'No date yet.'

'Is there anything you want me to do?'

'No. Thanks for coming to see me.'

'Thanks for the help.'

'You're still a mad cunt.'

30.

A little later, in a crisp clean shirt, he was walking down La Canebière, the street of which the Marseillais liked to boast, '*Si Paris avit une Canebière, ce serait un petit Marseille*'. When he reached the end and saw the masts of the little sailing boats in the old port before him like a leafless forest, he felt happy to be returning to an old haunt.

He'd spent most of the 1914–1918 war working there, waiting for shipments from his brother-in-law's armaments factory in Russia. His job was to check the cargo against the inventory once the crates had been unloaded from the hold, and then supervise their reloading onto the waiting trains at the quayside, ready to deliver the arms to the large depot in Avignon, or to the even larger depot in Clermont Ferrand.

Another aspect of his work had been to try and lighten the burden of import duties, and Artyom had soon learnt who was who among the custom officials of the Bassin de la Joliette. Back then, he'd been familiar with all their tricks, and knew exactly who it was most profitable to bribe. The glory of Marseille was that there were so many men ready to do you a favour for a reasonable price. The dockers were a corruptible bunch, and the scum in charge of security were even worse; an honest man was rarer than hen's teeth. Most of them were members of gangs, which, though fiercely independent, were highly persuadable when it suited them, and it usually did suit them when there was a promise of payment blowing their way.

But they were also easily insulted, and could bear a grudge for generations. Nevertheless, where the police were concerned, all mouths were shut on pain of death. Every now and again, the *flics* would come sniffing around, but more for form's sake than anything else. There was a tacit understanding that the gangs would sort out their own quarrels, and if anybody in the police thought otherwise, then a bribe was the most convenient way to make all that tedious paperwork float away as light as a feather on the air.

A big-bellied man with a thumb missing on his left hand came to sit opposite Artyom in the Café de la Terrasse. The face which stared at him from under the blue cap was covered with pockmarks, testament to a serious illness from his childhood. Although Pierre's face was bony, his shoulders were wide as an ox. His father had been a sailor, and his grandfather had been famous throughout Marseille for his ability to trim a sail in the face of a hurricane, but Pierre hadn't followed in their footsteps. Instead, he'd left school at nine to be apprenticed to a metalsmith, and made his living maintaining and mending ships' boilers while they were in dock.

Later that evening, the two of them sat in the rosy glow of the lamp in Artyom's hotel room.

'Where do you get your hands on this stuff these days?' asked Artyom, scooping up a nailful of powder and snorting it.

'From Beirut. Much easier now than it was in 1916,' Pierre replied. 'Back then the government wanted to make sure nothing came into the country that might send the boys in the trenches off their heads. Poor buggers. I lost three cousins in Verdun. Good?'

'Mmmm.'

'But since the war ended there's a big demand for all kinds of stuff. Morphine, Hashish. Opium, of course. Anything to dull the pain, eh? All those soldiers missing half their limbs. And all those women still missing their men. We get the odd shipment coming in through Corsica or Trieste, but it's mainly from Beirut. Most of it is grown in Turkey.'

Artyom stretched his legs out and asked, 'Why does opium from Turkey have to come through Beirut? Isn't that more complicated than it needs to be? You have to cross two borders…'

'Three,' corrected Pierre, 'If you count crossing from Beirut to Marseille as well.'

To smuggle the opium from Turkey to Beirut, you had to cross into Syria, then over the border to Lebanon which was quite an undertaking. In some places, families had made their livelihoods from it for generations, the wife and the children usually sharing the burden like so many mules, while the men sat around doing nothing but chew a bit of tobacco before spitting into the sand. They knew every mountain pass and path along the border like the back of their hand. That made buying and smuggling far easier for them than it would ever be for a Frenchman working on his own.

'But you still haven't answered my question. Can't it come straight from Turkey?'

'That's not how it's ever been done.'

'Well, it's time things changed.'

31.

Sebastien never got out of bed before two o'clock in the afternoon. Then, he'd have a good long soak in the round black-and-white marble bath. Alyosha was expected to be at the ready with two pink towels when his master stepped out. He'd dry himself inch by thorough inch, pausing often to gaze at himself, and once dry he would stand in the middle of the bathroom, and perform his stretching exercises, continuing to admire himself in the long mirror. Then, he would take his time to dress, selecting one of the silk shirts Alyosha held up, two at a time, for his perusal.

Once a month, every month, two tailors from the famous La Grande Fabrique would come to measure him, gossiping and drinking cocktails (which Alyosha had to learn to mix). A few days later, the new shirts and suits would be delivered, though

Sebastien would send them back if they were not exactly as he'd specified. At some point in the week, Alyosha would take delivery of beribboned boxes from Parfums d'Orsay on Boulevard des Italiens, or sometimes from Houbigant on Rue du Faubourg St-Honoré, full of little pots of pomades, pastes and creams for the face and hands, pastel-coloured tablets of scented soaps, bath salts in blue glass pots, and pot pourri. Sebastien had told him exactly how they were all to be laid out on his dressing table, in front of the mirrors where he spent hours anointing himself.

He had very soft hands, with beautifully manicured nails, and his skin was pale, almost translucent in its whiteness, but he wasn't a weakling. On the contrary, he was strong and sinewy, from his years in the *corps de ballet* at the Grand Opéra. He might still be dancing had the company's prima ballerina not taken a violent fancy to him, at a time when she was fast approaching the age when she would have to give up performing and turn to teaching her craft to others.

'You little angel, give Mummy a kiss.' Until her desire grew from bad to worse. 'My little man…'

She was fiercely possessive, and wouldn't share him with anyone, because he was hers and hers alone, night or day. He was seventeen, and she was nearly forty. She would whip herself into a jealous frenzy at the thought of another woman trying to get her dirty little paws on him. Just thinking about this possibility would send her into such a rage, she felt as though the blood pumping through the vein in her temple might explode over her nose.

'He's my sweet sugar lump, and nobody else's,' she'd say, stroking his cheek tenderly with the back of her hand. 'You're such a pretty little puppy,' she'd murmur, biting his bottom lip tenderly between her teeth.

When she did this in front of other people, he would die of embarrassment.

'Don't…' he'd tell her quietly and turn his face away.

Then she'd ask, 'Sebi, why? Why are you so mean to Mummy?'

His reticence only made him more desirable. As for his skin, it gave her some sort of second wind, so that she felt like a girl of eighteen again. She imagined herself shaving all the red hair on his groin and his testicles, until one night, she did just that, telling him in tones of wonder afterwards, 'They're like two eggs in my hand…'

When the time came for her to leave the Grand Opéra, she persuaded Sebastien to come with her. She wanted them to live together forever. Four years trickled by, spent touring all over Europe in an open-topped motor car, though they kept a home in Paris: Budapest, Bucharest, Berlin, Stockholm, Warsaw, Copenhagen and Madrid, never staying very long in one place. But for all the driving and spending, being every minute in each other's company did neither of them much good. The truth of it was that Sebastien soon became sick and tired of the selfish generosity which claimed his body in payment every night. What kept him with her so long was how much he loved their way of living: the dances, the operas, the plays and the parties. But she could sense that he was starting to pull away from her, like a ship gently hauling up its anchor, while she was still at the quayside. It made her beg him to love her all the more, which made Sebastien hate her all the more. Her emotions were too strong for reason. She could pounce on the least thing as an excuse for throwing a public tantrum of epic proportions. She had no compunction about picking a quarrel in front of everybody in the restaurant at the Ritz, or throwing a glassful of Sazerac in Sebastien's face in the bar of the Théâtre-Français, or storming out of the casino in Cannes, screaming obscenities at him which would have made a whore blush.

It was not as though he had ever loved her. That was the naked truth, and living in her company became more and more tiresome. One late afternoon, in a villa in Livorno, he woke from a nap and made himself a promise that he would, before long, find himself more agreeable pastures, come what may.

That happened in Monte Carlo. At a ball to see in the new year at the Hôtel de Crillon, the wife of the politician Henri Dupont fell head over heels in love with him. Telling her husband that Sebastien was teaching her the foxtrot, their raging affair was soon the talk of Paris. Caught up in her passion for the boy, she naively imagined – when she bothered to give it any thought – that nobody had noticed. Meanwhile, tongues were furiously wagging in the salons of the sixth and seventh *arrondissements* of Paris, and, after it had reached everybody else's ear, it eventually reached the ear of her husband. Reproaches and ructions, tears and tantrums ensued, but the greatest danger was that the scandal would gather so much momentum, it would crash into the corridors of power at the Quay d'Orsay. That was not to be borne.

'That is *not* going to happen,' Henri shouted furiously when he heard from the deputy-editor at *Le Figaro* (an old school friend) that the newspaper was offering to pay Sebastien for his story. Realising that there remained only a limited time to contain the situation, Dupont acted swiftly. A yellow envelope with a black rim (such as one would use for a letter of condolence) was delivered to Sebastien by hand. He had been expecting some sort of approach, but when he saw the amount being offered, even he was impressed.

After that, there was no turning-back, and teaching wealthy women the foxtrot became a way of life. It kept him very comfortably, and his apartment in the Bois de Boulogne was as luxurious and well-appointed as any in Paris. He had his standards, of course, and he wasn't one of those gigolos – there were all too many of them in Paris and on the Riviera – who negotiated a fee in advance and would only be paid in dollars. So vulgar. He didn't mind how he was paid. As far as he was concerned, a cheque from a bank in Boston or Berne or Liechtenstein was equally acceptable. He was also happy to accept gifts in kind – a gold cigarette case perhaps, or a watch. He still wore a beautiful pair of diamond cuff-links the President of Paraguay's sister-in-law had given him for entertaining her so well while her husband was buying guns from a factory in Rouen.

No wonder he was so contented. No wonder, either, that what Alyosha had thought was a generous salary to begin with now seemed nothing of the kind. His employer could have given him ten times that amount without making a hole in his account at Credit Lyonnaise on the Champs-Élysées.

'I'm not in the least demanding,' Sebastien had told him, and proceeded to make sure of his money's worth through the long hours he made his valet work.

One day, much to Alyosha's surprise, he rose before noon, and instructed Alyosha to pack for a trip. The two of them were leaving Paris for a very important appointment.

32.

From the welcome Sebastien was given, it was clear that he was a valued customer at the Hôtel de Belmont et de Bassano, on the outskirts of Orange. But Alyosha was finding the constant proximity to his employer hard to bear. It was as much as he could do to hide his contempt as Sebastien fiddled constantly with his curls, or played with his food instead of eating it, or sucked in his stomach and asked Alyosha whether he mightn't have put on a couple of pounds. To a man who had lived through famine in Russia, this kind of vanity was hard to bear.

Over dinner that night, Sebastien bored on at length about the strength of the dollar and the weakness of the franc, then went on to mock the inadequacies of American husbands, elaborating on how bad they were at lovemaking, good for nothing but banking and baseball. To cap it all, and to Alyosha's horror, he then took it upon himself to instruct him on how to seduce women.

'It's intimacy they crave. Whisper sweet nothings in their ear – that's the secret of success every time.'

That's what women liked, not the greedy kneading and fingering, sweating and grunting like a gorilla in the sun, but tender words and soft looks. The most erotic lovemaking took place only when the world inside her head was stimulated.

'The imagination is the most powerful force alive, Alexei Fyodorovich.'

Through the imagination, a man and a woman could create any reality they chose. Or they could break free altogether from reality. Sebastien thought that was why sex was very much like religion: they were both based on fantasy, which stemmed from some primitive need for escapism.

Later, before going to bed, Sebastien came up with a proposition.

The next morning, when they left Orange on the last leg of the journey, they were no longer master and servant, but two men on the same quest. This shift was signalled to Alyosha when Sebastien sat in the front at Alyosha's side, rather than in the back as he had done from Paris. He had made two appointments in Nice. The first was with an established client, a wealthy American who came to the Riviera every year on vacation. But there had been a discreet enquiry from a potential new client, and even Sebastien couldn't be expected to be in two places at the same time. That's when it had occurred to him to apprentice Alyosha.

When they reached Nice, Sebastien directed him to the Hôtel de la Méditerranée, where he had made reservations. He would have preferred the Negresco, he told Alyosha, only it didn't do to mix business with pleasure. That was a golden rule he never broke. Another important rule was to never work the first night after a long journey. Energy had to be conserved so that the flesh could be encouraged to total obedience. It was important to always be perfectly groomed and fresh as a daisy, and the greatest sin was to show fatigue. That was fatal, because being tired all the time was what *they* were guilty of. That was always the refrain: that their oafish husbands just wanted to work to fill their bank accounts, eat and drink to fill their stomach, and play a little golf. They had no energy left for their wives.

That evening, after dinner, Alyosha asked Sebastien, 'So who is she?'

He told him she was a rich merchant's wife from Tunis. Her husband was doing some business somewhere or other in Provence, but his wife and daughters preferred to spend the time in Nice, enjoying the sun and sea.

'And she'll pay me?' asked Alyosha.

'Of course she'll pay you, and handsomely.'

Sebastien told him that if he did well, this might be the beginning of a very lucrative career.

33.

The following evening, the two young men walked sedately to the pink-domed Negresco, as Sebastien had warned Alyosha on no account to rush, in case he started to perspire. It had been arranged that Alyosha would go straight up to the room of his client.

'What about her daughters? Where are they tonight?' he asked nervously.

'There's no need for you to worry, she'll have made sure they're out of the way. Now off you go. *Bon courage mon brave!*'

Alyosha felt every eye was upon him as he crossed the glass-domed rotunda and made for the lift. He got out at the third floor and walked down the long, thickly-carpeted corridor until he found the room. He knocked on the door and waited. He stepped back. Room 325. He felt he was still too close to the door and took another half-step back to be safe. He was already too hot, and his collar chafed his neck. He was horribly aware that his hands and armpits were damp, and he felt grubby in spite of his earlier bath. Why was she taking so long? Had she reconsidered? Or would he come face to face with her husband?

The door opened.

She wore a dark blue kimono with an orange trim. With her hair piled high on her head he felt as though he were gazing at a Japanese print.

34.

It felt marginally less awkward in a roomful of people than on their own. He hadn't known what else to do. Even then, what needed to be said was left unsaid, and they talked of other things. Alyosha unbuttoned his collar and felt a small relief. Sitting opposite her, he felt as though he was acting in a picture, waiting for the studio lights to be extinguished so that he could leave the set and walk back into his everyday life.

Little by little, Alyosha took in the changes in his mother since he last saw her. Her make-up was as expertly applied as ever, but a little heavier that it used to be, and her jawline was no longer quite so well defined. Her teeth weren't so brilliantly white either, and in the gap where she had lost one, there was a gold replacement. Her green eyes were still bright and beautiful but he noticed the two lines that now went from nose to mouth. Blowing her a gentle kiss, old age was coming to meet her.

With her head a little to one side she smiled at him a little defiantly 'You think I've aged, don't you?'

He bit his lip and shrugged.

His mother's smile faded, and a sort of terror seemed to come over her expression.

'Alyosha? Tell me – what are you thinking about?'

He asked after his younger brother, and they were saved for a while: Georgik was a safe subject, and Inessa enthusiastically told Alyosha all about him.

'He's not a little boy anymore. You'd be surprised how much he's grown.'

He was twelve now, in long trousers. In less than a fortnight, he would be coming to spend Easter with her, from his school in Le Rosey. Inessa chattered on about how well he had settled, how hard he worked, and what high marks and good reports his teachers had given him at the end of term. He was a talented sportsman, too, the best in his year at the high jump, and he played a very decent game of tennis. He was popular with his schoolmates and teachers alike, and was having a marvellous time.

Alyosha listened to her quietly. Then something occurred to him and he asked 'So I have a stepfather and two stepsisters from Tunis then?'

'Of course you don't,' she snapped, before taking a sip of her wine and adding in a softer tone. 'You don't have a stepfather of any description.'

To their relief, the waiter came over.

'Are you ready to order, Madame?'

'I'm ready,' answered Inessa. 'Are you?'

But once he had left with their menus they both sat there in an increasingly awkward silence.

'You'll have read about me, I expect?' she said eventually.

Alyosha frowned. 'Read what?'

Her hair was much redder now, and her eyebrows were thicker, which he thought made her look less feminine than when they were shaped into two fine bows.

202

'You must be one of the few people in Europe who *hasn't* heard what happened to me, then,' she told him sourly, and went on to recount how she and Alexei Alexeivich had arrived in Rome by train and gone straight from the station to the Hotel Campo de Fiori. There, he'd sat her down and told her that he had some news for her – bad news, unfortunately, but news he had to share with her before anybody else, because she meant so much to him. She still remembered his words, and his sickening dishonesty, which went through her like malaria.

'Are you listening to me, Alyosha? Or am I just talking to myself?'

He'd been gazing out at the Promenade des Anglais, where a large group of elderly men and women stood on one leg like a flock of flamingos, slowly turning their arms, following the movements of a needle-thin Chinaman who stood facing them. Alyosha turned back to his mother and said that he was listening.

Alexei Alexeivich hadn't been worrying about her at all, he was just worrying about saving his own skin. Before they'd left for Rome, he'd received a telegram from the editor of *Il Tempo* informing him they would be printing the story in the following day's edition. Did he have any comment to make?

The next day, the scandal spilled onto the streets of Rome.

'Are you sure you saw nothing about all this?'

Alyosha shook his head.

'Really? Not even that first picture of them kissing in Florian's on Piazza San Marco? He'd always promised to take *me* to Venice, but he never did.' A quiet contempt entered her voice. 'You'd never believe how many lies that man has told me over the years.' She raised her glass to her lips and he noticed the prominent blue veins on the back of her hand. 'She's the Marchesa Mariani Eugenio. She claims to be related to Mussolini on her mother's side. I have plenty of respect for him, of course, but she's nothing better than a whore.'

'Mother? Why did you never love me?'

She stopped. He'd already asked her once but she had changed the subject. 'Will you answer me?'

Inessa raised her voice slightly to prevent him from cutting across her again, and claimed it was no loss when he left her. She had become sick and tired of his behaviour – his constant drinking, his vulgar womanising – but the fact that the studio in Rome had broken its contract with her – now that had *really* hurt her.

'How could they? How dare they? An actress of my calibre, famous all over Europe.'

Then, as though the thing she most dreaded was an actual conversation with her son, she launched into a long monologue, jumping from one topic to another. The jealousy of other women towards actresses like her was only another form of desire, of course. But she sometimes thought that fame was just another word for loneliness. She had also come to the conclusion that marriage was a form of insincerity between two people, and the worst thing any man could do was feel pity for a woman, and that there was no friendship deeper than that between two women who hated the same man. Love was nothing but disappointment and betrayal, she wanted none of it. She lived and breathed for acting, that was her raison d'être, her staff of life, her only sustenance, her only living – and her only ambition was to spend her days in front of a camera.

To think it had all begun with *Russia's Altar*. She couldn't understand why the critics had been so unkind, but what did they know? It had been a sweeping success in some countries – Albania and Montenegro in particular, but Greece too. Of course, very few Russian films were produced in Berlin these days, and it was difficult for her to work in France because they didn't like her Russian accent, though she always insisted on speaking French with Georgik so that he wouldn't be held back from getting on in the world. She cursed the French prejudice against Russians, but then they were prejudiced against anybody who wasn't French. They were the most xenophobic and selfish people in the world. Which fool said *La France est la lumiére du monde?* Light of the world indeed! Such a high opinion they had of themselves! Only in France would you have a king who compared himself to the sun and thought he was the divine incarnation of the state. But she was more determined than ever to succeed.

Another bottle of Vouvray had replaced the first in the ice bucket. Alyosha felt sadder than ever.

'Mother, when are you going to answer my question?'

On she went, as though he'd never spoken. She'd show them all – the critics and the gainsayers who claimed she couldn't act. If she lived in Russia she'd be a star of the screen – but then what would be the point of making films there? Who wanted to pay to see a picture about a man in love with his tractor? Or a crew of young people with red handkerchiefs around their necks singing at dawn as they went on their way to plant a field of potatoes. Only birds were meant to sing at break of day. Young people should be safely tucked up in bed, they needed their rest to grow.

She had finally talked herself to a standstill. She looked down at her plate: her food had grown cold. Then, with that old fake affection that Alyosha remembered so well from his childhood, his mother said brightly, 'But never mind silly old me, tell me about you. I want to know all about you, find out who my son has become.'

'Me?' he asked himself. 'Me?' he puzzled again. What a bizarre question. What was he meant to tell her? At one time in his life, he might have thought he knew who he was, but by now he really didn't have a clue. Had he ever really known himself? What he had come to realise as he grew older was that his whole existence had been limited every step of the way by the exigencies of the moment. His life was one unholy muddle. Meanwhile, however much his mother pleaded poverty, it seemed that she could afford to pay for Georgik's schooling at Le Rosey near Lausanne, and for a room in one of the most expensive hotels on the Côte d'Azur. He glared at her.

'It's as much as I can do to keep body and soul together. I don't think further than paying my rent from week to week.'

She patted his hand and said, 'I know just how you feel; I have to fend for myself now.'

She gave him an ingratiating little smile and the dimples which had always given her face a charming youthfulness, momentarily appeared. But the wrinkles at her eyes were like the pattern of fine sand at the water's edge. She leant slightly towards him across the table.

'I'm living from hand to mouth, too,' she whispered looking surreptitiously around her to make sure nobody was listening at a nearby table. 'If I hadn't sold my darling mother's wedding ring – the very last thing I had left to sell – I'd have been out on the street. I'm only staying one night here.' She stifled her tears. 'If you could only see the place where I live from day to day.'

Still, she could pay for a gigolo to take her to bed. She had never been slow to spend on her own pleasures.

Alyosha looked out again towards the horizon where a storm was breaking above the sea: white forks of lightning sliced through the clouds, and just a weak light remained from the far side of the world, the black sky doing its best to blot it out.

Alyosha turned back to look at her and asked yet again, 'Why did you never love me, Mother?'

She was finally silenced by the heartfelt simplicity of his question. But, in spite of the hint of confusion in her eyes, she launched into a vigorous rebuttal, telling him that she had loved him from the first, had always loved him. She had loved him as a babe in arms, loved him when he was crawling, then walking, then running. She loved him every bit as much as she loved Georgik.

Alyosha suddenly lost his temper. He had heard enough of her lies, her justifications and self-delusions. 'Mother, we have to be honest with each other for once.'

'Yes, I know. Will you listen to me?'

'I've done nothing but listen to you. Why won't you listen to me for once?'

'Not with that hateful tone in your voice, I won't.'

They were lighting the lamps in the restaurant.

'It's something that you've always hated within yourself,' she whispered, 'that's why you're being so cruel to me tonight.'

Alyosha shook his head hopelessly. 'You just can't admit it because it makes you feel guilty.'

'I have nothing to feel guilty about...'

'Listen...'

'Not a thing, certainly not about *you* of all people.'

But he was determined to drag some honesty out of her, even if it meant offending her forever. He persevered. What about loving his father?

'What about loving your father?'

'You never loved him.'

'Never loved him? I *adored* him.'

'Mother, that's not true.'

'I gave that man so much love, you have no idea.'

'I know different. You don't have to lie to me.'

Inessa glared at her son. 'Very well. The whole truth. If that's what you want, I'll give it to you. Here it is, every word the truth. Back in 1915, my father was over his head in heavy gambling debts, and faced scandal and ruin. My mother saw an opportunity to save the situation by marrying me to an older man, who'd had his eye on me for a while. I was oblivious, of course, far too young to be aware of such things, but she had noticed. As you know, there was nobody more determined and single-minded than your grandmother when she'd set her mind on something. She was that sort of a woman. And that's how things were arranged. A girl of sixteen, I was barely consulted…'

Alyosha's bitterness subsided a little but he heard himself saying, 'That's still not an excuse for the way you treated him.'

'I was faithful to him throughout the marriage. To the grave.'

'How can you sit there and tell me such a bare-faced lie? I *remember*.'

She told him he must have imagined such things. A child's mind is a strange and wonderful thing.

'What about a diary entry? Did I imagine that as well?'

It took Inessa a moment to digest this and then she said balefully, 'You read my diaries?' With mounting anger, she made him recount what his thirteen-year-old self had done.

'How could you, Alyosha?' she fumed. 'Rooting through my personal possessions? Besides, I kept my diaries under lock and key.'

'It didn't take me long to find the key.'

'So, what did you read, you hateful child?'

'Every word. So I know all about Mita Golitzin. The officer in the Army's Medical School. He didn't come back from the war, did he?'

Because she'd hurt him, he didn't mind hurting her.

'Coffee and cognac?'

The waiter had been hovering at their table for a while.

'Not yet…'

Inessa ordered another bottle of Vouvray instead.

'To find some answers Mother. That's the only reason I did it. To try and understand what I meant to you. What I'd done to offend you. I thought it was my fault, that I'd done something unforgiveable, and that's why you were so cold towards me, always keeping me at arm's length…'

'Dearest Alyosha,' she said, seeming finally moved, 'My dear son…'

'You can make any claim you want here tonight... But you never loved me. You didn't, Mother.' He was overwhelmed with sadness. 'Not like other mothers love their sons. Not like you loved Georgik, and still love him. You're giving him a proper education, which is more than I ever had... Doesn't that say it all?'

It was too much for him. He stood up to leave.

'Don't go... Not yet... Alyosha, wait... Don't leave me... Not now... Darling, I beg you... Stay. Stay with me. I don't want to walk in there on my own.'

35.

The Hollywood Club jazz band was blasting out 'Choo Choo (Gotta Hurry Home)' in the Negresco ballroom, and, under the baccarat chandeliers, the party was in full swing. The doors had been thrown wide open to the night, and the dancers had spilled out onto the terrace. As he followed his mother, Alyosha felt as though he were walking through a gallery of faces from his youth. The past unfurled before Alyosha vividly, as nearly everybody there was Russian, some of them the children who used to run up and down the corridors of the Hotel Adlon in Berlin when he lived there with his parents.

His mother took him around the tables, introducing him to her friends, first whispering in his ear to remind him who they were. He recognised Baroness Witte, dressed soberly, with her hair plaited neatly on her head without any ornament, and her companion, Natalia Eristova, newly married after barely wiping the tears dry for her first husband. Then, there was Baron Chichagor, a man who professed sanctity, though in fact he was a selfish old goat. After a lifetime of heavy drinking, his health was starting to deteriorate, though he was still to be found in a backstreet bar with a glass of spirits in front of him at ten o'clock in the morning. As he greeted Alyosha, there remained some unruly energy about him, though his hand shook badly.

At midnight, with a full moon hanging high in the sky, the band stopped playing and they all sang 'God Save the Tsar' to the accompaniment of just the trumpet. Then, before cutting his birthday cake, Prince Maktuyev gave a short, emotional speech, his voice occasionally cracking.

When he declared that life was hard, he spoke for them all. He extended sympathy to everybody there who was struggling with life's complications, but that, unfortunately, was their fate, ever since they had been forced to turn their backs on their dear Mother Russia. Without a country of their own, their plight was a pitiful one. For even the strongest soul set adrift in a foreign land, the simplest endeavour could be insuperable, and all their dreams were broken dreams.

A few of the women had become emotional and one or two were weeping quietly.

'But what will it profit us to be downhearted? To live without hope? We must act!' Prince Maktuyev's voice no longer cracked, it boomed with authority. 'We must rediscover our faith that Russia, one day, will be restored to us in all her glory.'

From the back of the room, somebody heckled, 'If it was such a precious way of life, why didn't you fight to the death to preserve it when you had the chance?

'We did,' Prince Maktuyev roared, 'but who ever truly understands the worth of something until it has been lost?'

The voice shouted, 'Hypocrite! You and everybody else in this room! The Romans took their own lives in preference to living a life without honour.'

He had clearly been drinking and people turned on him angrily and told him to be quiet, but the Prince said 'I agree with you, sir. Friends, we may all hate the Bolsheviks, but as the gentleman over there is suggesting, we should rather hate ourselves for giving Russia up so easily. All the more reason, then, for every one of us here tonight to commit, with every fibre of our being, to winning her back. It is incumbent on every one of us who fought in the ranks of the White Armies to continue that fight, until our hands are stained red with the blood of the communists.'

After that, the dancing resumed and up in the balconies, the young people tugged at the netting which had been suspended across the ceiling, releasing balloons, buckets of confetti and strips of golden ticker tape onto the dancers below. Some of them had little whistles which they blew, clashing with the jazz in a noisy cacophony. The young women who took to the dance floor wore their hair shingled, exposing their white necks, and their dresses were also daringly short, coming just to their knees, while the eyes of the older women noticed everything above their old-fashioned fans.

Around the room were the remnants of the royal court and the hangers-on – distant relatives of the Tsar, his former ministers, princes and princesses, some former oil merchants from Baku, hopeful and hopeless capitalists. They were nearly all impoverished, many up to their necks in debt, managing somehow to obtain a little more credit on the basis of their aristocratic pedigree. So used to a life of luxury, they still continued to worship the golden calf with faith and hope, waiting for their luck to change – for the natural order of things to be reinstituted.

But, for now, life was an endless, exhausting struggle, lived in nondescript rooms in shabby houses along back streets. Some of them still clung by their fingernails to the sort of life they thought they deserved, spending as though there was no tomorrow. Unfortunately, there were many tomorrows, forcing them to sell their palaces and estates in Russia for a song. The bankers of Europe, like a pack of wolves circling their prey, were ready to pounce on their cheaply bought spoils the moment communism came to an end, but as it obstinately survived, it seemed as though their gamble, for once, would not pay off.

A bearded giant of a man was weaving clumsily towards Alyosha, bumping into people and swaying. He grasped his elbow tightly in an effort to steady himself.

'Who are you?' he asked, leaning so that his face was only an inch or two from Alyosha's. He wore a row of medals on his chest, and his epaulettes were as yellow as a canary. Without waiting for an answer, he launched into his experiences as a commanding officer in General Nikolai Yudenich's army during the attack on Petrograd, in the ice and snow of that harsh November in 1919, when they had been just a hair's breadth away from beating the Bolsheviks. If it hadn't been for the treachery of Baron von Mannerheim, who had promised Yudenich, 'on the life of his mother', that he would advance with his army from Finland, the city would have been captured, no doubt about it. But Mannerheim didn't keep to his word.

'Can you imagine?' he almost howled. 'Can you imagine how we felt, twenty thousand of us out under the stars, frozen stiff as corpses in the snow?' He went on to give his thoughts about the best way to win the country back. 'From the Baltic countries, young friend, that's where we need to mount our attack.' He kept staggering until he completely lost his footing and went crashing backwards, mid-sentence, into a table of champagne glasses.

Alyosha watched his mother dancing. When Prince Maktuyev led his wife onto the dance floor, Inessa and a few of the other women gave him a small curtsey. The Prince was not the best dancer, and his wife winced when he stepped on her toes, but they persevered. Alyosha had a boy's memory of him at the opera in Petrograd, in the box next to the Tsar and his family.

Inessa came over to him after the dance ended, and dragged him round to meet more of her many acquaintances. Mathilde Kshesinskaya was one, a former *prima ballerina* at the Mariinskii

Theatre, who used to be the mistress of Tsar Nicholas II. She was now a widow, having buried her husband, Archduke Andre Vladimirovich Romanov, some fifteen months previously. Mathilde Kshesinskaya, in turn, introduced them both to her companion, Duchess Vera Meshcherskii, who intended to open a house for Russian exiles in Saint-Geneviève-des-Bois. She was filled with compassion for the victims of the world, and kept referring to the horrors she had witnessed in the port of Izmit in Turkey shortly after she sailed from the Crimea in 1920. She wouldn't elaborate, but it was obvious the experience still weighed heavily on her.

They spoke to Prince Alexander Buxhoeveden, too, who had just moved with his family from Paris to Nice. Life had been hard in Paris, and they had been poor. But he had managed to raise a little capital and had begun to dabble in buying and selling; property, sailing boats, motor cars – anything and everything. Moving to the Côte d'Azur was the best thing he had done since leaving Russia, and he felt that his luck had finally turned, though he was more than sensible of the fact that it could change just as easily again. He was a man who had experienced the bad, as well as the good, that life can dole out. At one time, he had been very fond of dancing, but he no longer had any strength in his left leg, and his right leg was beginning to stiffen in the same way. His greatest fear was that he would become a cripple, and be a burden to his family.

At the same table sat Prince Felix Yussupov, enjoying a leisurely smoke with Archduke Dmitri Pavlovich Romanov. Alyosha listened to the hypocrisy of their small talk, so full of malice about their friends and acquaintances. These were the two who had been responsible for murdering Rasputin and throwing his body into the Neva. But that had been a long time ago.

It wasn't all spite and venom. There was also witty repartee, lively anecdotes, real affection and goodwill, and of course, among the younger set especially, flirting and romancing. But his eyes strayed to some of the older women who were accompanied by younger men. Boys like him, at work, dancing with women who could easily have given birth to them. He noticed how some of the elderly couples watched the dancers fondly, no doubt reminiscing about the balls of their youth. He gazed at their faces, thinking to himself that there was a sort of beauty to old age that was absent in the young.

Inessa persuaded him to dance with her. It was a slow dance, and she grasped his fingers in order to place his hand flat at the small of her back. He felt the heat of his mother's body mingling with his as she leant heavily into him. She had been drinking all night, and the champagne and wine seemed to have gone to her head.

He realised, not for the first time, how important it was for his mother to be seen and admired. That was the main attraction of this occasion for her, an opportunity to put her best foot forward. She had always been adept at presenting herself in the best possible light, because she thrived on admiration and attention.

She whispered in his ear that he was, by far, the most handsome young man in the room. Then, she told him how proud she was of him that night. She was sweating, he could smell it on her, mixed with her perfume and the slight wine-sourness of her breath. He felt the fluttering of her fingers on the nape of his neck, which was also damp with sweat. He whirled her around in a slightly unstable turn, and she threw her arms up, her hands stroking his cheeks, her eyes shut and her lips mouthing the words of the song. The drink had caught up with him, too, and an attack of heartburn made the pressure of her body against his chest unpleasant.

He realised that she was properly drunk, and suggested it was time to leave. Slurring, she agreed, and he decided he should see her safely back to her bedroom. She could barely keep her footing, and kept stumbling, so he put an arm around her and almost carried her from the lift to her room. She couldn't unlock the door either, and, giggling like a schoolgirl, gave him the key. He helped her to the bed, and she fell back, holding on to him so that he fell with her. He had the strangest feeling, as though he had left his body and was looking down on himself and her, with the sound of the sea crashing on the beach in his ears.

He tried to pull himself free, but she had grabbed him by his hair – two fistfuls of it, and mumbled something about how he was meant to stay all night. She tugged her dress over her head clumsily, pushed him on the bed, climbed on top of him and kissed him. He hesitated, then took hold of her waist, pulled her closer and kissed her back. She rummaged at the buttons of his fly, but he had to undo it for her, their fingers tripping over each other. She pawed at him and grabbed his erection, but she couldn't push it into herself. She gave up and started to kiss and bite his ear. Alyosha rolled her over onto her back and, half in anger, half in fear, he delved between her thighs, his desire mounting. He pressed his lips against her neck, her chin, her nose, he kissed her lips and her forehead. She cupped his testicles with one hand, her sharp nails catching at the flesh. He couldn't hold. He couldn't hold. Suddenly he was inside her…

Her breath was laboured in his ear. She ran her nails slowly along his back, sending shivers through him. His desire evaporated quickly now that he had come, and a shudder of cold horror replaced it. She moved slightly, before turning onto her side. They lay there without a word, with her light scratching of his flesh the only sound, like the beating of insect wings at dusk.

36.

In the cool early morning air, they were already hard at work wiping down the tables and sweeping the pavement outside the cafés in the Marche aux Fleurs and Place Gautier. The delivery boys in their grey aprons were heaving the flowers and fruit and vegetables down from their carts, while the market traders had started to unpack the boxes and arrange the produce on their stalls.

Alyosha hurried past unheeding, heading for the narrow streets of the old town. The watery early morning sunshine was abruptly extinguished by the confining walls of the Rue des Serruries, and he had lost his heat by the time he emerged back into the light at the Place du Carret. A refuse lorry rumbled past him slowly, but there were very few people about; a man walking his dog, a few early risers taking their morning constitutional. He crossed the Promenade des Anglais, went down the stone stairs and picked his way across the stony beach to the water's edge, where a light morning mist rose from the sea.

His mother had been lying on her stomach when he woke, a tiny bit of spittle at the side of her mouth, and her mascara smudged down her cheek. The sheet had barely covered her, and he'd surveyed her semi-nakedness for a brief moment before quietly dressing.

High in the sky, a faint blush of dawn remained. At the Hôtel de la Méditerranée, Sebastien would be waiting for him. He made his way back to the market, and stopped at a café for a cup of coffee. Then, he walked aimlessly down the Rue Droite. He remembered crying out between sleep and wakefulness, and the sweat and the heat and the weight of her body on his, the taste of her breasts, the saltiness of her armpits. He washed his hands, face and neck in a stone basin under a little fountain pouring out of a cherub's mouth – a fat-cheeked baby with voluptuous lips which had half birthed itself from the wall of the church. Her perfume still lingered on his skin. He pushed his hand down the front of his trousers, fingered his cock, and lifted his finger and thumb to smell her.

37.

A shipwright gave him a lift in his truck and told him cheerfully about his work maintaining pleasure boats, but Alyosha barely understood one word in ten because of his thick Niçois accent. Further along the coast, he asked to be dropped off at some nameless town, and wandered aimlessly towards the harbour, where old men sat under a café's parasols playing dominos.

When a woman in a white apron came over for his order, he asked if he could have a glass of water. He sniffed at his hand, then his arm. She was still on his skin. The sun hurt his eyes and his head throbbed. Even at the end of October, it was still hot; he felt his forehead prickle, and wished he'd thought to wear a hat.

He gulped down the water and set off again, leaving the town and walking a fair distance along the coastal road. Already, the previous night had started to bend, distort, escape to some other part of his memory: the blaring of the band; the rapt faces of the dancers as they escaped the reality of their lives for the length of the song. Everything was a charade. Fun and games, frenetic enjoyment, living in one perpetual present because the past had disappeared like mist from a mountain. How could anybody live in a perpetual present? Easily – that's what he was doing. What choice did he have? He was a boy from the lost generation, without a country, without roots, without anything. No wonder the Russians on the Riviera lived such chaotic lives, searching for the next thrill in a desperate bid to escape the yawning abyss which lay just ahead of them.

Several white villas stood among the dusty trees, their red pantiled roofs dotting the hillside. He passed a couple before reaching a stone by the roadside with *Manoli les Pins* painted on it. The villa stood high on the hillside, in a rather isolated spot, and the hard clay drive leading up to it was steep, so he was rather breathless by the time he reached the house. He hadn't had a crumb to eat all day; he was weak with hunger and his legs ached.

A little boy was playing ball on the terrace, and when he saw Alyosha approaching, he paused his game to stare at him. A middle-aged lady looked up from her seat in the shade, where she was podding peas, splitting the pods lengthwide with her thumbnail and tumbling the peas into a bowl. Seeing Alyosha, she turned her head and called to somebody inside the villa.

A young woman appeared.

Alyosha introduced himself, and she reciprocated, 'I'm Jeanette.' The little boy came to stand by Artyom's wife. 'And this is my mother, Madame Madeleine Theodore,' she nodded to the older woman.

'Pleased to meet you, Madame.'

'And this is Dimitri.' Jeanette placed her hand on the back of the boy's head.

Dimitri wore navy blue shorts, and looked younger than his nine years.

'What should I call you?'

'Alyosha.'

'Call me Jeanette.'

They all went into the villa.

When he told her he had come from Nice, she asked, 'What were you doing there?'

'Not much of anything…'

'Does your mother still live in Berlin?'

'Biarritz, I think.'

'Have you seen her lately?'

Alyosha shook his head.

'What about your brother – Georgik, isn't it?'

'I haven't seen him in years, either.'

After supper, where he tried his best not to fall on his food like a savage, Jeanette told him they always had their coffee in the living room. It was nearly dark outside, and the generously proportioned room was filled with soft shadows. Although the villa was modern, it had been decorated very traditionally, in rich rusts and reds. The furniture was incongruously heavy too; an old-fashioned mahogany chiffonier, a scrolled desk and chair, and a large glass cupboard displaying a porcelain dinner service decorated with pale blue flowers and a gold rim. Armchairs and a chaise-longue were arranged around the fireplace, with an ormolu clock on the mantelpiece. Green wall lamps lit the room with a soft glow.

Dimitri, who'd been brought up in the company of women, kept staring at him with a shy curiosity, until Jeanette rang the bell for him to be taken to bed.

'*Bonne nuit, Dima.*' She kissed her son. 'Sweet dreams.'

'*Bonne nuit, Maman.*'

Madame Theodore kissed both Dimitri's cheeks and squeezed his fingers.

After he'd left the room, Jeanette asked Alyosha if he thought he was like his father. He hadn't seen much of a resemblance, but pleased her by saying he was very like Artyom.

'He's a dear little man,' smiled his mother tenderly. But mentioning Artyom seemed to have upset her, and tears came to her eyes. Madame Theodore half rose from her seat but Jeanette shook her head. 'No, Mother, I'm fine.' She took a handkerchief from her sleeve and wiped her tears away. 'It's just that I still haven't come to terms with the fact that he's left me,' she told Alyosha. It struck him that he had seen nothing in the villa to suggest that his uncle had ever lived there. 'Though it's been a while now... hasn't it, Mother? Madame Theodore nodded. 'I'm still trying to make sense of what's happened... It was shameful, the way he treated me...'

She went on to say she had good reason to complain about what her husband had done to her. He'd been unfaithful to her for years – even before they were married, when he was carrying on an affair behind her back with some married woman. 'One of these women who likes to chase after other women's men. I'm not even going to say her name out loud: it would only leave a nasty taste in my mouth. I'd rather try and forget everything about her.' Sadness flooded her features. 'Do you know how I came to learn the truth about his carryings-on?' Alyosha shook his head. 'Let me tell you about it.' She wanted him to hear every last detail, so that he would know what an unprincipled cad his Uncle Artyom really was. 'This Spanish whore's own husband, no less – that's how I came to hear about the affair. It must be seven years ago by now…'

She became more and more agitated as she told him how the man had turned up at their door one evening. She didn't know how he'd found out where they were living in Paris, but when the maid had opened the door, he'd pushed past her and come storming through the house like a lunatic. Artyom hadn't stopped to reason with him, he'd just run for his life, with the husband giving chase, bellowing in anger.

Then, to Jeanette's horror, the Spaniard had pulled out a pistol, which he'd started to fire in every direction. She'd been convinced she was about to die. How she ever got herself under the kitchen table, she would never know, but there she'd found herself, screaming at the top of her voice.

'It was absolutely horrific.'

Madame Theodore echoed 'horrific' under her breath.

Jeanette had never been so frightened in all her life. What if a bullet had killed Dima? He was only two years old then; he'd been playing on the floor with his wooden blocks. And if the Spaniard hadn't happened to catch his shoe on the rug and bump his head against the chair, he would have shot Artyom without a doubt.

'Shame he didn't manage it.' She seethed quietly for a moment. 'Artyom fled the house without a thought for his wife and child.

Not that the Spaniard had a quarrel with us, and he said as much once he'd calmed down. He was rather charming as a matter of fact, apologised for the damage and said he wouldn't bother us again, only to be sure to tell Artyom that if he came near his wife again he would finish the job. But then, when Artyom slunk back home the next day, he had the bare-faced cheek to tell me he hadn't done anything wrong. Did he really think I was born yesterday? Your uncle is one of those men who will never own up to anything – or discuss anything either – if it will be to his disadvantage. He'll look after his own interests first every time, no matter who he's dealing with.'

Madame Theodore had gone to stand by the fireplace during this outpouring, leaning one elbow against the mantelpiece, with a grim expression on her face. She didn't open her mouth, apart from once, when she yawned, showing her rotten teeth, like stubs of nails left out in the rain to rust.

Jeanette blew her nose.

'Since he went to live with that Zepherine – they say she used to model for Coco Chanel; I don't know about that, but she's common enough – I've been so angry and bitter and vengeful. I'm quite lost. I have no more zest for life, I'm smoking more, I have no appetite. It's true, isn't it, Mother? I can't muster up the energy for anything. I can barely sit at the piano with Dimitri to give him his lesson. He plays so beautifully. Sometimes I feel as though I can't... I don't know what will become of me.' She blew her nose furiously before continuing, 'My marriage was everything to me. I had so much love for him, and felt so sure of his love. And what did the wretch do? Threw it all back in my face. Things will never be the same again. Everything now is ripped and ruined. I don't know how a woman is meant to get over something like this.'

She had obviously been cut to the quick, and her outpouring meant he could examine her without having to respond, beyond nodding or murmuring sympathetically occasionally. She was petite and a little hollow-cheeked and pale. Her curly blonde hair was cut fashionably short, and she had a slight cast in one of her eyes, which, beneath the heavy mascara, were full of pain. He guessed her to be in her late twenties, perhaps a little younger. Every now and again she'd glance across at her mother, as though expecting Madame Theodore to second or amplify what she had just said, but her mother remained impassive.

Eventually, Jeanette's diatribe came to an end, and she said bleakly, 'I'm so sorry. I'm ashamed of myself. It was wrong of me to unburden myself on you tonight, when we've only just met. It wasn't fair.'

'I really don't mind…'

'He's still your uncle. But I couldn't help myself. I hope you understand.'

'Of course.'

'But it's not your fault, the way your uncle behaves… The way he's treated me… The only thing I've had from him is this villa… A roof over our heads, no more… And he still owns the place. I'm pretty sure the only reason he offered it to me in the first place was to get me out of Paris. Forgive me for having such a low opinion of him, but he's a terrible man…'

She suddenly seemed to remember her duties as a hostess. 'Are you sure you've had enough to eat? Something to drink?'

'I don't need anything, you've been very kind.'

Behind her anguish, there was a warm heart. 'If you're sure. Perhaps it's time to go to bed, then.'

Jeanette rang the bell, and the maid showed him upstairs to where he was sleeping. After placing a lamp on the bedside table for him, she wished him a good night and melted away like a wraith. As soon as she'd gone, Alyosha kicked off his shoes and socks, and felt the coolness of the tiles under his aching feet. The long day had left its dirt and sweat on him, and he bent his head to the basin to wash his face and neck. Earlier, he had been exhausted, but now he felt totally awake and alert. He examined a painting on the wall of a young stag leaping dramatically across a glade in a dark wood by moonlight. He lay on the bed, but, restless, got up again and opened the window. There were pots of geraniums still in bloom attached to the balcony railing. He felt tense, and knew he'd be awake for hours, but he went to lie down again. Why had he hidden so much about himself? Why hadn't he made it clear to Jeanette that he wasn't made of the same stuff as his uncle? That he was different, a better person? He worried away at the puzzle. Why hadn't he felt he could tell her he was a good person?

He felt rivers of failure run through him, and he tried desperately to keep the images of his mother at bay. His thoughts turned inevitably then to Wisia. How he had wished for a perfect love with her. That had been the greatest disappointment.

His memory jumped back suddenly to an evening during the Civil War, when he'd been working for the Cheka in Kiev. He'd bought himself a cheap beer in Bessarabka market, and then he'd walked through the city beneath the silvery moon and the naked branches, the frozen fallen leaves crunching under his feet. He'd ended up in the Bazaar Galitskii, where the whores gathered, and bought himself a sloe-eyed young woman in a once-grand dark-blue evening dress. It had been a bitter night, so he'd taken her to the nearest café to drink tea served from a samovar, with two slices of lemon in each cup. After that, they'd gone back to his room, which was like a cave, undressed, and lain under the blankets, their teeth chattering. Her fingers had been like ice, and his cock had shrunk at her touch. It hadn't mattered what he'd said or done, she'd just laughed at everything, and, after a while, he'd had the uncomfortable feeling that she was laughing at him, rather than with him.

He felt a sudden flash of anger towards Jeanette for being so selfish, talking about herself all night. She had barely asked him about himself, and it was easy to see why somebody like his uncle would have become tired of her. He got up and went to the window again, staring out moodily at the silhouette of a great oak tree which dwarfed the pines with its bulk, and waited for the night to end.

38.

Sleep came at last, but it was restless and fitful, filled with dreams of the dead, a forest of skeletons rising up to walk, stretching their arms out to trap him.

The next day, he rose early intending to leave before the family were up, but Madame Theodore was already at the table. The maid brought them breakfast, and they ate without much conversation passing between them. When Madame Theodore chewed her toast, he couldn't help staring at her rusty teeth. Presently, she left the table and came back with a sepia photograph, which she placed on the table in front of him.

'This might be of interest to you,' she said.

She lit a cigarette, took a puff, and stood at his shoulder, holding the cigarette in her hand at her thigh.

'Thank you.'

It was a family portrait that his Uncle Artyom had taken at his childhood home in Petrograd. Alyosha gazed at the faces looking out at him. How had he forgotten that his father had a moustache? His mother had always complained that it was tobacco-stained. He examined the young faces of Margarita and Larissa. And Uncle Kozma, who had been full of cold that Christmas, and his mournful Aunt Ella.

His mother gazed out of the photo at him. He gazed back at her for a long time.

For a second, he felt panic engulf him, and thought he would suffocate. He realised that he was shaking, and he desperately needed some air. Excusing himself, he put the photograph down and made his way outside to sit on the steps of the terrace. It was early, and the air was cool, the morning mist still shrouding the tops of the pine trees on the hillside. Here and there, the red roofs of other villas were visible, and, in the distance, Nice curved around the bay, where a couple of white-sailed yachts were already out at sea. There was nothing to hear but morning birdsong and a dog barking somewhere further down the hill. He breathed deeply, trying to calm his racing pulse. He had to rein in his emotions, collect himself.

But he had to leave. Right away. This minute. Apart from anything else, he didn't think he had the stomach for any more of Jeanette's sadness. He longed to be on his own, longed to scramble along a shady path in the lee of a mountain, where mosses and rushes grew, and find himself a sheltered spot among the wild lavender, sharing it only with the bees. That's where he wished to be.

Without saying goodbye, he started to walk, sticking out his thumb whenever a vehicle passed him, in the hope of a lift. By midday, the sun was uncomfortably hot on his back, and it suddenly struck him: why on earth was he aiming for Paris? What did he have waiting for him there?

As he approached a family eating a picnic by their motor car, he fancied for a second that they were speaking Russian together. How hopefully every exile listened out for familiar vowels. Often on the streets of Berlin and Paris, he had imagined hearing his mother tongue in error, only to apologise, feeling like a fool, for startling a stranger with his greeting.

A motor-lorry carrying bottles of pastis eventually stopped for him. The driver asked him how far he was going, and laughed to hear his reply. As he pushed the gearstick into place, he told him he couldn't take him to Berlin, but he'd be happy to take him as far as Fontainebleau.

III

1928–1931

I.

Larissa had been visiting a friend, a girl she'd nursed with in the old days, and had stayed reminiscing longer than she'd intended, so she'd taken the shortcut through the park, along the tree-lined avenue which split the park in two. It was a cloudy evening, with rain in the air, so she made haste. She could hear herself panting lightly, and her shoes squelching through November's sodden leaves.

She thought she heard a noise, and glanced over her shoulder, but only long shadows followed her. She picked up her pace anyway, until she was fairly striding along. One second, she was admiring a scudding cloud obscuring the moon, and the next, her feet had left the ground, and she was being dragged backwards with great force through a gap in the bushes by the side of the path. She felt the leaves brush past her face and she tried to summon a yell but she couldn't – her voice was locked in her throat. She tried to twist herself free, but she was being held in an iron grip, arms locked around her, pinning her arms to her side. Then, she was hurled down to the ground and, instinctively holding out her arms to save herself, she fell clumsily and painfully on her wrists. Her flesh burned, but her assailant grabbed her by her hair and yanked her up onto her knees, so that she felt the damp grass soak through her stockings. Something flashed before her eyes. Some devil? There was no face, no eyes, nothing. A cap? A mask? The knife ordered her to undress. He punched her breast and barked something, but by now the only thing she could hear was a rushing sound in her ears, and her pounding heart.

'I'm expecting a baby,' she pleaded, but he roared at her, and she felt a pain in her arm. Blood. He had stabbed her. She started to shake as she realised she was going to die. Somehow, she found her voice, and, with one last effort, screamed with all the strength that remained to her. The black shadow leapt on her, pushed her savagely to the ground, straddled her, and began mauling her breast like a furious ape, his other hand pressed over her mouth to silence the desperate noise coming out of her. Then, a star flitted through the dusk, spinning closer until it crashed towards her. Larissa was already on her knees with her hands wrapped around her stomach when the cyclist reached her. He knelt at her side and asked her gently if she was alright. She said that she was, but the shaking wouldn't stop and she was terrified that the blackness which had disappeared would return from the shadows to attack her again.

When Bruno returned home, he was surprised to see one of the student doctors from the hospital sitting next to Larissa, who was lying on the sofa with a cashmere blanket over her, looking paler than he had ever seen her in his life. It was only then that he took in the two *schupos*. Larissa told Bruno what had happened, and how Simon had come to save her after he heard her screams.

Bruno tried to take control of the situation: comfort his wife, thank the stranger, talk to the *schupos,* but he felt oddly superfluous. He couldn't even make Larissa go to bed, clearly the best place for her, because she insisted on waiting up for Margarita.

She could have died.

A hair's breadth.

And the baby.

A hair's breadth.

The thought repeated itself over and over in Bruno's mind. He felt he had failed in his first duty as a husband: to keep his wife and child safe.

Simon left with the *schupos* and, as he saw him to the door, Bruno shook his hand warmly and thanked him from the bottom of his heart. He would be forever in his debt, and if there was ever anything he could do for him, he had only to say the word.

Once they were alone, Larissa started to reproach her husband. Why hadn't Bruno met her to go together to see her friend, as they had arranged? What had kept him? Where was he? Bruno had already decided he wouldn't make excuses, that he was going to tell the truth: that his colleagues had persuaded him to go for a drink with them after the boxing match, and one had led to another, and then another. But when it came to it, he failed. Instead, he lost his temper, and told her she had no right to rule his life for him.

'What if I'd been murdered tonight?'

A guilty Bruno accused her of being melodramatic, and Larissa was too exhausted to continue with the quarrel. She just wanted to see her sister Margarita.

2.

After the picture, they were both in such high spirits that they went to the billiards bar for a drink. Apart from the woman serving them, they were the only females there, but they'd been there before and were left alone. Then, they both caught the Mariendorf tram, still giggling as they re-lived the Charlie Chaplin picture. Sitting next to them was a grizzled old man, all hunched up in his seat, who every now and again would slip his hand into his pocket and pull out a a small, silver flask, winking at them before taking a long swig.

As the tram reached Seestrasse, on the corner of Togostrasse, Margarita and Natalya were arrested. The other passengers looked on impassively through the steamed-up windows as the two women were made to step down into the cold by a young man in a soft hat and grey raincoat. Margarita had already noticed him when he'd got on the tram at Rosenthaler, because his head looked too big above such a thin body. Then, when he had approached them to ask what language they were speaking, Natalya had giggled, thinking the man was trying to flirt with them. But Margarita hadn't been so sure, and her suspicions had been confirmed when the young man had taken out his leather badge from his inside pocket.

3.

Margarita crossed the cell floor and rapped on the door. She was sick and tired of sitting there with nothing to do. She tried again, louder and longer this time. Some time later, a hand appeared through the small hatch in the door offering her a glass of water.

When she was interrogated later on, she told the truth.

'Aznefttrust?' The policeman raised his head. 'When did you start working for them?'

'Is it illegal?'

'Less of your lip.'

'Is it illegal?' she challenged, staring him straight in the eye. 'It's a Russian trading company.'

'Depends what you're really trading.'

Natalya had thought it safer to lie, making things far worse for herself, as they proceeded to interrogate her for hours. By the early hours of the morning, exhausted and tearful, she had changed her story several times. The *schupos* had frightened her and she insisted on her rights as a Russian citizen to see somebody from the Soviet embassy. Around half past five in the morning, a consul arrived with a briefcase under his arm and a stinking cold. After a great deal of paperwork and stamping of various documents, Natalya and Margarita were eventually allowed to leave.

They walked out into the fresh morning air just after seven o'clock. Natalya was very shaken, so Margarita tried to make light of the whole thing, but her friend started to cry quietly into her hands.

'Things aren't that bad.' Margarita put her arm across Natalya's shoulder and hugged her. 'We're fine,' she comforted her. 'They didn't charge us with anything.'

But Natalya just kept repeating the same thing over and over: 'It's all over for me now.'

4.

As she hung her coat and beret on the hook, Margarita caught a glimpse of herself in the mirror, and noticed how pale her cheeks were. She peered at herself more closely and thought that she looked dreadful.

'Where in God's name have you been until now?' Bruno had appeared from upstairs, in his waistcoat and slippers, looking exhausted.

'Why? What's the matter?

He explained what had happened, and Margarita raced upstairs at once.

'Lala?' she called out as she opened the door.

The curtains were drawn and the room was in semi-darkness. Her sister was lying in bed with her back towards her.

'Are you alright?'

She went to lie on the bed, and the sisters clutched each other tightly.

There was a knock on the door, and the maid came in. 'There's somebody on the telephone for you, miss.'

'Take a message and tell them I'll call them back,' Margarita told her, and the girl disappeared.

'What happened Lala?'

Larissa had only just started to explain, when the maid popped her head around the door again.

'What is it?' asked Margarita irritably.

'They're insisting that they have to speak to you directly.'

She was instructed to come in to the office immediately.

'Rest,' she whispered to her sister, who was already dozing.

As she wearily put on her coat, Bruno appeared. 'Are you staying home to look after her today?' she asked him.

'I've already let the hospital know,' he said looking shamefaced.

'Good, I'm pleased to hear it.'

'It wasn't my fault,' he said as she opened the door.

'Did I say that it was?'

5.

At the office, there was no sign of Natalya, and Margarita was taken aback when she saw that her desk had already been stripped bare.

'She's going home,' Osip Nikitich explained, when Margarita asked why such a thing had been done.

'To Russia?'

He looked at her calmly and asked, 'Where else is home?'

The following week, a new girl came to sit at the desk opposite Margarita – a much quieter individual than Natalya, and not half such good company. Margarita felt the loss of her friend, and looked forward to the letter which she felt sure would not be long in arriving, but she didn't hear a word from her. When Margarita asked her boss for Natalya's address in Moscow, he told her he didn't know where she was living. From time to time, she would still bring up Natalya's name with other members of staff, and would make a point of asking any Russians visiting Berlin about her, but nobody ever knew anything. Occasionally, she would have the unpleasant feeling that Natalya had been swallowed alive by the Soviet Union.

She was no longer sent out on underground missions, and a few weeks later was transferred to the marketing department, where she was one of three. The work was very dull. When she asked Osip Nikitich about her future prospects, his answer was vague to the point of unhelpful. Margarita realised that she no longer had any meaningful role at Aznefttrust and, as a result, she found herself attracted back to her old KPD circles.

6.

It was the tiniest advertisement in the *Berliner Tageblatt*. *The early bird catches the worm*, Alyosha thought, and went for it without delay. He was interviewed by a young man, not much older than himself, who asked him at length about his previous experience. Alyosha found it simple enough to pull the wool over the man's eyes, and claimed to have experience in many clubs in France. He surprised himself with his detailed description of his work at the Flamant Rose in Montmartre. In his mind's eye, he saw Galina waiting on the tables.

'So, why did you leave Paris for Berlin, then?'

The young man got up from his seat and leant on the side of his desk. He crossed his arms and looked at Alyosha knowingly.

'Things became a little… complicated.'

Same old story. That's what Alyosha read in the man's eyes.

'Have you got a record?'

He shook his head.

'Never been in trouble with the police?'

'Never.'

'So you've never been in jail?'

'No.' Alyosha didn't feel the need to mention his time in Warsaw.

'Pity.' The man shook his hand and welcomed him to the Havana.

It was mainly a club for homosexuals, on the corner of Martin Lutherstrasse. There were another four clubs on the same street, three of them for lesbians. The doors opened at half past nine every night, and by ten, the band had started to play. Alyosha's work was primarily to control the drug dealers who sold hashish or cocaine. Only those who were paying a commission to the Havana were allowed to sell to the clientele, and he was shown who to welcome and who to turn away. The woman who owned the Havana never came near the place, and the manager only popped in now and again as the fancy took him, so Alyosha had the first and last say.

Before long, all the gangs had heard about the Havana's new doorman, and sent their men from every corner of Berlin. The Croatians, the Serbs, the Romanians and Poles – they all tried to buy him. He was promised money, a cut of the profits, a supply of the drugs, girls, boys; and, after the bribes didn't work, the threats began.

'A razor across your face…'

One of the barmen got up to show his hands. Running across his fingers from one hand to the other was a red scar

'Be prepared. Leather gloves with an iron mesh on the inside will save you,' he explained.

Alyosha bought a second-hair pair through a friend of the barman, but he couldn't get used to them. He felt like some crusader in the sands of Palestine, as the mesh rubbed against his knuckles and his fingers crunched every time he bent them. He hated the job of course – kicking his heels outside the door, keeping his eye on every coming and going – and counted the minutes until the early hours, when the club closed and he could set off for home. He'd only ever seen it as a temporary job, anyway. He checked the situations vacant columns in the morning and evening newspapers every day, looking for something better, but there was precious little advertised, and when when he leant on the bar to turn the pages of the newspapers, he could feel ten million hungry eyes looking over his shoulder at the same time.

He tried for anything he could, because he knew it was only a matter of time before somebody went for him at the Havana. He'd been told about plenty of other doormen who had been cut. Many of them had been badly scarred, and one had lost his sight. Alyosha decided for his own safety to keep a knife up his sleeve, just in case.

He hadn't even thought he was in any danger on that particular night. He had only just locked up, and was on his way home. Two girls came towards him, arm-in-arm, giggling when they bumped tipsily into each other, but, as they passed him, one of them swung her bag across his back, a bag as heavy as a chimney brick. A watery, colourless fog danced across his eyes and he hit the pavement.

7.

His white coat was spotless, though there was a lingering smell of iodoform. Like any busy doctor, Bruno Volkmann spoke plainly and without preamble. He was practically moving on to his next patient before he had finished talking. Alyosha found him dry and brusque, and, according to the other patients on the ward, he was a bit of a snob, and could be unfeeling just when somebody was at their lowest point, and craved a word of sympathy. If possible, it was better to talk to one of the other doctors or nurses.

Later that day, Alyosha was lying on his bed, unable to sleep because he was in so much pain, when Larissa came rushing into the ward, and squealed with excitement when she saw him. She bent over his bed and hugged him, and Alyosha couldn't help wincing from her over-enthusiastic embrace. Still, he managed a smile and she grinned back, delighted to see him. They hadn't set eyes on each other for years, since the spring of 1924, when Alyosha had decided to leave Berlin for Paris. With her hair tied back, her forehead looked higher and wider than he remembered, and she was heavily pregnant, but her high spirits seemed undimmed. There was so much to say and so little time, as visiting only lasted half an hour. Larissa wanted him to tell her everything, and insisted that, once he was discharged, he should come and live with them, at least until he'd found his feet. To this, he thankfully agreed.

8.

'How can we afford a place like this all of a sudden, Artyom? How did you find the money to buy it?'

'My investments on the Bourse have started to pay off. The last nine months have been the best I've ever had.'

'Luck is a fickle friend. What if it turns again? I don't want to find ourselves back where we were four years ago, not being able to make ends meet, and people after us for their money.'

'That won't happen again, Zephi.'

'How can you be so certain? Remember you have two little girls to look after now, as well.'

Six weeks previously, Bibi had been given a sister, a little girl they named Karina. Zepherine's labour had been a savage one, lasting nearly fourteen hours. She was only just back on her feet, and Artyom had no intention of telling her the truth about their new-found wealth.

They were standing outside a handsome villa situated in the countryside to the south-west of Paris, about to view the place. Artyom had already looked over it on his own, and had fallen in love with the house and the location, as the countryside around Paris, especially to the south, reminded him a little of rural Russia. He thought it wiser not to mention this to Zepherine, so, as they wandered from room to room, he pretended to be seeing everything for the first time. He could see her enthusiasm growing as she began to see the attractions of living there, although she continued to fret about the financial burden, and Artyom had to work hard to convince her that they could afford to buy it, and that she had no reason to worry at all.

'But *how* can we afford a place like this?'

'It doesn't matter how.'

Zepherine, convinced at last, turned around in a complete circle in the middle of the high-windowed *salon* and declared joyfully, 'This place is a wonder to behold!'

Artyom winced. He hated it when Zepherine used that expression. It had been one of his mother's stock phrases, but, for some reason, he found it horribly annoying when she said it in French. Perhaps it grated on him because it was so old-fashioned.

'I can't wait to show my sister.'

It had been raining heavily that morning, but the weather had lifted by the time they finished inspecting the inside of the villa. After she had made a tour of the gardens, Zepherine was in her seventh heaven. She had changed her tune completely from the morning, when she'd told him she didn't have the least inclination to leave Paris for the country. She was a city girl. Just hearing a cow lowing, never mind actually seeing one, would frighten her.

Why was Artyom insisting on taking her to this place when she really didn't have the slightest interest in seeing it at all?

'Why can't we buy a bigger place in Paris?'

'Just wait until you've seen it before you make your mind up.'

The journey to Yvelines had been very silent, as Zepherine was in a sulk.

Her father had been a Marseille man, a sea captain, who had drowned in the Bay of Biscay when his boat had been hit by a torpedo in November 1916. Zepherine only had two pictures of him. In one, he stood straight-backed in his cap and uniform, one hand in his jacket pocket, in front of a sturdy mast. The other had been taken in some *bal musette,* and, in this one, he was sitting next to his wife, his shirt collar open, his arm lying casually along the back of her chair, a cigarette between finger and thumb. There was a roguish little smile under his beard, and laughter in his eyes. Because of that, this was her favourite. It showed her mother and father as a happy and harmonious couple.

That, too, was the picture Zepherine always painted to Artyom, but it was all a fabrication. Avril, Zepherine's sister, let the cat out of the bag one evening, when a conversation turned into a quarrel out of nothing. It transpired that Zepherine had no idea who her real father was. There was no name on either of their birth certificates. From when they were tiny, their mother had sometimes mentioned the 'Sea Captain from Marseille', and they had convinced themselves that he was their father. So, Zepherine had learnt to create a fantasy life for herself, so much so that she often couldn't distinguish between what was true and what wasn't.

On the way back to Paris, thoroughly excited, she chattered on about how she intended decorating and furnishing the villa. Artyom didn't have to say a word, he just had to listen and smile.

Zepherine didn't have the faintest idea how Artyom made his money. For many months now, he had been careful to make a bit of a show of himself at the Bourse – nothing too obvious, he just made sure he was seen in those places, which would signal to the right people that he was brokering on the Stock Exchange. He made it known that he was buying and selling for several important clients, a few of them foreigners. It wasn't only Zepherine who could see a transformation, but his old contemporaries too.

'Good to see the old Artyom is back,' was a comment he often heard.

'It's good to be back,' he'd reply.

It was a perfect front.

9.

Alyosha gave an account of himself to Larissa and Margarita in dribs and drabs, although they were both so curious about his life in Paris, they would have preferred every last detail all at once. But they quickly grasped how precarious his life had been there. Bruno blamed the unstable times they were living in, and Alyosha agreed. He didn't say a word about Ludwika or his mother. He told them what he knew about Georgik, though, not that it amounted to much more than that he was a pupil at Le Rosey.

Alyosha could see how Bruno doted on his little girl, Ella. He adored being a father, and was very happy that his wife was pregnant again, and that there would soon be another baby in the nursery – a son this time, he hoped.

Alyosha didn't find his cousins so terribly changed. Margarita had cut her hair shorter (though not very fashionably), and she dressed like a professional young woman, but she was still intense and serious, weighing matters up carefully before coming to an opinion, especially when compared to Larissa, who remained ebullient and high-spirited in spite of her domestic responsibilities and pregnancy.

Alyosha asked Margarita about her work.

'It's a Russian company,' she explained.

'Selling what?' he asked.

'We don't sell anything. We just facilitate trading between the Soviet Union and German companies and corporations. Oil from Baku mainly. Agricultural machinery, too – tractors and so on.'

'So you're working for a Soviet company?'

'Yes. It's called Aznefttrust. What's wrong with that?'

Her expression was defiant. But he was taken aback and said, 'You know quite well what's wrong with that.'

'I'm of the opinion that communism is the only way forward,' she said without hesitation.

Bruno looked up at the small chandelier, blowing through his cheeks.

'Tell me you're pulling my leg.' Alyosha turned to Larissa for confirmation, but she remained silent. 'It can't be true.'

'It is true,' his cousin replied.

He was astonished, and, wanting to get to the bottom of it, fired a barrage of questions at her.

'Can't we discuss something else?' Margarita asked after a while.

'No, not until I understand what's happened to you. This is madness.'

Margarita sighed and said quietly, 'Communism makes perfect sense to me. It's so simple. Under capitalism, you have a dozen cows belonging to one man. The man has five servants to milk them, feed them and care for them. In exchange for their labour, the five men are given a wage. The cattle, or capital, are in the hands of one individual, to do with as he pleases. His employees can buy what is produced by the cows – the milk, the cheese and the butter – only if they have the means to do that, and if the owner is willing to sell to them. With this system, that one individual makes all the profit.' Bruno tutted, but Margarita ignored him and continued. 'Under communism, on the other hand, the cows belong to all six men. They belong to the whole of society, which decides what to do with them according to the needs of all. As far as the produce is concerned, there is no profit. The produce is simply distributed fairly between the six men, in a way that's acceptable to all of them. Why does that sound so unreasonable?'

She was of the opinion that Europe had to change.

'It would be disastrous if the continent slides back to how it was before the war, a world of monarchists, churchmen and aristocrats, with their secret diplomacy over brandy and cigars, willing to consign millions of men, women and children to a life of suffering.'

'As though everything was as black and white as that,' scoffed Bruno from the head of the table.

Alyosha had never been so surprised by the change in someone.

10.

Every morning, Artyom would make his way to his usual café to eat his breakfast, read the newspapers, and make his telephone calls, after which he'd stroll over to the Bourse to do a little buying and selling, though he was only dabbling in the market for the sake of appearances. He also went out of his way to build up a reputation for generosity, often paying the bill when he was dining with acquaintances – especially if it was somebody's birthday. In this way, he attracted lots of new friends, younger men mainly, who looked up to him, and often turned to him for advice. He quite liked the feeling this gave him of being very old and wise – in fact, he was in his element.

Every few days, usually late in the afternoon, Artyom would call in at the office of the Orphans of the Levant Charitable and Provident Society, which he had set up and continued to fund. He had appointed Charles Theberge to manage the charity, whom

Artyom had soon christened 'the Saint'. Charles Theberge's father and grandfather had run a little bistro by the Gare de Lyon for years, but he hadn't wanted to take over the family business. He'd always been a devout boy (taking after his mother in that respect), and, after leaving school, he'd hoped to be a missionary in Cochinchina. But he fell ill, and, once he was better, worked for a time mopping the floors of the Maison des Religieuses Augustines de Meaux, before securing a position as a clerk in the Rue Halévy branch of Société Général, where he learned how to look after other people's money. But he felt spiritually unfulfilled, and still wanted to serve his fellow man. As he was waiting for the tram one morning in a shower of fine rain, he was called by God. He resigned from the bank, and came to work at the charity.

Charles Theberge was a dedicated, industrious and modest man, and, like every saint, he pushed himself to his limits with no thought of sparing himself. The Saint was the first through the door every morning and the last to leave every night, working through many a weekend and never taking his holidays, but dedicating himself entirely to The Orphans' Friend, as the charity became known.

One night, when Artyom and Zepherine happened to drive past on their way home from the theatre, they saw a light on in the office. Artyom parked his Duesenberg outside and knocked on the office door. When the Saint answered, Artyom scolded him for working so late at his desk, and offered him a lift home, but the Saint smilingly but firmly refused.

Artyom's life was sweet as a nut. He grew to appreciate fatherhood at last, and doted more and more on his two little girls, Bibi and Karina. Playing with them gave him a sense of contentment he had rarely felt before, and, consequently, he became closer to Zepherine. The two went out together more often, for suppers or to the opera and theatre, and they never missed a new exhibition, as Artyom was beginning to buy fine art again. Back in 1916, he'd bought a painting from Picasso in the Café de la Rotonde, and given it to his brother-in-law that Christmas; now, he bought a further three paintings from the same artist for himself, and hung them in his villa in Yvelines. He also bought himself the latest Kodak camera, so that he could take up photography again.

He was doing so well that he had indulged himself with not one, but two new motor cars – a Rolls-Royce, the Phantom I silver model, and the Duesenberg model X. But then, with one car always sitting unused in the garage, it seemed high time he employed a chauffeur. It crossed his mind that he might offer the post to his nephew, but he hadn't seen Alyosha for such a long time, and didn't even have an address for him.

'It's lovely to see you so happy, Artyom.'

'My life could not be better, Zephi darling.'

He kissed Bibi and Karina's little heads, then kissed Zepherine. Even his sister-in-law, Avril, seemed less unbearable these days. In fact, he felt well disposed enough towards her to offer her a job at the office of The Orphans' Friend.

Thanks to the Saint's tireless work, the latest campaign to help the poor orphans of the Levant was beginning to attract the patronage of many prominent public figures. That suited Artyom very well. He was very happy not to put himself centre-stage; it was quite enough to know that the people who counted realised that he was the driving force behind the latest appeal. Artyom had a quiet word with one of his new acquaintances, who had a quiet word with his friend, the editor of *Le Petit Parisien*, and the Saint was cordially invited to write a monthly column about the work of the charity, and its long-term aims and hopes. This brought the charity into the public eye, and several other publications sent their journalists to interview the Saint for their own readership. Some of the articles written about him and his charity were syndicated, so news of the pitiful condition of the children appeared in some of the main newspapers in other French cities, and reached even further afield, to Spain, Portugal and the Netherlands. In the wake of such sterling publicity, contributions from churches, societies and individuals from every corner flooded in, all eager to do their bit to help the poor little creatures who had been abandoned to fend for themselves on the streets of Turkey, Syria and Lebanon.

Quite apart from money, they received clothes, tinned goods, books and educational supplies, and all manner of other things of varying usefulness. Artyom had to rent a warehouse – an old coco-matting factory in Bobigny – to store it all. Even then, it was difficult to find room for the daily arrivals, and it became a matter of urgency to send the donations on to Marseille, from where they would be shipped to the Levant.

The Saint was punctilious about recording every gift and every last franc. His inventories and accounts, written in his beautiful cursive script, were a sight to behold, and accessible to all.

'Impeccable,' praised Artyom.

'It's the least we can do for our donors,' was the Saint's modest reply.

More and more politicians and public figures tried to enhance their reputations by associating themselves with the increasingly fashionable campaign. No sooner had Albert Sarraut, the Home Secretary's photograph appeared in *Le Monde Illustré*, accompanied by a fulsome article about his generosity and public-spiritedness, than other members of the Republic's Chamber of Deputies came knocking on the door to 'render any assistance possible'. Artyom's new Kodak proved a very sound investment, paying for itself several times over. He took photographs of politicians of every stripe – and his picture of Aristide Briand, the Minister for Foreign Affairs, shaking hands with the Saint outside the office after presenting him with a cheque for two thousand francs, was reproduced many times, appearing in all the national and many regional newspapers and journals.

The charity went from strength to strength. A cross-party group of French deputies arranged a splendid fundraising dinner. It was a sweeping success, and more money flooded into the coffers. The Saint, as always, made sure that every last franc was accounted for. The charity's only expenses were the running costs of the office. The Saint paid himself a tiny stipend, although many of the charity's donors actually argued that no man should be expected to live on such a pathetic amount of money, least of all the Saint, who spent all his hours endeavouring to alleviate the suffering of others. He was held in high respect by everybody.

Nothing could have pleased Artyom better.

One evening he had an idea, and, the next day, he went to discuss it with the Saint. He wanted to publish the accounts in the press.

'So that nobody can ever doubt our bona fides,' Artyom told the Saint.

The Saint didn't even consider this for half a minute before saying, 'I don't see any reason why not. We've always been happy for anybody to see them.'

Artyom knew no more would need to be said, and that the Saint could be trusted to put the plan into action. 'Thank you for all your hard work,' he said, putting his hat on.

'The thanks are due to you,' smiled the Saint, 'for giving me the chance to do a little for my fellow man.'

'What you do here is remarkable,' Artyom told him sincerely.

'We are all Christ Jesu's servants,' was the Saint's simple reply.

II.

Alyosha was having fun playing ball with Ella, bouncing it a little higher with every throw.

'Reason with her? What's the point?' asked Larissa as she watched them. 'She won't listen to a word we say. To the point of tears, I've done my very best to knock some sort of sense into her head.'

'Perhaps I should try?'

'Really, Alyosha, I wouldn't waste your time. Take it from me, there's no point trying to make her change her mind, because she won't.'

Alyosha puzzled over this for a moment. 'This is so… odd.'

'I know. Margarita of all people.'

Larissa reminded him of how loyal to the Tsar her sister had been back in Petrograd. She told him of the time the two of them had been made by their mother to volunteer to nurse injured soldiers, supervised by Baroness Wrangel. Larissa still remembered it all as though it were yesterday: how the trolleys would arrive from the train stations from hour to hour, and the men lying on their backs under the green tarpaulins with the red crosses on them, whimpering with the pain of their injuries. There were hundreds upon hundreds of soldiers on the streets of Petrograd back then – some on crutches, some without arms, some without noses, others blind, clutching the shoulder of the soldier next to them, walking in a chain of brown overalls and stocking-less black slippers.

Then came 1917, when she lost her home and lost her father to the Cheka, and she, Margarita and her mother had escaped from Russia on a train belonging to the Red Cross, crossing the border into Latvia, and from Latvia to Poland. They had been advised to wear nurses' uniforms, and not to carry more than two suitcases between them, so that it didn't look as though they were running away. It had been such a long journey.

But it was as though Margarita had forgotten all of that.

'There must be something we can do.' Alyosha was adamant.

'No, there's nothing you, nor I, nor anybody else can do.

We're better off leaving her alone, and perhaps someday, she'll see sense again.'

'I'm going to *make* her listen to me.'

Larissa plaited her hands over her pregnant stomach.

'Every time I think about Papa, about what he'd say if he knew what she'd become, it upsets me dreadfully.'

'Uncle Kozma would be furious with her.'

'He'd be beside himself. You'd think she'd have enough respect for his memory, and everything he stood for. The Tsar. The Church. The Imperial Army. Russia's old values as she was in all her glory. But it's just too upsetting, so I try not to think about it.'

But what Alyosha was curious to understand was Margarita's inner journey to communism. How could anybody from her background embrace something as repugnant as Marxism? This was the credo which had led to so much unnecessary pain throughout Russia, Europe and Asia, without mentioning the suffering of the three million Russians who had been forced into exile from their country. 1917 had seen a whole generation turn their backs on their homes to live at the mercy of strangers in foreign countries.

12.

'Communists are such hypocrites, Margarita. The way they insist on everybody sacrificing their personal freedom in the name of a spurious equality which will never come to be. Their aim is to free people who don't wish to be freed. And they're so arrogant, thinking that they know what's best for everybody. Who gave these revolutionaries the right to act in anybody's name? Power for the people, they say. Power for themselves, more like. That's what 1917 was about. Look at the type of people who rule Russia today. When you agitate the waters of a lake, what comes to the surface is the mud from the bottom, and it dirties all the clean water. During the Bolshevik revolution, it wasn't the finest men who reached the top, but dogmatic intellectuals, pitiful failures almost to a man, narrow-minded fanatics like Lenin.'

Margarita smiled pityingly at her cousin, and asked had he'd got everything off his chest now?

'No, I most certainly haven't! A new society? The Soviet Union? Seriously? More like a society which has managed to attract all the dregs, the thieves and the murderers…' She snorted dismissively but allowed him to continue. '…while the Tsar and his family – not that they were perfect, or even close to perfect, I'm not claiming that, but then, who's perfect? – were doing their best under extremely difficult circumstances.' Margarita took a deep pull of her cigarette as Alyosha continued, 'They were the legitimate governing class, they were the upholders of Russia's best traditions, her scholarship, her religion and her dignity.'

'Her religion and her dignity indeed!' she couldn't help interrupting.

'Everything that was good about the old society before the revolution—'

'You're really throwing down the gauntlet here aren't you? You've been thinking about what you want to say to me Alyosha. You never used to talk like this—'

'These are the people, entire families, like ours, who were blown to the four corners of the world. But we're people who won't give in lightly. We're stubborn. We're determined. We will carry on bringing everybody together, to build a movement which will fight the communists, until we restore Russia to her former splendour.'

Margarita laughed softly and said, 'Seriously, Alyosha, where is this great resistance of yours? In that pitiful conference Duchess Lydia arranged in Munich a while ago? Or was that an example of yet more empty rhetoric from the Monarchists?'

'These things ebb and flow, I admit…'

'It's more than that, be honest.'

'We mustn't lose heart.'

He heard a distant echo from that evening at the Hôtel Negresco in Nice.

'This is exactly how I used to think at one stage,' Margarita replied, 'but it was all immature prejudice.'

Alyosha's anger wilted all of a sudden, and he felt sad and hopeless.

'How much do you know about what is really happening in the Soviet Union today, Alyosha? How much effort have you *truly* made to understand? With an open mind, in a spirit of sympathy?'

She stubbed out her cigarette and looked at her cousin earnestly.

'It's difficult to have a spirit of sympathy as you call it, with the whole country lying in ruins under the communists' rule,' he said.

'Lying in ruins? Who on earth is saying that?'

'That's what I've heard.'

'But from whom, Alyosha? Paris and Berlin émigrés, no doubt. People who have lost all their property and are feeling bitter. They're hardly going to be objective.'

'People who are suffering ill health and poverty, overwhelmed by their longing for home, you mean?'

'They are more than welcome to go home – nobody would prevent them.'

'And face instant arrest? Before being shot?'

'And your source for this conclusion?'

'You only have to read the newspapers.'

'That's just malicious scaremongering. Negative propaganda based on ignorance and spite.'

'So, they're all lying when they say there's no democracy under the communists?'

'Was there democracy under the Tsar?'

'But the Bolsheviks didn't replace the Tsar, they replaced Alexander Kerenskii's government, who would have held the first elections in the history of Russia, if the communists hadn't used force of arms to shut the Constitutional Assembly down and send everybody home.'

'Was there democracy under the Tsar?' Margarita repeated.

'Perhaps not. But Lenin and his gang made big promises that the new regime would be better than the old one.'

'And so it is, much, much better than the old one.'

'Is it democratic? Can you honestly tell me there is a democracy like the one Russia would have had if the Constitutional Assembly had been elected?'

'It depends how you define democracy.' Margarita lit another cigarette.

'Is it democratic?' Alyosha persisted.

'You're shutting your mind again. Try and be more receptive to other ways of living. Why is it only your way that's valid? If I explain to you the true nature of communism, will you promise to put your prejudices to one side and listen?'

Without even waiting for his reply, Margarita launched forth.

'There is a very great difference between bourgeois democracy and proletarian democracy. The first is based on the idea of the will of the nation, which unites the will of every class within the state. The truth of it is that, within a bourgeois state, there are several classes with different interests... I speak from experience. When I first came to Berlin, I found work – I don't know if you remember this – in a cake factory. There, on the assembly line, I saw for the first time in my life how the capitalist system operated. Why kill yourself working long hours only to put more profit in the bosses' pockets? Working more than ten hours a day certainly didn't benefit the workers.'

'Margarita, I've worked in awful jobs myself, I'm not denying there are bad bosses out there.'

'The raison d'être of all bosses is to squeeze as much work out of us as they can, for as little money as they can get away with, in order to maximise their own profit.

'I'm just not so sure it's that simple,' he said.

'But it *is* that simple. Talking about the common will is sheer folly. Essentially, the will of one class or another has to triumph. There is no middle way. Between the bourgeoisie and proletariat, where is the common will? Either the bourgeoisie will prevail or the proletariat will prevail, and whoever wins will impose their will on the state. The victorious proletariat wills a communist republic, a society which operates for the benefit of the many, and not for the few rich and privileged.'

He remained silent, reluctant to capitulate so easily, and besides, he wasn't sure yet what he thought. Margarita let him be for a while before saying, 'I can see from your face that what I said is beginning to make sense to you. There's nothing mysterious or complicated about communism. Anybody can understand it. Marxism is the answer to the age-old problems of the human condition and the tangle of history. Keep thinking.'

'What about?'

'Which class offers hope and deliverance from oppression, and transforms the world for the better? And which class wants to reinforce the old slavery?'

13.

Alyosha was lying on his bed when he heard the front door open and voices cross the hall. He sat up to listen, then went to the top of the stairs, but there was nothing more to be heard. As he padded downstairs, he noticed the thick protruding vein on his left foot, like a snail under his skin. That was the price for tramping the streets of Paris.

He went over to the parlour door and opened it, then froze, as the couple quickly drew away from each other. His cousin blushed deeply, and half turned her shoulder, her pregnant stomach very obvious. The young man jumped to his feet, but then just stood there awkwardly, and Alyosha felt that he should say something, but no words came. Larissa started fussing with the sofa cushions, and eventually said, 'I thought you were thinking of going out for the afternoon.'

'I had thought of going for a walk,' Alyosha answered, 'but I went to rest instead.'

Nobody knew quite what to say next. In the end, Alyosha managed to say, 'You've no need to worry... I won't say anything.'

'Not even to Margarita?' asked Larissa, a little too hurriedly.

'Not even to her...'

'Thank you. Alyosha, this is Simon – Simon, Alyosha, my cousin...'

'I've heard a lot about you,' said her lover, shaking his hand.

It was the maid's half-day, so Larissa made the three of them tea in the kitchen, as they tried to keep up the rather stilted conversation. Alyosha learned that Simon Schlünz was a junior doctor at the Charité Hospital, and had recently saved Larissa from being attacked – or worse.

'No, I'm not a Berliner, I come from a place called Schwalmstadt in Hessen... There's a castle'

'And a Spring Fair,' prompted Larissa.

'Yes, quite a famous one. Sells all sorts of things...'

Alyosha watched his cousin hanging on his every word.

'...pots and pans, crockery, fruit and nuts and foods of every description...'

There was admiration and love in her expression. After her initial embarrassment, she seemed pleased to be able to share him with someone else.

'What about you?' asked Simon presently. 'You were badly beaten, Larissa tells me?'

'These things happen.'

They smiled at each other, and then Larissa put her hand to her stomach as she felt the baby kick.

Bruno's baby, or Simon's? Alyosha wondered.

He felt he was trespassing on their time together, so he told them he would take that walk after all.

14.

It was almost three in the morning and Artyom was drunk. There'd been a great deal of flirting and kissing of wrists and arms at the bar, and then he'd tried for a proper kiss from the prettiest of the lot. She was staggeringly beautiful, but a nervy little thing, terrified of her husband's anger, though longing at the same time for some sexual adventure.

Artyom felt sure – on the basis of past experiences – that her lovemaking would be wild and uninhibited, however coy she seemed. He'd had enough women like her over the years, women who were sexually starved. But then, her husband appeared with a glass of Tzuica in his hand, stout and red-cheeked. He was an idiot, of course, his conversation dull and pompous, reminding Artyom of a saying of his grandfather's that men with small minds were very similar to bottles with narrow necks: the less substance they contained, the more noise they made in the pouring.

The man summoned his wife over to the roulette table, where Artyom had the pleasure of watching him lose. His own luck wasn't much better; he wasn't concentrating, as his eye still roved the room for a woman, though he was, by now, too drunk to do anything about it.

Leaving the Haussmann Club on his own, he felt thwarted

and irritable, and he lost his temper with the chauffeur when he tried to warn him against bumping his head as he bent clumsily to get in to the back of the Rolls-Royce. He wasn't aware of the hot lump on his forehead until he had crossed the threshold of the villa.

He stumbled up the stairs and crashed around the bedroom in the gloom, dropping his clothes on the floor as he undressed.

'Where have you been?'

'Sssshhh.'

'What's the time?'

His throat was hoarse with smoking, talking and laughing. He collapsed naked onto the bed, flung an arm around Zepherine, and immediately sank into a drunken sleep. Zepherine, furious that he hadn't even bothered to answer her, tried to wake him, shaking his shoulder and then, her temper mounting, kicked his leg.

'Don't…' he mumbled.

'Where have you been until now?'

'Need to sleep…'

'Artyom? You stink of cheap perfume. You've been carrying on with someone, haven't you?'

He rolled onto his side, turning his back to her.

'Well?' she asked, and continued to punch him. 'Who was she? Where did you go? I can smell her on you, you bastard.'

There was a knock on the door, and a sleepy maid poked her head into the room, saying there was somebody on the telephone asking for Monsieur Artyom.

'At this time of the night? Is it her?' asked Zepherine.

The fog of drunkenness cleared amazingly quickly when the maid gave Artyom the name. He wrapped himself in the coverlet from the bed and stepped past the plump maid, who was trying to stifle her yawns. Zepherine had hired her because she was the plainest of the six who had been interviewed – almost ugly in fact – and so was highly unlikely to be a threat to the lady of the house.

In the dark study, he gave himself a moment to clear his head before he picked up the receiver. It could only be bad news. What else had a call in the middle of the night ever been?

A lonely little voice reached him from the other end of the line.

There was a problem.

'What kind of problem?'

In the background, he could hear the voices of some stragglers wandering out into the night. In his mind's eye, Artyom could see Pierre standing at the booth in the corner of the Café de la Terrasse, and he could practically smell Marseille in his nostrils.

Pierre was gabbling away. There was something rash and reckless in his make-up which Artyom was already aware of, and he would often overreact and panic when the slightest little thing occurred – a dangerous cocktail.

Artyom tried to slow him down. 'I don't understand what you're trying to tell me…'

Pierre gradually became more coherent. L'Oreille had been due to meet him that night at the Stockholm, but hadn't appeared.

'Why? Where was he?'

Somebody had lobbed a bottle of petrol through a window of the cottage on the outskirts of Bandol where the heroin was prepared, and set light to it, burning the place to a cinder, with Louis Albertini, the chemist, and L'Oreille inside.

'Are they alive?'

That was why he was calling. L'Oreille had finally made contact with Pierre. Apart from some minor burns on their hands, he and Albertini were safe, but the main worry was that the entire latest load had been destroyed in the fire. All their equipment had gone as well, and the *flics* had been there already, searching through the smouldering remains of the cottage for evidence.

Artyom's mind was darting all over the place, but he suddenly heard his father's voice warning him that people who played with fire usually ended up being burned. He hadn't heard that voice for a very long time, but it seemed rather apt given the circumstances.

'Did you settle with them?' asked Pierre quietly.

'What do you take me for? I've settled with them every time.'

'Them' were François Spirito and Paul Carbone, who ruled the docks of Marseille. When they were younger, they had smuggled opium themselves, but these days, they simply claimed a hefty commission for every load of opium smuggled through the docks from Beirut, making a handsome amount of money without having to dirty their own hands.

If there was nothing owing to them, then they weren't responsible for the fire. But L'Oreille and Pierre had both warned Artyom that, for some months now, a rival gang had been trying to encroach on Spirito and Carbone's patch, and that Lolole and Meme Corse were becoming a force to be reckoned with. Several men had already lost their lives. Pierre had told him that in the little Vatican, a part of the Old Port which was like a city within a city, and which had been ruled by Spirito and Carbone for years – the atmosphere was tense.

Barely a month before, one of François Spirito's nephews had been stabbed in his eye outside the Nautique Club. Reprisal had been swift and savage. Tempers were running high, and it was only a matter of time until there was an all-out war, from which only one gang could emerge victorious, after which everything would settle down again. In the meantime, this fire was most likely a message to Artyom that he had picked the wrong side. Artyom knew that without the protection of one or other of the gangs, his business was totally impossible. It was a dangerous place to be.

Zepherine had come in to the study, but he half turned his back to her.

'I'll come down the day after tomorrow.'

Pierre asked why he couldn't come sooner.

'I can't. I have things to attend to here in Paris. But I'll be there the day after tomorrow. I promise.'

Zepherine watched him as he hung up.

'What?' he asked, his mind racing.

'Are you really going to try and claim that there's nothing going on?'

When she didn't receive an answer, Zepherine flounced out. Artyom sat down quietly, to try and clear his thoughts. He was still sitting there when morning broke, the image of the cottage going up in flames before his eyes, and all his dreams with it.

15.

To Bruno's great disappointment, the new baby was a girl, whom they named Clara. He and Alyosha went to a bar called Bauer, on the corner of Friedrichstrasse, to celebrate, along with four or five of Bruno's colleagues from the hospital. From there, they then went on to watch the bicycle racing at Plötzensee, where Bruno became very sentimental, and told Alyosha how much his little girls meant to him. He spoke of his love for 'my Larissa', and how he would be lost if something happened to her. He had slung his arm around Alyosha's shoulder, and it remained there, like a dead weight.

'There's nothing I ought to know, is there?' he whispered in his ear.

'Know about what?'

'You're in the house for most of the day. Don't look so clueless…'

Bruno squeezed his shoulder.

'You'd tell me? Hmmm? Man to man?'

'Why? What do you think is going on…?

'I don't think anything is going on, I'm only asking…'

'Well, no, of course…'

'So, there's nothing going on? You're sure?'

Alyosha was feeling increasingly uncomfortable, and was glad when Bruno let the subject drop. That night, he came to the conclusion that he had probably overstayed his welcome. It was time he stopped imposing on his cousin. He was used to living his own life, and he was starting to miss his freedom.

16.

Artyom instructed the chauffeur to park in the shade of one of the warehouses, and to wait for him. He walked past the seamen's hostels and the offices for sailors looking for a passage, and made his way to the Stockholm. From the babel at the bar, he was greeted by Doña Rosa, the strapping Spanish woman who ran the place with her son, Camilo José. He was not quite sixteen ounces to the pound, but was perfectly pleasant until his temper was up. Then, he became a murderous lunatic, and would snort like a pig as he stamped a man's head to porridge.

The beauty of the Stockholm as a meeting-place was that it was completely safe. Doña Rosa was discretion itself, wise as the three wise monkeys. As for the clientele, even if they over-heard something incriminatory, by the time the job was done, the potential witness would be safely back on his ship on the other side of the world. How were the *flics* to find witnesses, when there were no witnesses to be had?

The little man arrived. He pulled up a chair and Artyom lit his cigarette. L'Oreille didn't have much good news. Spirito and Carbone had decided to teach a lesson to the leader of the dockers' trade union, Jean Carré, in order to keep him in line. A man was sent round to his house and gave his wife and children a good scare, but this proved a miscalculation. Carré, far from being cowed, saw red, and vowed that Spirito and Carbone would pay dearly for threatening his family. Jean Carré ruled over four thousand men, so it was really not a good idea to cross him. The word was that he was going to throw in his lot with Lolole and Meme Corse. There was another rumour, as yet unconfirmed, that two of Spirito and Carbone's inner circle, seeing the way the wind was blowing, had already sailed on a whaler bound for Newfoundland.

'You can be away for eighteen months to two years at a time on those whalers,' said L'Oreille in his light cynical way. 'By the time you're back home, things will have calmed down, and everybody will have forgotten the reason you went away in the first place. Mind you, it's a rubbish job. You'll only get desperate men on a boat like that. You're almost bound to lose a couple of toes, or fingers – or your mind – because it's so fucking cold.'

'What do you think the outcome will be?' Artyom inquired.

'Spirito and Carbone are on borrowed time. Everybody knows that. If you want to carry on, and I know you do, you don't have much choice but to go the other lot and hear their terms.'

Artyom left the bar feeling unsettled. Quite aside from his business troubles, he was still feeling peevish about Zepherine, who was being ridiculously quarrelsome, reproachful and jealous. If he so much as looked at another woman, she'd accuse him of wanting to get into her underclothes. More often than not, of course, he did. But what business was that to her, he fumed, as long as he kept her in luxury, fed her, clothed her, and made sure not to humiliate her by being relatively discreet? That was how practically every other man of Artyom's acquaintance arranged things, and their wives didn't complain one bit.

He had promised her he would be back home by the weekend, but he was already dreading it, as he knew it would drag interminably; two long days of Zepherine being sulky, picking fights, hurling accusations, then long hours of moody silence. It would be unbearable. And what in God's name had he done to deserve such treatment? He couldn't win. The more attention and presents he gave, the kinder he was to her, the more suspicious she became. Now that she had made her mind up he had somebody else, whatever he did, he couldn't win.

He dined alone at the hotel that evening, but then, still restless, went for a walk, and ended up at a bar nursing a cognac. A slogan painted on the wall opposite in red announced that Europe's crisis was the world's crisis. On a whim, he took a taxi to the seventh *arrondissement*, just beneath the basilica of Notre-Dame de la Gare, to a three-storey house with roses growing around the doorway. He took hold of the lion-head door knocker and knocked three times. The maid ushered him in, and Mila, a tall, thin woman in her late thirties, stood up to greet him, taking his hands and kissing him on both cheeks. She welcomed him back, and told him it had been a while since they'd last seen him, but she never forgot a face.

'What brings you back to Marseille? Or shouldn't I ask?'

'Business.'

'Business is a good thing.'

Artyom agreed that business was a good thing.

'When business falls off, that's when we all need to worry.'

Mila liked to speak in clichés. She was thoroughly venal, but would pepper her conversation with all kinds of sentimentality.

The room smelled of beeswax polish and strong tobacco. Two or three men were sitting at the bar, smoking and talking loudly, but the four or five girls around them weren't saying much. One of the men, in a dark-blue velvet jacket, turned to look at him, then turned back to the girl at his side. Artyom remembered the curved bar; it hadn't changed a bit. The last time he was here, some old codger had tried to teach Mila's little spaniel to dance on its two hind paws as he sang a sea-shanty to it. It had been such a comical sight, everybody had been roaring. He'd laughed so hard, he'd very nearly wet himself.

He was introduced to the girls who were in the house that night, and picked the redhead, who took him upstairs.

Bed, chair, a basin and a jug of water. Paulina was from Bratislava, and didn't have a word of French. She had some German though, and with lots of gesturing and a few common words, they understood each other as much as they needed to. After she undressed, she undressed him, folding his clothes neatly on the chair. He felt like a child again. Naked, he lay back on the bed and mused idly on how monotonous and constant his desire was. The girl poured a glassful of cold water and a glassful of hot, and put them on the small bedside table. She knelt between his thighs. She worked the tip of her tongue over his body, starting slowly under his chin, moving over his chest, his stomach. Every now and again, she'd take a sip, so that she could lick the water slowly over his skin, until his flesh was tingling. But when she swallowed his erection in a mouthful of hot water, his willpower dissolved. He couldn't resist her, and he emptied himself into her mouth.

17.

The next day, Artyom left a message at the Artistic Bar for the two Corsican brothers, as L'Oreille had instructed. He then returned to his hotel room to wait for an answer. It was late in the afternoon before a knock came on the door. Zampa's hairline was receding, and what was left was streaked with grey, but there was the same old sly look in his eyes. He told Artyom that Lolole Corse would meet him at the Cave de Falcion at eight o'clock that night. He left, and Artyom closed the door. He remembered the messenger well from the days of importing his brother-in-law's arms through Marseille, during the war. At that time, Zampa, an Italian by extraction, though brought up in Nice, drove a motor lorry for the Trois Canards gang, and a rough lot they were. It was said they were the first thieves to wear balaclavas, though the only reason for that, Zampa had told him once, had been to keep themselves warm as they drilled through the wall of an icy cellar to the bank next door.

Wearing balaclavas then become the thing for a while, even in summer, when they made the skin sweaty and itchy. Thieves were never very original, and stealing and smuggling were as much at the mercy of fashion as any other human activity. If one gang thought of an idea for a new scam, within no time every other gang would follow suit, which, Artyom supposed, made the police's work that much easier.

Promptly, at eight o'clock, Artyom walked into the Cave de Falcion, where he was directed to a private room at the back. Lolole, drinking pastis, gestured towards the chair opposite.

'I understand your brother, Meme, is standing for election?' Artyom asked, after some small talk about fishing, Lolole's favourite pastime.

Yes, he was, in Zicavo, answered Lolole. An uncle, their mother's brother, was the councillor for Zicavo, which was a very primitive place. But then Corsica was a primitive island, as well as parochial – everybody knew each other, which was a virtue in many ways.

Lolole's French was thick with the accent of the south of the island, so it was not always easy to understand what he was saying. He was a short, swarthy man, in corduroy trousers and blue braces over a white sleeveless tennis shirt. He was running to fat, and he had a wattle, which shook like jelly on a saucer when he laughed. His breathing was short and shallow, and he kept his mouth open, the lower lip slack, as if to catch some extra air. He had two days' growth of beard on his cheeks, and his face was brown as a walnut, which made the whites of his eyes appear all the whiter. Artyom could smell the sun on his skin, and the grey of Paris on his own. As Lolole drained his glass of pastis, Artyom noticed a tattoo on his wrist – an aquamarine mermaid with the head of a red serpent and a black tongue.

Lolole told him that his brother had addressed a large open-air meeting at Bonifaccio a few days previously, and had received a warm welcome. But, fighting an election was an expensive business.

'I'd be happy to make a contribution to the war chest.'

Lolole, his eyes as hard as two rosary beads, said he was sure that Meme would be very grateful. After their glasses were refilled, he went on to say that he and Meme admired Artyom for showing a little imagination. That was in scant supply in Marseille these days. Although he was perfectly courteous on the surface, Artyom knew it was a veneer which hid violence and lies.

'Why did you burn my laboratory, then? Couldn't you have talked to me first?'

He denied that they were responsible for the arson. Spirito and Carbone did all sorts of things to other men – men like Artyom, who were paying them commission – and then spread the rumour that it was the two brothers from Corsica who were responsible. But the tactic was backfiring on them. Everybody knew the truth.

'The *flics* want us to put a stop to this crap. We will too.'

Artyom didn't have much confidence in this explanation but he had made up his mind.

'I'm an honest man, and I keep to my word. If you deal fairly with me, I'll deal fairly with you,' he said.

'Then we can do business together.'

Once they had negotiated the commission payable on every load, the atmosphere relaxed. Lolole even gave him some advice, telling him that he'd have no bother from them or the *flics*, but his own men would be the problem. Not right now, but within a year or two, as they vied among each other for power within his organisation.

L'Oreille and his three.

Pierre and his two.

Albertini and his problem with the bottle.

Did he know about that?

Artyom didn't, but said that he did.

'I've seen it a thousand times. The more money they'll see flowing through their fingers, the greedier they'll become.'

As Artyom rose to leave, he said. 'I'm glad we've come to an understanding. And thank you for the advice.'

Lolole wished him well, but he didn't offer to shake his hand.

18.

Alyosha had rented a hovel of a room for himself in Rüdersdorf, but paying for it was the problem. Being a foreigner in Berlin didn't help, and everywhere Alyosha went, he was told, 'If we had anything we'd give it to our own people first.'

He persevered. He was willing to do anything: sell newspapers from a kiosk, be a messenger boy, factory work – he didn't mind how lowly, he just wanted some sort of wage in his hand at the end of the week. He even tried for a job as a vacuum-cleaner salesman, commission only, but they said the housewives wouldn't trust a foreigner. Eventually, he was taken on at the Palast Hotel on Leipziger Platz, for three hours every afternoon, to scrape the burns off the bottom of saucepans with a knife, before scouring them clean until they shone. It needed strong arms, but not much more, and it was monotonous work. The only reason he was taken on at all was because the rest of the kitchen staff were reluctant to do such a thankless task. Scraping the burns off saucepans was even worse than having to peel a sackful of potatoes.

He also found some tutoring work, though again, it was only for a couple of hours a week, and not enough to make a livelihood. Worse still, the woman he taught was such a bad student, it was all he could do not to show his impatience. She simply could not grasp Russian grammar, and even conjugating a regular verb was beyond her, never mind the exceptions. He came to dread the weekly session, and, as he approached her house one evening, under a cloudy, storm filled sky, between one lamp post and the next, something came over him, and he turned on his heel and ran for his life.

Then, he stopped turning up at the hotel as well, and began to feel very low. He knew he was in danger of spiralling into hopelessness. Some days, he couldn't even get out of bed, and lay there all day, too listless to dress or wash himself. He went out less and less, and when he did, he felt snappy and irritable. Seeing healthy, happy people going about their day made him feel all the more inadequate.

When he looked in the mirror, the face staring back at him was pallid and thin. He could feel his ribs, as by now he was surviving on one meal a day. He felt weak, and was constantly famished, taking any opportunity that came his way to stuff his face, though he avoided his cousins, because he still had some pride, and he didn't want them to see him so down on his luck. Eventually, just when things were so bleak he thought he might actually die of starvation, he found a job selling cigarettes in the Mexico nightclub on Geisbergstraasse.

19.

As he lit his cigar for him, Alyosha could see the surprise grow on Baron von Haumer's bulging face in the light of the flame. He pulled in his chin and corked his monocle into his eye socket, and prodded Alyosha back so that he could look at him properly. The Baron proceeded to look him over minutely, but there were no two ways about it. He recognised him from the Hotel Adlon days of old, and it was more than he could do to hide his surprise at finding the son of Fyodor Mikhailovich Alexandrov, of all people, working as a cigarette boy in a nightclub. He promised to try and set him on his feet: 'I'll do my very best for you my boy, don't you worry,' he said, his voice slurring with emotion.

Alyosha's hopes were high for a few days, but, unbeknown to him, by lunchtime the next day, when the Baron's headache had cleared, all that remained of the previous night's conversation was a hazy memory of talking with somebody from the old days, the man's name completely eluding him.

The Mexico was housed in a low-ceilinged, long and narrow cellar. All along the walls were rows of small red lamps, which threw little pools of weak light onto the rose wallpaper and the red leather banquettes. The management had been at pains to create an intimate and stylish ambience, in order to attract a better class of clientele – people like Freiherr von Cramm, who liked to order jeroboams of champagne for his handsome entourage. They would sit huddled together like a nest of kittens, talking boisterously and smoking heavily, enveloping themselves in a fug of hashish smoke. Apart from his house in town, von Cramm also owned a place in the country, in Freienwalde, on the edge of the marshlands of the Oder, with the woody hills of the Märkische Schweiz nearby. Whenever there was a full moon, they'd all go out there, strip, and have an orgy. So went the rumour, at least. One Saturday night, after the Mexico shut, Alyosha was invited to go with them. He went expectantly, but was disappointed, as all they did was listen to jazz records on the gramophone, dance a little, and drink and smoke a lot.

One evening, a former mistress of his stepfather, Alexei

Alexeivich Dashkov, swept down the staircase of the Mexico, in a black-and-white strapless silk dress split to the thigh, and high-heeled red shoes. Svetlana Gosovska was the actress who had made his mother demented with jealousy back in Berlin, but, by now, even she was not in the first flush of youth, though she looked much younger than most women of thirty-five. Her hair was now a honey-blonde colour, with one little curl artfully falling over her eye. She was accompanied by an old general from the Kaiser's army, who limped, leaning heavily on the gold hilt of his walking-stick, and they were with another couple, Hermann Goering and his wife, Carin. Alyosha overhead them speaking enthusiastically about the performance of *Parsifal* they had just seen at the Deutsches Opernhaus. A bottle of champagne was placed in its ice bucket by their table, as Svetlana mischievously tickled her lover under his chin.

They raised their glasses, and the four of them smiled broadly as the flash lamp popped, illuminating their dark corner like lightning in a cave. Miss Gosovska had strong, good teeth, white and straight, very evident when she laughed, and there was plenty of laughter from her table that night. Goering bought two packets of cigarettes from Alyosha's tray, and told him to keep the change. The actress didn't notice him. All her attention was for the General. As Alyosha wavered, not sure whether to introduce himself or not, he saw somebody else who diverted his attention, but he couldn't get a good look at her before she disappeared out of sight up the stairs.

20.

On his return to Paris, Artyom called on Madame Prideaux. As they often did, they played a game of cards in her small back parlour, where one or two of her favoured customers were lolling.

She had opened a bottle of Haut-Brion, her favourite red wine. Madame Prideaux was a courteous woman, careful to ask after everybody's health and spirits.

'Whatever happened to that boy? What was his name?'

'Who are you talking about?' asked Artyom.

'Your nephew,' replied Madame Prideaux.

'Alexei Fyodorovich?'

'Yes, him. Don't you remember? You brought him here with you once. When he had just arrived from Berlin, it must be a few years ago now. And then he came again, on his own.'

'I haven't seen him in a long time.'

'Why?'

'It's rather a long story, but to make it short, he never forgave me for helping his mother get rid of some maid who was after his money.'

'There's nothing new under the sun.'

'He was besotted with her. Couldn't see through her. His mother and I got rid of Grete for his own good.'

'He'll thank you for it one day. I hope he's well.'

'No idea,' answered Artyom cheerfully, striking a match.

It was only after the last customer had left that they got down to business. The door was locked, and the table cleared to make room for some thousands of francs to be counted. Once that was done, Artyom, as always, settled her commission.

This was an arrangement which suited them both down to the ground. After every load reached Paris from Marseille, on a 'Pastis de Marseille' company motor lorry, usually, the heroin would be distributed from the Orphans' Friend's warehouse to a network of dealers all over the city. The money would then be collected by two young boys and delivered to Madame Prideaux, after which Artyom would call by to count the takings.

'It won't be possible for you to have the use of this place for much longer, Artyom.'

The *Sûreté* was his first thought.

'What? Are the police threatening to raid?'

'When I keep such a well-ordered house?' She pretended to be shocked at such an idea. 'The very thought, Artyom. No, but it's like this. This place has changed hands.'

This was news. 'When did this happen? Who's buying?'

'Somebody from Algeria, only he lives here, in Marseille. A Frenchman, naturally. I'd hate to think of some old Arab getting his dirty paws on this place.'

Did she know the name of the buyer?

She didn't. But he didn't want her and the girls there as his tenants, so she'd have to shut up shop.

'You won't have a problem finding alternative premises, though, will you?'

'That's just it. I've decided to retire. I've plenty of money thanks to you and the girls, and I'm getting too old for these late nights. I was thinking of moving out of Paris. But where will *you* go is the question.'

Artyom felt in his bones that the two Corsican brothers were behind this. The buyer from Algeria was just a frontman. Lolole and Meme Corse were placing their shadow over him, as much as to say that they had him in their sights, and could control him like a puppet. He'd heard enough from L'Oreille and Pierre to know that the Corsicans didn't so much smash the competition in Marseille as take it over. They had realised long ago that conflict was best avoided, and picking quarrels with people only led to the *flics* poking their noses in places where they shouldn't. That did nobody any good.

Artyom knew he wouldn't be able to cheat the Corsicans out of one franc, and he also knew they'd insist on coming in as full partners. He'd be sharing even more of his profit with them in the end, and he didn't want that to happen, because he was already paying them handsomely. But he could feel their fingers tightening around his throat.

21.

She was sitting on one of the high bar stools at the Mexico. He peered at her through the low light and thick smoke; her hair was a different colour, she seemed thinner, and there was something nervy about her, which made him think he might have made a mistake. He took another look at her bony shoulders and back, but when he approached her, he saw that it was definitely Galina.

Her eyes lit up when she saw him. 'Alyosha!' she squealed, and kissed both his cheeks and hugged him. She told him she'd been living in Berlin for almost three months already, after deciding there had been nothing to keep her in Paris. Alyosha asked her who was looking after Roksana.

'She's better off with her father.'

There was an awkward silence, which Alyosha broke by asking after her father and Duchess Lydia.

'They're well, thank you. They're married now.' She smiled. 'It's so lovely to see you again.'

She insisted that she was done with Montmartre, and done with cocaine. She'd also finished with Camlo, and was determined to start living her life again.

'I've made such a fool of myself, you wouldn't believe…'

Rather like Alyosha, she'd come to Berlin because, after spending a few years there at the beginning of the 1920s, she knew it as well as she knew anywhere.

'I want to make something of myself this time…'

She told him that she had tried her best to do that in Paris, and, for a while, had done very well selling perfume at Galeries Lafayette.

She sipped her drink. 'You would have laughed if you could have seen how I made a show of myself – I was well worth seeing.'

She'd won the award three times for Perfume Salesgirl of the Month. The manager, Monsieur Girard, had placed a blue sash over her shoulder, to wear all week, with the accolade printed on it in red letters. And she was allowed a small bottle of perfume for herself.

'Whatever takes your fancy, regardless of the price, you choose.'

That's what Monsieur Girard had said to her, his breath smelling of garlic, as he'd batted her behind. He was a notoriously lecherous manager, and his female staff all tried their best to keep out of reach of his groping hands if possible. She had chosen an Eau de Cologne on each occasion. She loved to spray a fine mist of it over her body, and the smell always reminded her of her aunt, Lazarevna Petrovna, whom Galina had always admired from when she was a small girl, because she was such a picture of sophistication.

Her sales figures had been so good, it had made the other girls jealous, and a few of them were real bitches, and had said terrible things about her behind her back, and to her face too.

Her high spirits seemed to drain away.

Her tone changed again, as she told him how much she loved acting – she loved it more than anything else in the world. Ever since she had been given that tiny part in his mother and stepfather's film, her greatest ambition was to be able to make a living as an actress.

'Do you remember me in it?'

He told her that he did.

'You're such a bad liar!' She slapped his arm playfully. 'You don't remember me acting at all, admit it.'

'I do have a faint memory of you…'

In the first half of the picture, she reminded him, she was standing in a group of aristocrats who were escaping from Russia. She was more or less at the front, only there was another princess, a cousin to the Tsar, standing in front of her – a rather wide woman in a tent of a frock, and there she'd been, on tiptoe trying to peep past her shoulder. But then some bad-tempered assistant, with a cap and a megaphone, had insisted she keep to her mark, which was chalked on the floor of the studio. And did Alyosha remember the other scene, where they were all doing their best to push their way onto the ship at Yalta, and everybody in a panic, shoving each other out of the way? She was in that one, too, in the crowd on the quayside, and she'd had to shout at the top of her voice, like this: and she placed her palms against her temples and opened her mouth in a wide silent scream.

'Do you remember the horses? They were properly wild! That was such a dramatic scene I thought. When Alexei Alexeivich killed the Bolsheviks, and they all dropped like flies at his feet? Dozens of them – wasn't he brave? He was such a handsome man, I was so jealous of your mother, the lucky woman. Then, there was one other scene – when I was in the nightclub in Istanbul. Now, what was it called, d'you remember?'

In his mind's eye, he saw his mother's naked back, and the dribble of saliva at the corner of her mouth.

'Do you remember me in that one?' she looked at him expectantly. 'In the nightclub in Constantinople?'

'Hmmm?'

'Alyosha! Are you listening to me?'

He suddenly looked at her and said, 'You were sitting at one of the tables—'

'Yes I was! Watching couples dancing the foxtrot. I was dressed like a princess from the Tsar's court, with rings and a necklace and earrings, but I was sad, because I'd lost my entire family and was living far from home. "Look sadder." That's what Alexei Alexeivich told me. That was one of only two times he spoke to me. "You're not sad enough. You need to look sadder!" And then, after we'd finished, he came over, and do you know what else he said?'

Alyosha was aware that the back of his neck was becoming damp with sweat under the strap of his cigarette tray.

'That I acted a sad person very well. That I was the best saddest person he'd ever seen.'

She looked rather lost and empty. A middle-aged man came

up to Alyosha and bought a packet of cigarettes from him. Then Alyosha remembered the name of the nightclub in Istanbul. It was called the Rose Noire.

'The Rose Noire. You're right! What a good memory you have.'

Galina was buoyant again, and asked him if he could introduce her to anybody in the film industry. She'd heard that the Mexico was very popular with actors, producers and directors, especially at the weekends, and that's why she'd come, in the hope of making some contacts.

'Svetlana Gosovska was here earlier in the week,' he told her.

'No, really? How I'd love to be like her.'

Alyosha promised if he ever had the opportunity, he'd do his best for her.

'Thanks, Alyosha. You're a love,' and she placed a feathery kiss on his forehead. 'You know I think the world of you. My parents told me years ago that I should have married somebody like you...'

He felt rather sorry for her.

'Never too late, you know,' she said and took a sip of her cocktail through a straw. 'Why are you smiling?' Galina tweaked his nose. 'I'm serious. Instead of marrying those two fools, I should have married you. You'd have made a far better husband.'

'*Two* fools? You remarried?'

'Yves. The bank clerk, remember? After Marcel finally agreed to a divorce. Unfortunately for me... and him.'

Not that she missed him. But she missed Roksana.

22.

Alyosha didn't see Galina Andreyevna for a while after that. When she next came in, on a Saturday night towards the end of the month, her eyes were rolling, her hair was untidy, and her make-up looked as though she'd put it on in the dark. She ordered a Martini, and then she wandered around aimlessly. The club was busy and full, and Alyosha was kept too occupied selling cigarettes to keep an eye on her. But, when things became a little quieter and he was allowed to take his break, he looked for her, and saw her sitting in one of the booths, her hand on Baron von Haumer's thigh. On a whim, seeing the adjoining booth was empty, he went to sit and eavesdrop. Galina was in the middle of telling the Baron about something that had happened to her in Russia… How hundreds upon hundreds had died of typhus on the way from Petrograd to Kiev, when the Reds had the upper hand… The train journey to Kiev alone had taken almost a month, and then another month to reach Odessa… Her father like a ghost, his hopes failing, and his will to escape becoming weaker by the hour. His greatest concern, though, had been for her and her little baby…

Little baby? Alyosha was all attention now because Galina didn't have a baby back then – what on earth was she talking about?

The Whites had been fighting the Reds in Vladikavkaz, so there hadn't been any boats to take the fugitives, and nowhere to stay. In the end, after many difficulties, her father had managed to rent half a room for a small fortune, from some old peasant who made her living by making kefir from goat's milk in her half of the room. There had been only one bed, and Galina and her mother had slept in it, with the baby girl between them. Alyona, the child, had been healthy for the moment, but they'd lived in fear that she would fall prey to typhus or cholera, as everything around them had been so unsanitary and squalid. One night, after they had gone to sleep, they'd been awoken by furious hammering on doors, and voices warning that the Red Army were on their way, and people should leave at once. Galina and her parents had thrown their things into their bags, but when they'd arrived at the station, Galina had realised she didn't have any water for the baby. She'd left Alyona with her parents, and run to the station tap, but it had been dry. Then, the whistle had blown, and so she'd squeezed her way onto the nearest carriage instead of fighting her way through the throng of people to where her parents were. But they had uncoupled half the train, and she'd realised with mounting horror that her parents and baby girl were in the front half, which was starting to pick up speed as it travelled down the track.

She'd been left behind.

She'd had no option but to walk along the track, trusting that the train would not go far before coming to a halt at a siding or the next station. Sure enough, half dead with fatigue after walking some twenty miles with no food or water, she'd caught up with the train where it had come to a standstill at a small station. However, her troubles had only just been beginning. Her parents had fallen ill with typhoid, and they'd had to bribe their way into a hospital. Galina had had to nurse them herself, as most of the staff had fled. Her milk had dried up, and she'd been unable to nurse Alyona, so she'd found a wet nurse locally, and given the child into her care.

Sadly, her mother had died, but her father had miraculously recovered, and, as soon as he had grown strong enough, they'd gone to fetch Alyona in order to resume their journey. The second Galina had seen Alyona's dear little face, her cheeks, her lips, her hair, all her troubles had temporarily melted away. But the woman had refused to give up the baby. She was Ingush, so they'd not had much common language, but she'd managed to convey to Galina that Alyona had fallen ill and died, and that this was not her baby. Galina had known the woman was telling lies – she recognised her own baby. Her father had taken what little money he'd had, and offered it to the woman for the return of the child, but the woman had just shaken her head, steadfastly maintaining that the baby was hers, and that her name was Aabish.

'She's my baby,' Galina had sobbed, 'and her name is Alyona.'

The woman had gone into her house, and returned with Alyona's clothes, blanket and rag doll, and given them to Galina, then gestured for them to follow her. She'd led them along a path which went through a cherry orchard, at the far end of which had been a little mound of earth on a small grave. Galina had knelt, and the sound of her heart breaking could be heard all through the sky. But, from that day to this, she was none the wiser whether her daughter was dead or alive.

23.

'You have to help me,' Galina begged him through her sobs. 'Alyosha, you're the only one I can turn to.' Her real story spilled out: she had left Paris in order to escape her debts, but her biggest problem had followed her all the way to Berlin. 'And now he says he wants to kill me… Those were his exact words… And if Camlo says he wants to kill somebody, that's usually exactly what he does. You have no idea what he's like.'

'Here, take this to wipe your nose…'

'Thank you. I went to the doctor yesterday. He makes my flesh crawl, but I never have to pay him, not if I…' She stuffed the handkerchief up her sleeve. '…and he told me I have syphilis. Can you believe it?

'*Syphilis?*'

Galina laughed through her tears. 'That's exactly how I said it too… *Syph-ilis?*' She wiped her tears with her sleeve. '"Are you sure?" That was the next question I asked him.'

The doctor didn't want his usual payment, so it was a safe bet he was sure.

She was warned, in no uncertain terms, to stop working at once – never mind what her pimp said – until she was better. '"You don't treat something like this lightly". That's what he said, the pig.'

That was all very well, but Camlo wouldn't see it like that. He'd lose his temper when he heard, and beat her black and blue. She was in no doubt of that. 'Doesn't matter what the doctor says, Camlo will make me work all the same.'

'Not if you're ill.'

'I won't have a choice, Alexei.'

Alyosha suspected another reason: if Galina refused to work, then Camlo would withhold the little bags of white powder.

'This is all his fault. He's the one who forces me…' she sniffed.

'You have to leave him. You don't have a choice.'

She gave a weary smile. 'I've already tried. Why else do you think I came back to Berlin? From choice? But it doesn't matter where I run to. Name any city, any country in the world, sooner or later, Camlo will be sure of finding me, no matter how far I go.'

24.

When the club doors were locked at half-past four in the morning, Alyosha felt he had no choice, and told Galina she could stay with him that night. As they walked back through the fine rain, she slipped her arm through his and said, 'You know I still dream about love?' She could always find the energy to discuss herself, even when she was exhausted. 'Do you Alyosha?'

'I'm not sure.'

'I long to feel those emotions you only have when you're in love, because they're the only ones I value. From when I was a little girl, as far back as I can remember, I learnt how to treat men. Perhaps I learnt it at my mother's knee. Every time Mother wanted something new, a dress, or something for the house, she'd always be especially sweet to my father when he came home from the bank. She usually got her way. Later on, I learnt about the advantages of going to bed with men, even though I didn't quite understand what I was doing half the time, or the effect it had on some of them. I only married Marcel in order for Yves to realise what he was missing. Instead of holding back, keeping him at arm's length, until his desire for me drove him wild, I just gave myself to him without winning any advantage. As for Camlo, he just played with me.'

They waited for an empty tram to rattle by before crossing the square.

Alyosha was practically asleep on his feet.

'Are you listening to me?'

'Mmmm–hmmm…'

'Sure?' She nudged him with her hip. 'Or are you just humouring me?'

'No, no. Carry on, I'm listening.'

'I'm so afraid. Afraid of what will become of me, Alyosha. Afraid of people. Afraid of Camlo.'

'We all live with regrets.'

'You've no idea how much I long for somebody to fill my life with love. Proper love. I can't bear to be on my own. I loathe my own company. The thought of growing old by myself like my Aunt Lazarevna terrifies me.'

He wearily unlocked the door and ushered her in. His room in Rüdersdorf wasn't much. 'You take the bed. I'll sleep on the floor.'

Alyosha remembered the morning when he'd first walked into this room – how empty and bare it had been, with just the iron bedstead, wardrobe, and a rough wooden table and chair. The threadbare carpet had smelled stale and sour, and the cat's hair over everything had made his nose itch until he started to sneeze.

Even in an empty room, traces of other people's lives remained. At the bottom of the wardrobe, there had been a pile of newspaper cuttings, including some reports of Soviet Union aviation breaking the record for flying over the Arctic. He'd also found a postcard from a girl called Zelda, addressed to 'V.' She'd written that she wasn't ready to leave Mannheim, and that she needed more time to think about their marriage. The picture on the front had been of a municipal park with ornamental fountains.

Alyosha had mused over the short message. Had V taken a train to Mannheim to find Zelda and convince her to give him a second chance? Or had she come back to him? Were they still married? Alyosha could only speculate. He'd read the card several times, before pinning it on the wall by his bed, the short sentences like the bones of some short story, one of thousands like it.

25.

At last, Margarita was in a position to leave Bruno and Larissa's house for a small apartment of her own, on the third floor of a block in Neukölln. Her commute to the Aznefttrust office was shorter and easier, but by far the biggest advantage was not having to bite her lip continually in front of Bruno. Living under his roof had become too tiresome.

A host of other communists lived in the building, some of them employed at *Die Rote Fahne*. So, when Vicky sent Margarita a message that there was a rumour that SA Stormtroopers were going to attack the block that night, as cell leader, she called an emergency meeting at once to alert everybody. The news came as no surprise, as some nights previously, three gunmen of the *Roter Frontkampler Bund* – a group of armed communists – had driven past a beer cellar where the SA were holding a meeting, and had opened fire. Two Nazis had been killed and seven injured, two seriously. There had been almost forty in the meeting, and everybody was surprised more hadn't died. The attack was a retaliation for an earlier SA attack on a KPD cell.

More than a hundred and fifty RFB men came over to the block, and by eight o'clock, there were guards on every entrance. Others went up onto the roof, to keep a lookout.

As Margarita went downstairs to relay a message to the two at the front entrance, she came face to face with Kai-Olaf, who was bounding up the stairs with his customary energy, as though he had a dog at his heels. They hadn't seen each other for a while, as he had been away in Italy. Margarita invited him to her apartment, and he said he needed to see somebody else first, but that he would call after that. When Margarita returned to her apartment, Paul, the out-of-work printer, was sitting on his haunches looking at her shelf of books, running his thumb along their spines in an abstracted way. His little white mouse, Rosa, was running up and down his arm. He turned to look at her, and asked, 'Is anything happening?'.

'No, everything's quiet outside.'

'We're bound to hear them when they come. There's always some commotion around the SA.'

After a while, Kai-Olaf arrived and put his leather bag down on the small desk. He took off his cap and scratched his head. Margarita thought he looked tired. But she had long since learned that Kai-Olaf hated being questioned about his movements.

'Does it have to come to this? Don't you think it's all rather a mess?' he asked her.

'What choice do we have?' she replied, surprised at the despairing tone of his voice.

'Who's created this situation?' was his answer.

Was it wise to speak so plainly in front of Paul? Margarita could see that Kai-Olaf was agitated, and that he wanted to thrash something out.

'I want us all to speak honestly.'

'Speak as honestly as you like,' answered Paul. 'Nobody's stopping you.'

'You're not going to like what I have to say.'

'Perhaps you should let me be the judge of that.'

'Fine then. What are we in the KPD doing? Attacking the socialists in the SPD. Slandering them, insulting them, calling them fascists... instead of fighting shoulder to shoulder against the real fascists. I think our present policy makes absolutely no sense.'

Kai-Olaf told them he'd read a story in *Die Rote Fahne* about the Prussian *schutzpolizei* raiding the SA headquarters first thing one morning. They'd found half a dozen hand grenades, and an attic full of guns, bullets and knives. The SDP had been outspoken in their condemnation, and had called for a ban on the wearing of Nazi uniforms. Rather than congratulate them, what did *Rote Fahne* do? Ignore this utterly, and, worse than that, the headline the following day was still peddling the same old line, that the Social Democratic Party in Germany were encouraging the Nazis.

Paul left the bookshelf and came to sit by Margarita and Kai-Olaf.

'The Communist Party has a long-term policy towards the SPD,' said Margarita firmly. 'Why do we need to change that in the light of one small incident?'

'Because that one small incident shows perfectly clearly that the SPD are against the Nazis.'

'You seriously think that?' Paul challenged him.

'Yes I do,' Kai-Olaf said. 'Facts are facts.'

Margarita frowned.

'It depends how you interpret the facts,' she said. 'Surely I don't have to tell you that – you've preached it yourself often enough. What if the police raid was a ploy? Have you considered that? What if they were pretending to act in order to hide the fact that they're in cahoots with the Nazis?'

Kai-Olaf sighed quietly.

'Even if some of the SPD leadership are subjectively anti-fascist, to all intents and purposes, they think the same as the Nazis,' said Paul. 'I'd even go further—'

'—yes, yes, I know exactly what you're going to say next, I don't want to hear anymore—'

'—because they claim to be socialists, they're the most dangerous of all our enemies. They're so two-faced, so dishonest, so fucking hypocritical—'

'—because they split the working-class vote. So you say! So everybody says!' Kai-Olaf had raised his voice in frustration, 'If you repeat something like a prayer every day, every night, every week, every month, every year, then it becomes all too easy to swallow it unquestioningly. But I have a longer memory. Back in 1919, it was us, the KPD, the Communist Party – we were the ones who went our own way. We split from the socialists—'

'Don't let anybody else hear you talking like this, Kai-Olaf,' warned Margarita.

'Talking like this about what?' asked Vicky, who had just walked into the room, a cigarette in her mouth.

There was silence apart from Rosa pitter-pattering lightly along the bookshelf.

Paul shifted in his chair.

'Nothing,' said Kai-Olaf.

'What?' mouthed Vicky to Margarita.

She shook her head as Kai-Olaf walked to the window and stood there with his back towards them.

Vicky unbuttoned her loose coat. Hanging around her middle were four Dreyse semi-automatics and a brand new Walther. From the inside pockets, she brought out several rounds of bullets. She distributed the arms, and Paul, Margarita and Kai-Olaf took them to designated comrades in different parts of the building.

When Margarita returned, Vicky was rolling herself a cigarette by the window and keeping an eye on the square at the same time. From the corner of her eye, she noticed that the second drawer of her desk was slightly open – not very much, just a little proud compared to the others, but enough to tell her that it had been opened. Vicky kept her back to her as she puffed on her cigarette.

Kai-Olaf returned.

Margarita dimmed the lamp, and the three of them sat to wait. Every now and again, one of them would glance out of the window, where shadows thrown by the lights from the cafés along the sides of the square wove together to form an intricate pattern on the statue at its centre. They talked, but sporadically, as if they were all aware they needed to conserve their energies. Margarita couldn't help wondering if it was Vicky who had been rifling through her things. Or was it Paul? Or had that drawer always been like that?

Ever since the trip to the Soviet Union, there had been a subtle shift in her relationship with Vicky. If Margarita submitted an article, under a pseudonym, to *Die Rote Fahne*, Vicky would be very non-committal, or would come up with a reason why she hadn't read it. Even when a whole series of articles by Margarita was published in *Die Rote Fahne*, for which she received a fair amount of favourable comments by those who knew she was the author, Vicky didn't say a word. She acted as though she hadn't even seen the articles, let alone read them.

Margarita knew that practically nobody – apart from Paul, possibly – read *Die Rote Fahne* with as much attention as Vicky. She swallowed it up from cover to cover, and would quote articles on various subjects from three or four years previously. She had an astounding memory for minor details and obscure facts.

The three of them sat up all night. There was no attack, but it was a night of realisation for Margarita. She comprehended one very important thing which had been eluding her: this girl, once her closest friend, was no longer a friend at all. Vicky was jealous of her – jealous of the respect she was given, as well as her relationship with Kai-Olaf.

Margarita would need to be more careful from now on.

26.

Camlo didn't come looking for Galina as she feared. Why bother, when he knew full well that, sooner or later, she would come back to him, like a puppy looking for a pat?

So Galina stayed with Alyosha in his shabby room. She was filled with self-loathing, and hated her appearance: her thin face, the skin stretched so dry and taut it reminded her of a skull. Her mood was erratic, suddenly swinging from gay to tragic, so that he never knew how she would be from one hour to the next. She could spend hours lying in the dark in deepest despair, only to be thrown into hysteria when she claimed Camlo was outside at the window, waiting to strangle her in her sleep.

'If you come back and find me dead, you'll know who was here.'

Often, she would beg Alyosha not to leave her on her own.

'I have to go. I have work…'

'Alyosha, wait!' and she would stand against the door with her arms wide.

'Galina, I can't stay…'

She had constant nightmares, and would often wake screaming Roksana's name. Sometimes she called out for Yves. One night, she imagined her mother was standing at the foot of the bed in a petticoat, reproaching her for having neglected her father.

'Papa,' she sobbed, 'Papa, Papa...'

She tried to live without the snow. She promised Alyosha she was making an enormous effort, fighting with all her strength and willpower to break her addiction to the white powder. Then she would become vile-tempered, and beg Alyosha to bring back just a tiny amount with him from the Mexico. On one occasion, at the end of his tether, he gave in and asked the barman to ask his friend for some.

Then Alyosha returned from his shift, exhausted, in the early hours one morning, only to find his door bolted from the inside. Assuming Galina was sleeping, he knocked loudly on the door to wake her, so that she could let him in. When she eventually opened the door a few inches, she asked him to wait just a little; she was with somebody. Alyosha sat at the top of the stairs, his head against the cold wall, fuming. By and by, a pair of legs walked rapidly past his shoulder, disappearing into the gloom of the stairwell, leaving a faint trace of lavender soap behind him. Furiously, he returned to his room and told Galina exactly what he thought of her, without holding back at all. But, with the cocaine in her blood, she was unreachable...

When he came back to a bolted door for the third time, Alyosha told her she had to leave. She was making his life miserable, and he'd had quite enough of her tricks. He expected her to be out by the next day. When she started to plead with him, he interrupted her.

'I don't want to hear another word.'

'You can't just kick me out...Where will I go?'

'That's your problem.'

'I won't be safe anywhere else...'

In her little girl's voice, she begged him, 'Don't be so nasty to me... I can't help it... Remember what happened to me...'

At this he lost his temper utterly.

'You never left a baby behind in Russia!'

'Of course I did!'

'No you didn't! *I* told you that story back in Paris. It never happened to you. It happened to Marya, who worked in the kitchen at the Grand Cercle Muscovite. Don't you remember?'

'What are you talking about?'

'Galina, I can't decide if you know you're lying, or if you've actually convinced yourself this happened to you.'

'Of course I'm not lying! What a foul thing to suggest. Of course it happened to me!'

'Galina stop this. It happened to Marya. Alyona was her baby.'

Galina wept, but he felt nothing but fury at her.

'What am I going to do?'

'That is entirely your problem.'

Then, Alyosha was given seven days' notice by the landlord.

'I'm not in the business of renting rooms out to whores and their pimps,' he said bluntly when Alyosha protested.

'I don't have anywhere else to go.'

'There are plenty of places for people like you to do your filth, out on the street.'

Quite apart from her addiction to cocaine, at some level, she was also addicted to Camlo, which made her deaf to reason and full of self-delusion. She had made a fool of him from the very first. And now, because of her and Camlo, he would be homeless. Alyosha felt the chill of disillusionment, and hated himself for having been so naïve. He hated Galina, too, but there was something pitiful about her, which meant most of his hatred was reserved for her pimp. He tormented himself by imagining Camlo laughing at him for giving his whore shelter and a bed to work from. He whipped himself up to such a state that he became unable to think of anything but how these two had wronged him. He raged and roiled at the unfairness of it, and cursed himself for letting himself be taken for a ride.

He started to imagine ways of getting his own back. He enjoyed devising various scenarios which culminated in Camlo on his knees at his feet, begging for mercy. He imagined himself tying him up in a weighted sack and throwing him into the Spree, and the pleasure he would experience in watching him drown.

The urge to teach Camlo a lesson consumed him. One night, he slipped into the kitchens at the Mexico and stole one of the knives. The next day, at twilight, Alyosha made for Nollendorf Platz, his resolve mounting with every step. The wrong had to be put right. *Wrong put right, wrong put right*, he chanted to himself amidst the noise of the trams and the crowds. He didn't have to wait long before he saw the man himself coming from afar. Camlo was swaggering along in a short grey coat with an opossum collar, like a young squire walking his land on a fine evening of summer. He had changed a little since Alyosha had last seen him, leaning against his Cadillac coupé convertible in Montmartre. Although his hair was still rather long over his collar, and his fingers dripped with gold like the pimp that he was.

Alyosha watched as Galina and another girl went over to him. Camlo lit himself a cigarette as they talked. Alyosha crossed over the tarmac. He noticed the last rays of sunlight creating pools of weak light here and there. He felt himself being pulled nearer and nearer, until he was being sucked faster and faster, as if by some huge force, to a place where he didn't wish to be.

Galina screamed, and the other girl crouched down, wrapping her hands around her head. Alyosha watched the expressions sweep over Camlo's face: astonishment, horror, agony. He didn't let out a gasp. He didn't shed a tear. He didn't make a single sound. Alyosha let go of the knife, but it stayed exactly where he'd planted it.

He was wrestled down onto the pavement before he'd run more than a few yards.

27.

Harmonious relations had been restored between Zepherine and Artyom. Things went even better when he told her that he'd just booked a suite in the Hôtel Metropole, and that he'd arranged a birthday surprise for her while they were there. Although Zepherine pestered him, he refused to reveal what it was.

'But I don't have anything suitable to wear for Monte Carlo.'

This gave Zepherine and her sister, Avril, the perfect excuse to go on a spree, and they spent three solid days shopping, bundling bag after bag into the chauffeur's hands to pack away in the Rolls-Royce.

'Have you left anything for the rest of Paris?'

'The odd thing,' Zepherine giggled, holding a floral summer dress in front of her.

'Artyom?'

'What?'

She mouthed that she loved him.

He had just come home after being to see his optician, who had confirmed what he already suspected: that he was shortsighted in his right eye. Nevertheless, he was reluctant to start wearing spectacles.

'Your sight will only deteriorate.'

'Spectacles are for old people,' insisted Artyom as he got up from his chair.

The optician picked up a purple velvet case and opened it. 'Why don't you wear one of these?'

Inside was a monocle with a gold rim. Artyom picked it up between his thumb and finger and pressed it into his eye socket. He examined himself in the square mirror and decided it gave him a certain gravitas.

He wore it for Zepherine and asked her what she thought. She considered him carefully, her head to one side.

'Mmmm. Suits you.'

'You took a long time to decide.'

'It's just you remind me of someone…'

'Someone famous?'

'One of my… admirers when I was working for Coco Chanel.'

'Would I know him?'

'I shouldn't think so. He wasn't a very nice man, nowhere near as nice as you.'

Artyom smiled and kissed her.

Most of the luggage was sent on the train, along with Bibi and Karina and their nursemaids. But Artyom and Zepherine drove to Monte Carlo in a white open-topped tourer with a dazzling silver rim. They drove through fields full of riotous sunflowers, and crops of oats and barley which became riper the further south they travelled, the fields stretching away towards the horizon under the azure August sky. It was impossible not to be in good spirits, bowling along those open roads, under that glorious sun; impossible not to be light-hearted and carefree; impossible not to be happy in each other's company.

The Hôtel Metropole stood just a stone's throw from the Casino gardens. As she walked through the door, Zepherine felt like a girl on her honeymoon. Their suite was enormous, with Bibi and Karina and their nursemaids close to hand in their own room.

On their second day there, once Zepherine had gone shopping, Artyom called on Inessa. He had neglected to tell his wife that his sister was here, or that he had bought her an apartment.

His nephew, Georgik, ushered him in to a spacious white room, furnished with light, modern pieces. The glass doors leading to the balcony were flung wide open, and the dazzling water in the harbour beneath hurt his eyes with its brightness. Georgik was dressed all in white: white shirt, white trousers, and white plimsolls. Throughout the conversation, he turned the tennis racquet on his lap over and over. He had small pink ears, like the ears of a piglet, and his fair hair was cut very short. He was a very shy boy, and hunched his shoulders and mumbled, obviously finding it torture to be on his own with his uncle.

'Mama should be back before long.'

'Is she out for a walk?'

'She's gone to the station.'

The conversation died. There was a sound of splashing from somewhere.

'Nice view you have here. Have you and your mother settled in alright?'

'Yes, thank you, Uncle Artyom.'

'How's school? Your mother tells me you're doing well.' He sat on a chair opposite his nephew. 'High marks in all your exams, and doing better than most of the French boys, even though it isn't your mother tongue…'

Georgik blushed.

'Is that true then?' Artyom teased him. 'Or is your mother puffing you up?'

'I can barely speak Russian. Mama and I always speak French together.'

Artyom flicked away an ant which was scurrying over his knee. 'Have you heard anything from your older brother at all?'

'Not for ages.'

'Not a letter or anything?'

'Nothing.'

'No more have I. It's a pity how Alyosha has cut himself off from his family. After all, we're all that he has… the people who care about him.'

Georgik winced, and buried his personality deeper under layers of shyness.

'I know your mother worries terribly about him. Though we all have the right to live our own lives, I suppose.' He flicked another ant from his sleeve. 'If he insists on ploughing his own furrow, who are we to tell him differently? He's a grown man, after all.'

Artyom smiled at a sudden memory. 'I remember Christmas of 1916. I drove the whole way from Paris back home to Petrograd. You were just a baby back then.'

A shy smile crossed the boy's face.

'How old would you have been, Gosha?'

'Christmas 1916? I was barely a year old, Uncle Artyom.'

'And your brother? What would he have been? Twelve? Thirteen?'

'Thirteen.'

'Ah yes, thirteen.'

He shook his head in wonder. 'Thirteen! Good grief! So Alyosha must be... what? Twenty-six?'

'Almost.'

'Who would have thought? Doesn't time run away with us without us noticing? Still, it's all ahead of you, of course. You're a blank slate without a scratch yet, Gosha. Though this old world has a habit of leaving its scars on you quicker than you might imagine.'

The boy didn't find this line of talk very interesting, though he didn't have the gumption to change the subject.

'I must have a picture of Christmas 1916 somewhere. I photographed the entire family with a brand new camera. Your parents, grandparents, your brother. Everybody together. Have you seen it?'

The boy blushed again, even deeper this time, and shook his head.

'There was so much snow outside, it reflected the sun, and the light flooded into the house. Your grandparents... I don't suppose you even remember them? After the Revolution, they chose to stay in Russia, though I'd gone to considerable trouble in Paris to arrange visas for them – I had to pay quite a premium for them, with so many people trying their best to get their nearest and dearest safely out of Russia. My father was the problem, Changed his mind at the last minute. Home was his place, he said. At the time, I was furious. I remember sending them a rather peevish telegram. I know Mama would have come away in a heartbeat if it had been up to her. Your grandfather could be a stupid old fool at times.' He smiled. 'Mind you, he was a fine hunter in his day, loved to shoot wild ducks, in particular. When I was a boy, about the same age as you are now, I used to go out with him sometimes to Ladoga Lake. Just the two of us, spending whole afternoons lying on our stomachs in the rushes.'

Like most boys in their teens, Georgik didn't have the slightest interest in hearing this kind of reminiscing. Time gone by was time gone by. Another age, full of people he barely knew and people who were already dead. He found it all so boring. Artyom realised this and changed the subject.

'Look, as your mother isn't here…'

He held out a little grey parcel.

'Something for you. A very special gift from your old uncle, all the way from a little place I know about in Montmartre.'

He gave it to his nephew with a wink.

'Don't you mention a word to your mother mind. If she finds out, I'll swear till I'm blue in the face that it was nothing to do with me.'

He winked again.

'Thank you,' the boy answered insipidly.

'Aren't you going to open it?'

The door opened, and Inessa walked in with her fiancé.

'Gosha, my love, go and fetch me a glass of something cold before I expire. Tomya darling, you're here.'

They kissed each other's cheeks.

'Mmmm. You smell of the sun. Such a good smell. Did Georgik look after you? Gosha, I hope you made your uncle feel at home.'

'Yes Mama,' he answered meekly.

'What's that you're holding behind your back?'

'Nothing,' he mumbled, and went to fetch the drink.

'I'm sorry I wasn't here when you arrived, Artyom, but I'd already arranged to meet…'

She turned and gestured at the tall man by her side.

'Tomya, this is Philippe – Philippe, this is my brother, Artyom.'

They shook hands.

'It's a pleasure to meet you,' said Artyom.

'The pleasure really is all mine,' Philippe said. 'I've heard rather a lot about you.'

28.

'What? Your sister and her fiancé? *That's* your surprise?'

Zepherine was holding up a pair of earrings to her ears appraisingly.

'You've brought me all the way from Paris to Monte Carlo to spend the evening with them?' she pouted.

'Tomorrow is when I give you your surprise. Tonight, we're celebrating Inessa and Philippe's engagement.'

'I just hope this one is better than the last one. Why does she go for such awful types?'

'We don't know what type Philippe is.'

'What is she doing here, anyway?'

'I told you, celebrating her engagement.'

'Pah!'

'Why the scorn?' he raised his eyes from the *Carte Bécherel* he was reading naked on the bed.

'Your sister gets engaged more often than I change my stockings.'

Artyom caught a fleeting expression in her eyes: something between anger and a deep unhappiness.

'How many men has she been with since that idiotic husband of hers left her?'

'Remember that you're talking about my sister,' Artyom chided her. 'However foolish she may have been, she's my flesh and blood, and always will be.'

'She's not much of a sister to you,' Zepherine persisted. 'It's always you who has to rescue her out from whatever hole she's managed to dig herself into.'

She turned to face Artyom with one earring dangling and the other still in her hand.

'You haven't paid for her to stay at this hotel, I hope?'

He shut the book with a snap. He certainly wasn't going to admit that he'd bought his sister an apartment.

'Oh, Artyom, you're such a fool…'

'I haven't paid for her to stay in the hotel, no.'

'I'm not sure I believe you…'

There was a light knock on the door. Artyom wouldn't have bothered to throw a towel over his lap if Zepherine hadn't glared at him.

'Enter.'

The two nursemaids had brought Bibi and Karina in to say goodnight to their parents.

'Good night, my darlings.' Zepherine kissed her daughters tenderly on their foreheads. Their hair was still damp from their bath, and they smelled heavenly.

'Good night, chicks.' Artyom patted Bibi on her head and ran his little finger along Karina's cheek, before the nursemaids took them off to bed.

'We should probably think about dressing,' Artyom said, and promptly lit himself a cigar. 'We shouldn't keep Inessa and Philippe waiting.'

Zepherine saw him examining his groin intently.

'I have a grey hair just here.'

'You're growing old.'

He showed her. 'Look…'

Zepherine took her scissors and cut the hair out. 'Oh but you have another one… here… and here…' she said, snipping them away.

'Do you still like it? Why don't you make it hard?'

Zepherine opened the blades of her scissors and balanced his penis between them.

'This is what you deserve really.'

They looked at each other for a moment, then Artyom leant towards her and kissed her lightly on her forehead, before going to the bathroom to run himself a bath. Zepherine heard him close the taps, test the temperature, and then step in, whistling to himself. She heard him add more water every now and again.

'Why don't you come in with me?'

She looked at herself in the mirror. Did it show on her face that she'd been crying? Her shoulders slumped forward; she felt like weeping all over again.

'Zephie?'

'No.'

She should really have cut his cock off when she had the chance. Earlier that day, Zepherine had come back to the Hôtel Metropole for lunch after a morning of shopping. As she gave her bags to a bellboy to take up to her room, the young man at the reception, in his light-blue suit and pink tie, waved at her discreetly to catch her attention. She went over, and he gave her an envelope: a letter from Paris addressed to Artyom. Zepherine wouldn't have thought twice about it, but on the way to her room, she caught an elusive trace of a perfume that was not her own. She waited impatiently for the boy to deposit her bags by the chaise longue, and the minute the door had shut behind him, she ripped open the envelope.

It was a short note, but unambiguous.

'*I will love you forever. P.*'

She looked and looked again at that single initial.

Who was she? This P, who was going to love Artyom forever?

Zepherine felt her heart die inside her.

29.

As they descended the white stairs outside the Hôtel Metropole, a balmy Monte Carlo evening welcomed them. Zepherine was not in the mood to enjoy herself, let alone celebrate the engagement of a women she had never been able to take to. Somehow, though, the night turned out far better than she'd imagined. Even the letter, which she hadn't shown Artyom, faded from her mind. New company always succeeded in taking Zepherine out of herself.

On the terrace of the Hôtel de Paris, Inessa introduced Philippe to her. Artyom pretended that this was the first time he had set eyes on the man. On the horizon, the sun slipped lazily into the sea as the champagne arrived, and Artyom toasted the happy couple.

'To Inessa and Philippe!'

Inessa and Philippe didn't let go of each other's hands, even as they clinked glasses.

It was a sultry evening out on the terrace, and the air was redolent with the scent of the flowers in front of the Casino. They smoked their cigarettes and cigars, they sipped their champagne, Zepherine admired the ring, Inessa asked after Bibi and Karina, and Zepherine asked after Georgik, who had been playing tennis all day.

Philippe was two yards tall, and although he was middle-aged, he had a young, scrubbed face, with a good head of dark hair and a neat moustache. When he spoke, his voice was slightly nasal, but there was something charming about the way he was ready to laugh at the smallest excuse, and he seemed to have a natural *joie de vivre*. From the way he'd look across at Inessa every so often, it was clear that he adored her.

Inessa was telling her brother and Zepherine how they'd met.

'I had an audition for a show they were putting on at the Odéon in Paris…'

They were going to stage a new translation of an American play, a musical with a chorus line. She'd sung her two prepared songs, and when she'd finished, a faceless voice from the darkness had thanked her and told her they'd let her know. Of course, they never did let you know unless you were successful, so after a fortnight, she'd known she hadn't been picked.

'So much for that…'

Inessa squeezed Philippe's hand as he smiled at her, and resumed her story. A few days later, she'd happened to be having her hair trimmed at Valentin's salon on the Rue Royal, and told the young girl who was cutting her hair about her disappointment. She'd been very sympathetic, and had assured her that her luck was sure to turn, but Inessa hadn't felt very hopeful. While she'd been waiting for her hair to dry, she'd flicked through a copy of *Figaro*, and read about a newly established drama company, whose first production was to be a comedy called *L'Argent n'a pas d'Odeur*. But what had attracted Inessa's attention had been that two Russian exiles – Georges Piteor and his wife Ludmilla – were part of the venture. She'd known their names from the magazines she'd used to read back in Petrograd. At one time, the two of them had worked for the Moscow Art Theatre, under Stanislavskii.

She'd contrived, through a mutual acquaintance, to have herself invited to supper. The only other faces Inessa had recognised around the table that evening had been the actors Marcel Herrand and Paulette Pax. It had become clear before the first course had been cleared away that they were far more concerned with trying to extract as much gossip as possible from her about her ex-husband, Alexei Alexeivich Dashkov, than in getting to know her. They'd been pruriently interested in the ins and outs of his sex life, and the circumstances surrounding his mysterious death a few months previously in Hollywood. They'd quizzed her relentlessly about the truth of various rumours that had been swirling around; had the press exaggerated the scandals in order to sell more copies? Inessa hadn't had the slightest desire to discuss him, and had been rather offended, so she'd turned to speak to the person by her side. That had happened to be Philippe, and he'd begun to tell her about the idea he had of establishing a truly multilingual theatre company.

'It's the only way forward in the Europe of today,' Philippe interjected. 'Artists of different countries coming together to form a group and working together in a spirit of fraternalism – a sort of theatrical United Nations.'

'I told him I thought that would be my ideal company,' Inessa told her brother and her sister-in-law, 'and he told me I was his ideal woman!'

'But in which language do you perform?' asked Artyom. 'French?'

'And Spanish, Italian, German, English and Russian...' Philippe replied.

'But it's in Paris you'll be performing mainly?' asked Zepherine rather impatiently.

'We intend touring as much as we can, all over Europe,' answered Philippe.

30.

In the baccarat room at the casino, Zepherine found a stool to watch the gambling, while Artyom went to buy chips for everybody. The gamblers were mostly elderly people: dinner-jacketed men with their bushy side-whiskers, and women in their old-fashioned floor-length evening dresses and white gloves, exposing the tired flesh of their upper arms, which hung loosely from their bones. They seemed so still and lifeless to her, their attitude to losing so impassive compared with the speedy cheerfulness of the young croupiers, lean young men with their hair plastered down with grease, so that they all looked identical.

Inessa wanted to try her luck at the roulette table, so the four of them made their way into the main *salle de jeu* and took their places along the mahogany gaming table. In no time, their drinks were placed discreetly at their sides: gin and it for the women, whiskey and soda for the men. Inessa announced that she only ever bet on single figures, so Zepherine put her chips on the doubles. The ladies had soon lost all their chips, Philippe took a little longer, but Artyom was on a winning streak.

'Why don't you stop while you're ahead?' suggested Zepherine as he put a sizeable bundle of chips down. 'Isn't that what the professionals do?'

Inessa, ever the contrarian, urged him to try his luck one more time.

Zepherine scowled at her suggestion, and squeezed his elbow. 'Cash them in. Buy me a nice surprise. Something to remember Monte Carlo.'

'You'll be having your surprise tomorrow.'

Artyom was staring at the wheel.

'Go on, Tomya,' Inessa was urging him. 'You're on a run.'

The croupier called for the table to place their bets.

'I just know you're going to win, something is telling me you will…'

He put all his chips on number three.

'I'm feeling lucky tonight,' Artyom said, kissing a fuming Zepherine.

The croupier spun the wheel around. The ball whirled around, before starting to rattle and click, and finally bounced once, twice, thrice before coming to a stop.

On number three.

Zepherine leapt up from her chair, clenched her hands in triumph, and brought them up to her mouth. 'You've won!'

Inessa stood up and said, 'What did I say?'

Philippe shook Artyom's hand. 'Congratulations.'

31.

It was a muggy evening on the terrace of Les Frères Provençaux. Zepherine's back was uncomfortably sticky, and her cheeks were too hot, even though she fanned herself with the menu, as she discussed her two little girls with Philippe. The brother and sister were talking together.

'I'm so happy, Tomya,' Inessa said. 'Happier than I've been in a very long time.'

Artyom told her he was delighted for her.

'You're obviously happy too. How could you not be, now that you're doing so well on the stock exchange? Who would have thought you would be so good at it? To accumulate such a fortune in such a short space of time. You've learnt how to gamble…'

Something Philippe had just said made Zepherine burst out laughing.

'See how he charms everyone?' Inessa smiled as she lit a cigarette. 'He puts a smile on my face every day.' She threw the match into the black water of the harbour below them. 'He loves me… and I know that I love him.'

'How can you be so certain after such a short time?'

'What has time to do with love?'

Artyom was curious to know whether Philippe had been

married before, and whether he had any children, but he decided not to ask any more. On a night as magical and tender as tonight, such questions could wait.

'Yes, he's the one for me. I've always thought, from when I was a tiny thing, that there was one special person for everybody in life.'

'Mmmmm.'

'At last, I've found my own special one…'

'I'm delighted for you,' said Artyom, tapping the ash from his cigar into a saucer.

'I'm the happiest woman in the whole world. I feel like I deserve this bit of happiness, too. Over the years I've suffered a great deal, and put up with an awful lot, in order to keep the love of men who didn't even come close to deserving me. And on top of everything—'

When she whispered, Artyom smiled broadly, and then he laughed.

'That good?'

'Even better.'

'What are you two whispering into each other's ears?' asked Zepherine.

'Nothing,' answered Artyom.

Far out to sea three rows of little lights could be seen.

'Do you see that boat over there?' asked his sister.

Artyom raised his monocle to his eye.

'Where do you think she's sailing tonight?'

'Who knows? Tangier perhaps, or Cairo, or Alexandria. Or to Oslo, or Copenhagen, perhaps, or further up the Baltic even, to Russia. She could be going to any port in the world.'

He blew cigar smoke into the night, and thought to himself that the path of every boat on the sea was the path of the stars at night. Inessa told him that the lights of the ship reminded her of being in Yalta once, long ago, when she was there on vacation one summer. It had been one of those baking Augusts, when the sun was as hard as stone and sucked the strength out of every living thing. It had made her fit for nothing apart from lying on the sand, with an occasional swim when her body had overheated in the sun.

'The only thing I can remember about that summer – and I'm ashamed when I think of it all now – is a feeling of hatred, pure hatred towards poor Fyodor. There was one night when I actually wished he would simply fall down dead. Can you imagine? We were all sitting out on the terrace of the Hotel Billo. Have you ever been there?'

For a brief moment Artyom felt as though somebody had winded him, and he couldn't answer her. Inessa kept on talking in her beautiful, melodious voice, but he didn't hear a word. Unlike most Russian exiles, Artyom never felt any longing for his home-land, but tonight, for some inexplicable reason, her question had stabbed him in the heart, and he was overcome with an agonising desire to see his mother country again. He hadn't been there for years, and it was unlikely now that he would be able to go back, to visit his childhood home, to walk the streets of Petersburg and the squares of Moscow on a snowy winter's day. His feelings of anguish engulfed him.

His sister was still speaking. 'There we were – Fyodor, me, Andrei Petrovich and his wife, that tall woman who was having an affair with some poet or other, and their daughter, what was her name now…? She was a plump, quiet little thing… Was it Galina? I can't remember… And Margarita and Larissa were there too… All the other tables were full, and all I could think of was how everybody else in that room was having more fun than me, and I was simply willing Fyodor to drop dead in front of me. If it had happened that night, I wouldn't have had a moment's regret. I was even imagining myself at his graveside. Of course, I can see now there was something else at the root of that desire.'

Her brother looked at her.

'It was a prophecy, Artyom.'

'Prophecy? What do you mean?'

'How much life did Fyodor have remaining before he died in Berlin? Barely five years. That night, without my knowing it, I was given a sudden glimpse of my future…'

Before long, families like her own would be on ships that were fleeing Russia for the night of foreign cities. As her voice faltered, Artyom put his arm around her.

'I've lost sight of things,' Inessa whispered in his ear. 'I've done something unforgiveable… Something utterly unforgiveable… I can't tell you… I can't tell anybody… But, will you forgive me?'

'Forgive what?'

Inessa began to weep, and Philippe rose at once and came round to where she was sitting, knelt at her chair, took her hands and spoke quietly to her.

The two of them said their goodnights shortly after that.

As they made their way back to their hotel, Artyom noticed that the moon had made silvery rail tracks along the surface of the sea.

'What were all those whisperings and tears about?' Zepherine asked him.

'She'd had too much to drink, that's all.'

The bay was so beautiful in the dance of the moonlight, and the sweet night breezes seemed to carry the aromas of far continents. Against the clouds, the tall masts of the boats in the harbour jostled with each other. But still lingering in Artyom's head was his longing for his mother country. He walked on silently, his mind wandering through the byways of his memories. As they approached the white façade of the Hotel Metropole, he tried to hold Zepherine's hand, but she pulled away from him.

32.

The next day was Zepherine's birthday. When she saw the motor launch with *Zepherine* painted on the side in a bright-blue cursive script, she had to admit that Artyom's surprise had been worth the wait. Once they'd left the harbour mouth for the open sea, the captain invited her to take the helm, which she did, pink with pleasure, as the birthday guests gave her a round of applause.

Later, full of caviar and champagne, they all lazed in the heat of the long afternoon. When evening brought some cooling breezes, the captain turned the boat for home, ploughing a white furrow of foam as it made towards the mainland.

Now it was Georgik's turn at the helm, his ears and cheeks red from the sun. Artyom looked indulgently at Inessa and Philippe, who were intertwined in each other's arms by the railing in the stern, where the French flag billowed in the wind. The engine purred, and he felt the deck throb tenderly under his feet. He went over to where Zepherine was sitting in the shade, and asked her, 'Did you enjoy your surprise?'

'It was just perfect.'

'Do you love me?'

'Yes, I do.'

He kissed her tenderly.

'I'm glad we didn't bring Bibi and Karina with us. Today would have been too much for them. Better that we left them at the hotel.'

Artyom was enjoying watching the waves at their tail. How quickly the sea reverted to its former serenity; a little distance beyond the boat, there was only a fleck of white here and there.

'What are you thinking about?' asked Zepherine, almost as an afterthought.

Artyom had been pondering his next steps in his attempt to float the bank he had set up in Beirut on the French stock exchange. That was the only way to attract honest capital, and the reason why he had spent so much money plying potential investors with his champagne and cigars amid the heat of the day. But there was a stumbling block: so far, the French Banking and Financial Regulatory Committee were withholding their approval of a flotation, and had even forbidden Artyom's Intra-Banque from establishing a branch in Paris, or anywhere else in the republic. This had been a setback, but he was determined to find a way to change the status of his bank. It would mean he would be able to call a halt to the heroin smuggling. Not overnight, but, little by little, he would be able to disentangle himself from illegal activity completely. Heroin was a dirty business, and a dangerous one, too. There was no knowing what might happen from one day to the next – or even from hour to hour. Being free of it would ensure a secure future for himself and his family.

It was Inessa's turn at the helm. Georgik stood in the bow, the sea spray splashing his face making him smile. This was the first time ever that Artyom had seen him looking like a boy having fun. As the coastline came into view, everybody's gaze turned to the soft early-evening lights of Monte Carlo. In the distance, the mountains were buried under a blue-grey haze, which had crept down to the lower slopes.

'A heavenly day.' Inessa squeezed her brother's hand. 'Thank you, Tomya.'

'I'm glad you enjoyed it.'

'And did you?'

'Of course. But I think what gave me the greatest pleasure was seeing everybody else enjoying themselves.'

They looked at the white buildings.

'To think that I have a place here for Gosha and me.'

Her brother smiled. 'You deserve your place in the sun. After touring so many theatres, you'll need somewhere you can call home.'

'Wherever Philippe will be, that's where my home is from now on. I'm so glad the two of you get on so well.' She shaded her eyes with her hand. 'Who's that? Over there…'

Artyom followed her gaze. 'Where? Who have you seen?'

Inessa pointed. 'There.'

Artyom couldn't see anything: he corked his monocle into his eye and looked again. Even with the lens, he failed to see what had taken his sister's attention.

'He's waving his arms…'

Artyom felt rather irritated with himself that he was so short-sighted.

'What is he trying to do? Is he trying to attract our attention?' she asked.

'Are you sure he's waving at us?'

Inessa turned to her son. 'Gosha, do you see that man over there?'

He nodded.

'Do you know who he is?'

Georgik looked and shrugged, not much interested.

'What *is* the matter with him? Why is he still making those gestures?' asked Inessa.

Zepherine had joined them.

'Can you see who that is?' Artyom asked her.

'Yes, of course. It's the boy from our hotel reception.'

'But why is he waving his arms around like that?' asked Inessa. 'What's the matter with him? Has something happened?'

Zepherine felt suddenly weak. 'The baby? Bibi? Do you think something has happened to her? Artyom? Or to Karina? Oh God…'

The same thought had crossed Artyom's mind, but he tried his best not to rush to conclusions.

'Say something! Artyom, do you think something has happened?'

As the cruiser drew nearer to the quayside, the boy was pacing to and fro. Zepherine could see he had something in his hand – an envelope, a telegram? She started to shake. Something awful had happened. Her world was about to be smashed to pieces. She thought, *After today, my life will never be the same again.*

'If something has happened to my babies, I'll never forgive myself.'

The boat had reduced its speed in preparation for docking. Zepherine was shaking with fear. Why was everything taking so much time? Why was the boat moving so hellishly slowly? By now, many of the other guests had become aware of her anxiety, though without knowing the cause.

The reflections of the pink and blue café lights bobbed on the surface of the water, throwing little waves of light against the white sides of the boats. The harbour noises were audible now. The sound of seagulls. Everyday life. The purring of a motorbike grew louder, and a young man with a girl riding pillion, her arms around his waist, drove along the quayside at a lick, before disappearing. As they finally docked, Zepherine and Artyom hurried off the boat. Through her tears, Zepherine gasped, 'Are Bibi and Karina alright?'

The tall young man, looking slightly puzzled, turned to Artyom and handed him a telegram.

'You'd better read this, Monsieur,' he said in an unexpectedly deep voice.

Artyom's guests were beginning to disgorge onto the quayside. He moved away from the gangplank, and turned his back on them to read the contents.

Artyom stood there immobile for what seemed like an age, until Zepherine went over to him and asked him what was the matter. He muttered something under his breath, but she didn't hear him properly. He turned to look at the mother of his children and repeated himself.

'Who?'

Zepherine was still shaking.

'Who's killed herself?'

'Jeanette.'

33.

A lanky Pole threw himself onto the lower bunk.

By his own admission, he'd been thieving since he was old enough to crawl, and his own father and grandfather had been his tutors – two sly dogs if ever there were. Even when he'd been forced into the army, he'd carried on pilfering all sorts of things as he hung around the barracks at Olsztyn, until he was caught with a gammon joint. The other soldiers had given him a hell of a beating for that, left him black and blue, and missing a tooth or two for good measure. On top of which, he was disciplined by the authorities: a whipping and three months in chains.

He'd been thieving in most of Poland's towns at one time or another, but his favourite region was Silesia, especially in the spring. Then, in summer, he'd return to Berlin for the tourist season. His stomach had been responsible for his latest calamity. He'd been starving, and hadn't been able to resist lifting the two yards of fat sausage which had been hanging in the window of a *delicatessen,* that one at the bottom of the station stairs at Frie-drichstrasse. But as he'd run away, he'd tripped and banged his head – and when he'd opened his eyes, he'd been sprawled on the floor of a prison cell.

Alyosha found Eustachy a very companionable cellmate. When he wasn't talking, he was reciting poetry, as he knew reams of Adam Mickiewicz's work by heart. Alyosha knew next to nothing about Poland's most important poet, but Eustachy was happy to tell him all about his sad life, and how Mickiewicz had spent the last months of his life in poverty in Istanbul.

Alyosha in turn told him about his time in a Warsaw prison.

'When exactly where you there?'

'A while back.'

'Maybe we were there around the same time.'

'I didn't see much of anybody. I was kept in the dark most of the time.'

'In solitary? You must have been a dangerous so-and-so. What did you do to deserve that?'

Alyosha told him about the disastrous ending of his relationship with Ludwika.

'I remember her father well,' said the voice from the lower bunk. 'He was a staff officer under Marshal Piłsudski when I was in the army. He was part of the force which gave Lenin's Red Army a good hiding back in 1920.'

He lifted his right hand up. 'Look...'

There were only two fingers left on it.

'I only wanted to lose one, but the barrel jerked. Mind you, it did the trick. I was given a dishonourable discharge.'

He even remembered reading about the magnificent wedding of Ludwika and Mateusz Kołodziejski in some magazine or other, and told Alyosha all about it, which made him wish he'd never mentioned her name.

34.

Another day dawned, and the morning crawled by slowly between the grey walls. Sometime around the middle of the afternoon, Alyosha was taken from the cell to a visiting room. When he entered the room, he saw his cousin, Margarita, sitting on the other side of the table, with some bald man with blue eyes that he had never seen before. His cousin gave him a wan smile, but she looked anxious.

'How are things, Alyosha?'

'As you can see.'

Margarita lit a cigarette for her cousin, and introduced him to Kai-Olaf, who asked him to tell them exactly what had happened. He gave a short account of the events leading up to the stabbing, but said it was he and only he who had stabbed Camlo. Margarita promised they would do their best for him. Kai-Olaf suggested that the first step was to sack the useless lawyer he'd been appointed by the police, and hire a better one. Margarita thought the first step was to find Camlo, who was still alive, and see which way the wind was blowing. Alyosha felt that his cousin was not very hopeful of a good outcome, though she tried to hide that from him.

35.

A man with a little mouse called Rosa replaced Eustachy as Alyosha's cellmate within a few days. Paul had come in that first night in a bad way, spitting blood through badly swollen lips, and so badly bruised from his beating that he grunted with pain every time he turned over. He'd been arrested during a fight with a gang of Nazis on Alexanderplatz, but that altercation was nothing compared to what happened to him after. In the back of their motor lorry, he'd been beaten to a pulp by the police.

The unemployed printer was delighted when he discovered that Alyosha was from Petrograd, and insisted on telling him at length about his trip to the Soviet Union a couple of years previously. It was the best place he'd been to in his life, he said, and the highlight had been attending the celebrations of the tenth anniversary of the Revolution in Red Square. Paul still had to pinch himself sometimes to convince himself it hadn't been a dream. There, before his eyes, in flesh and blood, had been Stalin himself.

From the upper bunk, Alyosha listened as he ranted furiously about the SPD – 'the social fascists' as he called them. He told Alyosha that, under all that bombast, they were babes in arms, the lot of them, and he had nothing but contempt for them. There could be no middle ground between the communists and the socialists, as their leaders were traitors through and through, as they'd demonstrated only too clearly several times. Even if the KPD were to make a common front with the SPD temporarily to fight the Nazis, sooner or later, the SPD would end up breaking their word. The only way forward was to show the working class what kind of two-faced hypocrites their leaders were, and win them over to the ranks of the Communist Party – the only party it was worth fighting for.

Although he thought they might have broken his jaw, there was no silencing him. Paul felt it was a privilege to be living through this period of history – even though the present was a period of rampant imperialism, the capitalist countries were too corrupt to endure. Their foundations were already rotting, and, very soon, they would be smashed to dust, and a new civilization would be established in Europe. Paul didn't want to underplay the task that lay ahead, or the obstacles that would lie in their path, but he was determined to cross the bridge to the riverbank on the other side in order to reach the country of light.

'You haven't fallen asleep, have you?'

'No…'

'I thought I heard you snoring.'

'Listening to you is keeping me awake.'

'I hope you've learned something.'

The future Paul wanted to see in his own country was completely possible, because it was already a reality in the Soviet Union. Communism was the key which would unlock the door to the problem of History. If only everybody shared the same ideals, and fought together to realise the same vision.

'If people could just see for themselves what's happening in the Soviet Union today, instead of being tricked by bourgeois propaganda…'

The great need was to inspire men to create a new kingdom; to build new schools, new hospitals, new houses and factories, new prisons even. It had been Paul's great privilege, in 1927, to be given a glimpse of the future, of a morality so different from the hypocritical morality of his own society. He longed to see his country stepping forward into a pure and clean future, where everybody could co-exist on a continent where unemployment wasn't sweeping like the Black Plague through Europe.

He stopped speaking practically mid-sentence, and the cell sank into silence.

'Are you alright?' asked Alyosha in a while.

There was no answer.

'Paul?'

Muteness.

'Can you hear me?'

Nothing.

Alyosha felt a lump under his back as Paul screwed his fist into his mattress.

'You,' hissed the communist.

'Me what?' asked Alyosha shifting onto his side.

'You can't trick me.' His former cheerful volubility had turned into a seething hatred. 'I know it's them who've put you here.'

What them? What was he talking about?

'I don't want to say another word to you ever again, you wanker.'

'I don't understand what you're talking about…'

'The fascists who run this shithouse of a jail. You've been put in my cell to try and get me to open my mouth about KPD business.'

'What on earth makes you think that?'

'Don't try to deny it.'

'I'm here because I stabbed a pimp.'

'Agent provocateur.'

'I stuck a knife into his chest. That's why I'm here.'

'Spy.'

'I'm not a spy.'

Silence.

'Are you listening to me?'

A second.

'Paul, will you listen to me?'

But Alyosha didn't hear a single other word from him. The next day, the cell door opened and the unemployed printer and his little mouse were taken away.

36.

Wiping her tears away with a handkerchief, Galina couldn't stop apologising.

'If it hadn't been for me,' she said in her little girl's voice.

If it hadn't been for this. If it hadn't been for that. If it hadn't been for the other. *If I hadn't been born*, he thought. Even though she clearly felt very guilty, she still couldn't stop herself from listing all her current misfortunes. He didn't have much patience, and had little to say to her. There's nothing in the world as loud as the sound of silent anger.

'Don't worry.' She made to touch his hand. 'Don't worry, everything will be alright.'

'How?' he asked. 'How the fuck will everything be alright?'

'If I'd only listened to you.' she wailed.

'Pity you didn't.'

Galina bristled. 'You're not my papa, you know.'

'Did he ever stab a pimp for you?'

'Why are you so mean to me?'

His head pounded, and his heart felt like stone.

'If you want me to leave, you've only to say so.'

'No, don't go… Not yet… Sit…'

He apologised.

She apologised.

There was an awkward silence, then, 'I do feel awful, Alyosha.'

'I'm sure you do.'

In spite of himself, his eyes kept wandering to the cleft between her breasts.

'What are you thinking about?' she asked him.

'About the life I would have liked to have lived. Days without storm clouds. A normal life. One without nightmares.'

'There's no such thing. Nobody lives a normal life,' was her reply.

When he was taken back to his cell, there was yet another new cellmate: a sick old man, prostrate on the bunk. He coughed feebly, the phlegm rattling in his chest, and croaked his name, too weak to move from his supine position. He was as frail as a baby, unable to even lift a finger over the edge of his blanket.

Lothar was a man who was a burden to himself, and seeing him there so broken, watching him weeping quietly to himself, Alyosha suddenly felt his own life to be a beacon of hope in comparison. The old man told Alyosha that he had fallen into a slough of despair. His life was a plenitude of poverty, a richness of nothing. His wife had died young, many years ago, when she was barely thirty. She had been a wonderful wife, and an even better mother, but when she died, the home died too, and the children scattered to the four winds. After that, his life was purposeless. He remarried briefly, but it was a mistake, and proved yet another disappointment.

In the darkness one night, he started to say in his short, choking sentences how similar everybody was to each other. Angels and thieves, reds and whites, feckless idiots and upstanding pillars of the community; all just minor variations of the same tune made flesh. You could always recognise another's nature, because you could always see something of yourself there, even in your enemy.

37.

The two Nazis, Max and Moritz, spent their time smoking and boasting about their prodigious capacity for drinking, fighting and fucking. They were two fine specimens, tall and strong without being too meaty. In their own way, they were open and kind, and during their conversations, it became clear that, at one time, they had been full members of the KPD. They had even been on a visit to the Soviet Union, which, in their opinion, was the arsehole of the world, full to bursting with Jews and whores.

'Too many Jews by half, and that's a fact.'

'Everywhere you went, there was some cunt wanted to tell you about some fucking farm or foundry or factory or other. It was a joke. They couldn't shut up. Claiming they had the best of everything. Morning, noon, and night, every fucking day.'

They had both been unemployed for years, but since they joined the NASAP, they had found an outlet for their unruly energy. They usually interrupted each other, their words tumbling out of their mouths like toys from a cupboard, but Max and Moritz were of exactly the same opinion: what their country needed was a strong leader who could put Germany back on her feet again, make her proud and vigorous once more, and, most importantly, restore her former glory in the eyes of the world.

They relished insulting the communists, the socialists and the Jews. Looking back, they claimed that Russia wasn't any kind of workers' republic at all – that was all a ploy. After visiting all those factories and foundries where the workers cringed under the bridle and the bit, punished for the slightest misdemeanour, and treated like dogs, the two had seen the communist regime for what it was. They couldn't understand why their former comrade, Paul, still had any illusions.

'Stupid bastard,' said Max. 'Fucking wanker …'

'I'd like to give it to his mother in front of him…' agreed Moritz.

'We will, too.'

'He can depend on it, because we know where the fucking bitch lives.'

'Why? Is she like Paul?' asked Alyosha.

'What d'you mean?'

'Is she a Bolshevik as well?'

'Who cares? She gave birth to one didn't she? That's enough of a reason to give it to her.'

They both knew his cousin Margarita as well, thought she was a right pain in the arse; a mouthy bitch who was asking for it. When they found out he was related to her, they thought he must be a communist as well, but once they understood that he hated the Reds as much as they did, Max and Moritz were as good as gold, always ready to share their tobacco with him.

According to Max, Kai-Olaf was 'the biggest wanker of the lot.'

'Fucking bald twat…'

'He needs his cock and balls chopped off…'

'Till the bastard's squealing for his life…'

'And stuffed into that big gob of his…'

'That would stop the cunt's bullshit once and for all.'

After spending nearly three days on his own, Alyosha was glad of their company. But after spending another three days with them, their extremely limited topics of conversation palled. They didn't have much talent for silence, and he longed to have the cell back to himself. The prisoner in the cell above them's constant marching back and forth, and the hoarse, persistent cries from another cell, were beginning to drive him mad as well. Anxious as he was about his own fate, his nerves were jangled by the slightest thing.

38.

Margarita came to see him again with good news: his new lawyer was convinced that Camlo would never come near a court of law to testify against him.

'What judge is going to set any store by the word of a pimp?' she asked.

It was a matter convincing the police of this so that they dropped the charges, and as they were realists, if nothing else, they would eventually agree. Alyosha didn't have to worry about facing judge, jury or more prison, but Margarita's greatest concern was how he would keep himself safe once he was released; there was no question but that Camlo would be after his blood.

'He'll kill you. You'll have to get out of Berlin the minute they release you,' was her advice. 'Why not go back to Paris? You'd be a lot safer there. Don't you think?'

'I'm not sure I want to leave Berlin.'

When Galina next visited him, she voiced the same concerns.

'You know what he's like. He always bears a grudge.'

'I can't ever go back to France.'

There were too many bad memories in Paris.

'Go somewhere else then. Anywhere.'

'Without money?'

He was strangely resistant to leaving Berlin, though he wasn't sure why. Did he want Camlo to kill him?

'For your own sake, I'm begging you to catch the first train out of the city once you're free.'

39.

Very early one morning, he heard the key turning in the lock of his cell door, and the heavy bolt being pulled back. When he stepped out of the prison into the fresh air, he was half expecting to see Margarita, but it was Larissa who stood there waiting for him. She slipped her arm through his, and they walked away from Moabit's high walls. Alyosha sucked the morning air into his lungs, and lifted his eyes to the sky, but it was a disappointingly cloudy day.

'Margarita wanted to come but they wouldn't let her have a day off work.'

'Why not?'

'She didn't say. She never really discusses Aznefttrust. You need feeding, Alyosha, you've lost weight. I could feel your ribs when I hugged you. Come on.'

Over a good breakfast in a café on Wiebstrasse, Larissa told him how she'd wanted to put a roof over his head, but Bruno had objected.

'I can understand why,' he told her.

They smoked a cigarette, and Larissa said it was because he was worried about the safety of his wife and children. His greatest fear was that Camlo might find out Alyosha was living with them, and come to the house when Larissa and the children were there on their own.

'Really, you don't have to apologise. I totally understand.'

Bruno probably wants to keep the stink of prison out of his respectable parlour as well, Alyosha thought to himself. So that she wouldn't worry about him, he told her he already had somewhere in mind to live. The café smelled of sawdust, and their little round table kept wobbling. Larissa told him she had to share her secret with him: she was in love.

'I know,' Alyosha said.

'No, you don't.'

'Yes, I do. Simon, the doctor… When I was staying with you…'

Larissa shook her head. 'Simon… That came to an end ages ago…' This was somebody else. She sighed quietly. 'But everything is so complicated.'

She hadn't been in love with Bruno for years. Looking back, she wasn't sure whether she had ever loved him, but she had married him because she'd been so desperate to put down roots; she could see that now. That had been a mistake, no two ways about it, but how was she to get out of the trap? She was in such a pickle, and now here was Bruno starting to talk about trying for a baby brother for Ella and Clara. Of course, he wanted a son; he was a Catholic after all, and having a large family was very important to him. Every time they were with his parents, the conversation would turn to more grandchildren. But Larissa could barely stomach him near her, let alone him touching her.

'So who is he?'

'Walter.' Her expression brightened at once. 'Let me tell you about him.'

40.

Margarita was distracted from her work by voices in the corridor outside her office, which became louder as they approached. She heard one of them excuse himself, and recognised the voice of her ex-lover, Stanislav Markovich. The next minute, he had walked in to her office without knocking, sucking on his pipe as always, wearing a mackintosh over his grey suit. They greeted each other, exchanging a kiss on the cheek, and then he perched on the corner of her desk, explaining that official business had brought him to Berlin, but he wouldn't be there for long – a couple of days at most – and then he'd be back in Paris.

'You're looking well,' Margarita told him, noticing his tanned face.

'Tatyana and I took a vacation in the Crimea.'

'Lovely.'

'Why are you smiling?'

'I just remembered something I did years ago. My sister, Larissa, and I were collecting seashells on the beach at Yalta. The two of us had wandered along the seashore, and had ended up all the way along past the headland…' She stopped, suddenly embarrassed. 'It's really not very interesting…'

He tapped his pipe into the ashtray on her desk. 'No, no, finish your story.'

'It's not important.'

Stanislav half smiled and gazed at her consideringly. She had noticed that his hair had some grey streaks now, and he had put on a little weight around his middle. He seemed to have slipped into middle age rather suddenly. But perhaps he was thinking something similar about her.

'I have a gift for you. Something I promised you back in Moscow,' he said, producing a small envelope out of his inside pocket. Before he placed it in her hand, he added, 'I know how much it was worrying you.'

'Thank you.'

She waited for him to leave before she opened the envelope. It was a black–and–white photograph of a grave, with some Michaelmas daisies at the base of the headstone. She studied it intently, but the inscription was too small to read, so she went over to the accounts department to borrow a magnifying glass. Back in her office, she shut the door and examined the photograph again through the lens.

On the headstone, she could just make out her father's name and the date of his death.

41.

It was almost seven o'clock when Margarita rang the bell of her sister's house. The maid showed her in. Bruno was in good spirits and seemed pleased to see her.

'Sit, sit,' he urged her benevolently. He was just on his way out to a wrestling championship at the Sportsplatz. Larissa saw him to the door, and Bruno claimed a kiss from her. The second she'd shut the door behind him, she rushed to the telephone in the hall and made a call. When her sister eventually joined her in the sitting room, Margarita said,

'Larissa... can I ask you something?'

'What?'

'You and Walter...' She hesitated but then went on. 'If you're serious, why all this deception? You don't love Bruno... Why don't you leave him?'

'It's not that simple. If only it were. But it's not...'

'Why?'

I'm frightened of how he'll react. What he'll do. I think he'll take the girls. And now Walter says his wife is becoming suspicious, even though we've tried to be so careful. I just don't know what to do.'

'You can't keep on living like this...'

'No, I know...'

Seeing her sister's distress, Margarita changed the subject, and told her about Stanislav's visit. She took the photograph out of the envelope and showed it to her. There was no magnifying glass in the house, so Larissa had to take her sister's word about the date of their father's death. On the back of the photograph, somebody had written the name of the cemetery in Lvov in blue ink.

'So Papa must have fought with the Red Army against the Poles?' mused Larissa. 'That's difficult to believe…'

'Yes, isn't it?'

It had been raining for a while, but the wind suddenly picked up, and from nowhere, a February storm of unusual ferocity whipped over Berlin. The rain pelted against the windows and the wind shook the branches of the trees. In spite of the weather outside, Margarita felt a deep peace inside herself. Her father had been a communist.

42.

One cautious hop at a time, some sparrows had been approaching his feet. He didn't have any crumbs to share and he shooed them away, but perhaps they were as hungry as he was, and they cautiously regrouped, coming closer again in twos and threes, until they took to the sky when a dog came scampering past.

Alyosha had just broken his thirst at the little fountain, one of four which spurted from the mouths of lions at the centre of Bayerischer Platz. The water had tasted odd, and he raked his tongue with his teeth in an effort to get rid of the bad taste from his mouth, and spat a few times. But the taste lingered, sour-sweet, redolent of something cadaverous – a dead seagull, rat, or a cat, probably.

He gazed around him at the mothers and their children, little scenes of fondness and laughter. Two nursemaids in uniform were pushing identical enormous perambulators side by side, gossiping away under their little round hats. And there were the unemployed men, who came every fine day to sit, sad and slumped, watching the hours inch past.

It was lunchtime, and he had just spent seven *pfennigs* on some crusts, a small lump of hard cheese, and a thumb-sized slice of Thuringia sausage. He never ate breakfast, as he couldn't afford more than two meals a day, and he preferred to keep his money to try and fill his stomach in the evening. At least that meant a reasonable night's sleep.

After he'd finished his frugal meal, he walked down the street on the southern side of the square. He stopped outside the Peltzer-Grill, and cupped his face in his hands against the window so that he could read the clock on the far wall. He still had twenty minutes left before he had to go back. Then he noticed that somebody was gesticulating at him to come in. He pressed his forehead against the cool glass to see who it was.

The swarthy young man who had been sitting with Stanislav Markovich was already on his feet, and left with barely a glance at Alyosha as he approached their table.

Stanislav ordered a coffee for him, and asked him what he'd been doing with himself. Alyosha noticed that he had become a little jowly.

'Are you working?'

Alyosha told him how he had recently lost his job selling cigarettes, but had come by a few hours of tutoring at a language school.

'Russian?'

'French.'

He asked if the work paid reasonably.

'I don't have any qualifications, so they don't pay me the going rate. So no, it doesn't.'

And Alyosha lifted up his elbows to show the untidy patches he had tried to sew over the holes in his shirt. After taking a few appreciative sips of his coffee, he asked, 'What brings you to Berlin?'

'I was in Moscow, so I'm just passing through on my way back to Paris. I've been commissioned to write a series of articles about the state of the bourgeois nations.'

'For *Pravda*?'

'*Izvestia*.'

Stanislav told him that what struck him most this time in Berlin, in the working class areas of Wedding and Neukölln, was the sense of hopelessness. The people there looked ravaged, in their shabby clothes and leaky shoes. 'For Sale'. 'For Rent'. 'Everything must go'. Street after street of poverty and deprivation. How did people make two ends meet? The answer, according to Stanislav, was quite simple – they didn't. And the police were so heavy-handed in arresting the homeless, so pitiless in their persecution of the unemployed, delivering savage beatings to anybody who dared raise their voices in protest.

'Everybody's heart must beat on the left while the enemy is on the right,' he said.

Alyosha glanced at the clock; it wouldn't do to be late. He thanked Stanislav for the coffee and told him he should get back to work.

'I hate to see you wasting your life like this, Alyosha.'

Alyosha thought of Galina.

'At least I'm still alive.'

'There's living and living.'

And dying too, Alyosha thought to himself. The newspapers had all reported the story about the young woman's corpse which had been fished out of the filthy waters of the Schifffahrtskanal. Galina, described as a known prostitute and heroin-addict, had been slashed forty-two times. There were the usual editorials urging the government to act at once to stop the heroin trade. And there was the usual, slightly prurient speculating about Galina's life and possible murderer.

Alyosha didn't need to speculate. He knew it was Camlo who had killed his friend, Galina Andreyevna, but how could he prove it?

As he made to leave, Stanislav grasped his hand with both his.

'You did me a great favour once,' he said with some emotion. 'In Kiev, during the Civil War, you saved my life, and don't think for a second that I've let myself forget that. I haven't. You shouldn't be scratching a living like this. You could live a different life, a much better life. Do you understand that, Alyosha? Look, why don't we meet again this evening?'

'I can't tonight.'

'Tomorrow, then? It's my last night before I go back to Paris. I can offer you something worthwhile. You won't regret it, I promise you.'

They agreed a time and a place.

'Until then.'

Alyosha extricated his hand and walked out.

43.

It was two of his fellow émigrés, Vlasich Pesotski and Matyev Sava, who had told him about the Russian concert nights at the Café Fürstenhof, insisting that he come along with them. The strongest attraction was the cheap beer and the free food.

His two friends had many years of exile behind them. In the early days, Vlasich Pesotski told Alyosha once, he had gone to sleep every night with his head resting on his suitcase; but, by now, after packing and unpacking so often, all of that unique smell it had which reminded him of Russia had long since disappeared. The only things that remained of his mother country now were his fading memories.

Vlasich had started to rant before they even arrived at the Café Fürstenhof. He was raging about the unfairness of the system, where all the unemployed Russians – and there were hundreds upon hundreds of them in Berlin – had to queue at the back door of that ugly old red-walled building on Ludwigkirchstrasse to register. And then, even worse, in order to claim the measly fifty *pfennig* food stamps, they had to make their way to another centre which was miles away. Was that fair?

Not a single Russian émigré had any hope of gaining German citizenship, but all those Jews from Galicia, who flowed over the border day and night, wangled it straight away, just because they had the wherewithal to slip a bribe to the right bureaucrat. Was that right?

Once they arrived at the café, Vlasich proceeded to drink himself into a stupor as quickly as possible, but Matyev was a teetotaller and a vegetarian. That didn't prevent him from squaring up to all and sundry like a policeman's son, swaggering and picking fights with gusto.

Alyosha sat at a table with four other Russians, and listened to them as they – inevitably – discussed Russia. Russia? What republic of workers? What destruction of capitalism? The true aim of the revolution was to give power to the swarming scum from Asia's underworld: the Slavs, the Muslims, the Tartars, the Huns, the Armenians and the Georgians, so that they could dilute the blood of Christian Europe with barbarian filth, defiling a whole civilization for generations – if not forever. That was the real tragedy of what the Antichrist had spawned in the city of Petrograd in 1917. 'How is it possible for us to work with the Germans, the people who allowed Lenin to travel on that train to Petrograd?' asked Vlasich, adding that Lenin was in fact a Jew by the name of Zederblum.

'We'll have to work with them because we don't have any other option.'

Vlasich wanted to spit in the face of every German. Moscow was by now nothing but a second Jerusalem for hothead Jews. The White Armies' fatal mistake had been to let so-called moderate socialists into their ranks, rather than treat them for what they were – traitors. Mussolini had the right idea, stringing up every last communist he could lay his hands on. Mussolini was Vlasich's great hero, though he thought the world of Adolf Hitler as well.

Alyosha concentrated on filling his belly with the free food, as did everybody else. Thankfully, there was more than enough for all. But he was glad when the balalaika orchestra started playing, to drown out the querulous voices around him. The musicians were all wearing the traditional red shirts, black trousers and leather boots. Soon, everybody was singing. 'Troika, Troika!' went down well, and they sang the old favourite, 'Trink, Trink, Brüderlein, Trink!' four times.

Encore!

Whistling and applause.

Encore!

They toasted the New Germany.

And the old Holy Russia.

'Holy Russia!'

By now, Alyosha was feeling warm and mellow, at one with the world for a change in this friendly atmosphere. Until he'd started to attend these evenings, he hadn't fully realised quite how lonely he was. Now, he had some company to sing along with.

'I'll look after you, Alexei Fyodorovich,' promised Vlasich, pulling him affectionately towards him with his arm over his shoulder. 'You're my friend for life.'

'And you're my friend for life, too.'

'Like the Jews, we have to learn how to watch out for each other.'

'We'll watch out for each other, that's what we'll do.'

'A new party!'

'A new party!'

'You and me.'

'You and me.'

Then they joined in with the chorus again and sang and sang until their throats were hoarse.

44.

The following evening Alyosha met Stanislav in the bar of the Hollstein Hotel on the corner of Möckernstrasse as they'd arranged. They hadn't been talking long before it became clear to Alyosha that Stanislav knew more about him than he'd imagined. He'd heard that things hadn't gone smoothly for him in Paris, and mentioned his romantic difficulties with 'the aristocratic Polish girl'. He even knew about the two months he had spent under lock and key in Moabit prison for stabbing a pimp. It was through Margarita, of course. How else? They'd obviously been discussing him. Alyosha felt a little annoyed, but obscurely glad, too, that there was actually somebody who took an interest in his life.

Stanislav took a big pinch of his tobacco, and packed it tenderly into his pipe. Alyosha noticed how carefully he sucked as he lit it, before extinguishing the match between his finger and thumb.

'I want the two of us to be completely frank with each other,' Stanislav told him.

'In which case, tell me frankly, are you going to try and persuade me to come and live in the Workers' Paradise?'

'Mmmm-hmmm.' Smoke curled from the bowl of the pipe.

'Because that's the only possible future?'

Stanislav ignored Alyosha's ironic tone and said, 'Look at me Alyosha.' His voice was quiet and warm. 'When I was living here in Berlin before and starting to think seriously about what I wanted to do with my life...' He coughed a dry cough. 'Excuse me. Everybody needs some structure to their lives. When I decided to go back to the Soviet Union, you'd be surprised how many people advised against it. 'Naïve idiot' was probably one of the kindest things I was called.' He wasn't smiling. 'Of course, some of my countrymen, the ones who couldn't forgive the suffering the revolution had caused them, also called me a traitor. And I'd be the first to admit, it wasn't the easiest decision in the world. I thought long and hard before I accepted a Soviet passport, but by today—'

'It was the *best* decision of your life,' said Alyosha with heavy sarcasm.

'Actually, it was the most sensible thing I ever did.'

'But you live in Paris'

'I do, though I'm often in Moscow.' Stanislav leaned back in his chair and sucked his pipe quietly. 'What of it?'

Alyosha heard the voices rising in his head, voices from the mists of the past mingled with those closer to home, like his friend Vlasich, who he knew would never forgive him for turning his back on the cause. How could he, of everybody, betray people who had suffered so much under the hands of the communists?'

'You wouldn't regret it, I promise you.'

Alyosha pondered deeply. What should he do? Stanislav was still staring at him. Alyosha sighed. He noticed there was a section of wall in the corner of the room where chunks of plaster had fallen away, exposing the lathes.

'I can't.' The suggestion of a smile on Stanislav's lips vanished. 'Isn't it obvious why I can't?'

'Rubbish. Nobody cares anymore on whose side your father fought during the Civil War. All that's unimportant now; it belongs in the past. The only thing that matter to the Soviet Union is that hundreds of thousands of our best people are scattered all over Europe, their talents wasted – from Sophia to Prague, from Prague to Paris, from Paris to Berlin. Worse than that, their bitterness is killing them slowly, when they should be burying the hatchet and coming home.' In his mind's eye, Alyosha saw Vlasich roar his opposition. 'I know as well as the next man what kind of a wound homesickness is, and how it can destroy a man's peace of mind. You're homesick, Alyosha. When I saw you peer through the window of that café yesterday there was something about you which told me at once how lonely you were. You're standing on the outside, longing to come inside.' Stanislav leaned towards him. 'Look. Isn't it a good feeling to be part of a society, instead of its enemy? The communists of the Soviet Union are hard at work trying to create a society quite different from anything that's gone before. This is the biggest enterprise in the history of mankind. This is the greatest challenge for every one of us, because this society, before too long, is going to transform human nature itself.'

'That's quite a challenge.'

'Yes it is, but the people have hope in their hearts. What do you have against it? How can you be against hope? Why are you so reluctant to join with us? Is it fear? Doubt? Individualism?'

'Perhaps I value my freedom too much.'

'Your freedom to live in loneliness.'

'It's freedom just the same.'

'But what about the price you have to pay? Hmmm? The loss of security. The loss of hope. Is it worth it?'

Alyosha couldn't answer that.

'Look, it's far easier to criticise than to create. When you commit to something, you shoulder a burden of responsibility. Like a marriage.'

Stanislav was offering to arrange his return. He had connections in the government – at a pretty high level. Alyosha had only to give the word, and Stanislav could smooth away all difficulties.

'You'd be back home in less than a week. In less than a fortnight, you'd be in a good job, earning a decent wage.'

'You've forgotten one important thing,' Alyosha reminded him. 'I'm not a communist.'

'Not at the moment, but you'd soon become one of us.'

Alyosha shook his head.

'You're speaking thoughtlessly, Alyosha. Nobody stands still. We all change, all through our lives. Look at your cousin, Margarita. Life is a journey for all of us.'

With an early train to catch the next day, Stanislav had already ordered a taxi. A word came from the door to say that it was outside waiting for him.

Alyosha was sorely tempted, there was no denying it. Everything Stanislav had just voiced was, in one sense, true. He had been just treading water for years, barely keeping his head above the water, nothing more. What had he achieved? Nothing. He was getting older every day, and any hope of a career was as out of reach as ever. But the thought of going back to the Soviet Union was troubling.

'What do you say?'

He felt the decision like a hand weighing heavily on his shoulder.

'There's a reason why returning to Russia would be dangerous.'

'What would that be?'

'I might be arrested the minute I arrived.'

'Explain.'

He wondered whether Stanislav was pretending not to understand.

'For what I did in Kiev.'

'Nobody's arrested me.'

'It wasn't you who shot the Commissar dead.'

Stanislav frowned and, lowering his voice, chose his words carefully. 'Who could ever accuse you? Who was in that little orchard that night, apart from me? Eh? You, me and the Commissar. Nobody else. Nobody saw what happened.'

Alyosha couldn't prevent himself from saying the obvious. 'You, Stanislav Markovich – you saw what happened and you could betray me.'

There was no sounder reason for not going. Someday, for whatever reason, there was no knowing how both their circumstances might change. But if he ever lived in Russia, his life would always be at the mercy of another man's will. And it was this particular man's will at that. Alyosha already knew that Stanislav wasn't a man to be trusted to keep to his word.

Alyosha stood up. 'Safe journey to Paris.'

Stanislav slipped his pipe into his pocket.

'Can I give you a lift?'

Alyosha sensed his anger. 'There's no need for you to go out of your way on my account.'

Stanislav fumbled for the sleeves of his coat as the waiter held it for him. He wrapped his scarf around his neck and put his soft hat on his head. The taxi driver was waiting patiently at the door.

'You can't take my word on trust, Alexei Fyodorovich? I'm disappointed. Personally disappointed.' He looked him in the eye for a long moment.

'I'm sorry, but no, I don't suppose I can.'

'Why?' asked Stanislav, looking affronted.

'Because I can't.'

'You're a fool, man. And do you know why? You're frightened of the future. That means you'll never be free. You know in your heart that the Soviet Union is the best chance for mankind. She's the truth which will one day free the human race from the oppression of the centuries, the only thing which can offer us all salvation. This is the best offer you'll ever have.'

Alyosha stood on the pavement watching the taxi as it drove off, Stanislav silhouetted in the back window, his shoulders wide and square as a table. He crossed the road, re-living the conversation in his head. Doubts flowered and withered in turn. Had he just made the biggest mistake of his life? If he had, there was no one to blame but himself. Yet, having made the decision, he felt strangely liberated. Whatever the consequence, he was happy that, just for once, he had executed his free will.

His body swelled with pride. He could sing. He could dance. He could jump for joy.

He could also starve to death.

45.

'Where are you going?' asked Zepherine.

'Business,' he answered, smoothing down his hair.

'When can I expect you back?'

He leaned towards her and kissed her. 'Shouldn't be too late.'

'Yes, but when?'

'When I come back.'

That night, Artyom had arranged to meet with Meme Corse. After the French Banking Commission turned down his application to expand his Intra-Banque Beirut to Marseille and Paris, Artyom felt he had no choice but to ask the Corsican for help. Since his election as Deputy, Artyom had already met him twice, but this time, they were going to talk terms.

The meeting went much as Artyom expected. Meme told him he'd be more than happy to ask questions on the floor of the French Senate – at a price. Then it was a matter of haggling over the amount of shares he'd be willing to transfer to the Corsican brothers – the more he gave, the more power they would wield on the board of his bank. That was the most difficult negotiation.

Meme Corse was as good as his word, and did his best for him in the Chamber of Deputies, and behind closed doors in various committees. But it was not enough, and the decision stood. Artyom was still in the same predicament, unable to float his bank on the Stock Exchange. That's when he started to realise that political power was a relative thing. Even the ostensible power wielded by the Chamber of Deputies of the French Empire, or the power of two gangsters from Marseille. True power ruled quietly somewhere else, as always.

Artyom was still a cuckoo in the French nest. That was the problem. Along with every other Russian exile, he still lived the déclassé life of the émigré. He was no fool; he knew full well what the French truly thought of people like him. Men who have lost everything are always held in suspicion by those who have never lost so much as a thimble. In their hearts, the French thought that the exiles were in some way responsible for their own fate.

Artyom remembered exactly where he'd been when he learnt about the fall of Pyotr Wrangel's Army in the Crimea in 1920: at the zinc bar of the Médova on Rue de l'Echelle. He'd spent the rest of the night drowning his sorrows, until he was filthy drunk. At some point, somebody had asked him, 'If your country's so precious to you, why didn't you lot fight a bit harder to save it?'

It's the truth that kills you.

'Easy enough to sit here feeling terrible, why didn't you go back and do your part?'

He hadn't been able to answer that at the time, and he had never quite shaken off a vague sense of guilt. He had betrayed his country in her hour of need, and his own family, too. He hadn't even managed to persuade his parents to leave Petrograd. The effort to save Russia had broken his brother-in-law, there could be no doubt of that. The constant anguish Fyodor Mikhailovich felt for his mother country had been responsible for sending him to an early grave.

And then there was Jeanette. Poor Jeanette, he should have done more for her, too.

Why did all these regrets meld with each other? His parents, Russia, Jeanette…

Zepherine hadn't come to the funeral, though he'd wanted

336

her to. Perhaps it had been asking too much to expect her to stand at the graveside. But he found her attitude towards Dimtry unforgiveable. She had put up every obstacle and objection possible to having him come live with them.

'Why can't he live with his grandmother? She's still alive.'

In the end she had – reluctantly – given in, but they still had awful fights over poor Dimtry because of the way she treated him. Jealous of any attention his father gave him, she was cold to the boy at best, and often unkind. Dimtry was frightened of her. He wet the bed nearly every night, which had the maid complaining about the extra work. Artyom begged Zepherine to be kinder towards his boy.

'Remember, he's still mourning his mother.'

Jeannette's mother had told him that it was Dimtry who had found his mother's hanging body.

'You'd be wetting the bed every night, too.'

46.

The train wended its way slowly through the Berlin suburbs, passing by gardens and allotments divided into long strips. Some early-risers were already busy tending their plots.

As usual, Alyosha hadn't eaten breakfast, but he didn't mind, because he was expecting a feast to be waiting for him at the end of the journey. Ever since Vlasich Pesotski had persuaded him to join a Nazi militia, these Sundays were the highlight of his week. He was half dozing, but it was impossible to fall properly asleep, as Vlasich, sitting next to him, kept breaking into raucous song. It was far too early in the day for the rest of them to want a sing-song, but his friend was a bundle of youthful energy, overflowing with enthusiasm and joy, and when he wasn't singing, he was talking nineteen to the dozen. Alyosha rested his temple against the window, and kept his eyes firmly shut, pretending to sleep through Vlasich's chatter.

The motor lorries were waiting for the Berlin train by the wooden gates of the country station, to take them the rest of the way. The men were glad to put the city behind them and enjoy the fresh air, especially on such a mild autumnal morning. Now, the singing was enthusiastic, everybody joining in with gusto as they turned off the road and drove through open iron gates up a long drive flanked by sycamore trees. At the wide cobbled courtyard, in front of the stables at the back of the great house, they all got out of the vehicles.

They rushed to the tables to fill their bellies, joining the twenty or so other groups who had already arrived. The estate servants waited on them, refilling the platters and glasses as soon as they emptied. Berlin boys were hungry boys, and it took some determined eating and several glasses of buttermilk before Alyosha began to feel full. With food in his stomach, he felt like a giant, ready for anything.

Drills and marches took up the morning, their hobnailed boots ringing against the cobbles of the courtyard. Officers of the *Reichswehr* whistled and barked at them to keep order. In the afternoon, they attacked the walls of an old ruin which belonged to the estate, an ancient ossuary from the twelfth century which had been allowed to go to rack and ruin. Real bullets were fired, their flash of heat close enough to make the earth leap before their eyes. Two of the boys were injured: one in his knee and the other in his shoulder, but nobody took it badly, and there was a doctor on hand to tend to their wounds. A scar was a badge of honour and a mark of courage.

As the evening sun sat low among the branches of the trees and the ravens cawed, the hundreds of men stood to attention in their formations, chests out, eyes forward, the Nazis in their brown shirts and the Russian auxiliaries in white shirts and black trousers.

Under the eaves on the wide stone balcony, Rittmeister Gunther von Kunz, in his hacking jacket and shiny black boots, his fist on the hilt of his sword, stood like a statue, where his ancestors had stood before him – those men who had served under the family coat of arms in the battles of the past: Tannenberg, Metz and Mollwitz. Rittmeister von Kunz was proud of his lineage, and loyal to the traditions of the Teutonic Knights of Marienburg, who had protected Europe's borders from the rapacious Slavs, the barbarian hordes from the bowels of Asia.

Night nudged the day away, and the soldiers returned to the long tables to feast once more, the eating and drinking interrupted by many toasts to the future of the new Germany, which was about to be reborn, pure and strong, out of the rotting flesh of the old Weimar.

'To the New Germany!'

'The New Germany!'

She would be a country to rekindle hope in every Russian. A country where the will would triumph. A country which would deliver the coup de grace to the thieves who had stolen dear Russia from those who loved her. Month by month, the great hour of revenge on the Jew-Communists was approaching. It was only a matter of time before the day would dawn, and the golden trumpets would call the Christian armies of Europe to save their heritage.

The drinking went from bad to worse. They lit an enormous bonfire, the sparks snapping and flying up into the sky. Near the thick, impenetrable blackness of the forest, they lit a circle of smaller fires, and many of the young men stripped naked. The first drunkard ran headlong through the circle of flames. Then, one by one, dozens followed suit. Alyosha stood with one heel resting on the side of the horses' water trough, watching the bodies flying through the circles of fire. Many of them were staggering about in their drunkenness, enjoying their pain, even

though their flesh singed and sizzled. Alyosha lifted his face to
the gentle breeze which rustled the leaves of the old beech tree
by the stable block. He fell into a reverie, and was overcome
by a profound loneliness. In the pinpricks of the sparks and the
yellow flames, he saw familiar faces, faces he had half forgotten,
and faces he had never met in his life. He saw a procession of
places, strangely familiar, though he couldn't recognise them. He
felt as though he was attracting the ruins of old, old memories
to him, and that half his life had been mapped out before his
birth. His misfortunes didn't stem from the circumstances of
living and being, or the force – or lack of force – of free will
at all. His fate had been decided a long time ago in Grendel's
black night.

47.

A powerful spotlight was trained on the ancient stone balcony,
and Alyosha looked up at Rittmeister von Kunz and General
Vassily Biskupskii, standing side by side. Standing there too was
the rich widow, Mathilde Scheubner-Richter, and Prince Cyril
of Coburg and his wife, the Grand Duchess Victoria Feodorovna,
who had contributed thousands to the coffers of the *Freikorps*
and the NASAP.

The meaty faces of men who already had blood on their
hands looked up towards the light, and a forest of arms shot out
in unison as the men roared:

'Heil Hitler!'

'Heil Hitler!'

'Heil Hitler!'

Then, an expectant silence fell. Rittmeister Gunther von
Kunz stepped forward, to welcome and introduce their guest
speaker, Alfred Rosenberg, who was to give a short address in

memory of the late Max Erwin von Scheubner-Richter. He, in turn, stepped to the front of the balcony, and, after greeting the men, said, 'In my mind's eye, I can still see him this second, see him in all his glory, marching confidently in the full military uniform of the Chevaux Leggers on that journey, that fatal journey to the Feldherrnhalle, when he walked side by side with his great hero, Herr Adolf Hitler.' His smile disappeared. 'Max Erwin von Scheubner-Richter, the first secretary of the Kampfbund in Munich in 1923, and the first, too, to fall for the cause. But for him, but for his courage and love and loyalty to his country, my elegy tonight would be for Herr Adolf Hitler. Max Erwin von Scheubner-Richter was felled in his prime, on the threshold of his fortieth birthday. A man need not live a long life to live a great life.' There was a quiver in his voice. 'Max-Erwin, my dearest friend, accomplished so much, even though his journey was a tragically short one, and to honour his memory as one of the first martyrs in the cause of our beloved mother country, I tonight christen this regiment of brave men the Freikorp Max Erwin von Scheubner -Richter.'

At the sign, everybody shouted in unison, 'Freikorp Max Erwin von Scheubner -Richter!'

'Heil Hitler!'

'Heil Hitler!

That's when Alyosha noticed a face at the back, between Rittmeister von Kunz and General Biskupskii – the face of his former tutor from Petrograd, Herr Professor Karl Krieger.

When the two came face to face, Alyosha and his former tutor gazed at each other in wonderment, neither having ever imagined they would see the other ever again, never mind under such circumstances.

'Alexei Fyodorovich, Heavens above!' They shook hands. Professor Krieger had heard about the death of his father. 'Your dear, dear father...' he said sadly, still holding his hand, the surprise of their meeting still fresh. He apologised for not having been able to attend the funeral, but his own brother had been gravely ill at that time, and shortly after died of septicaemia. 'Alexei Fyodorovich of all people...' He asked after his mother. Alyosha hesitated for a moment before saying that he hadn't seen her for a long while. 'And your younger brother? What is he doing with himself by now?'

'He's still at school.'

'And Larissa Kozmyevna?'

'Volkman, for several years now. She married a doctor from Berlin. They have two little girls, Ella and Clara.'

Professor Krieger tutted appreciatively.

'Delightful.'

'Margarita lives in Berlin as well...'

Clearly highly pleased to see his former pupil again, Professor Krieger insisted on introducing Alyosha to Rittmeister von Kunz himself, who told him that he had met his late father, Fyodor Mikhailovich Alexandrov, on more than one occasion.

'I'm very pleased to meet the son of such a patriot.'

Alyosha answered that the honour was his.

The Rittmeister ushered Alyosha and Professor Krieger to his library, which, he told them, housed one of the best private collections in Europe. They sat under the portraits of the Rittmeister's father, grandfather, great-grandfather and great-great-grandfather.

'We have a worthwhile young man here, Karl?'

'My former pupil. A very brilliant boy.' The small eyes of his former tutor twinkled at Alyosha. 'I would expect nothing less than total commitment to the cause from someone of his background,' he added

Rittmeister Gunther von Kunz clicked his tongue approvingly

'We can expect great things from you, young man, I'm sure.'

'Yes sir, you can,' Alyosha answered sincerely.

48.

The maid was serving Artyom and Dimtry at the breakfast table. Outside the large French windows, two gardeners were already at their work, filling their wooden wheelbarrows as they pruned and weeded. Since his son had come to live under his roof, Artyom had relished being given the chance to come to know him again, and he could see a lot of himself in his boy. Dimtry was very anxious to please his father, and had started to show an interest in his Kodak camera. Artyom enjoyed showing him how it worked, and Dimtry had taken a few good photographs.

Zepherine joined them, still in her nightgown and slippers. She was rather pale and her hair was lank. The taste of coffee turned on her and, irritably, she ordered some tea. Her third pregnancy was proving no easier than the others: she was sick most mornings, and felt constantly tired. She sat listlessly picking at her toast.

The chauffeur put his head around the door to ask if Master Dima was ready. Dimtry rose, kissed his father, and left for school, but Zepherine didn't pay the boy the slightest bit of attention. The minute his son had left, Artyom folded his copy of *Le Matin,* stood up from the table and asked his wife,

'How long have you been paying a detective to follow me?'

Zepherine raised her head sharply and spat, 'How long have you been deceiving me?'

'If he couldn't give you the answer to that, he's not much of a detective.'

Zepherine claimed that she knew about every detail.

'Then what else is there to say?'

'Are you thinking of leaving me?' she asked, and then, her voice dropped and she asked, 'Why do you treat me like this? I don't deserve it.'

'I was going to tell you everything before long,' Artyom told her quietly.

343

'You only say that because I've caught you. Because you can't wriggle your way out of it!'

Then the floodgates opened: she knew every last detail about every meeting, and had filed it all away in her head. Brasserie Métropole. Tabary on Rue Vivienne. Au Caneton near the Bourse, where Artyom had forked tasty little morsels from his plate into her mouth. The Marquery, where the detective had reported that they'd laughed and kissed openly. The Duval on the corner of Rue de Rivoli, and then a walk, hand-in-hand across the Pont-Neuf…

'Do you want me to continue?' She took his silence for a yes. 'Terminus-Nord. I see the attraction. Just one couple among the thousands flowing through the station every day. The Hôtel de l'Europe on Rue de Constantinople, where you took me for supper on my birthday, not long after we'd met. Lavenne. A very handy place to meet, at the foot of the monument on Place de Rennes. Terminus-Lyon on the tenth of last month for four hours. Do you want to hear more? Grand Hôtel du Pavillion for two nights, when you told me you had to go to Marseille. The Du Quai Voltaire between five and seven last Thursday. The night before last, you took her to Suzy's. What was that? Taking her to work?'

'She'd never been inside a bordello before.'

'I beg your pardon?'

'I shan't repeat myself; you heard me quite well.'

She rushed at him and slapped him, and when the first slap didn't elicit any reaction, slapped him again, harder.

'You've deceived me!' she shouted. 'I hate you!'

Many a woman would have wept, but Zepherine wasn't one for tears. Her way of expressing her anger was to throw things around. Before she had the chance to smash the entire breakfast service, Artyom had grabbed her.

'Wait a minute, just wait.'

344

She was the mother of his children, expecting another baby, and this is how he treated her? She did her best to kick and punch him, but he just held on to her tighter.

'Will you listen to me? Let me explain?'

She struggled and kicked all the more.

'What is there to explain, aside from you've been stuffing your fingers up some other woman behind my back?'

When Artyom told her there was a reason, she screamed shrilly, 'Of course there's a reason—'

She aimed a kick towards him, but Artyom side-stepped nimbly and she nearly lost her footing, grabbing the side of the table to steady herself.

'Let me go!'

'Not until you're willing to listen to what I have to say.'

'Let me go!'

'If you're still angry with me after that, you can kick me from here to the middle of next week.'

'You'll just come up with a pack of lies—'

'Just listen. That's all I'm asking you to do.'

'Have you been to bed with her?'

He hesitated for a moment, then answered that he had.

'I want to get away from here. I can't bear to look at you. Let me go.'

Artyom insisted that she listen to him.

'I never want to see you again.'

'Will you sit and be quiet for one minute?'

And then he was telling her about the Banque de France, of all things, and how important it was. That contrary to what most people thought, the Republic's central bank was, in fact, private. That although there were thousands of shareholders, only about two hundred of them mattered, the élite who were entitled to vote on anything of importance. This was a very select club, and, as Artyom knew from bitter experience, they weren't looking for new members. Even wealthy and successful businessmen like André Citroën or François Coty weren't welcome. This elite comprised the *haut* bourgeoisie, who had kept hold of the reins of power for generations, and were determined not to extend their privilege to outsiders, no matter how much money they had.

'Why are you talking to me about banking? What does that have to do with fucking this whore?'

'If you'd only listen, you'd find out.'

These two hundred men were the only ones who could vote to appoint the eighteen deputies who sat on the Bank's board. The Government appointed the Governor and the two Deputy Governors, and, following an old tradition, three deputies represented the Treasury. These three were the plutocracy within the plutocracy — *Inspecteurs de Finance*, civil servants invariably appointed from the country's best families, whose pedigrees went back for generations.

To the ignorant, the Chamber of Deputies was the heart of French Government, but in reality, the true government was the *Banque de France*.

'How?'

'It's as simple as withholding a loan to the Treasury.'

'Why would they do that?'

'If some policy or other isn't to their liking. Raising taxation on the rich, for instance. Or if some politician or other starts to draw attention to himself by making too much noise about the rights of the poor or the unemployed, it's the easiest thing in the world for them to take a man like that down a peg or two. Or even destroy him if necessary. This is the kind of world we live in. This is the reality of a country which makes such a song and dance about her democratic constitution.'

Zepherine still was none the wiser what all this had to do with anything.

'Why else would I have spent so much energy courting the daughter of the President of the Banking Commission? Without a friend at the Banque de France, which controls the Banking Commission, I don't have a hope of expanding Intra-Banque out of Beirut. Zepherine, I need to be able to open branches here in Paris, and float my bank on the stock exchange. Otherwise I'll be scratching a living on the outside forever. These men would be happy to have me rot in Beirut forever. But I know I'm every bit as good as them. Do you think Pauline means anything to me? She doesn't. From the start, she's only ever been a path to lead me to the door of her father's house.'

Zepherine looked unconvinced.

'So you say.'

'It's you I love, now and always.'

'So you say,' She repeated, though she looked slightly mollified.

'I'm doing this for you and the girls.'

'But what are her feelings for you?'

'Once the Banking Commission reverses its decision, I can bring the relationship to an end.'

'Artyom, that's not what I asked you...'

He hesitated then said, 'Once I've had what I want, Pauline will be a thing of the past.'

It transpired he had already dined twice at François de Wendel's table, who had promised he would have the Commission look again at the Intra-Banque application. Though he had not promised more than that.

'So once you have what you want, you promise you won't lay one finger on her ever again? On your honour? Do you promise me?'

'On my honour.'

'On the heads of your daughters? Do you promise me?'

'On their lives and the life of this one,' and he placed his hand tenderly on her stomach.

'Because… I'm telling you now… I'm telling you right now, Artyom,' she said, a wash of pink colouring her pale cheeks, 'if I hear as much as a whisper that you're carrying on with her after that, I will never forgive you… Do you hear me?'

He answered that he did.

'I won't be made a fool of. You can't walk all over me just as you please. My name is not Jeanette. You need to understand. I would take my revenge on you. I'd make sure you suffered.'

'You'd have every right.'

'Why do I still love you, Artyom?'

'Because I love you.'

49.

The late autumn sunshine was refracted through the blustery showers, and in the distance, a rainbow spanned the Berlin skyline. Professor Krieger strode in to his office, apologising for having left him on his own, but a student had kept him talking. Alyosha moved away from the window where he'd been gazing out at the world.

In his everyday clothes, sitting at his desk as he put his lecture notes away in a drawer, the Professor was much closer to the memory Alyosha had of him from when he was a boy in Petrograd. Since their unexpected meeting, Professor Krieger had been eager to re-establish his acquaintance with his former pupil.

'I see more of your dear father in you than ever, Alexei Fyodorovich. You really have grown to be the spit of him. I hope you have also inherited that strength of character which was such a part of his personality. Fyodor Mikhailovich was a man of great integrity. He stood solid as an oak when every other tree in the forest was being blown like chaff before the wind. I remember how he loved reading about the history of Russia, and many was the time I urged him to turn his hand to writing, but he always demurred.' Swiftly, his tone changed. 'What ever became of that reprobate of an uncle of yours? The one who lived in Paris and, if I may say, seemed to ape the worst habits of the French?'

'Uncle Artyom?'

'Where is he these days?'

'I haven't spoken a word to him for years.'

'Does he still live in Paris?'

'As far as I know. I haven't seen him since I don't know when.'

'By chance or choice?'

Alyosha shrugged and told him it was a long story.

'A story you'd prefer not to share?'

He nodded.

'Of course. I wouldn't dream of intruding.'

Professor Krieger adjusted the position of the small swastika flag on the desk.

'I'm so glad our paths have crossed again, Alexei Fyodorovich.' He stood up. 'What is a crime if the state is the criminal? What is justice if society is unjust? What is the truth if that truth is just a jumble of slogans, to justify the power of a despotic gang of communist Jews who today have their heel on the throat of Russia? Keep in mind, Alexei Fyodorovich, that the mortal enemy of every man is self-interest. Self-interest and nothing else drove Lenin in every decision of importance he ever took. The man who serves his country rather than his own selfish needs is the one who attains true greatness. Like Adolf Hitler.' He turned his head slightly to gaze with reverence for a moment at the silver-framed photograph of the man which hung on the wall behind him. 'Don't you agree?'

He did, wholeheartedly.

'The shoots of great things are starting to grow in you, Alexei Fyodorovich. I can see that clearly. That's one of the great

349

privileges lecturing to the young at a University confers – the ability to recognise the leaders of the future.'

One of the reasons Professor Krieger had invited Alyosha to visit was in order to show him the last letter his father had given him when he was forced to leave Russia – a letter of thanks. 'I treasure it greatly. Look—' He ran his thumbnail lightly over the sheet. 'Do you remember what fine penmanship your dear father had?' He told Alyosha how his father had placed the envelope in his hand on the platform at the train station, just seconds before he had to step into the train to leave Russia forever. 'Generally, I'm not an overly emotional man, but that final farewell had me almost in tears.'

Alyosha read the letter, but the words on the page didn't bring his father back to life for him. His memories of his own father, the man who had been responsible for his existence, were, by now, faded and vague.

In the meantime, Professor Krieger had gathered his papers together for his next lecture. As he had nothing better to do with his time, Alyosha followed him to the lecture theatre and sat with the two hundred students.

Professor Krieger took a watch out of his waistcoat pocket and placed it on the lectern in front of him. He scowled when a young man slipped in through the double doors a few moments late and proceeded to speak for exactly one hour – not a second more, not a second less.

It was a lecture on Platonism, and the concept of 'two worlds.'

50.

The following Sunday evening, as the shadows of the waning day lengthened around them, Alyosha and his former tutor visited his father's grave at the Saint Konstantin cemetery, Professor Krieger in his brown SA uniform as a mark of respect. They stood silently for a few minutes on either side of the gravestone, before the former tutor insisted on their kneeling to pray. When he finished reciting the prayer, he slowly stood to his feet, straightened his arm, and held it in a long salute with his eyes shut, deep in contemplation. Alyosha listened to the voices of some small children who were playing hide and seek among the trees on the other side of the cemetery wall.

As they left, Professor Krieger said there had never been an equal to Fyodor Mikhailovich Alexandrov on Russia's soil. He fully deserved to have a memorial statue erected here in Berlin, and he very much regretted it had not already happened. Professor Krieger told Alyosha that he should dedicate himself to realising his father's ambition, in order to give a purpose to his life. There was nowhere better to start than at his feet.

'How?' asked Alyosha, not understanding exactly what his former tutor had in mind.

'By putting your own house in order,' answered Professor Krieger, as they waited to cross the road. 'Why are you looking so confused, Alexei?' With a slightly impatient sigh, he went on. 'We know all about your cousin, Margarita. We have ears amongst the Reds here in Berlin. I'm surprised at her, of everybody. One understands to an extent why the unemployed and the unintelligent find themselves tricked by the superficial appeal of Marxism, but when somebody like Margarita Kozmyevna falls for their lies – somebody who was brought up to know better – it is simply deplorable. But then, isn't it a perfect illustration of how this Jewish ideology can bewitch anybody? These Marxists aren't men who gobble up ideas, so much as the idea gobbles them up – see how it's gobbled up your poor cousin. After I myself taught her of Goethe, Shakespeare and Schiller, of the masterpieces of European civilisations, the jewels in our culture's crown. And what does she choose to do? It's enough to break a man's heart.'

'Larissa and I have tried to make her see reason…'

'You must try harder, Alexei Fyodorovich! It's high time she comes to her senses. Now is not the time to stay your hand, or there's no knowing what will happen. Soon, it will be too late, and no quarter will be given. The situation is as critical as that.'

Alyosha couldn't remember the exact reason why his tutor had been forced to flee Russia before the Revolution, but he remembered something about his having been arrested in a billiards parlour for arguing with Bolsheviks. He also had a dim memory that he'd been beaten by the police, because they thought he was spying for the Kaiser. He asked the Professor to remind him.

'What? You don't remember what happened to me? How could you forget, Alexei Fyodorovich? I remember it all as though it only happened to me yesterday morning.'

Alyosha wasn't given any further explanation. His most vivid memory was of his frozen feet as he waited on the platform at Finland Station with his father at dawn. He remembered his shoes crunching against the frost. He remembered the dazzling white of the early morning and his own breath prickling his nose.

After they left the cemetery, Professor Krieger insisted on taking Alyosha to supper. The restaurant at the Gasthaus Reiter on the corner of Gendarmenmarkt was his favourite place in Berlin – it was a traditional guest house kept by Herr Helfferich and Frau Helfferich, their three sons, Udo, Ulf and Urban, and three daughters, Udda, Udele and Udine. It might be a family affair, but that didn't mean they were old-fashioned. The previous year, they had installed a lift for the benefit of their guests, so they no longer had to climb the stairs to their rooms on the upper floors. But luckily, there was nothing modern about the food; they served good, traditional German fare in generous portions, and this pleased Professor Krieger more than anything. Alyosha ordered the ham hock on his recommendation, and it was every bit as delicious as he said.

They were enjoying a cigarette with their coffees when, glancing around him, Professor Krieger suddenly stiffened in his chair. Alyosha followed his gaze to the young woman sitting at the next table. Professor Krieger glared at her and then, looking at Alyosha over his spectacles asked,

'Have you noticed this dishonest Jewess?'

Some of the diners at the nearest tables overheard him, and there was a barely perceptible shifting in chairs and nervous glances. Alyosha felt his heart start to race. The young woman must have heard too though she didn't show it, turning her attention instead to the young man in a grey jacket who was making his way briskly towards her. They greeted each other with a kiss. Apart from his still, dark eyes, his appearance was unexceptional. He sat down, coughed, and took his lighter and cigarettes out of his pocket and put them on the table.

'Look at them,' Professor Krieger said, with no attempt to lower his voice. 'In all seriousness, just look at the two of them.'

The lovers were talking earnestly together, eyes locked, voices low. Although their hands didn't touch, their feet under the table were playing hide and seek.

'The way they're behaving, no shame at all.'

Alyosha was mortified, but thankfully, his former tutor left it at that.

It was only when Frau Helfferich placed the bill on their table that Herr Professor realised that his wallet was lost. He became rather flustered, until the young Jewish woman at the next table lifted it from where it had fallen on the floor.

'Is it this you're looking for?'

She held the leather wallet out on her open palm. As if he feared touching her flesh, Professor Krieger snatched it from her and stuffed it into his pocket.

'Aren't you going to thank me?'

She smiled sadly at his discomfiture.

51.

Vlasich Pesotski couldn't believe Alyosha's luck.

'It's still who you know in this world,' he said bitterly, 'I don't care who says different.'

After all the long years of living so precariously, Professor Krieger had told Alyosha he would help him out of poverty, and, unlike other individuals who had made similar promises, his former tutor kept to his word. He was employed by the NASAP as a driver and, ahead of his wages, was given money to buy a suit, a smart tie and a chauffeur's peaked cap. It was a fine thing to wear such clothes, with his hair neatly cut and the smell of soap on his skin. He felt he cut quite a figure, especially when he caught the girls throwing him a quick sidelong look as they sauntered past the motor car. Some even paused to chat and flirt, and he ended up taking a few of them for a drive, which they loved. More often than not, there'd be an excuse to park in some quiet backstreet, before climbing into the back seat.

However, apart from his official duties, he was also expected to collect Vlasich Pesotski and two or three others from the usual rendezvous, the beer cellar on the corner of Rheinburg-erstrasse and Strelitzerstrasse, after dark, to hunt down known communists. The fighting would be bloody and violent, with fists pounding flesh and air, feet dancing on the cobblestones, before the gang took to their heels and hurled themselves back into the car.

'Go, go, go, go, go!'

He'd press his foot down on the accelerator and tear away at speed.

52.

Occasionally, he drove Joseph Goebbels, Berlin's Gauleiter, when his personal chauffeur had a day off. The man always worked on his papers for the entire journey, the only sound the squeak of his leather coat whenever he shifted. Long after he got out of the car, the smell of that coat lingered.

On one occasion, Alyosha drove him to a funeral. The Gauleiter's arrival was announced by a fanfare from the SA, and several hundred supporters lined his way as he limped along the gravel path to the graveside, where he made a heartfelt speech about the latest martyr to the cause, promising to avenge the wrong. But as Alyosha drove him back to his office, he overheard him asking the deputy editor of *Der Angriff*, who was about to interview him, to remind him again of the name of the man who had just been buried.

Alyosha worked long hours every week, day and night, and would often feel himself slump at the wheel. The days would be sedate enough, but after dark, it was a different matter, the motor car full of sweat and laughter after a successful night of communist-bashing. A couple of nights previously, Alyosha had nearly found himself in trouble when Vlasich Pesotski was arrested for breaking the nose of the old one-armed man who sold the *Arbeiter Illustriete* in front of the Potsdam Bahnhof. He'd punched him to the floor, then kicked him in the head, sending him flying down the steps until his body rolled to a standstill at the bottom. As Vlasich had run off, two or three workers had given chase, and when they'd caught him, they'd half killed him. Alyosha had driven away from the Potsdam Bahnhof without his friend that night.

Alyosha was always relieved when those nights came to an end and he had the motor car to himself again. On the other side of the windows the world was lonely and silent in the darkness, the wind whipping from the east, the cold from the north, but he felt safe and snug inside his motor car. And, for the first time in his life, he was being well paid.

53.

Very early one morning, as instructed, Alyosha arrived at Professor Krieger's apartment to drive him to Cologne. As it was such a long drive, he alternated the driving with Kaspar Strassburger, the Professor's bodyguard whenever he was on official Nazi business. Kaspar's face was a mess, as a French bullet had ripped a chunk out of it in Verdun, but he still had the straight-backed bearing of a soldier. On his chest he wore his Iron Cross, awarded for attacking and killing five French soldiers with his bayonet. When his blade finally broke he killed the last soldier – a terrified young lad who begged for his mother – by forcing him face-down into the mud and piss of the trench and suffocating him to death by placing his boot across the back of his neck until the mud stopped bubbling. When he heard that the war was over, that Germany had been betrayed, that his hopes had died prematurely, that it was all over, after the army's exceptional sacrifice, Kaspar couldn't eat for almost two months. He carried his fury and his bitterness with him, until he could put them in the loyal service of the Nazis.

It was late afternoon when they reached the city, and on Hohenzollern Bridge, Alyosha was forced to slow the Mercedes to a crawl because of the thousands of people making their way across to the new Messehalle, on the other side of the Rhine. It was a magnificent building, rising to an impressive height, and, brightly lit as it was, it looked like some peaceful modern white temple against the night sky. As they approached, the slogans on the suspended banners read, 'Marxism must die if Germany is to live'.

Alyosha and Kaspar accompanied Professor Krieger through the entrance, which was guarded by young men in khaki, who stood to attention smartly when they saw the uniform of an Oberführer. As they entered the hall, their ears were filled with the sound of a band playing Lützow's song – 'Wilde Verwegene Jagd'. Backstage, the Professor was welcomed by a local committee of Nazis, and Alyosha watched bemusedly as a deputation of young nurses put bloody bandages on healthy men, so that they could sit on the stage with their crutches and their dressings, witnesses to the fighting between them and the KPD or SPD.

Professor Krieger was ushered in due course to his place on the stage, where twelve rows of chairs had been set out. Suspended from the ceiling were the familiar Nazi banners with their black swastikas. Alyosha and Kaspar were told to stand out of view on the side of the stage. The hall was rapidly filling, and the galleries were already packed, with people leaning over the rails. Running here and there were little boys selling newspapers, and flashbulbs were already popping from the pen of photographers, while on a rostrum in the middle of the hall, two cameramen were preparing to film the speeches.

The band struck up another tune as mothers and fathers, dressed in black to remember their sons, martyrs for the cause, were led to reserved seats at the front. Stewards ran up and down the aisles, gesturing to each other above the noise.

When everybody had found their seats, the music stopped, and Professor Krieger stepped forward to the microphone, his voice booming out through the loudspeakers when he greeted the crowd. But the intense heat from the powerful spotlights was already making Alyosha feel lifeless and light-headed, and he consequently took very little in of the speech, which lasted almost half an hour. When his former tutor finally finished and sat down, and the applause came to an end, the stage darkened. The band piped up again as a spotlight swept in circles over the crowd, before travelling up the main aisle and coming to rest on a man standing on his own. The crowd roared and rose as one. Alyosha watched him make his way down the central aisle towards the stage, followed by a forest of flags. As he neared the stage, Alyosha lost sight of him for a moment, but then, bit by bit, he reappeared as he ascended the steps – his hair, his watery eyes, like the eyes of a postman on a cold winter's morning, then his nose, his moustache, his chin, his Adam's apple, his chest, his legs. He turned to face the crowd and the music stopped, but he stood there without speaking for some minutes, amidst the tumultuous applause and the clicking and whirring of cameras. He looked younger and slighter yet taller in the flesh. With his fists held against his hips he patiently waited, the roars of the ardent thousands engulfing him in wave after wave of adulation.

When he finally spoke his voice was pleasant, melodious even, and he had a homely, intimate way about him. The crowd was so quiet now that when he let out a long and level sigh, as if from the bottom of his heart, everybody heard it. Gradually, as he warmed to his subject, his diction became more staccato, and he began to hammer home his utterances like nails. His speech gathered momentum, growing stronger and stronger. He was clearly feeling great emotion, and sometimes his voice became low and hoarse, and his tone fierce, but the next minute, he sounded close to tears, his voice so tender, almost breaking. He started to shake as if from overwhelming pain, like a man who was carrying the twentieth century on his back. But his words were like sparks, igniting a fire, until he'd lit a bonfire of response as he excited, as he disturbed, as he awoke, winning over every heart and mind in that vast hall. He clenched his fists, he shut his eyes tightly and lifted his chin as the sweat ran down his cheeks in rivers of tears. He talked of faithfulness. He talked of the spirit of the community. He talked of a community of communities, of a land and people fused. He talked of fraternity and blood. He talked of hopelessness and hope, and of the curse of communism. He talked of his own country being torn apart by two dozen minor parties and of their rampant selfishness.

'We will never thrive until our country is united.'

Applause.

'There is no future until our country is as one.'

Stronger applause.

'*Kein Kapitulieren! Kein Kapitulieren! Kein Kapitulieren! Deutschland, sieg*—'

'*Heil!*'

Five thousand as one.

'*Sieg*—'

'*Heil!*'

'*Sieg*—'

'*Heil!*'

'*Sieg*—'

'*Heil!*'

They had to return to Berlin straight after the rally because the Professor was lecturing the next day. Alyosha drove the first leg, with Professor Krieger snoring in the back and Kaspar nodding off next to him. It had started to rain, and Alyosha cursed silently as the headlights of the motor car close behind him blinded him every time he looked in the mirror. He assumed the driver wished to overtake, and so he reduced his speed slightly so that he could pass. The motor car drew level with him, and as Alyosha glanced across, he could see the dark shadows of the driver and passenger. The next minute, the window next to him shattered, sending shards and splinters of glass everywhere. The motor car sped away, its back lights becoming smaller until they disappeared completely. With Professor Krieger yelling incoherently from the back, Alyosha brought his own motor car to a stop at the side of the road, shaken but unscathed apart from a few minor cuts from the splinters of glass. It was only then that he saw with horror the blood pumping out from Kaspar's neck in great spurts, drenching the rest of him in a sticky red mess.

54.

Through Pauline's father's influence, Artyom was finally granted a licence to open a branch of Intra-Banque in Paris. In exchange, he was happy to offer François de Wendel a seat on the board. Artyom felt quietly confident at last that a flotation on the Stock Exchange would soon follow.

Pauline had first introduced him to her father at the Longchamp races. He was a heavily built, melancholic-looking man, who moved his cumbersome body as slowly as the Pharaoh's chariot in the sands of the Red Sea, but his mind was as sharp as a razor. Luckily, he took to Artyom instantly. Artyom had presented himself as a widower with one son called Dimitri. That was technically true, and he'd made a song and dance about the death of his dear Jeanette. His mistress and her children was a detail he kept to himself.

At one time, François de Wendel had many business interests in Russia, and he had lost some millions in investments following the 1917 Revolution. The Banque des Pays du Nord had shares in the Russian Azov-Don Bank, and François de Wendel had been on the board for years, and his father and grandfather before him. The main concern in Paris had been how to stop the communists from getting their dirty

hands on the reserve capital – twelve and a half tonnes of pure gold that the Azov-Don Bank had given as a deposit to the Enskilda Bank in Stockholm at the end of the summer in 1918, as they raised a loan of thirty million *kroner* for the cause of the White armies. There had still been considerable optimism then that Wrangel's army in South Russia would muster the strength to defeat Lenin. But it proved misplaced. By the first week of January 1920, not one of the directors of the Azov-Don Merchant Bank remained on Russian soil. Every one of them had been forced to turn his back on his own country, most of them fleeing to Paris or Berlin. The Board of Directors had met on the twentieth of the same month in Paris, François de Wendel in the chair.

Not to lose hope, that was the most important thing, though the Azov-Don and all its assets – including the twelve and a half tonnes of gold in Stockholm – had been nationalised by the Bolsheviks on behalf of the people. Through the influence of the Banque des Pays du Nord, some small remainder of their capital was saved from being swallowed entirely by Moscow. However, since the French Government had acknowledged the Soviet Union *de jure* in 1924, the Kremlin had insisted that any disputed assets in French bank accounts should be frozen, until it was all returned to the People's Bank in Moscow. Already the legal disputes between the Board of the Banque des Pays du Nord and the Government of the Soviet Union had been dragging their way through the French law courts for months and years, with the spiralling fees of the lawyers eating up more and more of the disputed capital.

'How did we permit such a thing to happen? Who was responsible?' François de Wendel addressed this question to Artyom at dinner one evening. 'Somebody somewhere has to shoulder the blame. Was the revolution inevitable, as the Bolsheviks claim?'

'Circumstances, fate and fluke were responsible,' answered Artyom, aware that the guests around the table were all listening. 'The Jews and the communists are the only ones who crow insufferably about the supposed inevitability of it all.'

'Circumstances, fate and fluke,' echoed Madame de Wendel sadly.

'A man of no substance like Kerenskii can certainly shoulder his share of the blame,' added Artyom, stubbing out his cigar. Of course the revolution hadn't been inevitable.

'How to make sure that such a thing is never allowed to happen again, that's the most important thing,' said François de Wendel.

Pauline's home was a tasteful house on the Avenue du Parc-Monceau. Her three main pastimes were horse-racing, the ballet, and learning to fly. Artyom often accompanied her to the races in the Bois de Boulogne, and there he saw the Comte de Quincey riding Golden Hope – the horse which had already won the Prix de la Plage Fleurie in Deauville. Pauline was convinced she would win again, and bet heavily on her, but Golden Hope came in third, much to her chagrin. Then she betted on Sourbier and Zariba, but her luck did not improve.

That day had been her twenty-third birthday, although with her short blonde hair and little snub nose, Pauline looked even younger. She had been married for two years, but had separated from her husband because he beat her, and was now in the process of trying to divorce him. Artyom bought her a Louis XV locket inlaid with twenty-three gems as a birthday present. She was thrilled with such a pretty thing, and kissed him lovingly.

'A little memento of my love,' he told her.

'Thank you, Artyom,' she murmured, and kissed him tenderly again.

The 1929 Wall Street Crash didn't reach the shores of France until the last months of 1930. That's when the franc collapsed, and Artyom's bank with it. In no time at all, he was nobody, and after so much effort to lift himself up, to be dragged down, to lose everything, was devastating. He was every bit as unemployed and every bit as hopeless as millions of others all over Europe. There was no refuge or present help in trouble. François de Wendel's businesses had also been badly affected. With a feeling of dread, Artyom realised his only option would be to return to smuggling heroin. But this would be highly problematic, as in the short time since he had disentangled himself from that side of his business, everything had changed. By now, his men were all working for other gangs, there were different men in charge at the docks, and the system for unloading the ships had changed, too. Most of the cargo was now sent straight out of the docks to warehouses on the outskirts of the city, where the various companies employed their own men to guard their goods.

Gangs from Sicily had invaded the heroin trade, but the Corsicans had fought back. After a couple of shootings in broad daylight, the *flics* had decided they needed to assert their authority, and there had been a few raids and several arrests. Things were in the balance for a while, but Meme gained the upper hand. Unfortunately, the violence had alerted the authorities to the scale of the problem, and the French government were putting a considerable amount of pressure on the *Sûreté* to restore law and order in the city.

Artyom nevertheless saw returning to Marseille and the drugs trade as his only option.

55.

Artyom arranged a meeting with L'Oreille in the Stockholm, but even here, things had changed, as Doña Rosa and her son, Camilo, had gone home to Andalucía. The place was now kept by some real low-life who some called Shari and others Sidi, and yet others called Mohammed. He claimed he was Algerian, but L'Oreille said he'd heard he was Syrian.

Perhaps the greatest change was in L'Oreille himself. He seemed far warier now, his eyes constantly checking the comings and goings at the door. He told Artyom he feared he'd end up the same way as Pierre, who was already in the grave. He'd been stabbed in the back one night, over some woman. That, at least, was the story, but nobody had ever been caught and punished.

Over a cigarette and a pastis, Artyom was eager to discuss his new plan, but L'Oreille interrupted him.

'Who are you with? Corsica or Sicily?'

'I'm still with Lolole and Meme.'

'Their protection isn't as good as it used to be.'

'I need the money, so I'll have to risk it. Let's just get the first shipment in, through the Orphans' Friend like before. Once I'm in funds again, I can decide who needs paying off. But I need that first shipment. They're going to take everything I have, otherwise.'

'This is asking for trouble, Artyom.'

'We'll still need the labs. That's where you can help me. We'll have to find somewhere out of the way, and find the right people to work there. What do you think? Are you in?'

There was a long pause.

'I'm in.'

56.

Alyosha was having a coffee in the Laurentzsch on his day off, when he happened to bump into an old friend, Heinrich Erkleytz, a taxi driver who had lived in the same block as him when he'd first moved to Berlin. Alyosha had been trying to put Kaspar's murder out of his mind, but it had been weighing heavily on him, and he ended up telling Heinrich about it.

'I don't care how well they pay you, what the fuck good is money when you're *kaput*?' asked Heinrich. 'You're risking your skin every time you get behind the wheel for those bastards. You've already had one lucky escape. Think how close that bullet came to your skull.'

'Where would I find other work though?'

'As it happens, our firm are looking for somebody right now.'

'Am I in with a chance of getting the job do you think?' asked Alyosha.

'As good as any other fucker who goes for it.'

Heinrich drained his glass of Bock, leaving a trace of white foam on his abundant moustache.

'Go over this afternoon and ask the boss. You should leave it till he's had his lunch, he'll be in a better mood with a full belly.'

'You've told me often enough how bad-tempered he is.'

'He's a bad-tempered cunt, true enough, but what boss isn't? Oy!' The bartender was deep in conversation with a blonde young woman and didn't take any notice. 'Fucking hell, come on…' Heinrich said impatiently, tapping his empty glass against the side of the bar. 'Oy! Can you do your work and serve me, instead of flirting. I'm dying of thirst here.'

Alyosha was reflecting quietly to himself. 'I don't know if there's much point going for it.'

'What have you got to lose?'

Later that day, he went to see the boss. He was in his shirt-sleeves, reading the *Völkischer Beobachter* with his feet up on the desk when Alyosha entered his office. The man was a Berliner, born and bred, with a burly frame and a three-day stubble. The large desk filled the small room, and was covered in piles of messy paperwork and files.

He asked Alyosha impatiently for his work permit. 'Or the police will be on my back.'

The last thing Wenzel needed was any attention from them, especially after the hellish time he'd had with those bastards from the tax office. The boss took the precious grey card and examined it carefully. Alyosha had applied for the permit a couple of months previously and, to his surprise, it had been granted, on condition that he renewed it on the third Wednesday of every

365

month. He had never experienced anything coming to him so amazingly easily as that permit. That was one of the advantages of working for the NASAP.

'Why are you applying to work here,' asked Wenzel suspiciously, 'when you already have a driving job?'

'I never know when they'll need me,' he lied. 'I don't know where I stand with them; they're really unreliable.'

How could he tell him the truth: that he was sick and tired of promoting the cause of pure blood by spilling blood. Supporting the cause of the NASAP had become too violent. His needs were simple, he thought: he just wanted a secure job with regular working hours and good pay, without having to put his life in danger every day. Was that too much to ask?

'Russian?' Wenzel asked coldly.

'We've all got to be something or other. Russian, Polish, Hungarian…'

'You a fucking Bolshie on the sly?'

He denied it. Was he sure? Perfectly sure.

'I hope you're being straight with me. Tell me lies and I'll have you. I'm not letting a single Bolshie bastard near my taxis, not with all their crap about unions and rubbish about workers' rights, got that?'

The room stank of strong tobacco, cheap perfume and sex. Heinrich had told him that it was an open secret that the boss and his secretary had been rubbing against each other for years. If the door was shut everybody knew to keep well clear, if they valued their job. 'Going over the accounts,' they called it. Poor Agna had tried her best over the years to persuade Wenzel to leave his wife, but with no success so far.

Alyosha, feeling he had nothing to lose, as the man clearly had no intention of giving him a job, asked, 'So is it just Bolshies you hate? Or all Russians?'

'The last one I employed cost me a packet…'

He didn't elaborate, and Alyosha didn't ask. He felt too dispirited.

'Right then.' The boss wiped his nose with the back of his hand. 'You're on a fortnight's trial.' He threw the permit back at him and picked up his copy of the *Völkischer Beobachter*. 'But you fuck me around, you little bastard, and you're out on your arse.'

57.

Artyom returned to Paris with a lighter heart, having arranged the first shipment.

Zepherine, meanwhile, had been thoroughly upset when some man called at the house and shouted at her aggressively for his money. As he left, he told her he'd be back.

'Artyom, what was that about?' she asked.

'Just a temporary nuisance,' he told her soothingly.

'Are you sure that's true?'

On her birthday, he took her to the Hôtel Continental on Rue de Rivoli, under a pale-lemon winter sky. She was put out when she was accosted by an old tramp, dressed in a filthy mustard coat tied around the waist with a rough piece of twine, his fluffy white hair blown everywhere by the wind. He had the gait of a man who had been walking for many years down roads beset by difficulties and obstacles. The doorman shooed him away, and Artyom watched him trudge off, talking sullenly to himself, his gestures suggesting some empty boast. *He must have had a home once*, thought Artyom. *A father and mother.* Had they always scratched a living an inch or so away from destitution? Had he been forced to work when his bones were still soft? Had that been the beginning of his troubles? How had he come to beg? A family breach? A marriage break-down? A disappointment in love? Who knew?

A few weeks later, Inessa and Philippe returned to Paris after touring the Netherlands. Artyom and Zepherine were due to accompany them to the annual dinner dance for the Russian community in Paris, which was held in the George V. Artyom was waiting to hear whether all had gone well with the first shipment, and was irritable and distracted, but couldn't think of a good enough excuse to cancel.

The Grand Duke Nicholas Nikolayevich Romanov – his face red and glistening – and his wife, Princess Anastasia of Montenegro, greeted the guests as they arrived. Her dress was as dazzling as a harvest sun, leaving her shoulders and arms bare, and her hair was piled high on her head, crowned with a narrow tiara. She was a tall, fair woman, with nut-brown eyes and smooth skin, without a wrinkle to be seen.

The master of ceremonies – a short little hassock of a man – stood at their side, announcing the guests, and the Grand Duke and Princess murmured exactly the same greetings to everybody in their turn. It was a laborious task, and neither of them showed much enthusiasm for it, the Grand Duke sniffing his disapproval every now and again.

Many eyes turned to look at Inessa when she was announced. She was arm-in-arm with Philippe, who wore a dreamy, almost drowsy expression. Her dress, from Coco Chanel's latest collection, looked slightly too young for her, but undeniably chic. A pink feather boa was draped over her shoulders, and dangling coral earrings accentuated the length of her graceful neck. Her eyes, thick with mascara, were a smouldering black, contrasting with the powdered whiteness of her skin. Her nails were painted black as well, and as she moved into the room, she left a cloud of Chanel No 5 behind her.

They found their table, and Inessa placed the little silver bag which had been hanging on her wrist on it. Philippe sat at her side, and opposite were Artyom and Zepherine, who had been placed next to Prince Alexander Buxhoeveden, there with his wife, Princess Olga, and their five daughters. Princess Olga was in her forties, with a round, compact face under ringlets so densely and uniformly black, it was obvious they were dyed. The Prince, a small man, square of body, with a weathered face, now sold houses and apartments in Nice for a living, but had very little to say for himself.

Before a phalanx of servants brought the food out, a woman stepped onto the low stage in front of the orchestra and began to sing 'Arise, Russian Land, Defend Your Faith!' Everybody joined in the chorus:

> *Again, march ahead!*
> *Again, the bugle calls!*
> *Again, we'll join the ranks*
> *And all march into the holy battle.*
> *Arise, Russian Land, defend the faith!*

Between the fourth and fifth course, Artyom motioned to one of the waitresses and whispered something to her. In no time, more wine was brought and his glass refilled.

'Artyom,' chided Zepherine, 'What *is* the matter with you tonight? Can't you enjoy yourself without getting blind drunk?'

He told her he was enjoying himself very much, but in fact he was in a foul temper. The taste of uncertainty filled his mouth, and he was engulfed in a dark cloud.

Inessa was animated and charming, and the Princess was a cheerful little thing, so Zepherine tried her best to be their equal.

'That hour you spent being happy, you didn't spend being sad,' said the Princess, appearing very pleased with her own cleverness. 'That's what my mother used to tell us when we were children.'

'True enough,' smiled Inessa, 'I must remember that. With your permission, I'd like to put it in my diary, so I don't forget.'

This pleased the Princess very much.

A man in dress uniform strolled past their table and put his hand on Artyom's shoulder. It was General Vladimir Dmitrievich Kuzmin-Karavaev, and Artyom stood up to greet him.

'I hear things have been difficult,' the General said.

'A little,' answered Artyom.

The General tapped his elbow and said, 'The two of us will have to have a proper talk.'

'Yes indeed.'

A date and time was arranged at a brasserie on Rue de l'École-de-Médecine.

'I look forward to it,' said Artyom, though, for some reason, he felt that there was some evil spell in the man's voice.

'Until then.'

For a little while, Artyom managed to slip away to sit on his own at the bar, pondering why he had such a strong feeling of dread, but Zepherine found him.

'What are you doing here? I thought you'd gone and left me,' she told him crossly.

They returned to their table where Princess Olga was talking in platitudes about how important it was when dancing to allow oneself to let go, to give oneself up to the euphoria of the purely physical.

'I'd love to be able to dance the Charleston like Josephine Baker.'

Artyom had barely spoken a word with his sister all evening, or Philippe for that.

'What a tedious evening,' said Zepherine in the taxi.

Artyom grunted his agreement.

Early the next morning, he was arrested.

58.

He was given ten minutes to dress. Zepherine stood by, looking wild and bewildered.

'What has he done? You don't have any right to take him.'

Artyom admonished her gently to be quiet. He held her face

tenderly and kissed her, telling her he'd be home in no time. The motor car sped away through the empty streets of Paris. It was the hour before dawn, and the gloom of the streetlights gave a desolate look to everything. They took him to the *Sûreté*, where he was put in a cell without being questioned. At seven, he heard doors being unlocked and the chatter of the prostitutes as they were released, but still nobody came for him. Hours went by. Had they forgotten about him?

Artyom cursed himself silently for his recklessness. Someone came and looked in at him, then sloped off again. He paced up and down the cell restlessly. They hadn't let him wash when they'd come for him, and he felt sour and stale. He kicked the bottom of the cell door until his foot was sore. Still nobody appeared.

Eventually a policeman brought him food, and after another hour or two, he was finally taken from the cell, upstairs to an office. Sitting there was a short, bald, sour-faced man in a black suit and tie, who looked like a funeral undertaker. 'Monsieur Artyom Vasillich Riuminskii? he asked.

Artyom nodded.

'Monsieur Artyom Vasillich Riuminskii?' the man repeated, still smiling.

Why ask twice?

'That's the name I was christened.'

'Is that still your name?'

'That's what I call myself.'

'That's what other people call you?'

'To my face, at least. I don't know what I'm called behind my back.'

The man began at the beginning. How had a Russian such as himself come to France in the first place? The interrogation went on for hours. When the sour-faced man flagged, towards evening, another individual took his place. This one had a sober, intense expression, and a detailed but dreary way of questioning, but by then, Artyom had realised exactly what was at stake. A little before midnight, he was taken back to his cell, and given something to eat. He barely had the strength to lift the food to his mouth, he was so tired.

The next day, the door was opened and the Saint was ushered in by a policeman. The door was locked, and the two men stared at each other. The Saint looked terrible.

'They've just accused me of importing and distributing heroin. They say I brought it in from Turkey,' he started to gabble. 'Even if I knew how to go about such a thing, why would I do something so evil?'

Ears in the walls listened to every word.

'Why would they accuse *you* of such a thing?' asked Artyom, taken aback.

The Saint explained everything, but Artyom was dismissive.

'I was dismissive to begin with, too. But I believe they're serious. It's such a disgusting accusation: that I would use the charity's ship – a ship carrying the necessities of life to those poor children in the Levant – in order to import morphine through Marseille. They say I'm in cahoots with you. Forgive me… but is there any basis at all to what they say?'

'No, of course not,' answered Artyom in a clear voice, so that everybody could hear.

But the police had shared the details of Artyom's racket with the Saint.

'They say they know everything,' the Saint said. 'They say they have evidence and witnesses, and that I'm a part of it. But the whole thing is completely repugnant to me. I've told them that, but they won't believe me. Won't you tell them?'

'I'm in the dark,' said Artyom, 'just as much as you are.'

'I'm glad to hear you say that, tremendously glad. Because the things they've been saying about you, horrifying things…' He trailed off.

'There's obviously been some ridiculous misunderstanding about the both of us.'

'That's what I told them. But they won't listen.'

Three days later Artyom was brought before the judge, to be formally charged with importing nearly half a ton of opium into France. They had evidence that he had brought it in through Marseille, and had stored it in the Orphans' Friend's warehouse in Paris. Artyom denied the charges and the judge ordered for him to be kept in custody until the court case.

The Saint was locked in the next-door cell to Artyom in the Santé prison, accused of being an accomplice. He was distraught, and Artyom would hear him through the wall, writhing and praying for deliverance from this unjust imprisonment for hours at a time. He wished he could do something to help him, but he had plenty on his own plate to deal with. It was quite plain that the police were very confident that they had a watertight case against him. Somebody had opened his mouth. Somebody had betrayed him. L'Oreille? No. The Sicilians? Probably.

Lying on his wooden bed that night, Artyom imagined himself in a monastery. But around him he could hear low murmurings, the odd indistinct knocking, and someone above his head howling for release. He wasn't in a monastery after all, but a lunatic asylum. Apart from the daily wailing, and doors being locked and unlocked, there was no other sound to be heard inside the Santé walls. No twitter of birds, no laughter of children, no evening breeze rustling the leaves of the trees. Nothing but iron and stone and sorrow. The world outside had sailed away.

59.

The sky above Berlin was a vault of blue that Saturday. Alyosha parked the Austro-Daimler at the rank opposite the picture house on Hauptstrasse, after a quiet enough day. The motor car had seen better days and was covered in scratches and small dents, while the rust underneath the motor was gobbling it up like cancer. He got out of the vehicle to stretch his legs. There were six other motor taxis already parked at the rank. Two or three of the drivers were chatting outside their taxis, but the rest were sitting at the wheel, their noses in their newspapers, reading the racing results. Horses were their religion.

Alyosha was just locking up his taxi and looking forward to having a bite to eat at the nearby *bierstube,* when he heard them. Looking up, he saw a flock of children of about ten to twelve years old, streaming out of the picture house's double doors into the daylight. In their red caps, they looked like a troop of dwarfs, and he smiled as he saw them break out of their lines to form little groups, chattering away, full of energy and mischief. He saw from the billboard that they'd been to see Eisenstein's film, *The Strike*.

He jolted upright when he saw Margarita coming down the stairs with three other young women, and watched as they chivvied the children to form a choir. All the other taxi drivers looked up as well when the little voices started to sing 'The Internationale'. Leaning back against his taxi, Alyosha crossed his arms across his chest and listened. But as the song continued, it had to compete with the sound of heavy marching growing ever louder as it approached, accompanied by harsh voices shouting out a song:

'*Heute gehört uns Deutschland*
Und morgen die ganze Welt…'

The young voices were quickly drowned out, and Margarita's face filled with panic when she saw the squad from the SA marching towards them. Alyosha saw her lean to whisper something in the ear of the child nearest to her. He immediately turned to the child next to him, and the message spread from ear to ear as the choir lost the rhythm and the singing trailed off.

With no quarter given for women and children, a hailstone of fists started battering them. Those who could, scattered to the four winds. It happened so quickly, it took Alyosha a moment to collect his wits, but then he sprinted across the road to save his cousin. Two or three of the other drivers followed him across the asphalt.

In a frenzied rage, two yards of Nazi had hold of Margarita by her hair. With her hands wrapped around his fist, he slammed her down onto her knees, and then spun her savagely around him. Reaching them, Alyosha kicked the tall Nazi as hard as he could in the small of his back, sending him flying against the concrete steps, hitting his forehead. Then, he grabbed his cousin's arm. She looked at him with a confused half-smile. As she was opening her mouth to say something, somebody made a lunge at Alyosha, grabbing him around the throat.

'Let him go!' she shouted.

He was choking.

'Let him go!'

Alyosha was dimly aware of Margarita fumbling in her bag and then she was flying at his assailant. Howling, Vlasich Pesotski let Alyosha go, and staggered backwards, stamping his feet frantically like a wooden puppet. Squealing like a stuck pig, he staggered backwards two or three steps, and then ducked down, his hands supporting his face as something viscous flowed through his fingers. His squeals turned to something almost unearthly as he writhed on the pavement in agony. Alyosha didn't know what had happened until he looked at Margarita, standing there stunned, holding a small pair of blood-soaked nail scissors in her hand.

Only as Alyosha was turning the nose of his taxi down Bayerischerplatz – the police truck, with its sirens wailing, rushing towards him – did he become aware of the throb in his stomach growing hot and sticky. His breath was coming in short, uneven gasps, and he felt hot and cold in turn. He swallowed hard, once, twice and again – but more and more bile filled his mouth and he started to shake, and felt himself go colder by the second. Margarita, meanwhile, was feeling in her hair, with clumps of it coming out in her hands.

He somehow managed to drive almost to Margarita's apartment block and bring the Austro-Daimler to a stop, before the world went dark. When he came round, Vicki was there, too, and the two women somehow got him up the stairs as he was fading fast from pain. They took him to Vicky's apartment as it was the closest, and they put him on the sofa and tried to staunch the blood, but the depth of the slash made it impossible. Margarita had to keep rinsing the cloth in the bowl, turning the water red, before placing it as gently as she could back on his flesh.

Alyosha whimpered softly, his fingers gripping the side of the sofa. His lips blue and his cheeks bloodless, his eyes fluttered as he drifted in and out of consciousness. As more and more blood continued to flow over her fingers, Margarita was desperately afraid that the blade might have caught his kidney. Vicky ran out to fetch a doctor, someone they could trust.

He was a Russian, and after examining the wound, he stitched it up and dressed it. Putting his equipment back into his bag, he told Alyosha he had been very lucky. The cut was deep, but he was pretty sure that there was no damage to any major organs.

Margarita followed him to the kitchen, where they had a murmured conversation. The doctor agreed she had done the right thing in not taking him near a hospital. That would not have been wise, given how many more doctors and nurses supported Hitler's party these days. The doctor knew of more than one communist who had gone to seek treatment, and had never been seen again. He gave them instructions on how to tend Alyosha, and left. Margarita said she should go and see what had happened to the children.

'I'll stay with him.' Vicky had just rolled herself a cigarette.

Margarita thanked her.

Very gingerly, Alyosha shifted. Vicky propped him up with some cushions, so that he could sit up a little. He asked for more water, but he could barely hold the cup, and he spilt most of it down his chest. She went to sit by his side, her body against his. She put her fingers over his, steadied the cup, and brought it up to his lips. He slowly drank the rest sip by sip.

Vicky sat herself in a chair, lit a cigarette and held it by her cheek. She wanted him to give her a report of what had taken place outside the picture house.

'Didn't Margarita tell you?' He felt exhausted. 'Why do you want to hear it all again?'

He closed his eyes, and she let him rest while she finished her cigarette. Then she dragged her chair closer to him, a notepad and pencil in her hand, and gave him a little nudge. In spite of how weak he felt after losing so much blood, Vicky insisted that he tell her everything that had happened, without leaving out a single detail. Alyosha tried his best, but he felt his throat drying up, and she brought him another glass of water. This time, he could smell tobacco smoke on her fingertips, and noticed how stained her fingernails were. He shut his eyes again, and rested his head back in the hollow of the cushion, his throat working, his cheeks hot and red as the blood rushed to his face. The next minute, he vomited over his lap, his insides roiling, his body ice-cold, his teeth chattering. He saw once more Vlasich's eyeball dripping through his fingers.

60.

In the prison yard, Artyom was walking with the Saint, who was a broken man. His eyes were red-rimmed and bloodshot, his skin had an unhealthy pallor, and his nose was dripping.

'Artyom, you have to rescue me from this agony.'

'I've already told you a dozen times, I can't. If I could, I would.'

'Would you?'

What have they been putting in the man's head? Artyom asked himself.

'I don't know what to think. You tell me one thing, and I hear something completely different. Almighty God, what is the truth? When we stand before our betters, I hope they will judge that a very grave wrong was done to the both of us. But if there is as much as an iota of truth in these dreadful accusations, then you must own up to it. You must acknowledge your sin openly, however excruciating that may be, and for the good of your soul, you should beg for mercy – not only the mercy of the court, but the mercy of the Lord Almighty, and accept your punishment with humility.'

'If I understand you correctly, what you're asking me to do is confess that I'm guilty?'

'If you are.'

'Do you think I am?'

The Saint was very quiet.

'Do you think that I have done what they are accusing me of? Do you think me capable of importing heroin? Seriously?' Artyom walked on and the Saint followed him. 'I'm disappointed. I thought we knew each other better than that. I thought it was the same zeal for helping those who most needed it was what brought the two of us together in the first place.'

'I'm so sorry, Artyom, please forgive me. But it's a terrible thing when a man can't recognise his own degradation. Better always to light a small candle of hope to illuminate a corner, than curse all the darkness.'

Artyom walked on again, head bowed, like a man cut to the quick.

'I beg your pardon. Forgive me for doubting you. But I've been facing dark nights of the soul, and I've found it hard to see deliverance. I feel that my Saviour has turned his back on me.

Although I beg him every night to open the cell door to the daylight of justice, it's the dark which engulfs me always.'

Artyom was interrogated again. It was clear that the case against him was strong. He and the Saint would be looking at ten years of prison with hard labour. And that would be in Guyana, in South America.

61.

'Lying on that sofa all day won't do you any good.'

'I do try my best to get up.'

'You have to try harder.'

'You can be a hard woman.'

Vicky smiled. They both knew she was very kind to him.

His only visitors were Margarita and the Russian doctor. His cousin never came empty-handed, and usually brought a bundle of magazines or newspapers with her – *Das Tage-Buch*, *Montag Morgen* and *Die Rote Fahne* – and every now and again, the *Arbeiter Illustrierte Zeitung*, Alyosha's favourite because of the pictures.

Margarita was very grateful to him for rescuing her, especially as they both knew that Vlasich and the SA would be slow to forgive. The Nazis would be after his blood forever, as Alyosha realised only too well. He didn't dare go back to his own room, as they would be sure to come looking for him – if they hadn't done so already.

62.

Inessa and Philippe visited Artyom at the Santé.

'Is it true?' whispered his sister across the table, looking distressed.

Artyom was smoking one of her husband's cigarettes, luxuriating in a long pull of smoke into his lungs.

'Is what I've heard about you true, Tomya?'

Philippe was scrutinising him minutely.

'If my own sister doubts me,' Artyom said lightly, 'what hope have I in front of the judge?'

She turned to her husband. 'What did I say? I told you, didn't I? I told you my little brother wouldn't be involved in such a thing.'

Looking at his sister, the slight softening of her profile made her look more like their mother, Artyom thought. Was he starting to resemble his father, he wondered? Was he starting to speak like him?

'Why don't we change the subject?' Artyom flicked the ash from his cigarette on the floor. 'Where have you two come from today?'

Inessa told him enthusiastically about the rehearsals for their latest production, a light comedy, which they would tour in Lyon, on the Riviera at Menton, then Beausoleil, Juan-les-Pins, Saint Raphael, Nice and Cannes.

Artyom felt the sun warm on his back as she named the towns, and it raised his spirits.

Philippe offered him another cigarette.

'We'll have a week's break before going on to Toulouse and Pau, and then we'll finish the tour at Biarritz.'

'Let's hope I'll be out of here in time to see it,' he said cheerfully.

The bell rang to signal the end of visiting. The three stood there awkwardly for a moment, then after Artyom had shaken hands with Philippe and thanked him for coming to see him, Inessa flung herself on her brother.

'It breaks my heart to see you in a place like this,' she said through her tears. 'You've been so kind to me...'

'Are you sure there's nothing we can to do help you? Just say the word,' said Philippe, 'and we'll do our best...'

'Thank you. I'm sure I'll be alright but perhaps you could

look out for Zepherine and the children? I've asked her not to come here, I don't want her upsetting herself.'

'Of course, we'll do our best for them.'

'Have you seen the new baby yet?'

'No, not yet.'

A second passed.

'But you have a good lawyer?' asked Inessa. 'It's worth spending the money on a good one…'

'I think he's able enough, thank you.'

That wasn't true: with not a *sou* to his name, Artyom was defending himself.

63.

There were two other men with his usual interrogator this time. He could see at once that these two came from a world beyond the greasy walls of the *Sûreté*. They both had soft, white hands and clean nails, and they had about them the smell of luxurious homes, tranquil wives, pretty little children and obedient dogs. They pulled documents tied in legal ribbon out of fine leather briefcases, placing everything neatly before them on the desk. They were the only ones to speak, the policeman a pale shadow in the background.

'On whose authority are you making this offer?' Artyom asked after hearing what they had to say.

'That's neither here nor there. What we want is an answer.'

'And then what? If I were to agree, how would I live my life then?'

One of the civil servants tapped the document in front of him.

'Very few men return to France after ten years of hard labour in Guyana. Those who do are broken in health and spirit. Alternatively, the earth and maggots of South America can be your home for ever.'

'Why don't you think our offer over?' suggested the other one in a reasonable voice.

64.

Margarita decreed that he was well enough to risk a short walk. It felt strange to be out in the fresh air. His body still felt heavy, and he moved hesitantly and slightly jerkily, veering from one side of the pavement to the other.

'Lean on my arm,' she told him.

They hadn't gone very far before he was tired, and she suggested a rest and a drink at the Grosser Kurfürst. It was clear that Margarita had been there often from the warm welcome the roly-poly of a woman behind the bar gave her. After sitting at one of the wooden benches, Alyosha saw why: on the windowsill at his elbow were some of the flyers and pamphlets of the *Roter Frontkämpferbund*. Then he took in that while the two or three young men standing casually by the door looked perfectly relaxed, they were keeping an eagle eye on the comings and goings outside. It was quiet enough, with little traffic and few people passing by.

Two glasses of Bitburger arrived, and Margarita fetched a chess set. Setting out the pieces, she spoke of her worries for the Soviet Union. It was clear that Adolf Hitler meant war; that much was obvious enough simply from reading *Mein Kampf*. The Soviet Union needed to arm itself, and quickly.

'Why is the rest of Europe so blind?'

Alyosha didn't have the energy to engage with her.

By the time his white bishop had succeeding in taking her black knight, the sky had darkened outside. In a move he hadn't anticipated, her second knight jumped over his pawns to knock his queen into his lap.

'I'm pregnant,' she said.

Curious, he looked up from the board at her. The rain was beating down by now and gurgling into the gutters. Several office workers had come scurrying into the bar for shelter, their shoulders and backs dripping, filling the place with a smell of damp cloth mixed with petrol fumes. The hum of voices and clinking of glasses on the zinc bar gradually grew louder. Half a dozen thoughts flitted through Alyosha's head.

'This is good news?' he asked carefully.

Margarita avoided his eye, turning her head to look out of the window. She clearly wasn't jubilant.

'Have you told Larissa?'

She shook her head. 'Not yet. I've been meaning to. But… I'm finding it difficult.'

'But you two are so close. I can't believe you've told me before her.'

'We are and we're not. Since Bruno joined the NASAP a couple of months ago I've barely seen her. It's just too… difficult.'

This was news to Alyosha

'Why are you surprised?'

'I thought he was a member of the *Deutschnational Voklspartei*?'

'So he was. But, like so many others, he'd been leaning towards the Nazis for a while.'

Margarita had joined them for supper one Sunday evening, and Bruno had launced into a diatribe about how society was going to the dogs, and how much he sympathised with the Nazis' hatred towards the girls who danced naked in nightclubs for filthy-minded old capitalists. What right had men like that to buy young flesh? And he hated the discordant noise of the negro's jazz that you heard in those clubs as well. What was the negro apart from the link between ape and man? Their music was an affront to the ear – if you could even call jazz music at all – and not suitable for the Teutonic nation. Was jazz appropriate for anyone with a

European aesthetic, a people for whom the splendours of Bach, Mozart and Beethoven were part of their inheritance? He'd gone on in that vein for what felt like hours, and of course she hadn't been able to stop herself from arguing with him, and things were said on both sides that would have been better left unsaid, and after that, the welcome when she visited was distinctly lukewarm.

Alyosha considered this, and then asked, 'Does Vicky know that you're expecting?'

She shook her head.

'Are you going to tell her?'

Margarita sipped her beer. 'I don't know. It depends...'

She seemed so uncertain about everything; so totally unlike her usual self.

'There's not much – how shall I say? – intimacy between Vicky and me. Not really. I've realised that she's never told me anything personal in all the time I've known her. She's never once discussed her family, for instance. I can't say I know her better today than on the first day I met her. I don't know if anybody knows Vicky, really.'

'I'll help in whatever way I can,' he said, placing his hand over hers and squeezing it tenderly.

'Thanks 'Lyosha. You're very kind to worry about me. There's nobody else much who does.'

'But what about Kai-Olaf? What does he say?'

She told him that Kai-Olaf thought that their political work was more important than anything, and that having a baby would be an added burden on lives which were already running close to the precipice – lives that the weakest breeze could blow over the cliff edge.

'The cause is more important to Kai-Olaf than anything else.'

He had told her that she should get rid of the baby as quickly as possible. But, in her heart, she didn't want to. She loved her sister's children, and knew how she would love to hold her own baby in her arms.

'If you were in my position what would you do?'

65.

The police made sure that the Saint heard everything. Artyom
had never seen him so furious.

'You're a wicked man, a truly wicked man. You've told me
nothing but a pack of lies. But there's an opportunity now for
you to make amends, and save us at the same time. Do what they
ask of you. Save us both.'

'Do you understand what they're asking me to do?'

'Do it.'

'I might as well just hang myself tonight and have done with it.'

'Are you willing to see an innocent man suffer because you
insist on saving your own sinful skin? Why are you smiling? I
don't have a reason to smile in the hell I'm in. It's all up on us.'

When Artyom was next brought before the two civil servants,
they told him his time had run out and he had to give them an
answer: was he prepared to give evidence in court against Lolole
and Meme Corse?

'Are you ready to do what we want? It's a disgrace that a
criminal like Meme Corse is sitting in the Deputies' Chamber.
He's poison, and there are some individuals very high up in the
Government who are determined to get rid of him. If you do
us this favour, you walk free, and we won't forget you helped
us. You will be doing a great service to the Republic of France,
which has given you so much. Otherwise, your trial goes ahead.'

'Neither of the two brothers will ever forgive me, as you well
know.'

'They'll both be under lock and key – for a very long time.'

'They'll have plenty on the outside to do their bidding. Where
would I go? Where would I live? And be safe?'

'You'd be a free man, so that would be a matter for you to decide.'

Silence.

'We won't be asking again, Artyom.'

'This is your last chance.'

One of them was already gathering up his papers in a neat pile. 'Very well, I'll do it. But I want you to protect my family.'

Immediately following his decision, he was kept apart from the other prisoners for his own safety. As he prepared for the trial, he had plenty of time to consider his situation. He wrote to Zepherine asking her to visit, but she refused. Artyom could understand her decision perfectly. The two Corsican brothers were brought before the court within a couple of months. Artyom was the main witness for the prosecution, and he recounted his dealings with them in full. It took three days for him to give his evidence. Several times, he heard heckling from the public gallery, though the two brothers sat impassively in the dock. Thanks to Artyom's damning evidence, Meme and Lolole Corse were both sentenced to fifteen years' imprisonment. Immediately after the trial, a sum of money was transferred into his bank account and, as he requested, a passage on a boat to Tangier was arranged for him. He was being forced to leave Paris, his home for so many years. He could still remember his first afternoon in the city, when he had leant his elbows on the parapet of the Pont des Arts, charmed by the little sails of the pleasure boats, like swans on the Seine.

He went to the house, but Zepherine wasn't there, and it felt as though it had been empty for some time. He sat and wrote her a letter, but when he read it over, he realised that everything he wanted to say had remained unsaid. Why did he find it so difficult to put his feelings into words? What was the matter with him? He felt furious with himself, but left the letter on the mantelpiece for her anyway, without knowing if she would ever read it.

He had so little time.

He made his way to the Gare de Lyon, and when his train reached Marseille, he made straight for the port and boarded the ship. He stood on deck as the ship's whistle pierced the air, as the anchor chain was hoisted over the capstan, and as the vessel moved slowly away from the quayside. As the ship gathered speed once it left the harbor, he was the only one who remained there, soaked to his skin as raindrops fell like bullets, watching the lights of France gradually disappear in the distance, as the rain hissed across the sea.

He was a free man, but his future looked bleak.

66.

When Alyosha finally dared to return to his shabby little room, every piece of furniture had been smashed to kindling. Even his suitcase – his father's old suitcase, the one he had taken all the way to Zürich when he was a student – had been slashed with a knife into long, ugly strips, and his pitiful collection of clothes and his second pair of shoes had also been ripped to shreds. A tornado of revenge had descended, a clear warning that the SA were after his blood. The word was already out that Vlasich was going to find him and the red bitch who had stabbed him in the eye, and kill them both. Alyosha was in no doubt that he would carry out his threat if he found them.

He was still staying at Vicky's apartment, and had barely left it since the fight. To begin with, he'd slept on the sofa, but over the summer, they'd felt themselves being more and more attracted to each other, and it hadn't taken long before he was sharing her bed. When he'd broached the subject of rent with her one morning, Vicky told him there was no need for him to contribute as much as a *pfennig*, because the KPD paid for the place.

Vicky's life ambition was to visit the Soviet Union again, perhaps even to study there, so in the few free hours she had free from working at *Die Rote Fahne* and her Party duties, Vicky took Russian lessons, as she was desperate to speak the language fluently.

'Don't go paying for lessons,' Alyosha told her. 'I'll teach you for nothing. It's the least I can do.'

'I want somebody who can teach me properly,' she teased him.

Nothing gave Alyosha more pleasure than introducing Vicky to the treasures of his mother tongue, though she was impatient when he tried to introduce her to Pushkin, and told him she had no time for poetry unless it was revolutionary.

Alyosha slowly regained his strength, and one Saturday afternoon at the beginning of October, he managed to borrow a yellow tandem, and he and Vicky set off on a bike ride out towards Potsdam, to eat hamburgers with mustard and drink beer at Heiliger See. He was exhausted at the end of the day, but it was a good indication of how far along the road to recovery he had come. But the better he felt, the more bored and frustrated he became, so Vicky suggested he might earn some money tutoring some of her comrades who were also eager to learn Russian, and told him to meet her after work one day so that she could introduce him to them.

He arrived too early, of course, and Vicky was late as usual, but as he was hanging around outside Karl Liebknecht Haus, two men in their shirtsleeves – their jackets hanging by their fingers over their shoulders, as it was such a mild October – approached him. Alyosha guessed what they were even before they held out their identity cards under his nose.

Two plain-clothes policemen both wearing sunglasses – one a blue pair, the other dark green. Blue Glasses asked him what he was doing loitering outside the doors of Karl Liebknecht Haus.

'I'm not breaking any law,' he answered stoutly.

Green Glasses asked calmly, 'Are you waiting for somebody?'

'What's that got to do with you?'

Blue Glasses asked, 'Do you understand what this place is?'

'No,' answered Alyosha as nonchalantly as he could.

'You're not a red then?'

He didn't want to give the two of them any reason to harass him further, so he muttered something and slunk off. He crossed the square and went to sit on a wooden bench, which was covered in bird droppings, keeping an eye on the entrance of the German Communist Party headquarters.

A swarm of midges were whirling about in the branches of the trees when Vicky and her comrades stepped out. Usually, she wore a leather jacket and a red scarf, but the weather was still unseasonably warm, and she wore a light summer dress which gave her an uncharacteristically girlish air. The dress fitted her perfectly, as though it had been grown onto her, and Alyosha thought how attractive she was, though Vicky never took much interest in her own appearance. She already had a cigarette in her hand. She always had a cigarette in her hand.

As he walked to meet them, he noticed that her shoes were shabbier than ever. Summer and winter, she always wore the same old pair of shoes. She said to waste money on new clothes, when the movement was desperate for funds, was unacceptable, and if she ever had any money left at the end of the month, she would insist on giving it back.

Meeting Vicky after work was a rare event, however, as she normally went straight to a meeting, not returning home until late. Alyosha was left to his own devices for much of the time, and even with his new pupils, tutoring only filled a few hours. One evening, sick to death of skulking in the apartment, he went to Café Romanische for a beer, nursing his glass of Edwinger at the bar so it lasted as long as possible. He was so bored, he thought about calling in on Vicky at her office, even though he already knew there'd be no welcome for him. He made his way to Karl Liebknecht Haus, but then he had second thoughts and ended up in the bar opposite. Late as it was, all the lights in the office building were still blazing. He was reminded of an illustration he'd seen in the *Arbeiter Illustrierte Zeitung* of the Titanic.

A third beer bolstered his resolve. After giving his credentials, and being thoroughly frisked for weapons, he was accompanied upstairs. At the head of the stairs, another guard sprang up from his chair in order to unlock a door, which opened onto a nicotine-stained corridor. He walked along the frayed carpet past the hustle and bustle of offices, with the click of typewriters to be heard over everything, and was told to wait.

The word came back: Vicky was too busy to see him.

He caught a glimpse of her through the glass door. She saw him looking at her and held his glance, but she looked abstracted and distant, and he felt that he was invisible to her. The room was full of men of various ages, and a few young women; there weren't enough chairs for them all, so some of them were perched on tables, or were on their haunches on the floor, or standing at the back of the room. Nearly all of them were smoking. Why were communists so fond of arguing in smoky rooms? Vicky was sitting at the front, under posters of Marx, Lenin, Stalin, Ernst Thälmann and Heinz Neumann. Two men were furiously debating, hurling words like 'traitor' at each other across the office.

Alyosha recognised one of them as the unemployed printer, Paul, who'd shared his cell in Moabit. He listened to him call the Social Democrats dishonest pigs, men who did nothing but feather their own nests. They may have been the great heroes of the working class, thundered Paul, but they betrayed them without a thought back in August 1914, when they voted for war credits, and sent overflowing trains of young men to the front through salvoes of flowers and hats, and crowds shouting 'Victory!' When all those husbands and wives and mothers and sons were kissing each other for the very last time, what were these politicians doing? Filling their bellies in cafés as they gossiped spitefully about each other. With such scum in their ranks, why was anybody surprised that the Social Democrats had voted for the Imperialist War?

'Why do you insist on going over the same old ground, Paul?' asked someone impatiently.

'Because their betrayal was unforgiveable,' shot back Vicky.

'It's in the past,' piped up somebody else.

'Perhaps it is, but the effects are still felt today. That's why we can't make a pact with the SPD,' insisted Vicky.

There was some protest at this.

'Vicky's right!' insisted Paul. 'We never can!'

Vicky warmed to her theme. Had they forgotten 1919? When Karl and Rosa announced a revolution on the streets of Berlin in the name of the working class? Who gave a free rein to the *Freikorps* to destroy them? Who was truly to blame for the vicious murders of Karl and Rosa?

Alyosha had heard enough. He must have heard Vicky rehearse this argument a thousand times, that it was the Social Democrats, and not the Nazis, who were the biggest enemies of the communists. In their hearts, all but the zealots thought by now that it was necessary to change policy, but the discipline of the KPD and the order from Moscow bound them all to the party line.

He left them to it.

It was mid-morning the next day when Vicky finally returned to the apartment, Margarita and Kai-Olaf in tow, after working all night.

While Vicky was in her bedroom, changing her stockings, Alyosha asked his cousin how she was.

'I'm fine.'

'How are things at Aznefttrust?'

'All well. I'm on my way there now – but we have things to do first.'

'You've made a good recovery.' Kai-Olaf made this a statement, not a question, and Alyosha was reminded of why he had never been able to warm to him.

'The wound is nearly healed. Thanks to Vicky. She's a very good nurse.'

Vicky came out of her bedroom and said smilingly, 'What are you doing? Talking behind my back again?'

'I'm praising you.'

As the three made to leave Alyosha asked, 'When will I see you?'

'Don't stay up for me,' Vicky told him, 'And whatever you do, don't come by work again.'

The door shut behind them.

67.

That autumn, he started to go with her on Sundays to canvass in the working-class districts of the city. He went slightly reluctantly, out of a sense of obligation, but also because he was worried Vicky might be attacked. Seeing her argue at people's doorsteps made his hair stand on end. She would take on even the most out-and-out Nazi, who often seemed about to take a punch at her.

One rare weekend in December when Vicky wasn't working, he persuaded her to come shopping with him. Alyosha actually had a little money in his pocket from his tutoring, and he wanted to buy her a new pair of shoes. The Christmas displays in the windows of the big shops, so colourful and pretty, gave Alyosha a delightful warm feeling. It had been snowing a little and there was already a white carpet underfoot.

As they entered the KaDeWe, they passed a man standing with a cap in his hand, singing drunkenly,

'Hoch soll'n Sie leben
Kinder soll'n Sie kriegen
Frei-mal hoch.'

Alyosha had come to a decision. He was sick and tired of his life in Berlin. 1931 was nearly over, and he knew if he didn't act, he would be in exactly the same place in a year's time, still living hand to mouth, still looking over his shoulder with the constant fear of being wounded or killed. He longed for a less haphazard existence. The more he thought about it, the more apparent it became, that the first step he should take, which might give him the security he longed for, would be to marry Vicky.

The week before Christmas, he barely saw her, because she was so busy arranging a rally at the Sportsplatz, working tirelessly to ensure the stadium would be full to bursting with red flags. He went with her to the rally, which was a success, and as they all poured out of the Sportsplatz, still singing, they brought the traffic to a standstill. Vicky and Alyosha were on their way to a small party Margarete Neumann and her sister Babette Gross were holding for their husbands and their co-workers at the Aschinger, a bier keller on Friedrichstrasse. As they wove their way through the lines of cars which had been forced to slow down, the streets were full of bad-tempered drivers and horns were blaring, but Vicky was in good spirits, pleased that everything had gone off smoothly, her cheeks rosy as she strode on energetically.

Alyosha suddenly grabbed her hand and pulled her towards him.

'What a place to ask!' she exclaimed.

A horn blared behind them until the bonnet shook.

'I didn't think you'd appreciate my going down on one knee – much too bourgeois.'

'I don't appreciate you asking me at all.'

Alyosha had imagined her throwing her arms around his neck, and going on her tiptoes to give him a passionate kiss, but Vicky just said,

'I've already tried marriage once. It didn't work.'

He pulled her towards him again, the leather of her jacket cold in his hand. 'Will you, though?'

She tried to pull away. He seemed to be singing to the deaf. 'Vicky, put the KPD to one side for a second.'

'You don't know me at all, do you? After living together all this time. You don't. Or you wouldn't be asking something so idiotic. Marriage exists to protect and transfer property from generation to generation. Private ownership is the basis for all greed and selfishness. Without the family and without property, the world would be a better place by far. Even Jesus Christ saw the benefits of turning his back on his family.'

'But it's just a normal impulse to want to have something of your own,' he answered.

She tutted again.

'I'm only saying. I wouldn't mind having my own house and motor car.'

'Alyosha, have you learnt nothing? Are American factory workers who own motor cars free? Or are they forced to buy one because that's the only way they can get to work? How do they pay for a motor car anyway? By borrowing money from the bank, probably. Just as they borrow to buy their little house and strip of garden. But once they've done that, they've chained themselves even tighter to the order which exploits them.'

Having expressed her fury at his idiocy, she relented a little, as the depths of his disappointment started to dawn on her.

'I like it that you and I are together...' she squeezed his arm. 'And together we'll be.'

Which perhaps for Vicky was the nearest thing to being married, Alyosha thought, slightly comforted that she still had a warm corner in her heart for him.

From the front seat of a Wanderer convertible – the patch on his eye like a black hole in his head –Vlasich Pesotski was glaring at him. Alyosha caught his eye. Vlasich's face was thinner and paler, his cheeks hollowed out and sunken, his chin surprisingly small and narrow. Vlasich dragged his finger slowly across his throat. With thousands of communists like a warm blanket around him, in that moment, Alyosha didn't feel so much as a smidgeon of fear.

IV

1932-1933

I.

The same familiar smell of polish and hot-house flowers wafted a greeting when he walked in through the main entrance of the Hotel Adlon. The foyer hadn't changed at all, the same black-and-white tiles, the same wallpaper, the same furniture and the same round glass in the door to the bar on the right. Even the magazine and newspaper rack was in exactly the same place.

Alyosha recognised the receptionist, but the one-armed porter was no longer there, and he didn't know any of the other staff. He passed an old couple, arm in arm, both feeble and hobbling, moving step by decrepit step while he bounded swiftly up the stairs, past the big plant pots in the alcoves. As he made his way, he half expected to see Grete coming round a corner of the corridor with her arms full of clean linen.

Grete the maid, as she had been before their world changed. He remembered how she would pad around as lightly as a cat in a gutter, in a negligee or, more often, naked. Even when she walked in a pair of shoes, she longed to be barefoot. Their afternoons in bed came back to him, her flesh sweeter than a nut, before she vanished from his life, leaving him heartbroken. Lovely Grete, his sweetheart, who, by now, belonged to another time, when he himself had been someone else.

He pulled his shoulders back, cleared his throat and rapped lightly on the door. Number 32. His father's old suite.

A thin man in a sober suit opened the door and, when Alyosha gave his name, motioned him in. From the butler's bored expression, he guessed he was one of many to be seen that day. 'And the name again?' He looked Alyosha over with a hint of a sneer.

'Alexandrov. Alexei Fyodorovich.'

The butler ran his finger over a list on the desk, then unscrewed the cap of a black fountain pen and neatly put a tick against his name. He disappeared into the adjoining bedroom, and Alyosha had a moment to glance around him. The room, like the foyer, was unchanged. The same discreetly luxurious furnishings. And there, on the wall still, the oil painting of Bismarck, and opposite, the rural scene of two pheasants pecking under the shadows of a beech tree by a lake. The cheval mirror, and on the desk, the same bronze blotter and the two inkwells on either side. Was it just a coincidence? Or had fate brought him back once more to the Adlon?

He was aware of somebody half whistling, half humming in the bathroom, and the sound of a razor being tapped sporadically against the edge of a porcelain basin. Years ago, Alyosha had sponged his father's tired back in that bathroom.

With a dressing gown folded over his arm, the butler knocked on the bathroom door and entered. Moments later, his master emerged wearing the burgundy velvet dressing gown, tied with a tasselled gold rope around his middle. The butler was at his tail with a black brush in his hand.

'This is the last one?'

'Yes sir. Alexandrov.'

Sinking down into a pile of cushions on the sofa, he sighed, 'Thank goodness. I don't want an afternoon as pointless as the morning we had.'

He crossed his hairy legs. They were solid, like tree trunks.

The room drowned in his *Eau de Cologne*, and although it was only midday, the butler poured his master a large Armagnac from a crystal decanter.

'Stand up and go over there so I can see you properly. No, no. Not there, you half-wit. What's the matter with you, boy? You're *right* in my light there. Move over. That's it, there — *there*. Stop exactly where you are.'

Captain Malinowski swirled the Armagnac around in his mouth as he ran his eye over him, exactly as though he was appraising a bullock he was thinking of buying.

'I have absolutely no patience with a whole lot of pointless questions and answers, life is too short. I'm a plain-speaking man. Sit. Not *there*. That one. That's it.'

Alyosha sat in the mahogany chair as instructed.

'I much prefer looking a man straight in the eye and letting him give me a fair account of himself. Give me one good reason why I should employ you.'

He gave as good an account of himself to Captain Malinowski as he could. He was asked briefly about his family, and his time in Paris. Then, so abruptly it took Alyosha a moment to take it in, he was told the job was his. There were no further questions about his work experience, or requests for his references, and on top of everything, he was offered a salary significantly more than what had been mentioned in the advertisement.

'I don't want anybody accusing the Poles of being a miserly nation.'

His voice was loud and booming, better suited to the barrack yard than a hotel suite.

He was a truly ugly man, with a purple pincushion of a nose, small black eyes set too close together, and yellow, snaggled teeth. He also had a birthmark which spread across his left cheek and down his neck. But he had a good head of hair, and when he lifted his head to light his cigar from the match his butler proffered, his dressing gown opened to show a thick reddish-black pampas across his chest. He carried some excess flesh around his waist, but he was a powerful-looking man nevertheless, and when he stood up, he had a straight-backed, military bearing. He told Alyosha he had never learnt to drive a motor car,

'And I'm too old to learn.'

There was something combative in the way he said this, as though daring Alyosha to disagree. The Captain went on to say he liked the old ways best, and he kept as much as he could to the old traditions of his youth.

'Nobody sensible likes to see change in anything. That's why you see so many old women with the same hairstyles that they wore when they were young.'

Captain Malinowski would far rather have been born at the beginning of the previous century than his own ('…things were so much better then, everybody knew their place.'). He'd practically been born in the saddle, and his favourite smell was that of horse sweat ('…a cloud of nature's own glory…'). He used to exercise his horses until he was stiff as a board and every bone in his body ached.

When he was only a boy ('…a strapping twelve-year-old…'), he claimed he could catch a year-old roe by running the animal until it was winded. He'd been brought up to a life of hunting and fishing on his father's estate, and had been a pupil at the same *gymnasium* in Wilno as Feliks Dzierżyński and Jozef Piłsudski. Later, under Marshal Piłsudski, he had fought off Lenin's Red Army in 1920, though he had been shot in the leg, and bore the scar still.

By now, the butler had poured his master a second glass of Armagnac.

Captain Malinowski went on to tell Alyosha that, while family tradition was important, the most important thing of all was his Catholic faith, and defending that faith. After carrying on in this vein for some time, Captain Malinowski abruptly asked Alyosha what was his opinion.

'My opinion on what?'

'What I've just said.'

He'd only been half listening so he said, 'I can't disagree.'

'I loathe flatterers. What's the matter with you, you fool? You don't have to butter me up or agree with everything I say, like a puppy looking for a pat. I've given you the job. Say your mind freely, I'll respect you all the more for it. I want you to be straight with me. D'you understand? There's nothing I hate more than the shilly-shallying of people who bend this way and that, trying to please everybody, but pleasing nobody in the end. Being relative about everything is just a way of trying to avoid conflict.'

Alyosha answered that Catholicism was not something he was very familiar with.

'What about the history of Poland? How familiar are you with that?'

Alyosha has a sudden image of Ludwika wrapped inadequately in a towel.

'Not familiar at all,' he answered.

Captain Malinowski was snappish, but for the occasional peal of bright laughter – a sudden warm bout of merriment.

One thing wasn't clear to him, Alyosha ventured.

'What's not clear to you?'

The Captain was on his third Armagnac by now.

'Am I being employed just as a chauffeur? Or as a tutor as well?'

'What?'

Was he a little hard of hearing?

'Am I being employed just as a chauffeur? Or as a tutor as well?'

'No need to shout for heaven's sake, I'm not deaf.' The Captain settled back on the sofa. 'You'll only be expected to work as a chauffeur to begin with. I might need your services as a tutor in a month or two. It depends.'

'What does it depend on?'

'Every great event in life is a bend in the road. What is round the next corner? Who knows?' He stood up. 'Remember that every nation on the face of the earth lives within narrow walls of possibility, even the most powerful and arrogant. The existence of a nation is not a fact, but a painful question, because history has taught us all that annihilation is a very real possibility. When one nation decides to impose its will on another, that is not a sign of strength, but a clear sign of weakness, and it will only ever be a matter of time before another bigger nation comes along and conquers that one in turn. That's why your future, lad, depends on which way the wind will blow.'

What *was* the man jabbering on about?

The Captain took another swig of his Armagnac.

'When it comes – and it's sure to come sometime, sooner than we think perhaps, it'll be one warm blast from the east, and a warmer blast from the west, with those in the middle roasting in the heat.'

2.

Motorcycles and rows of policemen were blocking the top of the street, which gave onto Bülowplatz, so nobody could enter the square. Alyosha made his way past more and more of them, standing in pairs at every door, until he came to a solid wall of *schupos,* their guns across their shoulders and their helmets tightly strapped under their chins. He was stopped from going any further.

The square itself was also cordoned off by more policeman. He was due to meet Vicky in the bar opposite Karl Liebknecht Haus, but how was he meant to reach her? From the amount of police, something big was afoot. Were they planning another raid on the KPD headquarters? The *schupos* had been there several times already, poking and prying from the attics to the cellars. The first time they came, Vicky had been very roughly manhandled by two policemen twice her size. Alyosha was worried about her, and turned down another street, hoping to slip through the cordons, but when he reached the entrance to the square by the park, there were *schupos* there, too, on horseback, and it was impossible to get past them. More and more motor lorries roared past, their side flaps bolted down, so that the policemen inside could leap out quickly if the need arose. People were already gathering to shout and protest, but they were herded firmly back on the pavements, so that the road was kept clear for the motor lorries to enter the square.

Alyosha found himself in the middle of a crowd who were pushing forward slowly towards the square. He asked one of the protestors what was going on, and was told that the SA intended to march in front of Karl Liebknecht Haus. This was clearly an inflammatory act, and it was sure to lead to people getting hurt, if not worse.

'Red Front!

The shouting became louder.

'Red Front!'

A long whistle was the signal for the mounted police to turn and urge their horses forward into the crowd, to the outraged and panicked shouts of those directly in the path of the trotting hooves. Now voices were raised in anger.

'Red Front!'

'This is our street!'

A young worker was the first to be grabbed in a stranglehold under the armpit of a *schupo*. He was given a good kicking by another, and then flung into one of the motor lorries. This set off a fresh storm of protest and booing, and soon, batons were flying and shouts turned to screams. Alyosha felt himself being momentarily carried along by the crush of the retreating crowd, until there was enough space for it to disperse. People were still being beaten and dragged to the lorries.

Then, the first column of Brownshirts marched into the square, accompanied by a double cordon of policemen at their side. Their voices rang out:

'Die rote Front, schlagt zu Brei,
SA marschiert, Achtung die Strasse frei…'

The man at the front, his black cap planted squarely on his head, and his leather straps pulled tight across his shoulders, held a flag aloft. The crowd of protestors pressed against the ranks of policemen, booing and heckling, but they were kept firmly in check. The flag-bearer heading the column marched past Alyosha, his shirt a paler brown than the ones behind him, his breeches of a finer material, his boots a softer leather, and the silver buckle at his waist shinier. It was Bruno Volkman.

'Red front! Red front!' shouted voices from the crowd.

'Sod off, you Nazi scum!'

The protestors finally managed to breach the police cordon, and dozens of them rushed headlong into the middle of the SA, kicking, punching and shoving. The police whistles calling for reinforcements were deafening, and it didn't take long for the *schupos* to regroup, herding the protestors back against the walls so tightly that many of them were in danger of suffocating, and started panicking.

'Can't breathe…'

'Give me some air…'

'My little boy is here,' screamed a young woman.

Those on the outside tried their best to break free, and the *schupos* started to back up a little as the dark boots marched further along. Then, some of the residents in the apartment block overlooking the square started hurling potted plants down at the marching Brownshirts from the balconies and window sills above.

The schupos were quick to react, aiming their guns up and shouting,

'Shut the windows!'

'Now! Or we shoot.'

The tail of the procession was passing by, though the voices of the SA swelled louder than ever.

Vicky, out of nowhere, was suddenly at his side.

'Follow me,' she said urgently.

'It's impossible to get in,' he shouted at her back.

'Come on!'

'Vicky.' He ran after her. 'Vicky – wait!'

She was fairly sprinting along.

'We'll never get in this way…'

She was as sprightly as a squirrel, and he had difficulty keeping up with her. He followed her into a side street, but others were running ahead of them with the same idea. Alyosha put on a sprint to catch up with her, and, panting, asked her what they were doing, but she didn't bother to answer. She was conserving her strength. She picked up speed again, and he managed to stay close. At the far end of the street, there were still more *schupos*, double-banked, head to head with a group of workers who were trying to gain entry to the square. Over their shoulders, Alyosha saw the columns of the SA marching purposefully: row after row of tough men. At the head of one regiment marched Vlasich Pesotski, with his black leather patch over the empty socket.

'There's another way,' urged Vicky. 'This way – come on!'

'We don't have a hope. We'll never get in…'

'There's always hope.'

They were running down an even narrower backstreet, when they heard the guns being fired, followed by screams and shouts.

They turned around and saw terrified people running towards them. 'What's happening?' Vicky shouted at one of them, but nobody stopped to anwer her. One or two of them stumbled and fell, sending the people behind them flying, too, but they all struggled to their feet and ran for their lives.

Then came the *schupos,* the ones at the front firing their guns. A woman fell to the floor, and Vicky and Alyosha dragged her into the shelter of a doorway. More protestors ran past, some flinging their red flags down. Alyosha pushed against the door and when, to his enormous relief it opened, he pushed the woman and Vicky hastily through it.

'What are you doing?' she said furiously. 'I have to go – get out of the way.'

'What do you think you or anybody else can do?'

They heard horses' hooves clattering on the cobblestones outside and gunshots.

'Alyosha, I won't tell you again – move!'

'Vicky, just think for a minute. What can you possibly do? You're no good to anybody dead.'

3.

They were decorating the Christmas tree with glass birds, bells and candles. Larissa kept an eye on Ella, who was standing on a chair and getting crosser by the minute because her little sister was being more of a hindrance than a help.

'Mummy, take her out.'

'She just wants to pass the things to you...'

'She's a nuisance.'

Ella stamped her foot. She was very close to tears.

'Now look what she's done! She just spoils everything...'

Larissa sighed, and told Margarita it would be easier if she rang for the maid to take Clara away, but Margarita, seeing Clara's crestfallen little face, took her hand and suggested they go and play upstairs. Clara cheered up at this, and took her aunt to her bedroom, where she introduced her to all her dolls, explaining who were best friends and who always quarrelled. Then she found her favourite picture book, and in no time, she was cuddled up on Margarita's lap, listening to the story. But somebody else was hovering at the door. With her thumb in her mouth, Ella came in, clutching her rag doll, and, her quarrel with her sister forgotten, she shared Margarita's lap for the remainder of the story. After playing with her nieces a little longer, the maid came in to give the girls their bath, with a message for Margarita that she was expected downstairs.

Bruno had arranged a small party at the house, for some thirty or so of their friends; doctors and their wives for the most part. By the time Margarita went back downstairs, most of them had arrived, and there was a lively hum of talk coming from the drawing room. Margarita helped herself to a glass of punch and then stood for a moment, feeling slightly awkward, as she didn't know any of the guests very well. She hadn't really wanted to come, but she had used the occasion to see her nieces and bring them their Christmas presents, as there were only two days until Christmas. Then, a familiar face came towards her, and she felt rather pleased to see her old tutor. Professor Krieger had a glass of wine in one hand, and he extracted the other hand from his jacket pocket to shake her hand.

'Margarita Kozmyevna…'

'Herr Professor.'

'How are things at Aznefttrust?'

He knew all about her. He had heard that the company was doing good work as far as trade went. There was a great need for new trading and business opportunities, in order to create more jobs, get the unemployed back into work and get the country back on its feet.

'Have you happened to bump into your cousin lately?'

'Alyosha? No, I haven't seen him in a while,' she lied.

'Neither have I.'

Margarita was silent.

'He was with us for a while. I found work for him. But… he left.'

'Wasn't there some incident?' she asked. 'A shooting?'

'There was.'

'Then perhaps it's not surprising he left you.'

'We all need to be careful with things as they are.'

Margarita felt that, behind the small talk, he was sizing her up somehow. Then, Bruno came to greet her, though he seemed more interested in talking to the Professor about some meeting they had both attended earlier in the week. She waited until after the Christmas carols, and then she told her sister that she was leaving. As she said goodbye, Larissa whispered, 'Things have come to a head. In the new year I'm going to leave Bruno.'

4.

An icy, mid-January shock of cold came off the Spree as Alyosha locked Captain Malinowski's motor car. It had been bitter for some days, the whipping frozen wind coating everything with a stubborn rime. He was glad to step in to the warm fug of the café after his brisk walk through the cold. Vicky hadn't arrived, of course, so he told the waitress he would wait for his friend before ordering, and sat there, gradually thawing out. Vicky was late for everything apart from KPD meetings or committees. She was never late for those.

Alyosha smoked his cigarette and studied the menu on the blackboard. The Aschinger was a good place for cheap food. Almost three-quarters of an hour went past before Vicky appeared, her cheeks red and her hands cold, the old and ragged gloves she wore pitifully inadequate.

'We have to go.'

'But I'm starving.'

'No time. Where did you park?'

He followed her out.

'I can't take you far,' Alyosha told her as he started the engine. 'I'll be lucky to get to the Adlon without being late as it is.'

'This is really important, Alyosha, you have to give me a lift.'

'Vicky, can I ask one thing? Why is every last thing you do so very important and everything I do not at all important?'

'It was you who chose to work for that that Polish bourgeois.'

'He's an aristocrat.'

'Same thing.'

'Not at all.'

'Well, you can split hairs if you want. Come on, drive.'

'Says *you* who does nothing but split hairs with me!' He laughed as he turned the Mercedes and began to drive through the icy streets. Pulling him up on his many solecisms was second nature to Vicky, and by now, Alyosha felt he was familiar with every Marxist precept in existence.

'Can't you drive faster?'

She was rolling a cigarette on her knee.

'Certainly, if you want me to crash.'

In the early days, Alyosha used to capitulate, because she knew Marxism like the back of her hand, and would always beat him in any argument. But the constant questioning of his every statement had sharpened his mind, and by now, he could sometimes win his point. So now, he told her that Marx had never mentioned the importance of the aristocracy as a class, only the bourgeoisie. 'Someone can grow to be bourgeois, it's not important where you came from, but you have to be born an aristocrat. Pride is the root of aristocracy, a pride in your own lineage. That's why the

409

genealogy of the family and the heroic deeds of valour of their ancestors are so important to them. They're outside the class war.'

'The aristocracy stands outside the class war?' she asked incredulously. 'You talk such sentimental rubbish. They've always been an elite in favour of perpetuating social, political and economic inequality and they'll use schools, universities, the church, theatres, parliaments, all those institutions and more, to make sure it continues, just like the bourgeoisie. There's nothing to choose between them, or if there is, it's inconsequential. So why on earth would you want to work for one of them?'

'Because the wages are better than any I've been offered in a very long while. I only have to drive him. It's easy work. I'd have been stupid to turn it down.'

'I'll give you a better offer.'

He laughed.

'Don't laugh, I'm serious. You can help by selling *Die Rote Fahne* for us'

'Vicky, seriously, how can I do that when the SA are still after me?' Vicky wouldn't accept his reasoning, and kept on trying to persuade him, as she was determined to see Alyosha join the KPD. Nothing was more important to her than that, and if he truly loved her, as he claimed he did, why was he still so resistant?

She directed him to the Welfare Centre in Charlottenburg. Alyosha had been there once before, with their neighbour, Franz, Frau Kempowska's son. It was housed in an old shoe factory which had closed in the slump of 1929, and to reach the room on the ground floor where the dole was distributed, one had to cross a wide cobbled courtyard. In one corner, the old night watchman's hut had been turned into a rough and ready soup kitchen by some charitable society, so that the poor could fill their bellies with a bowl of greasy broth while they waited to be seen.

A bear of a man was loitering on the pavement outside when Alyosha came to a stop outside the gates. He'd lost an eye and part of an ear, and on the breast of his greatcoat was the Iron Cross and the gold medal given to a badly injured soldier. When he saw Vicky in the Mercedes, he came over to her window.

'We can't talk inside. They've got ears sitting in there.'

He spat out a mouthful of chewing tobacco and climbed into the back.

'Vicky, Captain Malinowski is expecting me,' said Alyosha, irritated.

'Just drive us around the corner first.'

Sighing, he put the motor into gear.

'How did it go in court this morning, Erich?' she asked the man in the back.

He told her he had put in his glass eye to look respectable, worn his medals, and had taken his military record. That had probably saved him from a prison sentence for painting anti-Nazi slogans on factory walls. Erich had the rasping voice of a man who smoked too much for his own good. He was a stalwart communist, turning out in all weather in spite of his weak chest and hacking cough.

Alyosha kept the engine running, but they didn't take the hint.

'It's so cold, let us stay,' she wheedled.

'Five minutes, no more.'

She and Erich discussed tactics for agitating the workers at the foundries of Aron, Zweitusch, and Werner, and at the large power station at Siemensstadt, with a view to all-out strikes. They divided up the work of liaising with other cells between them.

Alyosha gathered that Erich had worked at Siemensstadt until, along with several other communists, he had been sacked for being too active in the union.

'Vicky, I *have* to go now.'

'Alright, alright. Thanks for the lift.'

She and Erich stepped out into the January cold.

5.

After taking Captain Malinowski back to the Adlon from his dinner at the Polish Embassy, it was two in the morning when Alyosha parked the Mercedes near his apartment block, and Nehringstrasse was unusually quiet. Vicky was already fast asleep when he got into bed, curled up on her side with her back to him, her hands under her cheek. Sleep eluded him, so he lit a cigarette and lay there, listening to her even breathing. They hadn't made love since he didn't know when.

He stubbed out his cigarette and turned on his side to try to sleep, but as he shut his eyes, there was a knocking on the door.

Vicky woke immediately and jumped out of bed.

She was back in a moment and told him to get dressed as quickly as he could.

'They're on their way.'

Vicky rushed out to warn other comrades in the building. Alyosha's first thought was that he'd better move Captain Malinowski's Mercedes out of harm's way, as he was meant to park it in the Adlon's garage at night and make his own way home. As he sprinted down the stairs, the lights were on in several of the apartments. A dog barked, and set several others howling in sympathy. He could hear frantic knocking, voices raised, doors opening and shutting. Out on the street, a white-haired man in a nightshirt ran past him – to where, God only knew. Some others were already out on the street, and there was the odd rallying shout of 'Red Front!' to gather everybody together.

Alyosha jumped into the Mercedes, but as he began to drive down the street, he heard a rumbling sound, and then he was suddenly blinded by strong lights. Squinting, he made out a convoy of motor lorries coming towards him. Panicking, he reversed at speed, though it felt painfully slow. The he heard the revving of motorcycles, as they approached from both ends of the street, and wild voices shouting from the block, 'They're here…' He just managed to slam on the breaks and turn the Mercedes into a courtyard, before stones and the odd flower pot started crashing down into the street from the balconies of the apartment block.

He extinguished the engine and the lights and sat there, his heart pounding. He could see a section of the street from he sat, and saw dark shadows flying past. Voices shouted, doors opened and banged shut, and there was a faint knocking, an echo on an echo, from inside the building, swiftly followed by the sound of blows and screams and shouts. Then a gun fired, and fired again, and then the sound of pounding feet. Then, as quickly as they arrived, the SA left, leaving two corpses in the street.

The next day, the two dead men were identified as a middle-aged *schupo* and Vlasich Pesotski of the SA. The Nazis weren't overly concerned about the policeman, but Vlasich Pesotski was the latest martyr for the cause, nothing less than another Horst Wessel. Their loud outrage began at once, as well as their demands for swift retaliation: this latest atrocity must be avenged.

There was not a word in the press to suggest that it had been the Nazis who had instigated the attack, or who had been the only ones shooting that night. According to *Der Angriff*, members of a communist cell from Nehringstrasse were responsible for both murders.

But as Alyosha saw it all, he knew the truth.

6.

The room was packed, stuffy, the heat coming in waves from the stove in the corner where newcomers gathered to warm their hands. Alyosha was standing in front of the Nehringstrasse Defence Committee, facing three dozen men and women, many of whom looked exhausted. He told them that he had seen the *schupo* and Vlasich Pesotski, in the confusion and panic, shoot each other. One or two laughed scornfully.

'Would you be prepared to say this publicly?' asked an old woman wearing a floral apron.

He wasn't blind to the danger.

'Would you?' asked Vicky, who was chairing the meeting.

'I would.'

A low murmur broke out through the room.

'We won't give our street over to the fascists without a fight.'

Fritz Kempowski was on his feet, a hot-headed young man with wide shoulders and a thatch of blonde hair. He had lost his left hand in the 1914–1918 war when he was only eighteen. After he'd been demobbed, he'd wandered from town to town scratching a living before ending up in Hamburg. As an ex-soldier, by his own admission still politically naïve, he'd joined the *Volkswehren*, the regiments the Government formed in 1919 under the name 'The People's Army,' in order to quell the Spartacist Uprising, which Karl Liebknecht and Rosa Luxembourg were attempting to ignite. Franz had thought he was only keeping law and order. After all, that's what every officer had told him, and he'd still respected them enough back then to take their word for it. But everything had changed for him in 1923. He'd been employed as a night watchman in a factory, though his wages had barely bought half a loaf, never mind any butter to put on it. With his union, he'd started to organise strikes for higher wages, and, following a run-in outside the factory with his employer's bully-boys, had ended up in prison for six months, where an old Marxist who had attended Rosa Luxembourg's classes had been his cellmate. He'd changed Franz' world view forever.

'We have to show everybody who the real murderers are,' he told the meeting earnestly. 'We need to use every means at our disposal to get the truth out: newspapers, pamphlets, slogans – the medium doesn't matter, as long as the message reaches the people loud and clear.'

Vicky agreed, and the discussion went on at length about how to proceed.

7.

Adolf Hitler himself attended Vlasich Pesotski's funeral service, along with many prominent members of the SA and the SS. Alyosha gazed at a photograph of the Russian lying in his coffin in his SA uniform, his hands crossed on his chest, his leather patch over his eye. The man who had been set on killing him had now met his end, and there were long reports in the newspapers; obituaries, tributes and photographs of the mourners. Even the *schupo's* widow was used in the campaign against the communists. There was a rumour going around that she'd had little choice in this, as she was afraid of losing her widow's pension, with three children to raise alone. On the wireless, there were countless items about their life together, until the myth-making grew wings and became outright lies. A story was also peddled in most of the papers about a peaceful march by the SA through Nehringstrasse in order to show their respect to Vlasich Pesotski, and their contempt towards the communists who murdered him, where they had been shot at by cowards hidden on the rooftops. When further enquiries were made, nobody was quite sure from where exactly the shots were fired. But, in any event, it was only a matter of luck that nobody had been injured. Wasn't it high time to re-establish law and order by bringing the communists into line?

When Vicky arranged to meet him in the bar opposite Karl Liebknecht Haus, Alyosha assumed she wanted to discuss the KPD's continuing campaign to counter such lies, and expose the truth about Vlasich Pesotski's shooting. So far, things were going badly: all their pamphlets and red slogans on the walls of Berlin had either been ignored, or dismissed as propaganda from 'Moscow pigs, trying to save their own skins'. At the same time, the real lies were fast becoming truths in the Nazi newspapers, and worse still, among the general public.

From the door, Alyosha spotted her standing by the bar, smoking and talking to some man who had his back to him. She was so deep in conversation, she didn't notice him coming towards her, and he heard Kai-Olaf's name being mentioned, though she broke off when she saw him.

'At last — where have you been?'

'It's not me that's late, it's you that's early for once.'

Had he heard the news? Hitler had just been made Chancellor. Paul turned to face him. He had grown a thin rim of beard, as white as flour, down the sides of his face and on his chin, which accentuated the grey hollows of his cheeks. As he ran his eye over Alyosha, he didn't so much as lift his elbow from the bar. Alyosha felt it was no coincidence that he was there. For whatever reason, Vicky had arranged for Paul to come face-to-face with him. But why?

The three of them went to sit at a table where they would not be overheard.

'The revolution,' Paul lifted his glass.

'The revolution,' seconded Vicky.

The burning issue was what Hitler's promotion would mean, and, particularly, how it would affect the KPD. Vicky underlined how important it was to have a correct communist interpretation of the situation. Alyosha felt strangely uneasy. Eventually, looking from one to the other, he blurted out, 'Have you two got something you want to say to me?'

Vicky turned to Paul and gestured for him to speak.

'One or two things, yes,' he said, putting Rosa down on the table. 'There are one or two things to discuss.'

As the mouse sniffed around the glasses, Paul reminded Alyosha of the hours they'd spent together in Moabit prison. By the time the ex-printer had finished, Alyosha was facing a litany of accusations, including being an *agent provocateur* and a Nazi spy.

With a cigarette dangling between her lips, Vicky asked Alyosha what he had to say.

'I'll answer each accusation in turn, if that's allowed.'

'There's no need to be like that.'

'Like what?'

He received a severe look from Vicky. Incensed that she had so obviously aligned herself with Paul, he longed to kick the man where it hurt.

With a sigh, Alyosha denied the accusations made against him, one by one.

'And every word is the truth.'

'What about the SA?' asked Paul as Rosa climbed up his arm. 'Do you deny that you were associating with them too?'

How was it possible for him to deny that he had been exercising with the auxiliaries on Rittmeister von Kunz' estate? He admitted it, and told them about his job as a driver to the Nazis, but emphasised that he had turned his back on them a long time ago, and that he no longer had anything to do with them.

And another thing for them to chew over: hadn't he testified to the KPD about the *schupo* and Vlasich Pesotski shooting each other on the night of the attack on Nehringstrasse? Hadn't he also put himself in danger outside the picture house when he rescued his cousin, Margarita, from being badly beaten, or worse?

'You know I was badly injured myself in that fight. What more is there to say?'

'That could be a trick,' suggested Paul.

'A trick?'

'To hide the fact that you're one of them.'

Alyosha pulled his shirt out and held it high above his chest.

'This? A trick?'

'I've seen worse scars,' answered Paul indifferently.

Alyosha itched to plant a punch in the middle of that loath-some face.

'You think I'd jump towards a razor in my guts? You stupid bastard.'

'Hey, hey!' Vicky placed a restraining arm on his chest, as he seemed about to go for Paul 'None of that. No fighting.'

But Alyosha was furious, and in a great torrent of words, he told them everything he knew about the SA, listing their strengths: plenty of money, plenty of arms and plenty of discipline and order. More men were likely to throng to the Nazis, especially now that their leader had been made Chancellor. Their greatest strength was their motor cars and motorcycles, their trucks and lorries, which could transport them efficiently from place to place: the *Roter Front*kämpferbund couldn't hope to match them there. He felt the communists' battle against them was already lost. No wonder Hitler was in the place he was.

'How dare you talk like this?' Vicky asked him furiously.

'Vicky, when an enemy attacks you, you need to listen to what they're saying instead of turning a deaf ear. More often than not, an enemy can expose your weaknesses, and far more honestly than any friend would dare.'

This only made her hackles rise all the more.

'We've got *nothing* to learn from the Nazis,' she spat.

'Why are you always so self-righteous?' Alyosha turned to her.

'I'm not self-righteous. You're talking rubbish.'

For the rest of the week, Vicky worked even longer hours than usual, perhaps to avoid seeing him. She was very nearly caught one evening smuggling KPD pamphlets into the barracks of the *Reichswehr*. She was also trying to organise a strike in the Sie-mensstadt Power Station, in order to plunge much of Berlin into the same blackness that she was beginning to feel in her heart.

8.

As Captain Malinowski never bothered to rise before midday, being his chauffeur was very pleasant work. Driving him to his various appointments around the city, Alyosha realised that, beyond the unemployment, the demonstrations and the fighting, the pleasant world of lunches and teas and dances in luxurious hotels continued as usual. While people were out on the streets, begging and whoring, the tables at the best restaurants were fully booked, night after night, for dinners and theatre suppers after the curtains had come down on whatever performance the Schauspielhaus Theatre was showing. The young officers of the *Reichswehr* were smart and handsome, and their girlfriends, in their white gloves and drop earrings, beautiful, as everybody mingled with members of the SA.

Captain Malinowski was a highly sociable man, with appointments almost every afternoon and evening. He often instructed Alyosha to stop at the Polish Embassy to pick up his great friend, Colonel Flezar. Alyosha would listen to them laughing at their private jokes in the back of the Mercedes, the Colonel's quiet chuckle a counterpoint to the Captain's loud guffaw. Neither of them ever neglected their stomachs, and Colonel Flezar especially, a carnal, healthy man, was a stranger to self-restraint where it came to his pleasures. He adored the company of women – the flirting, the dancing, the tried and tested jokes to make them laugh, the ogling of curves covered by thin dresses. He particularly admired opera singers, with their generous figures and exuberant breasts. But, the Colonel, in spite of his earthy tastes, was a man who had been polished by years of expensive education. He was an inveterate gossip, and took a perverse pleasure in undermining his friends and acquaintances by pulling them down a peg or two in company. He had never married, and his only true love was to his country.

One Saturday night, Alyosha drove Colonel Flezar and Captain

Malinowski to a reception held by the President of the Reich at his official residence on Wilhelmstrasse, a lavish affair for some hundred and fifty diplomats, all in gala dress. Several hours later, as Alyosha drove them both home, he listened to them discuss the evening. The Colonel had thoroughly enjoyed himself, as he had been seated between the wives of the Russian and Italian ambassadors. The Russian was a simple woman of the people from Rostov-on-the-Don, but the Italian was a very refined woman, with a glorious embonpoint. Captain Malinowski had talked to President von Hindenburg for some time before dinner, but had found him rather unimpressive. But what had pleased both men particularly was that, after dinner, when the company had with-drawn to one of the beautiful reception rooms, decorated with eighteenth-century tapestries, they had both had a short conver-sation with the new Chancellor. They agreed that what had struck them both about him was his humility; indeed, he was almost shy. Even though they hadn't talked of anything very consequential, they'd both felt glad that they had introduced themselves to him, and had enjoyed the pleasure of Herr Hitler's company greatly.

9.

Every Wednesday afternoon, Alyosha would be sent to Wannsee. Captain Malinowski had given him clear instructions, which he was to follow to the letter each time. After turning off the main road and parking at the top of a tree-lined lane, he was to extinguish the engine and wait. On no account was he to stir from the motor car. Usually, he had to wait ten minutes or so, but once, a few weeks ago, he'd been smoking in the motor car for almost half an hour.

As he never left the Adlon until late in the afternoon, by the time he reached the banks of the Havel, it was always dark. On this particular occasion, there was not a sound to be heard, not even a bird's song. It was the middle of February, and earlier in the day, it had been snowing, the flakes whipped up by a keen east wind.

A knock came on his window. It was the same ghostly young woman as always, her scarf covering her face, her black eyes just visible under a velvet hat pulled low over her forehead. He lowered the window and took the envelope without greeting her, as instructed, and she immediately turned on her heel, leaving him to watch her until she disappeared back through the gates of the villa. Then he turned the Mercedes around, and made for Berlin.

10.

To judge from the miasma of smoke, Paul had obviously been in the apartment for a good part of the afternoon. Since the evening in the bar on Bülowplatz, Alyosha couldn't bear the sight of him. He had no doubt that he was poisoning Vicky's mind against him, and he hated the fact that the two of them did so much together, though he was powerless to prevent it.

'Can't you keep him more at arm's length?'

Impossible, was her answer to that and then, infuriatingly, 'Why are you so jealous?'

There had been a warrant out for some days for Paul's arrest. The SA was doubtless responsible for planting the rumour that he was the one who had shot Vlasich Pesotski. With the police hunting for him, Paul was sleeping at Vicky's apartment temporarily.

Waking that night, Alyosha slid his hand along the mattress to Vicky's side of the bed and felt a cold emptiness. He opened his eyes, and heard a low murmuring coming from next door. He crept over to the door on tiptoe, and stood listening. The door was slightly ajar, and by the dim moonlight, he could just make Vicky out, crouched down on her haunches next to Paul, who was lying on the shabby sofa.

421

As the two were only inches apart, he could only catch the odd word, along with a muffled laugh. One word, though, he did hear clearly: his own name.

When he saw Vicky get to her feet, he quickly jumped back into bed. She came back with a glass of water in her hand, but he pretended to be asleep.

After Paul had left the next day, he insisted on having a word with her before she left for work.

'You think I'm in love with Paul?' she said, looking surprised. 'What on earth makes you think such a thing?'

'What were you discussing last night then?'

'What do you think? You.'

'At least you're honest.'

'And you know why, too. He's still not sure about you.' Vicky lit a cigarette. 'The night the SA attacked us. Why did you rush out onto the street?'

'I've already told you, because I was worried about the motor car. You know I'm not allowed to drive myself home in it.'

'Paul thinks that's a poor excuse.'

Alyosha felt himself grow warm with indignation. 'He actually thinks I went out to meet them? That I would give SA information? Tell them who lived where in the block? What doors to knock? Who to arrest? Is that what he's insinuating?'

'Why are you shouting?' asked Vicky quietly.

'Don't you see what he's trying to do?'

'He feels you might be a danger to me. That I'd be better off without you.'

'Do you believe him?' he asked her.

She looked away.

'I see.'

'He's threatening to report the whole thing. I could find myself in hot water.'

The KPD disciplinary committee. By now, Alyosha knew exactly what the final authority of that committee was.

'You understand what that would mean for me?'

He understood, but that wasn't what worried him. 'Vicky, be honest… Are you happy that Paul is driving us apart?'

She smoked without giving him an answer.

'I'm not, and I've never been, an agent provocateur. If I was working for them, don't you think Paul would have been arrested by now? Or some of the other communists in this block?'

Vicky considered this for a moment before saying, 'You can't deny you were in the SA though?'

'Yes, because there was food and drink to be had, that's why. That was the only reason. I had a job that paid nothing, I was practically starving.'

'And the brotherhood? Didn't you say there were other Russians there with you?'

It felt like he was reasoning with a stranger.

'You don't have a choice, Alyosha. The only way out of this is if you prove yourself to us.'

'Prove myself how?'

'By showing us beyond a shadow of a doubt that you're not one of them.'

'If you don't believe me, what hope have I got?'

'Prove whose side you're really on.'

Even Vicky didn't believe him anymore: that was clear as day. Paul's poison had proved its strength, and he felt sure he was going to lose her.

11.

By now, the old Community Centre at the end of their street had been turned into a barracks for the SA. Just two hundred yards away from the apartment block, there they were, day and night. There were always a couple of them swaggering on the pavement in front of the building in their brown uniforms, stopping people on the slightest pretext, and generally throwing their weight around.

It was a dark-enough morning, a dirty drizzle falling over the city. Vicky and Franz had called a meeting of the Street Defence Committee, and Vicky had insisted on Alyosha attending. That's when he heard for the first time that there was an intention to rename the street Pesotskistrasse. Franz told them that the Nazis were also going to erect a marble memorial at the spot where the martyr had fallen. The tenants agreed that they should oppose this vigorously. Somebody proposed laying flowers where the *schupo* fell. But they all knew they were losing the propaganda war.

At the end of the meeting, Vicky asked Alyosha to stay behind. Franz shut the door.

'As you know, Alyosha, the situation is worse than ever,' she started, in a rather formal voice. 'What we desperately need is eyes and ears in the SA.'

'A spy at the end of the street,' seconded Franz.

It was crucial for the Communist Party to know what the fascists were up to. If they could place somebody among them, it would be possible to make a lot of trouble for Hitler's men. The hatred between Goebbels and Otto Strasser was no secret, and there were still socialists in the NASAP. The KPD's Central Committee was of the opinion that such things could be manipulated in order to weaken them internally.

Did they realise what they were asking of him?

'If you send me to them, you're sending me to my grave. Vicky, I know I wouldn't last more than two seconds in the SA.'

He could hardly believe that she would even suggest such a thing.

'Do you have to be so selfish?' she asked.

The life of every communist in Berlin was in danger, she told him, and Franz put his good arm around Alyosha's shoulders and urged him to help them. Alyosha drew away because his breath was foul. His mother, Frau Kempowska, had often begged him to go and see a dentist, but Franz always refused because of the cost. He'd much rather spend what little money he had on more important things – like printing KPD pamphlets.

'We're all in danger of being imprisoned, or worse. Think of Paul. Every *schupo* in Berlin is after him, and the SA too. If they get hold of him, do you think he'll get a fair trial?'

And how was he meant to explain to the SA that he had saved a prominent communist like Margarita from being beaten up by the Nazis? Vicky argued that he could convince them how that happened.

'It was just an instinctive thing, to save your cousin. Everybody will understand that.'

Vicky and Franz did their best to persuade him. After all, there were so many things working in his favour. Hadn't his father been a prominent White Russian, a man who had done his utmost to defeat the Bolsheviks? On top of which, he knew Oberführer Krieger, who was now working for Joseph Goebbels himself.

As she spoke, it was Paul's voice Alyosha was hearing. He was behind all this. Did Paul want rid of him? Was that the true reason?

After Franz left, he took Vicky's hand and noticed her fingers were cold.

'I love you.'

'I know you do.'

'No, you don't. Listen to me. I'll say it again…'

The truth was that Alyosha was sick and tired of living in Berlin. He didn't tell Vicky, but Captain Malinowski had hinted he might have other clandestine tasks for him shortly, which he was none too thrilled about, but in any case – and this he could tell her – he had no desire to spend the rest of his life as a chauffeur. He had been saving his money for the two of them, and he had already made enquiries about two tickets on a ship bound for Buenos Aires.

Vicky shook her head emphatically.

'But what kind of a future do we have here?'

With an election on the fifth of March? The most important election ever? It stood to reason that here was their place, especially now that so many of their people had already been imprisoned – for their own good according to the Nazis, to protect them from the people's anger. This was the most important election in the history of Germany, and it was absolutely imperative that the parties of the left – the SDP and KPD – beat the Nazis.

'That's why I have to say here. Stay and fight.'

'I know, but...'

'What else is there to say? How could you ever think I would leave?'

Vicky spoke passionately about her commitment to the working class, and how important it was for everybody to give their all to beat the fascists conclusively, instead of trying to save their own selfish skin by running away abroad.

'I think the battle is already lost,' he told her.

Defeatism maddened her more than anything. Harsh words were said on both sides, but it was clear that South America didn't hold the slightest attraction for Vicky. Without a shadow of a doubt, if it came down to it, the only place on earth she would flee to would be the Soviet Union. How could he have thought anything else?

12.

When the Captain's butler let him in, Alyosha saw that there were three others in the room. They had obviously been there for some time, as the room stank of smoke, coffee and cognac. Colonel Flezar looked up from his conversation, but looked away at once when he saw it was only the chauffeur. He was mid-flow in an anecdote about the Italian Ambassador's wife. Fiorella had telephoned him more than once after that evening when he sat next to her at dinner, and then, three nights ago, he had bumped into her at a gala dinner held by Ernst Roehm, head of the SA, at his palace on Mattäi-Kirchstrasse. At the end of the night, the two of them had left in a taxi for the Herren Club to continue their conversation.

A blonde woman with large breasts chuckled as she tapped the ash from her cigarette.

'And where did you go after, I wonder?'

'Home.'

She laughed again. 'Home indeed!'

'I assure you.'

'Since when do you sleep in your own bed?'

Captain Malinowski noticed Alyosha standing there.

'I want you take Baroness Kosub and Countess Kołodziejska…'

Colonel Flezar's broke off at the look of shock on the face of the chauffeur.

'What is it? What? Do you two know each other or what?'

Countess Kołodziejska had risen from her chair. 'Hello, Alexei.'

He kissed her blue glove. 'Hello, Ludwika.'

He ran his eyes over her and stammered, 'It's been a long time.'

She smiled sweetly, 'A long time.'

In spite of himself, he lowered his eyes to take her in all over again.

13.

Through the darkness, he heard knocking, and a woman's voice calling his name. He had absolutely no idea where he was, nor what was happening around him, and it took several seconds to drag himself back into the present. Then, he remembered where he was. He remembered who he was and that his life, as always, was at the mercy of fate. He rubbed his eyes, before grabbing his trousers where he'd left them on the floor and throwing them on quickly. The floor was cold under his soles as he padded over to the door.

It was Frau Kempowska, Franz at her shoulder. 'They're here.' She turned back to her own apartment, and Franz rushed past Alyosha into his apartment, with a small package in his hand. He slammed the door shut, just as heavy boots were heard stomping up the stairs, followed a moment later by insistent banging on the opposite door.

'They're not stupid,' whispered Franz hurriedly, 'My bed will still be warm.'

They had a minute or two at most before they'd be knocking on Alyosha's door. Franz was already unbolting the window.

'Be careful. It's slippery,' Alyosha helped him clamber out.

They were already banging on his door.

'Open up!'

'Good luck.'

'Look after my mother,' were Franz' last words as he disappeared into the night.

Alyosha bolted the window shut, and took as long as he dared to answer the door, although the banging was now louder and angrier.

'Where have you been?' He was blinded by a strong flash lamp being shone in his face. 'Why were you so long?'

The first one barrelled past him, and the rest swarmed inside behind him: four secret policemen, two *schupos* and a great slab of a man from the SA, who had hold of a terrified Frau Kempowska. Alyosha could hear doors being hammered on the floors above his.

'Is this Ida Kempowska?' someone asked Alyosha as the flash lamp waved in front of his eyes. 'Have you seen Franz tonight?' asked the voice.

'Yes, it is, and no, I haven't…'

It was difficult to shelter under the shadow of lies: he felt an instinctive compulsion to confess the truth in order to get rid of them.

'Where is he?' the SA man bellowed into the old lady's face.

'And Hedwig Eisenberg?' one of the others asked. 'She lives here doesn't she? The one the Reds call Vicky. Where is she? Do you know?'

'I don't have the slightest idea.'

'When did you last see her?'

From the corner of his eye he saw the bedclothes being tossed onto the floor and the mattress being lifted off the frame before being flung aside. He could hear crockery being smashed in the kitchen. And then, the sound of a cupboard being dragged, bumping along the floor. Clearly they were intent on maximum destruction and a thorough search. One of the secret policemen stood at the bookshelf, carefully leafing through every book. He threw most of them onto the floor, but put one or two on the table. There was so much noise and movement, and so many questions being fired at him, that Alyosha didn't notice for a while the uniformed *schupos* were removing the pictures and tapping the walls behind them with little hammers. Whoever had been arrested from the block and questioned in the Vlasich Pesotski barracks at the top of the street had started to name names.

'Who are you then?' asked the SA man.

Alyosha told him.

'What are you doing here?'

'Lodger.'

So unknown and dark were they to each other, he thought. Strangers who wanted to know everything about him in a matter of minutes. But nobody believed a word he said. What was his full name? What was he doing in Berlin? How long had he been living there? How long had he been living here? Was he related to Vicky? Were they lovers? Was he a red? After a while, the *schupos* came over to the man from the SA to report that they hadn't found any arms.

The interrogation began again, and his papers were closely examined. Then, he was ordered to get dressed.

14.

There were three motor lorries with their engines still running outside the block, a few *schupos* in green sitting on the wooden benches guarding the tenants that had already been rounded up, who all had their heads down dejectedly. Alyosha was ordered to climb up and looked for somewhere to sit, but the back of the lorry was already full. Some more tenants climbed up behind him all the same, but it seemed Franz had managed to escape.

They drove through Berlin in the winter gloom, the lamps reflected in the icy streets. He had been too harried to have time to dress himself in warm layers, and the cold was punishing, despite his coat and corduroy hat. Even some of the *schupos* and the SA were pulling the collars of their greatcoats up.

Their destination was the inner courtyard of the police headquarters, from where the prisoners were escorted into the building, to a dimly lit corridor with yellowing walls, where there were already other prisoners waiting, mostly men. Everybody looked exhausted, with some of them practically sleeping on their feet.

Alyosha saw one of the *schupos* who had ransacked the apartment go by with some of Vicky's possessions in his arms. Many of the prisoners knew each other, and were talking quietly. Another lorry-load of men arrived, a rough-enough crew, dishevelled and down at heel. But they were all riff-raff as far as the police were concerned, and were treated as such.

It was later, in the cell, that someone told Alyosha about the fire at the Reichstag. He dozed, dreaming about Ludwika. He re-lived his shock at seeing her there in front of him, in flesh and blood. His heart filled with disappointment all over again as he remembered how he had suffered because of her. It wasn't that he wanted to have anything to do with her anymore, he told himself, it was just thinking about what could have been in place of this emptiness. That was the sadness. But then, who lives his life exactly as he would like? Sooner or later, what comes to everybody is disillusionment or disappointment.

It was impossible to sleep properly, as there wasn't enough room to lie down. During the night, sixteen men were squeezed into that one cell. They were mostly communists, but one was a SDP member of the Reichstag. Without mincing his words, he said that, whatever they printed in the press, they should know it was the Nazis who were responsible for lighting the fire, of that he had no doubt. Keen-eyed Carl von Ossietski was another, and the rest of them were surprised that a prominent pacifist like him had been brought in. They all shifted along to make room for the old philosopher Hermann Duncker when he was thrown in with them. He leaned heavily on his stick but, undaunted, he refused to stay silent, and started protesting loudly, though to absolutely no effect.

All through the night, more men were brought in to the corridors, and later, they learnt that several hundred, if not thousands, had been arrested all over the city.

It was mid-morning before Alyosha was brought out to be questioned. *The same type of table, the same type of chairs, the same bare soulnessness*, he thought to himself as he entered the room – he could easily have been back in Poland. He stuck to his story.

Stuck to what he and Vicky had agreed they would say if either of them was ever arrested.

Although they had no evidence to counter his claims, they were very unwilling to believe him. He was exhausted and desperate for them to let him go, so he decided to try and win their sympathy by telling them his life story.

He did so, emphasising how much he loathed and despised communists and all their works. He surprised himself at how readily a tear sprang to his eye as he told them that they had been responsible for killing his father, stealing his house in Petrograd, his *dacha* in Crimea, his armaments factory, forcing the family to flee to Europe, to scratch a living in foreign cities. As he continued with his account, he felt some genuine emotion, and a hard lump growing in his throat.

He went on to tell them of his longing to return to Russia – that he often dreamed of being able to walk down Nevskii Prospekt with his mother tongue being spoken all around him, of tasting Russian food on his tongue again, and breathing in those unique smells of his old home. More than anything, he wanted to see the fall of Stalin and his gangsters, and that's why he'd been drilling with the SA in the ranks of the Russian Auxiliary on Rittmeister Gunther von Kunz' estate. It would give him an unparalleled satisfaction to cross over the border in the military uniform of the New Germany to fight the communists and the Jews, and restore Russia to its former glory. To cap it all, he told them that Oberführer Karl Krieger, who worked for Doctor Joseph Goebbels, would be happy to vouch for him. If they still had any doubts about him, the best thing would be for them to lift the telephone. It was a bravura performance.

When he returned to the apartment, he saw that there were hours of work ahead of him restoring some sort of order. Before facing the chaos, he made himself some tea and listened to the wireless. It seemed Berlin was holding its breath, waiting for the communists to rise as one.

As the hours ticked by, nothing happened. The burning of the Reichstag was having all the attention, and some communist from the Netherlands was being blamed – although there was a strong suggestion that Ernst Torgler, Chairman of the KPD, and the leader of the communist faction in the Reichstag, was also implicated. According to the Nazis, this was on the basis of some highly incriminatory evidence which had been found in Karl Liebknecht Haus. Hence, the arrests had unfortunately been necessary, so that they could establish the truth about the fire.

As the days went past, still nothing happened, apart from the odd slogan painted on a wall here and there. They didn't even call for a general strike.

One night, Alyosha happened to drive past the Reichstag. The building didn't look too badly damaged, not on the exterior at least.

The arrests and imprisonments continued. Torgler was one of the first they locked up. Ernst Thälmann was on the run. Heinz Neumann and his wife succeeded in avoiding capture, and found refuge in the Soviet Union. Willi Münzenberg retreated to Paris to continue fighting the Nazis from there. Those who could, got out of Germany as quickly as possible.

15.

Captain Malinowski was a rabid anti-communist, and hearing of the persecution of the Reds following the burning of the Reichstag was music to his ears. He would often voice his pleasure at these developments when Alyosha was driving him somewhere. Stamping out Stalin's riff-raff was entirely a good thing. Communism was a disease of the heart, one which had given a nasty and unforeseen turn of events in the countries of Europe. Marxists were the scum of the earth, and hanging them slowly was far too good for them. He was delighted that Hitler was locking them up, and so much the better that he'd caught so many of them, he'd had to put them in a new prison outside Munich, a place called Dachau. Colonel Flezar, who was sitting at his side, murmured his agreement and then asked, not for the first time, 'Why do the working classes have to smell so badly?'

The group of Polish aristocrats living in Berlin seemed, to Alyosha, to be a sybaritic lot. Many of them were attached to the embassy, but their conversations were mostly inconsequential and superficial, full of accounts of visits to spas at Marienbad, Bad Freienwalde or Carlsbad, jaunts to Venice or Paris, or to Vienna for the balls. Alyosha heard so much about the Kiel regatta, he felt he'd been there himself, and knew all the gossip about the tennis tournament in Dalmatia, the swimming in Corsica and the croquet in Prague.

Alyosha was nowadays expected to divide his time between driving Captain Malinowski and tutoring Amelia, Ludwika's six-year-old daughter, in German and French. He had discovered that the Captain was, in fact, Ludwika's cousin. But every Wednesday, he was still expected to drive to the villa at Wannsee, returning to the Hotel Adlon with the white envelope from the silent girl. One time, he tried to talk to her, but she only gazed at him for a moment with her mute eyes, before turning and walking away.

Alyosha had heard nothing from Vicky, and was anxious about her. She was on the run, of course, moving from one hiding place to another, no doubt. But his thoughts were also full of Ludwika. He was still astonished at the coincidence of them meeting once again, and, of all places, in his father's old suite at the Hotel Adlon.

He had gone over that first meeting often in his head.

'Hello, Alexei.'

'Hello, Ludwika.'

Her bearing had been confident and relaxed, and she'd been beautifully dressed. With a half-smile and mischief in her eyes, she had turned to her cousin, and told him calmly that the two of them had known each other in Paris, known each other rather well.

'Didn't we Alexei?'

'Yes.'

'Are you going to tell us how you met then?' Baroness Kosub had asked playfully. She liked nothing better than finding out about people's sexual peccadilloes, and passing it all on to Colonel Flezar.

'I'm not sure,' Ludwika had smiled. 'What do you say, Alexei?'

Her words had sunk into his skin.

'I'd rather not.'

As he'd stood gazing at her, some old emotion had clenched at his stomach, something painful and primitive. With something between joy and dread, he'd realised he was feeling exactly the same as when he saw her for the very first time, back in Paris. Nothing had changed. She had hardly changed either. A little older, and her hair was shorter, but she was every bit as beautiful as before, her smile just as lovely. From the second he'd kissed her blue glove, he was defenceless against her.

16.

Larissa was already waiting outside for her when Margarita left Aznefttrust. She said she didn't have long, as Bruno would be home within the hour.

Over a cup of coffee, the two sisters caught up on each other's news.

'How safe are you?' Larissa asked her sister.

Margarita tried to reassure her sister but Larissa said doubtfully,

435

'But Bruno was savage about the communists after the Reichstag business.'

'If they'd wanted to arrest me, they'd have done it by now.'

'And Kai-Olaf?'

'He's still free.'

'Is he keeping his head down?'

'He's working in a bakery.'

Margarita, however, would be out of work by the end of the month, as Aznefttrust were closing their Berlin office. She told her sister how the SA had paid them a visit one morning. They'd all been questioned, and a few of them had been arrested. After that, they heard officially from Moscow that every contract was terminated, and the company would shut its doors.

'What will you do?'

Margarita had already had a word with the her boss, Osip Nikitich, and he was going to try to transfer her to the Amsterdam office.

'Amsterdam! Is this definite?'

'As long as they give me a visa.'

The same old problem.

'What does Kai-Olaf say?'

'With things as they are, he thinks it's for the best.'

'It's awful to think you're being forced to leave Berlin.'

Larissa said this with a certain innocence, and added sadly that it would mean they'd see even less of each other.

'We can write, Lala, and visit. It's not so terribly far.'

'I suppose, but it won't be the same.'

Margarita certainly didn't hold out much hope of finding any kind of other work in Berlin. The prejudice against foreigners – Russians, Poles, Slavs and especially Jews – was deepening. Germans now had the first refusal for any job, no matter how big or small it was. Besides, the thought of having to work in an office from nine to five every day, where everybody was heil-Hitlering

436

each other, made her feel quite sick. 'Heil Moscow!' was her greeting every time.

'How are things between you and Walter?' Margarita asked her sister.

'He's wants to leave his wife, but he feels guilty.'

Margarita considered this for a moment.

'It's a big decision,' Larissa said, 'I know that. But we feel so… We love each other. I know he'll come to me.'

'What about the little girls?'

That remained her greatest worry.

'I just know that Bruno will be completely vile. He'll do everything he can to keep Ella and Clara. I wouldn't be able to bear it.'

'You have a difficult time ahead of you.'

'Yes, I know. To be honest, I don't know what will become of me.'

17.

When Ludwika came to collect her daughter, she turned her head at an angle, touching the brim of her new hat lightly.

'What do you think?'

Alyosha dropped his gaze from the hat to the rest of her, enjoying the sight of her until he felt his appreciation turn to something more carnal, and felt the faint stirring of an erection. He swiftly turned his attention back to her hat.

'Suits you.'

It did, too. Ludwika smiled. She lifted Amelia in her arms and gave her a light kiss on her cheek.

Initially, Alyosha had been in two minds whether he should refuse to have anything to do with her, or to confront her with her behaviour towards him after she left Paris. But she had said to him in that direct way of hers, 'I want you and I to spend some time together. What are you doing tonight?' And that was that.

She introduced Alyosha to everybody as 'an old friend'.

'You and me,' she said, smiling, as they sat in her box at the opera. Ludwika told him her marriage had been unhappy almost from the start, and after barely two years, Mateusz had left her for an actress from the Rozmaitości Theatre. He'd used to meet her every lunchtime in an obscure little hotel, but it had not been obscure enough, and their entire circle in Warsaw had soon been enthusiastically discussing the affair.

Ludwika hadn't wasted many tears on him, but she'd been far more anguished when her Catholic parents had refused to countenance a divorce. Mateusz's family had been just as intransigent, insisting that, if the young couple couldn't reconcile, then they must come to some civilised 'understanding' which would preserve the good name of both families.

With her mother and daughter, Ludwika had taken a vacation on the Baltic coast, spending a month in Jurmala, near Riga. There'd been nothing very charming about the place, but it had been a chance to escape the gossip and clear her head. They'd hired a beach hut by the sand dunes, and Ludwika had become friendly with the couple from Prague who'd had the adjoining hut, a successful lawyer and his charming wife. They'd been a liberal couple, staunch believers in the rights of women, and over a glass of port one evening, the husband had told her he'd be prepared to fight her case. He'd been as good as his word, and Ludwika had been duly divorced, but she'd lost her family, and very nearly lost Amelia, though after months of tense negotiations, her ex-husband had finally relented, and she'd been allowed to keep her.

Captain Malinowski was related to her on her mother's side, and it was he who'd persuaded her to move to Berlin. He'd felt she needed a change of scene, and that it would be beneficial to put some distance between her and her family, especially her father, who was even more of a heavy-handed patriarch in his old age than before. According to Captain Malinowski, he had ruined his wife's life for years, and it was no wonder her health was so bad. When the visit to Berlin had been broached, her father had withheld his permission unless she went with an escort. Ludwika had complied with all his terms for the sake of peace – though she'd had every intention of ignoring every one of them once she was safely away – and Baroness Kosub had agreed to be her chaperone, although they'd both laughed at such old-fashioned nonsense between themselves.

'What about you?' she asked him. 'Are you married yet?'

'No.'

'Do have a lover?'

'I did have.'

'But not any more?'

He explained that things were rather complicated.

'Don't tell me… She's married?'

'No, it's not that.' he smiled.

'Oh, I know what it is. No need to say more. She's in love with somebody else? Or are you in love with somebody else?'

'I'm not in love with anybody.'

'What about her?'

'I'm not even sure if I'm still with her by now.'

Vicky was on the run. He hadn't seen her for some time.

Ludwika didn't offer a word of explanation or apology for what had happened in the past. Could she begin to comprehend the pain and the agony she had caused him he wondered? Alyosha tried to raise the subject, but she made it quite clear she was not interested in discussing anything of their former lives in Paris.

'That's all water under the bridge.'

From the opposite box in the opera, somebody half lifted his hand in greeting – a middle-aged man with something impressive in his stillness. Some SA lads were going round the opera house, raising money for the cause by selling postcards of Hitler, Goering and Goebbels. One of them, thick-set and swaggering, stepped through the divide in the curtains into their box, and Ludwika went into her purse and gave him nine *pfennigs*, leaving the card of Hitler face down on her lap.

'Just water under the bridge now,' she repeated when he'd gone. 'It all belongs in the distant past.'

'Distant past or not,' Alyosha persisted, 'There are still a couple of things I'd like to ask you about.'

She let out a little sigh, as though a small stream of sadness was flowing out of her.

'I do think I have the right Ludwika. The right to know why you acted like you did.'

She fumed a little, 'The right?'

'There's nothing worse than dashing somebody's hopes.'

'Tonight? Must we?'

Although he was desperate to hear her side of the story, he wilted under her displeasure.

'Another time, then.'

'Another time, you're right. Let's discuss it another time. Why don't we just enjoy each other's company without anything spoiling tonight's happiness.'

The second act was about to begin.

'You were a student when we met for the first time.'

She smiled.

'I used to love hearing you talk about your subject.'

'Are you teasing me?'

'Not at all. You gave me a taste for philosophy.'

He reminded her how they'd sit in the Luxembourg Gardens after her lectures, discussing what she'd learnt. He repeated her example of the two brothers who enlisted in the army, one because he was a patriot and the other because he was afraid of what people would think of him if he didn't volunteer. Both of them had acted in exactly the same way – for two entirely different reasons. What, then, did this prove? That the moral worth of an action wasn't always implicit in that action?

'Wasn't I insufferable, though?' laughed Ludwika, blowing smoke out over her lower lip.

'I didn't think so. I learnt so much from you.'

She smiled at him.

'Did you really?'

'Really.'

'What else did I teach you? Try and remember.'

'That it's not economics, or politics, or religion that drives History. It's emotion. And that Europe's dreams have always been emotional ones.'

She was no longer smiling.

'You were an excellent teacher, Wisia.'

When he called her that, she held his glance for a long moment, and then smiled that radiant smile of hers.

After the opera, they went to the Hotel Kaiserhof for dinner. As they walked in, he took a quiet pride in the fact that every eye in the place was fixed on Ludwika. With her at his side, his whole body seemed to fill with a delicious feeling of quiet contentment. He felt they slotted together perfectly.

Once they'd ordered, she was eager to hear more about Vicky, and wanted him to give a full account of her.

'You? Living with a communist? Who ever would have thought?'

'She's totally committed to the cause.'

'I'm sure she's sincere. But she's deluded. Whatever your girl may say to the contrary, Alexei, every society has to have an elite, even communist Russia. Think of Caesar's bureaucrats in ancient Rome. Or the priesthood in the Egypt of the Pharaohs. The Communist Party of the Soviet Union is a religious sect, which

441

exists in order to spread its own truth over the face of the world. It has its missionary wing, the Comintern, and its Inquisition, the OGPU, to hunt down and punish heretics. It has it gospels in the works of Marx and Engels, its holy texts from lesser scribes, and its saints, martyrs, and prophets. And, like all true religions, it demands unquestioning obedience from its acolytes, on pain of excommunication – or worse.'

It wasn't surprising that Ludwika thought like this, he thought. After all, she was still aristocratic, Polish and Catholic. She was of the opinion that there were two world views in conflict with each other in Europe: Christian Nationalism and International Marxism.

'It will be a fight to the death. So many intelligent people are being tricked by Karl Marx's hypocritical lies. Communism threatens every civilised country.'

Alyosha listened carefully.

'And equality?'

'What about it?' she asked after he'd lit her cigarette.

'Isn't that what International Marxism is offering everybody?'

'That's the noise coming from their propaganda.'

'But will it ever be possible for us to realise the idea of social equality?'

'What are you trying to ask? Will it ever be possible for us to legislate our way to a perfect world?'

'Will it?'

He was fascinated to hear her answer.

'This idea of social equality has always had a sort of mystique over the centuries,' was Ludwika's response, 'but as long as political freedom exists, economic inequality will exist. In order to establish some sort of economic equality among men, political equality would have to be completely stifled. That's why such an order would be the worst kind of oppression. Which is what we see in the Soviet Union.'

He told her that there was a sentence in *The Communist Manifesto* that had stuck in his mind. It said that everything that was established and solid today would vanish into thin air tomorrow. That had cut him to the quick, because it encapsulated his own experience of life. Where had the security of his childhood gone? The innocent fun of all those summer holidays? The long hours at his desk, waiting for lessons to end? The warmth and comfort of his home? A mother and father's love? His homeland?

By now, a new order had taken the place of the old. Could that really be a better way of life, as Vicky claimed? Or was Ludwika right?

18.

Kai-Olaf and Margarita were about to go to bed, when there was a low knocking on the door. Margarita darted a hurried look along his bookshelves. Marx, Engels, Kaustsky, Lenin, Bukharin and Trotsky, they had long since been removed, but she had a second of worry wondering if there was one she had overlooked, still sitting incriminatingly on the shelf. She went to open the door

It was Vicky, but it took Margarita a second to register who it was, as she had cut her hair very short and dyed it a light blonde. She wore an old coat, the sleeves splattered with spots of paint, a thick scarf around her neck, and a pair of shoes which had been cut from the rubber of an old tyre. She'd battled her way to them through the heavy snow.

Margarita gave her some tea. Vicky had been sleeping in a wooden hut on one of the allotments out in the suburbs for some weeks. She called the neighbourhood Little Moscow. She felt she was safer there than anywhere else. She slept on a bed of sacks, with a smelly old quilt which had seen better days to pull over her, and old clothes rolled under her head did for a pillow. It was alright, she could sleep anywhere, but she had to share the hut with the Strubbels and their little girl, Heidi. The family used to live in Nehringstrasse, but he'd been unemployed for three years, and, eventually, they'd been evicted for rent arrears. Members of his communist cell had built the wooden hut for them. There was no room to turn in there. They were like rabbits cowering in their warren, living in fear of being hunted down one night by the lamps of the SA.

Nearly everybody on the KPD central committee had been arrested. Vicky had been within a hair's breadth of being caught more than once. Only a couple of nights ago, she'd been spotted painting a slogan on a canal bridge, and had narrowly escaped arrest, taking to her heels under the gas lamps of the dark March night, running until she was gasping for breath, her chest tight and her heart pounding. It had been a close shave, and she felt that her luck was wearing thin. It was a hard struggle to live like this, constantly on the alert for danger, like an animal. There were black days ahead, but it was important not to despair, to keep the rebellion alive. They had to continue to resist, but how? Strikes, pamphlets, slogans on the walls of Berlin – and what else? What could withstand the flood of Nazi propaganda being churned out so relentlessly on the wireless, in cinemas and in the press?

Vicky eventually told them why she'd come. They'd heard that there were to be fresh arrests when the men went to claim their dole the next day. Margarita needed to spread the word to as many as possible to keep away.

'Have you heard about Paul?' she asked them then.

'What about him?' asked Margarita, and looked at Kai-Olaf, who shook his head. Paul and Franz had been delivering pamphlets in an area where many government clerks and minor civil servants lived, in Wilhelmsdorf. They'd noticed a man with a dark complexion appear from somewhere, but after hesitating for a moment or two, he'd disappeared. They'd carried on with their work, though Franz had felt increasingly nervous, and had wanted them to get out of there. True to character, Paul had insisted that they finish the work. Afterwards, Franz had still felt as though they were being watched, so they'd split up, and walked on either side of the street until they'd reached a row of shops. In order to check whether he was being followed, Paul had slipped into a dairy, where a queue of women had been waiting. From the other side of the street, Franz had seen the man with the dark complexion rush past, followed by four members of the SA. Paul hadn't seen them, Franz had been convinced of that. He'd been unable to cross the street to warn his friend of the danger without being caught himself. The SA had come back and began to question people. Paul must have panicked, because he'd tried to make a run for it out of the front of the shop, but he'd run straight into more of the SA.

'Where is he now?' asked Kai-Olaf.

'Under lock and key in the Vlasich Pesotski barracks.'

The three of them fell silent. After a while, Vicky asked if was alright for her to stay the night.

'I've nowhere else to go.'

'Why don't you turn to your own people?' was Kai-Olaf's quiet suggestion.

Margarita frowned at him.

'Where are the KPD that they can't help you tonight?'

He was finding it difficult to disguise his anger, and added, 'Why come to class enemies like us for help?'

Margarita scolded him softly, 'Not tonight, don't…'

'Why not tonight? This one was more than ready to throw me out of the KPD less than six months ago. I didn't hear her speak up in my defence then, when I was dragged in front of the Disciplinary Committee. She was happy to throw me to the dogs…'

Even now, Vicky couldn't stop herself from saying, 'Because you deserved to be thrown out.'

'Did I really?'

'You know you did. The things you were saying.'

'It was high time somebody said them.'

'It's perfectly clear to me what kind of a man you are. By ridding itself of rubbish like you, the Communist Party can only become stronger. Stalin himself said so.'

'Every time there's a revolution, some third class becomes more powerful,' Kai-Olaf replied. 'When the slaves rebelled against their masters, who won? The feudal class. And when the peasants rose up against their lords, who won the day? The bourgeoisie. And when the proletariat rose up against the bourgeoisie and created the Soviet Union, there it is again: a bureaucratic party-state, like a ton of lead over everybody, and Stalin the tyrant at its head. Why does it always have to be like this?'

Margarita hissed at Kai-Olaf to keep his voice down.

'He's acting in the name of the working class and for the interests of the working class,' Vicky answered back, 'That's what Stalin is doing! And that's what we're doing in the KPD.'

'Oh really?' Kai-Olaf snapped, 'So you still think the KPD line was correct do you? In spite of who is Chancellor today. How many thousands of you has he thrown into prison by now?'

'We won over seven million votes in the election back in November last year.'

'And how many voted for Hitler's lot?'

'Over seven million people voted for us.'

'Against the eleven million who voted for him. And on the fifth of March this year, which was the biggest party? Hitler's party. 196 seats in the Reichstag.'

'Which couldn't please a Trotskyist like you more.'

'The Nazis will go after the trade unions next, you'll see. Leipart, Grassman, Wissel; and after that it will be the SPD's turn.

446

Think how marvellous it will be for you all; you'll be able to quarrel about what went wrong all day long, in Dachau, more than likely.'

'That's enough! Be quiet!' Margarita hissed.

Kai-Olaf stomped back to bed, and Vicky made a bed for herself on the sofa with the blankets Margarita had fetched for her.

'Thanks,' she said, squeezing Margarita's hand. 'If I can ever pay the favour back…'

'Sleep.'

Margarita turned out the lights.

'Margarita?'

She turned.

Vicky swore that she wouldn't rest until *Die Rote Fahne* was back in circulation. That would have been Paul's dearest wish. Somehow or other, she was determined to put the newspaper back on its feet, so that the truth could be read once more on the streets of Berlin. Without that, there was no hope.

19.

In the bliss of her company, every other worry disappeared, and the days trickled by. As Alyosha spent more and more of his time with Ludwika, Amelia's language lessons became shorter and shorter, until her mother found another tutor to teach her.

Every minute he wasn't driving Captain Malinowski, he spent with her, much of it in her room in the Hotel Kaiserhof. He was spending most of his nights with her now, too. They always slept together naked, and, in the warmth of the room, the languid smell of their lovemaking was salty on their tongues. In the morning, nothing gave him more pleasure than waking up to see her face next to him on the pillow. He'd stroke her cheek, very lightly, so as not to wake her, and smooth her hair back from her face.

When she woke, Ludwika loved to have breakfast in bed with him. Then, she'd have her bath, which Alyosha would run for her. Through the open door, he'd listen to her humming to herself as droplets ran from her skin into the water, and even with the *Deutsche Allgemeine Zeitung* in front of his nose, his mind was still on her. He'd usually end up going over to the bathroom door to look at her. But though she was happy to share her bed with him, she wasn't willing to share her bath. Alyosha's only comfort would be to kneel down, and lean his head on his arm at the side of the bath, his other hand in the water searching for her thighs.

Or he'd soap her back for her: that fragile nape and her soft shoulders. Then, he'd hold out a towel for her to step into, wrap it around her like a child, and watch her again as she sat at her little dressing table, dabbing perfume behind her ears and between her breasts, and putting her make-up on.

But his enjoyment would darken when the past would insist on intruding on his thoughts. He'd remember that night, when they'd gone to the fair in Montparnasse and she'd told him about her engagement to Mateusz Kołodziejski. He'd remember how he'd felt when she'd told him his family's estate was near her grandmother's. Most of all, he'd remember her coming out of the cabin.

Over and over in his head, that image of her would torment him, filling him with angst. He'd be transported back to that corridor, surrounded by the smell of oil and polish, with the engine purring under his feet, and he'd be back in an instant outside the door of her cabin. He'd be gazing again at the deep velvety sky above the Baltic, at its scudding, heavy clouds, and he'd be overwhelmed by every sadness and longing he'd ever felt in his life. And that other image of her being driven from the port in Gdynia in her family's Rolls-Royce, leaving him shouting for her on the asphalt. And then, across everything, that communist, the girl from Lvov, forced to drink her own boiling piss…

448

'It wasn't you I wanted to hurt, it was my own family…'

'Why?'

'Because I wasn't brave enough to stand up to them.'

'And that's why you slept with that officer?'

'I understand it's a difficult thing for you to understand. When I left you in Le Havre, I knew they'd never let me come back to Paris. My instincts were right: my father wasn't even ill – that was a ruse to get me to go home. He'd heard about the two of us – how, I don't know to this day – but somebody in Paris snitched. Of course, he wasn't happy that I was having anything to do with a boy like you. My mother thought it was just some girlish romantic nonsense, and she tried to persuade my father that's all it was, but he wouldn't have it. He thought I was starting to see myself as some second Ludwika.'

'Why, who was the first?'

'Ludwika Śniadecka. She lived in the last century. She was meant to have been utterly beautiful. My grandmother saw her once, in a New Year's dance in Dobrzyń. She said when she walked into the room, everybody fell silent. Nobody knows how many lovers she took. The young poet from Vilnius, Juliusz Słowacki, was mad about her, but he was just one of many. Michał Czaykowski was so in love with her, that even living hundreds of miles away, in exile in Paris, if somebody so much as mentioned her name, he would be transported. Adam Mickiewicz was another one besotted with her, but the only thing she promised him in his poverty-stricken exile in Constantinople was her friendship.'

'What became of her? Which one did she marry?'

'She died all alone, and was buried far away from Poland, in a lonely grave on the edge of Asia.'

They gazed at each other.

'But she was loved?'

'More than any other woman who ever lived.'

He kissed her shoulders and caught her eye in the mirror.

'How long will we be together this time, Wisia?'

'Forever, Alexei.'

'That's what you promised me the last time.'

'This time, I mean it.'

Every other day, Ludwika would receive a letter from her mother telling her about household matters, her husband's health, and their social engagements. She always asked about Amelia. It seemed the family rift was healed. Ludwika read every letter intently, and kept nothing from Alyosha. This time, she promised, there would be no secrets between them.

20.

Plays, concerts and operas filled their evenings. Then, they often went on to a nightclub, to dance until the early hours. During the day, they liked to watch the motorcycle races in Plötzensee, or the horse racing in Grunewald, where Ludwika introduced Alyosha to one of the jockeys, an aristocrat by the name of Georg von Nałęcz Sosnowski, and some other Poles in his entourage. Günther Rudolf was one, tall of body but short of temper, with a big heart and little patience. There was also a young aristocratic German woman called Renate von Natzmer; she laughed at the least excuse, and although she had broken her leg and was hobbling around on crutches, she was more than ready to enjoy herself.

Ludwika liked Alyosha to dress smartly, and she bought him clothes for various occasions. These days, he walked in a cloud of expensive *Eau de Cologne*, and the silk handkerchief in his breast pocket always matched the tie around his neck. He felt quite the dandy, and nothing gave him more pleasure than people's readiness to admire them as a couple as they attended their parties and dinners. He couldn't care less about the snide comments he knew people made behind his back, though everybody was pleasant enough to his face. The warmth of her love made him invincible. Compared with Ludwika, every other woman fell short in all respects – dress, appearance and intelligence. When other men bent their heads to lift Ludwika's hand to their lips, she belonged to him and only him.

One occasion where he thoroughly enjoyed himself was a dinner at the residence of Luis de Zulueta, the Spanish Ambassador. The Spaniard was a talkative man, and was highly critical of the restless spirit that seemed to possess so many of his countrymen. Workers' rights, shorter hours and more pay, and strong anti-Catholic sentiments were starting to gain ground, as the young people in particular fell prey to the lure of socialism or anarchism. Mistresses were being harangued by demands for more wages by their maids, ruining their former good relations with their greed.

'Very true, they tell me it's becoming impossible to find a good maid in Zaragoza,' added Señora Zulueta, an ivory-skinned woman with abundant black hair and large dark eyes.

'And babies born out of wedlock everywhere,' her husband said.

'The country is becoming immoral through and through,' she agreed. 'We no longer hear the wings of angels beating on the wind in Spain's dreams, but rather a proletarian clamour from the gutter, made up of the hoarse roars of covetous men who want to spit at the world.'

Alyosha was placed next to Frau Drexler, a young woman (much younger than her husband, who was something important at the foreign ministry) originally from Amsterdam. Unlike her rather patrician husband, she liked to tease people, in a high voice which seemed to draw attention to itself.

'Nothing's ever as important as it seems, nothing, and nobody,' she declared confidently.

'How so?' asked Alyosha.

'For the simple reason that time slips by, people grow old, circumstances change, new ideas are born, technology comes up with a new toy, and everybody is sure to die some day.'

'Very cheering,' he answered smilingly.

'But isn't it true?'

'I daresay it is.'

'Of course it is. Just think. Where we used to be, there's a younger generation now with their own preoccupations. Torturing themselves just as we did when we were young, but if they could only realise that nothing is ever as important as it seems at the time, because time keeps on slipping by. There's nothing new under the sun. Life is constantly repeating itself.'

The twitter of conversation continued round the table. There were several senior officers from the *Reichswehr* present, and two or three Spanish businessmen. A minister from the Belgian government expressed his concern at rumours that Germany was intending to go against the terms of the Versailles Treaty and re-arm. He spoke well and with authority.

'The future of Germany is the future of Europe,' he said, 'and has been since it unified under Otto von Bismarck.'

He was fearful of the future, but Herr Drexler brushed his concerns aside as nothing more than malicious lies, and reassured him that Europe had nothing to fear from Germany. But Monsieur François-Poncet, from the French Embassy, said that he, too, had heard the country would be re-arming. Under the formal courtesy, there was something in his manner towards Herr Drexler which was slightly contemptuous.

'The Kurfürstendamm is nothing but a weak imitation of the Avenue des Champs-Élysées,' he said at one point, when their exchange was becoming rather heated.

'There's far too much nonsense talked about Europe,' was somebody else's opinion. 'America is the country to watch. What is Europe, after all, but a little inconsequential peninsular on the continent of Asia?'

And everybody laughed, leaving him looking very pleased at his own brilliance.

21.

One morning, Ludwika wanted to go the Paul Cassirer Gallery on Viktoriastrasse for a vernissage. The gallery had kept its name, in spite of the fact that the man who established it had shot himself a couple of years ago when his wife, Tilla Durieux, divorced him. As Ludwika was applying her make-up, the telephone rang.

'Can you answer that, Alyosha?' she asked.

He was knotting his tie.

'Let's leave it ring.'

'But it could be important.'

Alyosha sighed, and picked up the receiver.

'Hello?'

Captain Malinowski was bellowing at him, but he was slurring so badly, it took Alyosha a little while to understand that he was being ordered to report to the Hotel Adlon that second.

'D'you hear me, you scoundrel?'

Alyosha was all for not going, but Ludwika persuaded him that he should. She stuck up for her cousin, saying the poor man had been a slave to morphia for years, since his leg injury from the war against the Red Army in 1920, and the reason for all his drinking was to dull the pain. Of course, in drinking to the degree that he did, starting pretty much as soon as he was awake, on top of the morphia, he only made things worse for himself. She had seen him stay in bed for days, the curtains tightly shut against the world, too depressed to get up. There he'd be, until the crisis passed, smoking, drinking and playing his mouth organ all day long. He always blamed his old wound for these various indispositions, but she knew better.

Captain Malinowski was standing in the middle of the room with a glass of Armagnac in his hand when Alyosha arrived. His eyes were red, his lump of a nose was purple, and he looked sluggish and irritable.

'Must you stand there in my light? What's the matter with you? Are you trying to annoy me?'

He sat down heavily on the divan, and his dressing gown opened.

'Listen carefully to what I'm going to say to you now,' he began, then told him what he expected him to do, adding that, if he valued his life, he shouldn't say a word to a living soul. 'On pain of death,' he repeated as he drained his glass, 'you're to tell nobody.'

Alyosha told Ludwika at once. He wasn't going to keep anything from her, because he was in love with her, and they had both agreed there were to be no secrets between them. He had already told her about his trips to Wannsee, to the twilight villa and the mute girl in the white scarf, who delivered the envelope before melting back into the woods.

'But this time…'

He hesitated.

'This time what, Alexei?'

He hesitated again.

'He expects something else from me – something more.'

She asked him what exactly he was expected to do, and he told her. When he had finished, she didn't seem to share his doubts.

'I don't think you need to worry at all. I know Przemek well.'

He always found it odd when Ludwika called the Captain by his Christian name.

'The last thing he'd do would be to put your life in danger.'

454

She soothed his fears to a degree, and he agreed to carry out Captain Malinowski's instructions. Nevertheless, he couldn't help feeling uneasy, because he was aware that it was not without its dangers – he could be imprisoned, or even executed. They still used the old-fashioned method of placing a man's head on a wooden block and cutting it off with an axe in Plötzensee prison.

22.

He drove to Nehringstrasse in Captain Malinowski's Mercedes. Or rather, to Pesotskistrasse, as the blue gothic letters high on the wall at both ends of the street now proclaimed. It was a sunny August evening, and Alyosha had barely locked the door of his motor car before one of the small boys of the Jungvolk was rattling his collecting tin under his nose. They were collecting for the *Auslandsdeutschen*, he said, and the smaller boy at his side held out his basket of little blue and white flags. Alyosha shook his head, and the two boys ran off.

There were far more swastikas hanging from the windows now, though not from every one. He looked over to the Pesotski Barracks. In the wide window by the main entrance, there was a picture of Adolf Hitler, his arms folded, staring belligerently out at the world – though the frame had been decorated with colourful flowers.

Alyosha walked to the tobacconist. Parked in front of the barracks were rows of motorcycles and two motor lorries. The building, recently repainted, gleamed in the late sun, and two members of the SA guarded the entrance. Alyosha lit himself a cigarette and made his way to the apartment. He hadn't been there for a few days; everything was exactly the same as he had left it, and there was still no sign that Vicky had been there.

He recognised the light knock as belonging to Frau

Kempowska, and he invited her in. She looked completely broken, and he suspected she was finding it a struggle to provide for herself. She told him that Franz had been arrested, and she'd heard they were keeping him in the Barracks.

'I went there to ask about him.'

They'd said he wasn't there, and were very flippant with her: 'If he hasn't come home, maybe he's found himself some skirt. Probably got sick of living with his mother.'

Frau Kempowska knew they were lying. Franz was locked up in the cellar, she was convinced of that. Then, the boy in the bakery confirmed it for her. He had been forced by his employer to join the SA. He told her he had seen Franz, and that he wasn't looking too good. And the worst of it was that one of those responsible for his mistreatment was Paul. Had Alyosha not heard? Soon after his arrest, he went over to their side. Now, he was worse than any of them, as though he wanted to prove his total loyalty to the SA. According to the baker's boy, he'd whipped poor Franz until his back was mincemeat. Sometimes, in the night, some of the tenants swore they could hear the screams from the prisoners. After all, the building was only two hundred yards away. They suspected that the SA wanted them to hear the screams, in order to intimidate them.

He comforted Frau Kempowska as best he could, and pressed a little money into her hand. Before returning to his car, he climbed the stairs to the fourth floor, where Margarita shared an apartment with Kai-Olaf. He always called on her, but she was rarely in. This evening he was in luck, and when she saw who it was, her face broke into a wan smile, but she was very pale, and had dark shadows under her eyes. The summer sun hadn't left much of a mark on her. She invited him in and made them some coffee, and although she asked him about his life, she seemed distracted and nervous.

'Are you going to tell me what's wrong?' he asked at last.

Just after five in the morning, a week or so ago, there'd been the furious knocking on their door that they'd been dreading for some time. They'd been questioned by two detectives while two more had rifled through their things, and had been asked for their papers, of course. When Kai-Olaf had come to live with her, he hadn't registered his new address with the police as he was meant to. When they'd discovered this, they'd become very suspicious, and when she'd spoken up for him, it had only made them suspicious of her as well. They'd asked her about her Nansen passport.

Margarita had asked if they were going to arrest Kai-Olaf.

'Who said anything about arresting anybody,' one of the detectives had said to her smoothly.

That's exactly what they'd done.

'Where are you taking him?'

'For a ride.'

Margarita had been informed that her passport would be returned to her within two or three days. Then they'd left, taking Kai-Olaf with them.

Her cup of coffee had long gone cold as Margarita went on to say that, in that second, she had held out very little hope of ever seeing Kai-Olaf again. So she'd been stunned when, the next day around noon, he'd walked through the door with not a scratch on him, and with his papers amended with the correct address and stamped officially. He'd been clearly very shaken by the experience, and had told her he couldn't believe he wasn't already on his way to Dachau. She'd asked him if he'd brought her passport back with him, but he'd said they hadn't given it to him. Without her passport, she wouldn't be able to apply for a visa to work in Amsterdam.

Kai-Olaf had told her he'd had no choice, it was time for him to leave Berlin. Margarita hadn't had a choice either – she'd have had to go to the police, and ask for her passport back. But

Kai-Olaf had advised her to wait a few days, in case they sent it back to her as they'd promised.

'So, have you had it back yet?' her cousin asked her.

'I waited a couple of days, and then I went in person to enquire, but I was told they wouldn't be returning my passport to me, "not for the time being, at least". That's what he said. They're still making their enquiries.'

'What enquiries?' asked Alyosha.

'I have no idea, he wouldn't say. So now I'm terrified I'll be stopped every time I leave the building, of course.'

Alyosha felt anxious on her account.

'In a café, in a shop, it happens all the time. People get arrested and dragged off for no reason at all. In the meantime, I'm meant to show this.'

She showed him the temporary identity card she had been given.

'Can you use that to apply for a visa?'

She shook her head. A prison wall was being raised brick by brick around her, and the door out of Germany was locked. Margarita looked sad and old as she sat there hunched with misery.

'So, where is Kai-Olaf now?'

'We decided he should leave without me. He's made it safely to Paris. We discussed whether I should try and get out without papers, but he thought it was too dangerous. I don't want to put the other members of the group in danger by being caught.'

'What group?'

Margarita told him briefly about the work of the IKD – the *Internationale Kommunisten Deutschland* – a group Kai-Olaf had joined when he was expelled from the Communist Party. He'd been very bitter because of the way he'd been treated, especially after all the work he'd done for the Comintern. Hitler had smashed the KPD into the dust, and was fast doing the same to the SPD, but they had to fight on. Kai-Olaf was hoping that he'd be able to work for the International Secretariat with Trotsky in Paris.

'What about you?' he asked her. 'Are you still in the KPD?'

'Yes, officially, but for how long, I don't know.'

She, too, had been called before the Disciplinary Committee and questioned at length, but they hadn't expelled her. Not yet, anyway, but she thought that was only because of Vicky, though she couldn't be sure, as she hadn't seen her for a while. In her heart, she felt more drawn to the IKD.

The police must have their eye on her. Margarita was sure of that. Why else would they be keeping her passport? Perhaps they were waiting to see if they could arrest all the members of the IKD at once, though the group rarely met now; it was just too dangerous.

As she saw him to the door, she hugged him and said sadly,

'These aren't the easiest of times to be living through, are they?'

23.

Once upon a time, the whole wide world had been at his feet, but for years now, Alyosha had been under the feet of the world. He was sick and tired of being treated so shabbily, and he felt more and more strongly that Captain Malinowski was taking advantage of him. Ludwika sympathised with him, and put her arms around his neck and kissed him twice – once on his lips and once on the tip of his nose. Every time he stood this close to her, his skin danced. He had never been so happy. He had never been so unhappy.

Time was running out, and the decision had to be made.

'I don't want to work for the Captain anymore. He doesn't give a damn about me, not really, I'm just his messenger boy.

Why should I feel any loyalty to him? He should do his own dirty work.'

A few days previously, Alyosha had driven to Frankfurt Tor, in the east of the city, as instructed by Captain Malinowski, and parked under the tower. When the audience spilled out of the small theatre just adjacent after the performance, two men in grey suits slipped into the back of the car. They told him to drive them down Thaerstrasse, round Baltenplatz, and carry on until they reached Landsberger Chaussee. A voice from the back suggested he park in the shadow of a tall wall. He extinguished the lights of the motor car and heard the back doors opening and shutting.

He waited in the silence for almost three-quarters of an hour. When they got back into the car, they were out of breath, and told him to drop them off at the Hauptbahnhof. They also gave him a roll of film, and told him to deliver it to the Captain.

Alyosha later made some discreet enquiries, and found out that the factory making tanks for the army that Hitler was re-arming was situated on Landsberger Chaussee. It didn't take a genius to work out that they were taking photographs of the tank designs.

'If I was caught,' he told Ludwika, 'how could I deny that I was a spy?' She stroked his hair lovingly. 'I'm not happy.'

She told him she could understand.

'Can you?'

'Of course.'

'Whatever's going on, it has nothing to do with me.'

'You'll have to talk to Przemek.'

Captain Malinowski was dressing for dinner, when Alyosha arrived to see him. His butler was fastening his cuff-links and arranging his silk handkerchief in his breast pocket. He barely glanced at Alyosha, beyond throwing him a quick look in the mirror as he combed his hair. As Alyosha stood there, the light in the bathroom was extinguished and the mute girl from the villa in Wannsee walked into the room, stopping for a moment to give Alyosha a blank look. She crossed over to the bed, picked up a pair of silk stockings, and rolled them up her legs. She didn't speak a word, and the Captain didn't acknowledge her presence. Alyosha couldn't stop himself from watching her as she fixed her garters in place.

It was only when he said 'I'm leaving' that Captain Malinowski put down his comb and turned to look at him properly. He lifted his glass from the drinks trolley, and rolled it slowly between his palms.

'When do you mean to do that?'

'Tonight.'

'Am I to understand why?'

'I think you know why.'

Nevertheless, he expanded by saying he wished to be master of his own fate. Captain Malinowski looked unconcerned and a little impatient, as though he were trying to hold a conversation with a child who had lost his ball and was sulking at the end of the garden.

'Every man should want to be the master of his own fate. There's nothing wrong with that. It's a good impulse.'

The butler brought the decanter over and refilled his glass.

'This isn't a sly way of asking for more wages, I hope?'

'No.'

'No, you wouldn't be one to play tricks like that with me,' he said, sipping his Armagnac. 'Why, then?'

'You always said you wanted me to speak out, not to mince my words,' Alyosha said, 'Well, that's exactly what I'm doing. I don't want to do your dirty work for you any more.'

'There we are, then, there's nothing for it but to say our goodbyes.'

Alyosha held out his hand, but Captain Malinowski had already turned away.

24.

After Kai-Olaf fled for Paris, Margarita found it hard to make ends meet, as they had both been living on his wages from the bakery, so she decided to let the second bedroom in the apartment. It was the last thing she wanted, but under the circumstances, she had no choice – if she couldn't pay her rent, she would be evicted. A young couple with a baby took the room. Julius was unemployed, and relied on the dole. Thankfully, the baby didn't cry much – she would hear him mewling in the middle of the night every now and again, but he always quietened once his mother put him to the breast.

She gave them the bigger room that she and Kai-Olaf had slept in, and moved her things to the smaller room which they had used as a study. They kept out of each other's way as much as possible, but living with a baby brought all sorts of conflicting feelings in Margarita to the surface. Usually, she felt sure she had done the right thing in aborting, but sometimes, she felt it was the worst thing ever.

She still hadn't summoned the nerve to go back and ask about her passport. She longed to hear more from Kai-Olaf, and to be able to share his news with the rest of the IKD, but messages from Paris were sporadic, as they had to be passed along a network of couriers. When one of them was caught, tortured, and sent to Dachau, there was a long silence until they could be sure the rest of them had not been identified. She never knew when the next message would come. Even then, much had to be left unsaid, to protect the membership of the IKD. Even in the part written in invisible ink, real names were never used, only the codenames they all had.

In the meantime, Vicky had come to her again, asking for her help. Firstly, she wanted to establish a link between the IKD, the KPD, and the most progressive elements within the SPD, with the intention of creating a united front against the Nazis. Secondly, she wanted to see Alyosha. Was it possible for Margarita to arrange a meeting?

25.

Above the doors of some of the bars and dancing halls, the neon lights still winked, but the Kurfürstendamm was virtually deserted, aside from a few late birds making for home. Alyosha rang the bell twice, and the door clicked open. He walked along the corridor and through a kitchen of bright white tiles, to reach the large room with the wooden dance floor. The place smelled of sweat and spilt alcohol. The stub of a cigar still smouldered in an ashtray, and several wine bottles in their raffia baskets remained uncleared on some of the tables.

Two young men and an older woman were on their knees, busily cyclostyling leaflets. They worked intently and silently, pressing the leaflets flat between two boards and smoothing them with rubber rollers. The title was *Die Rote Fahne*.

'She's through there,' said one of the young men, barely lifting his head from his work.

Vicky's skin was sickly, her eyes bloodshot, and dark roots were creeping through her blonde hair. She was deep in discussion with two comrades, and it was obvious from their demeanour that they were all dispirited.

'Thank you for coming.'

When she hugged him, her breath smelled of drink. Alyosha asked her directly what she wanted him to do.

'Deliver copies of *Die Rote Fahne*. You're the only person I know who drives a motor car.'

He told her that he no longer worked for Captain Malinowski. She frowned. 'Are you telling the truth?'

'What reason would I have to lie?'

He suddenly felt very sorry for her. 'Why are you still doing this Vicky? It's so dangerous. Wouldn't it be safer for you to leave for Moscow?'

'And let those Nazi scum have the upper hand?' Her old spirit flickered into life, 'There are powerful articles in this edition.'

'I don't doubt it.'

Vicky smiled, and sat to light a cigarette and reflect for a moment. This was nothing new for her, she told him, she'd been in a similar situation after Kapp's *putsch*, back in 1920, when the streets were filled with murder and mayhem. She had lived in constant fear through that, too, living from hand to mouth, sleeping somewhere different every night.

'Will you help us?'

'I can't.'

She asked why.

'I'm not prepared to risk my life for a cause I don't believe in. While I live, I'll oppose communism. You're trying your best to impose a moral order on everybody. You say your Marxist ethic is relevant to everybody, everywhere under the sun. But I just don't see how that can be.'

'What do you see in its place then?'

'I don't know. I don't think there are any laws within history, just layers of reality – zigzagging sometime, inside-out at other times, and all jumbled up.'

'Anything else?'

'Yes. That every one of us, in my experience, at least, under-values the role of chance.'

'What are you trying to say?'

'That any meaning someone discovers in his own life is something that's unique to him.'

'So what is the meaning in your life?'

He paused for a moment. 'I don't know for sure… Not yet, anyway.'

'Of course you don't! And you never will. The truth about an individual's life is outside himself, in other people or ideas or situations. Those are the things that shape the reality you live in. That's where the meaning of your life lies. In order to understand yourself, you have to understand everything else as well, by analysing the processes which work through history. That is the only reality. That is the only truth.'

'I'm sorry, but I can't help you.'

Vicky looked at him longingly. 'I miss sleeping with you, Alexei.'

She placed the back of her hand tenderly on his cheek.

26.

In mid-October, hundreds of Berliners made their way to Pesot-skistrasse, to gather under the swastikas, which seemed to hang from every window. A brass band gave them a brash welcome, and on the erected platform stood two rows of the SA, Bruno Volkmann among them. Oberführer Krieger introduced the main speaker, Dr Goebbels, who pulled the cord to uncover the plaque which had been placed high on the wall.

Vlasich Pesotski
Er fiel für Deutschland

As he picked his way through the crowds, Alyosha became aware of a shadow at his shoulder. It was Paul, now clean-shaven and with a little more flesh on him than before, though his cheeks were as bloodless as ever under his brown peaked hat. They looked at each other for a second or two, then Paul looked furtively around him before muttering that he had to see her.

'Who?'

Vicky's name was almost drowned by the notes blaring out from the band.

'Will you tell her?'

'I don't know where she is anymore.'

Paul sniffed sceptically. 'But you know how to get hold of her. This is important. There are things I have to tell her. Important things. Things she needs to know.'

'On my honour, I don't know how to contact her.'

'But you can ask around?' The SA's man stared him in the face challengingly. 'Can't you?'

Alyosha was torn. He couldn't decide if Paul had become a Nazi through and through, or whether the anguish he seemed to be expressing was genuine.

'I'm not what you think I am,' Paul said earnestly.

The band stopped playing and the crowd whistled and applauded.

'Vicky has to understand that. My loyalties are still with the working class.'

'Where's your mouse?' asked Alyosha.

'Rosa died.'

27.

Margarita had long since put any thoughts of a wage packet behind her, when her circumstances changed for the better. One afternoon, she bumped in to a girl who used to work in another section at Aznefttrust, as she was pushing her baby in his pram outside the KaDeWe. She told Margarita she'd heard there was a job going, and if she didn't have the baby, she would have gone for it herself. Margarita duly applied, and was invited for interview at the Soviet Union's Department of Trade in Berlin. She was called back the next day for a second interview, and was told at the end of it that the job was hers.

In her desperation for work – any sort of work – she had buried any misgivings, but as she sat at her desk on her first morning, all sorts of doubts came into her head. Had she stepped into the lion's den? Was working here inadvisable, as she was still an important contact point between the IKP members in Berlin and the Paris office? Had she taken leave of her senses, in fact?

'Hitler or not, trade is still important. Though we don't know how long they'll let us stay of course,' her boss, Anton Kovrin, told her. 'The 1926 agreement between our two countries is still in force, so Russia has every right to trade here, though they've imposed the requirement that we don't employ any Germans. Of course, you know that, it's the reason why Aznefttrust had to shut.'

Doubts or not, Margarita was very thankful to be earning again. The Department of Trade was housed in a substantial building, a small, square mansion, with grounds, surrounded by tall walls, and two handsome gates of decorative cast iron, where a young man checked their credentials every morning before letting them through. All the members of staff were given identity cards.

For the first three weeks, Margarita shared the office with two other women – both ardent Stalinists – typing and translating letters. One, who was the same age as Larissa, had two children, and her husband had been arrested. She showed his picture to Margarita, who thought he looked familiar, though she didn't say so. There was no knowing when, or if, he would be released. He'd already spent the last five months in Dachau.

Margarita's experience of working in a bank came in useful, and she was soon transferred to the Finance Department to work for Anton Kovrin.

A regular visitor from Paris was Stanislav Markovich Feldman.

28.

Margarita had just put on her coat, ready to leave for work, when her tenant told her that the post had arrived, and there was a letter from the Gestapo for her. She took the letter and left the apartment without opening it. After shutting the door behind her, she stood at the head of the stairs and stared at the letter, pulling her coat around her as if to protect her heart. She opened the envelope and squinted in the poor light at the black type, and had to look again, as the few words swam before her eyes. It was a bald instruction to make herself available for interview at the time noted. Her mind raced. She must get out of Berlin for Paris, Amsterdam, Norway, anywhere at all, it didn't matter, just as long as the German border was behind her. She shouldn't catch the tram to work, shouldn't go back to the apartment either, ever again. Who could she turn to? She considered what members of the IKP might be able to help her. But was it fair to even ask? Wouldn't she be putting them in danger, too? She knew she was already in a desperate position. She had heard enough about the Gestapo's methods to doubt that she would be able to withstand interrogation. But why the letter? Why not pick her up and arrest her as they usually did, given that they knew where she lived? It was very odd.

Her nerves were so jangled that she couldn't think straight. She stopped at a café on Nollendorfplatz, and ordered a coffee. She was aware of a painful and insistent throbbing between her temples. She tried to steady her thoughts, but her headache was a distraction. *Why* hadn't the Gestapo just arrested her? Why send that letter? It made absolutely no sense at all. There was some stratagem at work here, but what? If only she could talk to Kai-Olaf, ask his advice. She missed him more than ever. He would have been able to think things out logically, and find a way out of her predicament. She sipped her coffee, but it tasted bitter.

29.

Alyosha felt like a free man now that he was no longer at Captain Malinowski's beck and call, and he walked with a lighter step. Life went on as before, though he was now a kept man. Ludwika even hired a car, and they took trips out of the city into the countryside. They had started to discuss their future together, but Alyosha still felt that Ludwika only half belonged to him. She spent some of her time with her own people without him, reporting that Baroness Kosub, Colonel Flezar and the rest of the Poles were becoming increasingly anxious about Adolf Hitler's intentions. The Soviet Union might well have reason to be wary, but Poland, as ever, was like a small child squeezed in a bed between two greedy men. If another war broke out, who knew what the fate of her mother country would be. Poland's fate was Europe's fate, as Talleyrand had told Metternich at the Congress of Vienna. Since the Treaty of Versailles, the bone of contention between Germany and Poland was the Danzig corridor, Upper Silesia, Teschen, East Galicia and Vilna. Hitler was eager to claim all this land back, and he was set on punishing Poland for claiming them in the first place.

Prophesising the future of Europe was the last thing on Alyosha's mind. The only thing of importance to him was a future where two became one: he wanted them to start a new life together in Paris.

'And Amelia, remember.'

'Of course, Amelia too.'

In the torpor of the night, with the taste of her flesh still on his tongue, and the noise of the SA wolves drifting in from the street, he would stroke Ludwika's back, cup her breasts, pull her closer, the sweat in the small of her back damp against his stomach. He'd kiss the nape of her neck, whisper endearments in her ear, and she would mumble something under her breath – something he didn't catch, but which would comfort him nevertheless.

30.

When she reported to Prinz-Albrecht-Strasse, she was interviewed by a bald, middle-aged man in a leather waistcoat. His
shirtsleeves were rolled up, and on the desk in front of him was
a manila file. He told her to sit pleasantly enough, and offered
her a cigarette, which she accepted, hoping it would calm her
nerves,

Throughout the subsequent interview, Margarita assumed the
Gestapo agent was laying some trap for her. The questions were
general to begin with, before concentrating on the whereabouts
of Kai-Olaf. Margarita claimed ignorance. She took on a vague
air about everything, as if she was rather forgetful. She even
plucked up the courage to tell him how inconvenient it was to
have to keep renewing the permit which allowed her to work
in Berlin.

'That does sound like an unnecessary nuisance.' He looked at
her benignly, before rummaging inside the file and producing her
passport, which he placed on the desk in front of her.

'That's why I'd like to offer my assistance.'

Margarita stubbed out her cigarette. *Here it comes*, she thought.

Sure enough, the man pulled his chair up closer to the desk,
and proceeded to tell her what she'd have to do effect the return
of her passport. As a loyal citizen, he felt sure she would be more
than willing to report on the internal affairs at her workplace.
Naturally, he was asking a great favour, he fully understood that;
he didn't want her to give him an answer that second, she should
think it over. He added that an intelligent young woman like her
surely understood what was at stake. After all, there was more
than trade going on at the Soviet Union's Department of Trade
in Berlin, was there not?

He threw her passport back in the file, and told her that the
interview was concluded.

31.

'Did he say anything else?' asked Anton Kovrin, after listening closely to Margarita's account of the meeting.

Margarita passed him the card with the telephone number on it. The bald man had placed it in her hand – like giving sweets to a favourite niece – as she left his office.

Her boss thanked her for bringing the matter to his attention so promptly.

'You did the right thing. We'll let you know in due course how we want you to proceed.'

That was all very well for him to say. But as the days went past with no instructions forthcoming, she became increasingly worried, so when she saw Anton Kovrin one morning in the corridor, she asked if she could have a word with him. He lifted a finger to his lips and asked her to follow him to his office, but after shutting the door, he was quite short with her.

'What is it?'

'Has any decision been reached about my case yet?'

'Not yet, no. Why?'

Because she needed to know what the next step was. What they would expect her to do.

He dropped his voice and told her the matter had been 'passed on'.

That was all very well, but what if the Gestapo picked her up in the meantime? What then? What was she meant to do?

But all he would say was, 'The answer will come in due course.'

32.

Late one November afternoon, Alyosha went over to Pesotskis-trasse. It was some weeks since his last visit to the apartment, and he wanted to collect his winter coat, as the weather had turned. Everything was in its place exactly as he had left it, and he was just taking his coat out of the wardrobe in the bedroom when he heard a knock on the door. Thinking it must be Frau Kempowska, he opened it without thinking twice, only to be hurled back as if by a tornado, banging his head on the corner of the table and sending an empty plant pot crashing onto the floor, where it shattered in pieces.

A blonde man in a sharp suit held a razor under his chin. A second man in a mackintosh closed the door quietly after him. He took a chair and sat on it backwards, slinging his legs either side of its back.

'Who the hell are you?' spluttered Alyosha.

They didn't seem to want to chat.

'There's no money here, if that's what you're after.'

Alyosha tried to sit up but the blonde man pressed the razor against his flesh: he felt a sticky wetness as blood trickled down the side of his neck. Then, the second man bent over and stubbed his cigarette slowly and thoroughly on the back of his hand. Alyosha screamed with pain, but was too aware of the razor at his neck to try to move.

The man in the mackintosh spoke quietly but menacingly. He had betrayed the Polish cause – he was a coward of the first degree. More than that, he was the most unprincipled, underhand bastard that had ever walked God's earth, not giving a shit about anything or anyone but his own yellow skin.

'Ever heard about making a sacrifice for a cause? Eh?'

He had twenty-four hours to disappear, and if they saw him on the streets of Berlin after that, they'd carve him up properly.

Ludwika was shocked when he told her what had happened. She ran her finger over the narrow cut the razor had made on his skin, which was already knitting together. Alyosha was shaken, but furious, and was all set to confront Captain Malinowski, until

472

she persuaded him to wait. He shouldn't rush over there while he was still so angry; better to calm down, and then decide how best to proceed. That was important. In the end, they decided between them that it would be wiser if Ludwika went to speak to her cousin first, in order to get to the bottom of what had just happened. If Przemek was in any way behind those louts threatening him, he would see a very different side of her. But in spite of her bravado, Ludwika was clearly worried, and the last thing Alyosha wanted was to have her put in any danger on his account. He walked her over to the Hotel Adlon.

'Don't wait for me,' she told him, 'and don't worry, I'll be back in no time.'

They kissed, and Alyosha spent the next couple of hours loitering around the Hotel Kaiserhof. After considering the matter further, he thought perhaps Captain Malinowski might not be involved after all, and that Colonel Flezar had been responsible. When she still hadn't returned, he became so restless, he decided to go outside for some air, even though Ludwika had told him to say in the hotel room so that she could telephone him. He only walked as far as the square, and sat there watching the minute hand of the clock inching forward, his thoughts turning back to Ludwika constantly: how much influence did she really have? Could she persuade them that they could trust him, and that he would never betray their secrets to the *Reichswehr* or the Gestapo or anybody else?

The lights around the square came on, and around him, people with their own troubles hurried by. He sucked the cold air into his lungs and walked about aimlessly. He was desperate to see Ludwika, to find out exactly what was happening. He felt an overwhelming urge just to hear her voice. He found a kiosk and dialled. As he was waiting to be connected, he watched an old beggar trying to settle his dog to sleep at his side.

'Hello?'

It was a woman's voice, but not Ludwika's, and it took him a few seconds to recognise it as belonging to the Baroness, as she sounded different over the telephone.

'It's Alexei Fyodorovich... Is Ludwika there?'

There was a loud click. Had she dropped the receiver? In his mind's eye, he could see Ludwika clearly, see her mouthing, 'Who is it?' as she got up from her chair. He could hear some low murmurs, and a sound like a drawer being opened and shut, not that he was certain of that...

'Alexei?'

Had she spoken to her cousin yet? He found it difficult to follow the thrust of her answers: her words were ambiguous, and he didn't understand what she was trying to tell him. He kept asking Ludwika questions which she wouldn't answer. What had she said to Captain Malinowski? More importantly, what had he said to her? Had she seen Colonel Flezar? Was he there? Her answers seemed to be coded, only he didn't have the cipher, and felt he as though he was going mad. Then, she said something so quietly he barely caught it.

'...not safe.'

Her voice shrivelled.

'What?'

He could barely hear her against the roar of the traffic. He pressed the receiver closer to his ear. Was there anybody else in the room with her apart from Baroness Kosub?

She was whispering now, 'Alexei? Listen... Alexei? Are you still there?'

He told her he was.

'Are you listening?'

'I'm listening...'

'Closely, are you listening closely?'

'Closely, yes...'

Ludwika didn't want him to go anywhere near the Hotel

Kaiserhof; he should keep well clear, and meet her later outside Frankfurter Allee station. Had he understood what she had just told him? Yes, he knew the place well, it was by the fields of the Stadtpark.

33.

He arrived half an hour early, and walked along the platform, to the very end, where it stopped in the gloom, though the red spot of a signal was visible further down the line. There were just one or two people waiting for their train. He went down the stairs, into the underpass, and emerged into the twilight of the street, which appeared greyish-yellow under the lamps.

It was utterly silent. Four motor cars parked nearby looked like monsters, huddled there for the winter. Opposite him were the black park railings, and beyond them, the silhouetted bushes and the stillness of the trees. He crossed the street, and stood in the shadows of the park, frost already chill beneath his feet. He kept one eye on the hands of the station clock, measuring the minutes ticking away one by one. Five trains slowed to a stop, before thundering off once more, bright ribbons into the night, their roar gradually fading into the distance. He stamped his feet, and did up the top button of his coat, under his chin.

At eleven o'clock, he saw a yellow light flashing along the railings from the furthest bend of the road. The motor car came to a halt in front of the station. Alyosha watched the red tip of a cigarette like a firefly, before it disappeared into the dark. He looked again intently, and he recognised the shape of her head: she was keeping an eye on the street, looking out for him. After waiting a while, she eventually got out of the car, and was about to climb the stairs up to the platform, but, by then, he had crossed the road and had grasped the sleeve of her coat. He gave her a shock, and she let out a little gasp, but then she hugged him tightly.

He kissed her, and smelt the cognac on her breath. Alyosha held her face in his hands and looked searchingly into her eyes. Her lips were slightly parted, showing her white, even teeth.

'This way,' he said, taking her hand and leading her into the park, making for where the bushes provided cover. It was only then that he started to question her.

'What's happening?'

'I tried my best, I promise.'

'Who sent them, Flezar or Malinowski?'

'For your own good I'm saying this...'

'Answer me, Wisia. Who set those two on me with a razor?'

'I can't do anything for you,' she said mournfully. 'They're determined to kill you.'

He was listening to her with one ear, the other alive to the sounds of the street.

'Alexei, you have to leave Berlin. If you don't get out...'

'Hush!'

She whispered, 'What is it?

'Hush!'

Ludwika whispered sadly, 'Go far enough away.'

The sound was approaching and Alyosha pressed his hand over her mouth.

'Ssh!'

A kind of rustling came nearer, step by step. Alyosha held his breath, every hair on his body raised, until he realised it was only a stray dog. Alyosha caught Ludwika's hands in his. Her hands were never cold, because she always wore gloves. Why not tonight?

'What's the matter?'

He didn't trust her. The sickening realisation swept over him in a wave of agonising disillusionment. How had he been so blind? He knew what she was, knew exactly what kind of a person she was, after Paris. She hadn't changed at all.

Now there was something else moving in the dark.

He grabbed her and yanked at her savagely for her to follow him. Low-hanging branches were scratching her face, and she tried to shake herself free from his grasp. He was white-hot with anger.

'Will you come with me to Paris tonight?' he demanded.

'Alexei, listen.'

'We'll take your car and drive to the border…'

'Stop, Alexei, stop!'

'We'll find a way over somehow.'

He couldn't see her eyes in the darkness.

'Me? Or your own people? Who is more important to you? You have to choose.'

Instead of answering him, Wisia pulled him to her and kissed him hard.

'There's your proof,' she whispered in his ear.

Alyosha kissed her – kissed her with all the strength of his creation.

'Too hard – don't…'

'Wisia…'

'You're hurting me, let me go, I can't…'

Over her shoulder, Alyosha saw the glint of a pair of eyes for a moment between the branches. He flung Ludwika away from him furiously, and she fell backwards, half screaming something in Polish. Alyosha was already running for his life, crashing purblind through twigs and branches, as men shouted behind him. At the edge of the trees lay level fields, their edges blurring into the darkness, but he would be too visible crossing such an open space. He turned abruptly on his heel and plunged back on himself, into the rhododendron bushes. He heard the voices approach. Then, a gun being fired. He ran on through the trees, his heart thumping, until he reached the iron railings at the park's boundary. He leapt over them, catching his leg on the spike, though he didn't feel a thing, and collapsed heavily onto the other side, He heard a motor engine accelerating.

'Ludwika!'

The motor gathered speed down the street: she was driving, but she didn't stop.

'Ludwika!' he shouted again.

He heaved himself back to his feet and ran after her, but the distance between them grew. She was driving as fast as she could. Then, he noticed a train pulling into the platform. He sprinted through the tunnel, chased by the echo of his own feet, and took the steps two at a time, until he reached the platform, and continued running to the end. He leapt through the open door of the last carriage and crouched out of sight, praying for the doors to shut, praying and praying.

Once the train had started moving, he peeped out of the window and saw Captain Malinowski and two or three men capering like madmen, rushing up and down the platform, their coats whirling like dancers, shouting and firing their guns into the air. He could still feel her Judas kiss on his lips, and without warning, hot tears filled his eyes. He felt the need to hide his face under a handkerchief, so that nobody saw them fall.

34.

Margarita was still waiting for Kai-Olaf's reply to the last letter she had sent him. In the meantime, she had been discussing her situation with members of the IKD. Most of them thought she was playing with fire by staying. Then, as if she didn't have enough on her plate, she returned from work one day to find Larissa, Ella and Clara standing outside the apartment block, waiting for her, with two suitcases There was something pitiful about the three of them, and poor little Clara was shivering with cold.

After giving them all hot drinks and settling the children with a puzzle and a picture book which Larissa had packed, Margarita asked her sister what had happened. Larissa told her that Bruno had found some letters from Walter that she had hidden. Their contents were unambiguous, and Bruno had lost his temper with her, shaking her violently and shouting so loudly the entire household must have heard. Larissa had crumpled and confessed her affair to him.

'However frightened I was, I was relieved to tell the truth. It's been unbearable these last few months, living a lie all the time.'

'What about Walter?' Margarita asked, 'Does he know you've left Bruno?'

'No, not yet, I'll write to him at his work to explain what's happened. I'll give him this address. We can stay for a bit, can't we?'

Margarita's tenants were none too happy that they were expected to share the apartment with three extra people. That was not part of their original agreement, and if they'd realised that this was going to happen, they'd never have become her tenants in the first place. Margarita tried her best to keep the peace, and reduced their rent, but the couple took an instant dislike to her sister, while Larissa was too bound up in her own worries to care what they thought of her. She was very low, and felt that her future was unravelling in front of her. Every time Walter called by (and he did so frequently, sitting with Larissa on Margarita's bed, where they talked earnestly for hours), the couple looked at him with utter contempt. They hated him even more than they hated Larissa, because he was a Jew.

Walter was a quiet, thoughtful man, as different from Bruno as it was possible to be. There was nothing pompous or ponderous about him. He was unassuming, kind to the little girls, and tenderly protective of Larissa. He was an engineer by training, but had not been able to find work in the field, and made a modest living working in a shop which sold string instruments. It was when Larissa was looking for a child's violin for Ella that the two had met. He was desperate to make a new life with Larissa and

479

her children, but he felt responsible for his wife. But, after a long discussion one evening, he seemed to have come to a resolution.

'He's going to tell her,' Larissa told her sister once he'd left, 'But we'll have to leave Berlin. We've decided. It's impossible for us to live here. We have to go somewhere where he can work again, where he can make some sort of a livelihood. And I have to get away from Bruno, too.'

'But where will you go?'

'Wherever he'll be treated with more respect than here.'

For Margarita, the answer was obvious, but she spoke tentatively, unsure of how her sister would react.

'The Soviet Union. That would be the safest place for the two of you and the girls.'

'Really?' asked her sister, looking doubtful. 'Do you know, Walter said the same thing. His family came from Russia originally, before settling in Germany. And that's where I came from, of course. And you, a long time ago…'

Larissa knew she would find it hard to leave Berlin. This was her home. Here, she had given birth to her girls; here, she had settled, put down roots, and made a life for herself.

'But I suppose it will be hard wherever we go,' she said sadly.

'I know,' said Margarita, squeezing her arm comfortingly.

But circumstances might not give them any choice.

'I'll make enquiries about visas for you.'

'Will that be difficult?'

'I'm sure it can be done.'

35.

This time, Stanislav Markovich was there too, smoking his pipe.

Margarita was asked to repeat what had happened when she went to Prinz-Albrecht-Strasse.

Stanislav kept his eyes fixed on her throughout her account, and as soon as she had finished speaking, told her he wanted her to phone the Gestapo.

'And then what?'

'Do whatever they suggest.'

Her wooden chair felt very hard.

'They might want to interview you again,' said Stanislav, 'or they might arrange to meet you somewhere else. They'll probably be expecting you to smuggle documents out of here for them to copy,' he said neutrally.

It went without saying she should report back everything the Gestapo told her at once.

'To you?' she asked Stanislav.

He half gestured towards Anton Kovrin.

'When should I do it?'

'The sooner the better.'

She used the telephone on the desk to call the Gestapo – with Stanislav Markovich at her elbow listening to every word.

By the time she received a reply from Kai-Olaf, the first rendezvous with the Gestapo had already been arranged. Too late, he wrote that on no account should she play the NKVD's games for them – they didn't care one iota about her safety. He emphasised this; they would see her as totally expendable. Kai-Olaf had crossed Stanislav Markovich's path many times over the years, and knew that he was not to be trusted. He wanted Margarita to arrange through the IKP to leave Berlin without delay.

She knew what he said was true, and she desperately wanted to leave herself. But it was difficult, if not impossible. She had already asked Anton Kovrin whether it would be possible to arrange four visas for the Soviet Union. He had promised to do what he could, but had added that such matters could take time. Until Larissa and Walter were safely over the border, Margarita felt she had no choice but to stay in Berlin. She wrote an answer

481

to Kai-Olaf explaining her situation, and promised to come to him the minute everything was settled. She added that she longed for him, hoped he was healthy and well in Paris, and that he was always in her thoughts. She had been rather hurt by the tone of his letter – he hadn't mentioned anything about his feelings for her. But he was busy, no doubt, as the letter seemed to have been written in haste. Once they were together again in Paris, everything would be as it was.

36.

They had told Margarita to go to Dahlem, and find the farthest greenhouse in the Botanic Gardens, out of sight of the road. She was to sit on the wooden bench nearest the waterfall which poured down over the big rocks. She followed their instructions and waited, watching the fat orange-and-black koi carp swimming under the white foam in the pool. The fine spray sprinkled her face and hair with a film of moisture. A gang of schoolchildren wandered past, their feet crunching against the gravel, giggling and squabbling. It was so humid that Margarita was already sweating, even though she had taken off her coat and folded it by her side.

The wooden bench creaked when he sat down beside her. She asked him for a light. He wasn't a smoker. He was a young man, younger than her, wearing frameless spectacles. He told her his name was Manfred, and then, without further preamble, questioned her about her work in the Trade Department. He was interested in the correspondence coming into her office, and he wanted to know the names of all the companies and organisations they had dealings with, who visited the offices, and who was who in Moscow. He was also very interested in her boss, Anton Kovrin, and even asked about his background and his education.

Margarita told him that she didn't really know him very well and – less truthfully – that their paths crossed very rarely. The young man said that in the last eight months alone, Kovrin had been seen in Stockholm, Vienna, Budapest, Milan and Sofia. On three of those trips, he had met with Stanislav Markov Feldman. Did she know Stanislav Markov Feldman?

Margarita thought fast and decided to tell the truth. This was a wise decision, because the Gestapo knew they'd been lovers. When was the last time she'd seen Stanislav Markov Feldman?

'A year or two ago... I can't remember exactly.'

He observed her keenly, and waited for a hunch-backed old man, leaning on his stick, to totter past them painfully slowly.

'Has Stanislav Markov Feldman visited the Trade Department at all?'

Not that she knew of.

Had anybody in the Department discussed him at all?

Not with her, no, nobody.

Then he asked her if she had heard of the Special Department.

'No.'

Had anyone in her office mentioned anything about the Special Department in front of her?

'No.'

'Never?'

She shook her head.

The young man's main interest was the Special Department. He wanted Margarita to see what she could find out, and report back.

37.

Bruno came round to the apartment, banging on the door insistently.

'Open the door,' he shouted.

483

'Don't,' Larissa told her sister. But the knocking continued, and then he started kicking the door, shouting loudly that he had every right to see his wife and children. One of the tenants shouted at him to shut up, but as he was making such a row, they didn't have much choice but to let him in. He was scarlet and short of breath after all his shouting and kicking, but he pushed past Margarita, and, pointing at Larissa, said, 'I want a word with my wife. On her own.'

He glared at Margarita's tenants, who were staring at him nervously. 'Who are they?' he snapped.

'Who are *you*?' asked Julius.

'Larissa, take Bruno into the kitchen, you can talk there. But for heaven's sake, Bruno, try to calm down, you're frightening the girls.'

She might as well have talked to the wall. Within half a minute, Bruno was bellowing for the whole block to hear that if she didn't come back to his house immediately, she would never see her daughters again, he'd make damn sure of that. Margarita could hear Larissa's supplicating tones, but then there was a loud crash. She rushed in to the kitchen to see a bowl shattered in pieces on the floor and Larissa looking shaken. Bruno, with a muttered oath, barrelled past Margarita and stormed out of the apartment.

'He threw it at my head,' Larissa told Margarita. 'If I hadn't ducked…'

When Walter heard what had happened, he felt wretched that he hadn't been there to protect her. After that, he tried to come by the apartment every evening after work, which left Julius and his wife sullen and cross. When Bruno came round again a few nights later to find him there, he didn't mince his words, and called Walter a dirty lying Jew to his face. After every bruising encounter, Larissa begged Margarita to do her best to move the approval of their visas on. She was afraid of what her husband would do next. Margarita had been asking Anton Kovrin about

484

them almost every day, but he always had an excuse. Feeling she didn't have a choice, she decided to go above his head and ask Stanislav Markovich if he could help, but his mind was on far more important matters – such as duping the Gestapo.

On the way to the apartment one evening, Walter was badly beaten up. From then on, Larissa was convinced that it was only a matter of time before Bruno would arrange to have him arrested or killed. It wouldn't be so difficult after all – in fact, it would be the easiest thing in the world.

They *must* leave, there was no time to lose. Why were the visas taking so long? Why was her sister having so much trouble getting them? Couldn't she persuade whoever was in charge how precarious their situation was?

38.

On their second meeting, Manfred gave Margarita some photographs, and asked her to identify everybody she knew. Margarita put a name to every face. The next time, she gave him a list of all the German communists who used to work at the Department of Trade. Manfred was visibly delighted. But, in fact, the names were all of former employees who were now members of NASAP. Stanislav Markovich had rubbed his hands when he thought of the fascists arresting fascists, accusing them of treachery and spying, beating them and mistreating them. It was a small blow for all the communists who were rotting in Hitler's prisons.

Once the next meeting with Manfred had been scheduled, Margarita went to see Anton Kovrin. She told him she would not be going until she was given the four visas as he had promised. He told her harshly that he didn't appreciate blackmail, but she held her ground and reminded him that they had made a bargain, and that she was the only one carrying out her side of it. Her sister, her sister's lover and her two nieces were desperate to reach the safety of the Soviet Union.

39.

When Larissa held the four visas in her hand, her emotions were mixed. Although she was filled with relief, in her heart, she didn't want to leave Berlin. Until recently, she and Walter had been so at home there. Berlin was the axis of their lives, where all their friends were. Here, was everything that was comfortable and familiar, and although she'd been born in Russia, the place was like a foreign country to her now. Would there even be a welcome for them there?

'Don't look so worried. Of course you'll be welcomed. They're desperate for men like Walter over there,' Margarita said reassuringly.

When Larissa thought of the Soviet Union, the picture in her head was of an enormous steelworks spreading for miles, belching smoke and steam. The Soviet Union. Even the name made her nervous. But it seemed the only option if she and Walter were to have any chance of a happy future together.

Meanwhile, Margarita was still meeting Manfred, but how long would it be until he realised he was being duped? He wasn't a stupid man. Sooner or later, he would work it out, and at that moment, her value to both sides would be zero. But whenever Margarita voiced her anxieties to Kovrin, he would throw back her words in her face, and remind her that a bargain had been struck. She felt as though she was nothing more than a flute for somebody else to play. The Director of the Department of Trade and Stanislav Markovich were happy to risk her safety while she was still being useful to them.

The night before Larissa left for the Soviet Union, the

two sisters stayed up very late talking. They reminisced about arriving in Berlin with their mother, and the confusion of those first weeks, when they were living in an empty barracks, with forty or more people in one room, squashed together like sardines, and sleeping in two long rows of beds on either side, a stove in the middle for them all to dry their clothes and cook their food.

'We were lucky to bag the three beds in the corner, d'you remember?'

Margarita remembered her mother being mortified that there was so little privacy and that the only place to dress and undress was behind a screen in the bathroom. There'd been only six basins for all of them, and they'd always been filthy. It was while they'd been there that their mother had had all her money and jewellery stolen.

'It all feels so long ago,' sighed Larissa.

'Because it is.' Margarita exhaled smoke from her cigarette. 'It's almost fifteen years ago.'

That first Easter in the barracks, their mother had somehow found a couple of eggs, and hidden them outside so that the girls could keep to the old tradition, and hunt for them in the long grass behind the building. Then, they'd been moved from the barracks on the outskirts of the city to a refugee centre in central Berlin – an old school which had been shut for twenty years or so, with a leaky roof. That's how Margarita had found work in the cake factory, when some man had come to the centre one afternoon looking for cheap labour. Her wages had meant they could at least move into their own apartment.

'I don't want to leave.'

'I know.'

'This is my home, Gretushka.'

'I know.'

'Here's where I'm happiest. Here is where my children are

happiest. When I think about having to go back to Russia, it makes me feel so frightened.'

She wiped her tears with her sleeve.

'You'll be fine.'

'Do you think so?'

'I've been there, remember. It's a different country for sure. But it's a better country.'

40.

It was a damp and miserable morning, with a December fog squatting over the city, the light dull and weak, when Larissa and Margarita stood on the platform at Stettin Station. Porters went rushing by with their piles of trunks, cases, and boxes of all shapes and sizes. By the bar, a row of men stood smoking with their backs to the world; two lovers kissed; children ran here and there, spinning round, playing hide and seek behind the pillars while their mothers scolded; weary travellers nodded off, their cheeks resting on their bags on their laps; and a tall young man clutching a violin case stared vacantly into space as he ate an apple.

The train hissed and snorted as it built up a head of steam, jerking once as though to prove its strength for the journey. The guard started banging the doors shut as the long whistle sounded. People hugged and said their goodbyes. From inside the train, Larissa held Ella and Clara up to the window. Margarita put her hands on the glass and the little girls held up theirs on the other side.

'Remember to write,' mouthed Larissa.

Margarita took a step back and waited with Walter's brother and his parents, who were standing arm-in-arm, his mother clutching a balled-up handkerchief in her fist. The father's forehead was deeply wrinkled, and there was pain in his face.

They waited. The train gave a jolt, and then another, before slowly moving down the line. The train's whistle pierced the air again, and Margarita closed her eyes and choked back the sob in her throat. She didn't know how long she stayed like that, but when she turned to go, there was no sight of Walter's family.

As she crossed the main concourse and went out on to the street, she had a feeling that she was being followed. She crossed the street, quickening her pace, and slipped into a shop. She waited there for a moment to get her breath back, then resumed her journey.

A blonde woman drew level with her and walked at her side.

'You have to leave Berlin today,' she said without looking at her.

Margarita stopped in her tracks and asked, 'Who are you?'

'Keep walking. I'm Tatyana,' she answered. 'Stanislav's wife.'

'So is he telling me this?'

'The Gestapo are waiting to pick you up at your apartment. Don't go back there.'

'So what should I do?'

'Leave.'

'Today?'

'Now. Any way you can. Just get out.'

Tatyana, without another word, peeled away and disappeared from sight.

41.

Margarita knew that she could not afford to hesitate, she must act. It took her only a few moments' consideration to decide who was best placed to help her, and she caught the tram immediately to the leather factory in Bielfeld where Eggert, a friend in the IKP, worked.

'What am I going to do?' she asked him.

He told her she should certainly leave Germany immediately, but better aim for Prague, not Paris. The border was easier to cross without papers.

'I don't know anybody in Prague.'

Eggert gave her the names of a young couple in the movement whom she could trust, and their address in Reichenberg.

'And remember, it's illegal to take money out of the country with you.'

'That's the least of my worries. How am I going to get across the border?'

Eggert thought he had the answer – though it was fraught with danger.

42.

The picture house was warm and snug, and Alyosha was glad to take off his coat and scarf and settle into his seat. Once he had thawed out, the warmth soon enveloped him, and he started to feel sluggish and sleepy. His chin kept drooping towards his chest, before jerking up again, and in spite of his valiant efforts to concentrate on the images on the screen, his eyes would inexorably shut. He started awake after a few minutes, but his head felt like lead and kept lolling in every direction, like a newborn, until, against his will, he sank deeper into a blissful blackness. On the screen, endless torches burnt the darkness, their flames making a mockery of the night by turning it light as day. Thousands upon thousands of them making a river of light, shoulder to shoulder, column after column, marching, marching, marching for ever. On either side of the central procession, the spectators applauded and saluted, their faces, illuminated by the torches, shining with hope and longing for a better future.

He left the cinema, blinking as the bright Christmas

decorations on the Champs-Élysées dazzled his eyes. He trudged on, but he still felt exhausted. His feet were sore and blistered, and after drying out in the cinema, his leaky shoes made his socks soggy within no time. He sat down wearily on a bench to rest for a minute. He watched the crowds swarming past, and they all looked so clean and tidy, it made him feel more bedraggled than ever.

He'd been walking since first thing, and was sick and tired of it. He stank too, sour and rank, like dog's piss in straw, so pungent that he could even smell himself. He sat there listlessly, shivering as a windy blast blew over his head. It was like broad daylight on the Champs-Élysées, but he looked up at the dark night sky, and felt his whole body grow limp as the last of his remaining strength ebbed away.

Alyosha felt he was living once again according to his own calendar. Within time, there were several types of time: the steady cycle of the seasons; the daily rhythm of the Parisian day, with its peaks and troughs of business and bustle, the metro doors opening and the metro doors shutting; but his own time was, for all purposes, outside time, as he didn't count for anybody. In the enormity of the city, he was completely isolated. The most difficult thing for an exile was learning how to stay. The longer the stay, the worse the pain and the homesickness, especially when hope was so elusive, lurking somewhere on the horizon, only to slip ever further away the more one chased it.

He hoisted himself to his feet and walked from one shop window to the next, looking without seeing, though he caught the eye of a couple of policemen, whose suspicious looks followed him for a while. He stopped for a moment and thought, *Tomorrow, what will I do tomorrow?* As the frost did its work concreting the night, he felt his toes freeze. He lifted the collar of his coat and walked on alone into the black forest of the city.

43.

Prague felt less oppressive than Berlin, its streets and squares unadorned by black swastikas. She found the building in a street off Wenceslas Square, a small brass plaque by the door noting that the Centre was on the third floor. As she climbed up the narrow stairs, Margarita had to pause for a moment because of the stitch in her side. On the landing at the top of the third floor, an old man and woman were sitting on a wooden bench, holding hands with a distant look in their eyes. She gave her name to the receptionist, and was told to wait until she was called, so she joined them on the bench.

'Margarita?'

She turned when she heard her name, and couldn't hide her surprise to see Vicky standing at the door. Her hair was copper-coloured now, and had grown to her shoulders. Vicky offered her a cigarette and they both smoked.

'How did you arrive here?' Vicky asked.

'I could ask you the same thing.'

She took Margarita to an office at the back of the house, which must have once been a bedroom. Vicky wanted to hear how Margarita had reached Prague, so Margarita had to relive it all. How she had bought a pair of second-hand skis to take with her on the train from Berlin, so that she could say she was going on a vacation to the mountains. The ruse had worked, and nobody had challenged her on the train. It was after that her troubles had started, especially the two days she had spent hiding in a house by the border, so tantalisingly close to safety. They'd told her it was better to wait for a cloudy night, and she'd spent the time hidden in the attic, too nervous to sleep, aware of every tiny sound or movement outside. She'd been able to hear the river, which signified the border between the two countries. On both sides, there'd been coils of barbed wire, soldiers and dogs.

The second night, there'd been only a sliver of moon keeping an eye on the world, so the son of the house had led her to the crossing place, where the water was shallow, and shown her the gap in the barbed wire. He'd told her to be wary as she'd walked over the Sudeten, as many of the farmers there were already Nazis and were suspicious of anybody crossing their land.

Vicky asked who the boy was.

'I didn't ask and he didn't say.'

Even when she was safely over the border, the danger hadn't passed by any means. She'd been starving, and had ventured into an inn to ask about the next train, but the woman had advised her not to catch it at the nearest station, but to go further down the valley to a smaller station. An old man who'd been carrying a load of hay in his cart gave her a lift.

Vicky persisted with her questions. Who was the old man? Had any arrangements been made from Berlin for her to meet anybody? Did she have any contacts? It became clear to Margarita that there was more than one path out of Germany, and more than one group helping fugitives to escape. Margarita didn't say a word about Julik and Käthe Kozlecki, who had given her shelter on the outskirts of Liberec. The two had been highly active in the KPD in Berlin at one time, before becoming disillusioned and joining the IKP. Vicky knew them both well – and hated them.

Vicky asked her where she was staying in Prague, and Margarita told her she hoped to find lodgings in a cheap hotel, but she had no money, which was why she had come straight to the Centre. Again, she had no intention of mentioning the address that Julik had given her. She duly filled in a form so that the committee could assess if she qualified for financial assistance as a destitute refugee.

'Take this for now.'

Vicky pressed a small sum of money into her hand, and Margarita thanked her. But as Vicky saw her out, she told her that her case would be expedited if her presence at a branch meeting was noted.

'As it happens, there's a meeting tonight. 36 Moravska Street, on the ground floor. You'll come?'

This only confirmed what Margarita had already guessed. The Centre for Dispensing Aid to Refugees Fleeing Fascism in Prague had another purpose. Its proper work was to be the ears and eyes of the KPD in exile.

'What time?'

'Eight o'clock.'

She didn't go near the place. Nevertheless, within a couple of days her claim had been processed, and Vicky told her that she was eligible for financial assistance.

'Here you are,' she said, giving her the money, 'but what happened? I didn't see you in the meeting the day before yesterday.'

'I'd intended coming but I was exhausted and I fell asleep.'

From her sceptical expression, it seemed that Vicky knew she was lying.

'It's important you come. There's so much work to do.'

But Margarita kept away. She didn't intend dirtying her hands with the KPD ever again. Her main preoccupation was securing a visa to enter France. Kai-Olaf had warned her in a telegram that, without one, she would risk being deported straight back to Germany. But Margarita was finding kicking her heels while she waited for a decision frustrating. She spent most of her time reading, or talking to people at the Centre who were in the same boat as herself.

One morning, as she was reading the *Prager Mittag*, a shadow fell over the newspaper. Looking up, she saw Vicky standing there. Direct as ever, she asked Margarita why she hadn't been to a single meeting of the KPD branch since she'd arrived in Prague. This was the third she had missed. Missing one was bad. Missing two was reprehensible. But missing three was unforgiveable. Margarita didn't have a ready answer to hand. Vicky looked down at her with something like contempt and said, 'Either you're with us through and through, or you're against us.'

She dropped the butt of her cigarette into Margarita's coffee cup where it hissed and died, turned on her heel without another word, and walked away.

Margarita bought herself another cup of coffee and tried to calm her fury. She realised that she was vulnerable, and that the committee could leave her destitute. This fear spurred her on to look for work, as she had no idea how long it would take for her visa to arrive, even with Kai-Olaf doing his best for her in Paris. However, all aliens had to fill in the requisite paperwork to work legally, and she needed to prove she was a genuine refugee. She left the form at the Centre for them to vouch for her, but when she went back to pick it up, the young girl in the office broke the news to her. Angry, but remaining calm, she asked if she could talk to Vicky about it, but was told that she wasn't there. She said she would see somebody else, and didn't intend leaving until somebody with authority talked to her.

She went to sit on the bench at the head of the stairs.

Eventually Vicky appeared.

'Why have you refused to vouch for me?'

'We don't have to explain our reasons.'

Vicky turned away, but Margarita grabbed her wrist. 'Tell me!'

'Because you're supportive of the enemies of the working class.'

Margarita stared in disbelief at the narrow face in front of her. 'How exactly?' Vicky sucked slowly on her cigarette. 'I don't hear anybody else accusing me of being supportive to the enemies of the working class.' She could feel herself losing her temper. 'What? You're going to punish me... for not coming to the meetings? You're just looking for an excuse not to support me. Fine.' And she added defiantly, 'I don't want your money. But at least give me the chance to try and earn my own crust.'

Vicky considered this for a moment and then asked, 'Why should we?'

Margarita could barely contain herself. 'Do you remember last year in Berlin? That cold winter's night when you came knocking at my door because you had nowhere else to go? What did I do?'

'Why should we give you any help?'

'After everything I've done for the KPD – and for you Vicky?' Vicky said nothing. 'How else can I live until my visa is granted?'

'That's a matter for you and the IKP.'

'This is the only Refugee Centre the Czechoslovakian government acknowledges. Without your cooperation I don't have a hope.'

Out on the pavement, Margarita nearly screamed with frustration. She was so angry she would have burnt the place to ashes, if she'd only had the means.

She wondered desperately where she could turn for help.

44.

Lili's hands were covered in flour when she opened the door. She went back to making her dumplings as Margarita told her what had happened. If the committee had turned its back on her, where did that leave her? Lili told her it would be best if she wrote to the committee members asking them to reconsider their decision, and hope for the best.

Margarita drafted and re-drafted the letter, explaining why she had been forced to leave Berlin with only the clothes on her back, and delivered it by hand to the Centre. But two days later, before she'd received a response, Lili's husband came back from work and asked Margarita to leave.

'But why? What have I done?'

He showed her his copy of *Lidoré Noviny* and translated the report on the second page of a Gestapo agent operating a circle of spies against Czechoslovakia. There, in print, was her name. Margarita's knees turned to jelly.

'I don't want you here,' he told her. 'You can stay until tomorrow morning – not an hour more.'

'It's all lies.'

Lili took the paper from her husband to read the article for herself.

'This isn't true.' Margarita insisted. She gripped the edge of the table and tried to stand up, but her legs were useless. For a second, the kitchen went dark, as though she had been struck blind.

'Not one word of this is true, please believe me.'

'Hitler's spy,' he said.

'Never.'

'It says here that you were working for the Gestapo in Berlin,' added Lili, 'That you betrayed a Bolshevik and turned him over to them.'

'I was working for the cause in Berlin. Ask Kai-Olaf. Or Julik and Käthe. They'll vouch for me; I was *against* the Gestapo. Against Hitler. That's what I was doing, until it became too dangerous. Why would I need to flee if I was working for the Gestapo?'

The next day, the story was on the front page of the *Prager Montagsblatt*.

Lili and her husband sat mute and fearful with her over breakfast. They'd packed a bag for her with a few borrowed items of clothing – all her worldly possessions.

The door shut after her with a thankful thud.

45.

Margarita sat on a stone bench under the shade of a sycamore tree in Stromovká Park. As she gazed out at the lake, she imagined for a moment how lovely it would be to watch the sun set over it on a warm summer evening, but her thoughts were soon back to her predicament. Her greatest concern now was not herself, but Larissa. If as much as a whisper of the story that she was a Gestapo spy reached Moscow, it might make things extremely difficult for her sister. What if they thought Larissa was a spy, too? She could be arrested and imprisoned. What would become of the little girls then? She had to protect her good name, not just for herself, but for her sister's sake.

She decided to pay a visit to the *Prager Montagsblatt* offices and speak to the editor. But when she got there, he was in a meeting, and refused to see her. She tried to stand her ground, but found herself being accompanied out of the building between two of the clerks. She went straight to the nearest café and wrote an angry letter to the editor, but then she reasoned that if he wouldn't see her, then no more would he publish her letter. She found the nearest kiosk and telephoned him, using a false name. Before he could hang up, she blurted out that he had been manipulated by the KPD, and that they had fabricated the story to punish her for not attending their meetings. He told her irritably that, as far as he was concerned, the information came from a reliable source, and he had no intention of publishing a retraction and apology without incontrovertible proof.

'But what about my good name?'

Margarita hated the desperate tone she could hear in her own voice. The editor told her it wasn't his responsibility to protect her good name. If she happened to be telling the truth – which he doubted – then she should call the KPD to account, not him.

'You've ruined my reputation. I'm homeless and friendless thanks to you.'

He didn't have an answer to that.

The same accusations were reprinted in other newspapers, where she was described as the daughter of an officer in the Tsar's army, who had left Russia in order to work for the counter-revolution in Europe. She was a cunning and wily spy, who had managed to embed herself within the Berlin proletariat in order to betray communists to the Gestapo. Now, she had turned her sights to undermining the government of Czechoslovakia.

Vicky's fingerprints were all over it.

46.

Prague became a cold and hostile place. Margarita stood on Karlov bridge, watching winter swimmers diving into the Vlatva from the steps on the riverbank. One of the men reminded her of Kai-Olaf, and she realised she hadn't seen him for almost a year.

Somehow, she had to leave Prague and go to him in Paris. Apart from anything else, if she stayed, it was surely only a matter of time before she was arrested as a Gestapo spy. She carried on walking aimlessly through the narrow streets of the Old Town trying to think of a way of doing it, when she suddenly came face to face with Eggert, and hopelessness turned to hope. Eggert took one look at her, before whisking her off to the Koruna and buying her a meal, which Margarita tried not to stuff down too quickly, starving as she was. He told her that the Gestapo had smashed the IKP in Berlin, and most of the members had been picked up and arrested. He had managed to escape, but he had no intention of staying in Prague. Like Margarita, he was set on reaching Paris. Margarita told him her own troubles, but Eggert was very reassuring. He said he had already read the newspaper reports, but hadn't believed a word of it, of course. Vicky had done far worse things to other people.

'Like what?

'She's sent individuals back to Germany to undertake underground work, but somehow or other, the Gestapo are waiting for them. At least seven have been caught that I know about; there may well be more.'

Margarita couldn't believe even Vicky to be capable of this.

'It's true, every word,' Eggert told her. 'The KPD have been lost for years. That's why the work of the IKP is more important than ever. Trotsky will carry the day. Of that, I'm certain.'

'Is he in Paris?' she asked.

'He was there for a day last month. That's where he'd like to be, if they let him. I'm not sure what will happen. His son, Lev Sedov, is already there, since he had to get out of Berlin.'

That night, they slept in a studio flat a stone's throw away from the Jewish cemetery, where another émigré from Germany was living. Eggert didn't explain how they knew each other, and Margarita didn't need to know. She was just grateful to be sleeping on a sofa, rather than out on the streets. The next day, she and Eggert left for France, without visas.

They crossed Czechoslovakia by train, slipping over the border to Austria easily enough on foot, and then made another train journey, on the uncomfortable wooden benches of third class, to Vienna. There, they stayed a week, and, thanks to Eggert's contacts, left with forged passports and visas, given to them by a man named George. They still had no legal right to live in France, however, as although a passport with a visa would allow them to enter the country, without a *permis de séjour*, they were of limited value. George warned them that the authorities were being particularly draconian at present because of the constant flow of refugees arriving from every corner.

From Vienna, the two crossed the border to Switzerland hidden in the back of a lorry transporting carpets. After spending three nights in Geneva, they were instructed by a local contact to be ready to leave on the Thursday night.

Spending so much time together, Margarita and Eggert had plenty of time to exchange stories. He had been born into a wealthy family, one of three children, and had been brought up in the Black Forest. Along with his two brothers, he'd been educated at the famous Cistercian seminary in Maulbronn, but, unlike them, he'd loathed the wealthy elitism, the snobbery and the restrictive and petty rules, and had run away. He'd decided to live the life of the open road, and had followed his nose from place to place. He'd eventually found himself in Paris, working in a cast-iron factory at Creil. That's where his true education had taken place. In the end, he'd been sacked for organising strikes for better wages and conditions.

He'd taken to the road again, and had walked the coastlines of France, Portugal and Spain, through those small impoverished towns where fishermen scratched a living from the fruits of the sea. From there, he'd wandered the continent, and had found himself one day in Antwerp. He'd found lodgings in a room on the Rue du Sac, where he'd taken a fancy to the daughter of the owner – a fifteen-year-old schoolgirl, who'd spent most of her leisure time on a window seat with her nose in a book. Whenever her parents had called her, she'd raise her head slowly, as though she was waking from a deep dream. She'd had still green, unsmiling eyes, a mane of long black hair and a smattering of freckles over her nose and cheeks, and her most prized possession had been a narrow silver bracelet, which she'd never taken off her wrist.

The Rue du Sac was situated opposite the docks, and Eggert had soon found himself frequenting the bars along the Scheldt, discussing communist ideas with the sailors. Somebody – working for the Comintern, Eggert assumed – must have noticed him, and had a word in somebody's ear, because he'd been approached and offered a job with the KPD in Berlin. That's where he had first met Margarita, shortly after the rally in the Sportplatz.

He'd been expelled from the Party around the same time as Kai-Olaf.

By now, he'd put enough distance between himself and the KPD to be able to interpret what had happened more objectively. The Communist Party was not so dissimilar to his old school in Maulbronn. At the heart of Marxist-Leninism was an elitism every bit as hierarchical and dictatorial as had prevailed there. Whilst it proclaimed the right of the millions to rule their own lives, in fact, the real power lay with a handful of men. It proclaimed freedom, but operated in an authoritarian manner. When had a despot every ruled democratically? What dogmatic ideology had ever allowed freedom of thought? Its *raison d'être* was to ensure happiness and freedom – but what makes people happy and free? How do you measure happiness? Or freedom? Can any human mind ever comprehend the whole meaning of life?

The two left for the French border by moonlight.

47.

The French sky was so changeable. One minute, a bank of fat clouds rolled along the horizon, the next, there was nothing but blue sky and spring sunshine, winking through the branches of the poplars on either side of the tracks in an alternating pattern of light and shadows. Every now and again, one of the branches would brush against the carriage. Margarita poked her head out of the window, and her hair was whipped around madly in the breeze. Some lilac trees passed her eye in a moving blur of colour, and she managed to grab a couple of blossoms in her fist.

When they reached their journey's end in the early hours, the Gare de l'Est was noisy and bad-tempered, its cavernous space filled with the echoes of pistons and brakes competing with the shouting of the porters and the whistling of the guards.

Outside, low clouds hung over the city and the early morning air was damp. Margarita and Eggert separated, promising to meet soon, and Margarita found herself on Rue de la Huchette, where she went in to the Café Saint Michel which had just opened its doors to ask for directions. A woman they called Eugénie was serving coffee and croissants to three or four early workers in her slippers, her legs bare. She had a blowsy look about her, and stank of cheap perfume, but she was friendly enough and took the piece of paper from her to ask the other customers if they knew where the street was. Margarita suddenly started to shake, though she wasn't cold, and she wrapped her coat more tightly around her. Eugénie must have had a good heart, because she came back with a coffee, which she slapped down in front of Margarita, telling her she looked done in, and that it was on the house. Margarita drank it gratefully. The street wasn't so far away – one of the men on the other table gave her directions. Thanking him and Eugénie for their kindness, Margarita set off feeling suddenly hopeful.

She waited for the messenger boy on his bike to peddle past before crossing the road. Already, the last few weeks seemed to be fading away, as if they had happened a long time ago. The streets were becoming busier now, and she started to pass people hurrying along, on their way to work. She was suddenly engulfed in a cloud of soapy-smelling steam which had escaped through the open doors of a laundry as she walked by, and then found herself smiling at a waiter in a long white apron, smoking a cigarette contemplatively by the entrance of a café. She turned the corner at the bottom of the street into a much wider street, where men and women were busy setting up their stalls for a fruit and vegetable market. Further on down, she started counting the numbers until she reached the correct building. She stepped through the wide double doors into a cobbled courtyard, and climbed the stairs to the first landing. She found the right door, and knocked. In a minute or two, a woman with tousled hair, still in her nightdress, opened it. Tatyana's sleepy expression turned to sheer astonishment when she saw Margarita on her doorstep. Margarita apologised for the early hour, but was given a warm hug and told to come in. Over tea and bread, she told Stanislav and Tatyana briefly about her journey. There was nothing very new in it; they were all familiar with such journeys. She was far more concerned with telling them about the accusations made against her in the Czech press. Stanislav listened to her carefully, smoking his pipe.

'You know better than anybody that I wasn't working for the Gestapo,' Margarita said and he nodded. 'But what worries me more than anything is Larissa's situation in Moscow.'

'I quite understand,' Stanislav said, and told her there was no need to worry.

'But I *am* worried. That's why I came straight here. I know from experience how these things get back to the Kremlin. And I don't want my sister to suffer.'

'I'll explain everything.'

'Do you promise?'

He nodded then asked, 'What are you going to do in Paris?'

'I'm not sure.'

'If you need anything, you know where we are.'

'Thank you. And thank you for saving me back in Berlin.'

'You can thank Tatyana,' answered Stanislav.

Margarita smiled, knowing full well he was behind it all.

She didn't have far to walk – just down Rue des Deux-Ponts, and then she was in Rue Saint-Séverin. The concierge opened the door and told her where to find Kai-Olaf's room.

She climbed the narrow stairs, then knocked the door, and heard a fumbling from the other side.

The door opened.

It was Kai-Olaf standing there, staring at her in disbelief.

They hugged, holding on to each other for dear life.

Margarita felt, at last, that she was home.

ACKNOWLEDGEMENTS

Both the author and translator would like to thank English PEN for the financial and promotional support they have provided towards the publication of this title.

Wiliam Owen Roberts was born in 1960 and educated at the University of Wales Aberystwyth. He worked for various theatre companies before joining HTV as a script editor in 1984. Since 1989 he has been a full-time writer and has written extensively for theatre, television, radio and film. His first novel *Bingo!* (1985) was described as the first postmodernist novel in Welsh. His second novel *Y Pla* (*Pestilence*; 1987) won the Welsh Arts Council Literature prize in 1988 and was subsequently translated into 10 languages. His third novel *Paradwys* (*Paradise*; 2001 was set on an imaginary Carribean island on the eve of the French Revolution and was short-listed for the Welsh Book of the Year Award in 2002. *Petrograd* (2008) won the Welsh Book of the Year Award and the ITV Wales Readers Choice Award in 2009. He is a Fellow of the Welsh Academy.

Elisabeth Roberts was born in Cardiff and educated at Oxford University. She has been a freelance translator and editor for many years. She is married to Wiliam Owen Roberts and has translated three of his novels into English: *Pestilence*, *Petrograd* and *Paris*.

ALSO BY WILIAM OWEN ROBERTS

"…an epic novel… you can almost smell Russia."
BBC Arts

PETROGRAD

It's the summer of 1916 and the Alexandrov family prepare to
embark on their annual holiday, accompanied by an army of
staff primed to cater to their needs.

Teenage, precocious Alyosha Alexandrov has never known anything but a life of privilege. He spends his days avoiding study
and pursuing pretty young maids. But Russia is poised on the
brink of epochal political upheaval and within a year Alyosha is
separated from family, security, and the innocence of youth.

Set against the backdrop of the Russian Revolution and its
aftermath, spanning the turbulent years from 1916 to 1924,
Petrograd is a vast, ambitious novel from an award-winning
writer. The first in a trilogy, and winner of the Wales Book of
the Year Award (Welsh Language), it tells the compelling, convincing story of the Alexandrov family as they each struggle to
adapt to the ravages of war and revolution.

"This is a novel with a huge international appeal."
BBC Cymru

978-1-909844-56-8 • £8.99 • eBook also available